T0103992

UNWANTED HEART

T.J. WOLFE

Order this book online at www.trafford.com
or email orders@trafford.com

Most Trafford titles are also available at major online book retailers.

Print information available on the last page.

ISBN: 978-1-4907-6752-9 (sc)
ISBN: 978-1-4907-6754-3 (hc)
ISBN: 978-1-4907-6753-6 (e)

Library of Congress Control Number: 2015920562

Trafford rev. 01/14/2016

www.trafford.com

North America & international
toll-free: 1 888 232 4444 (USA & Canada)
fax: 812 355 4082

This book is dedicated to the GLBT community—in particular, the stud, butch, or boi lesbians who have the courage to stand out and be who they truly are in spite of society and the beautiful femmes who love and support them every step of the way. Be it embracing their masculine side by sporting all-male attire or finding balance in androgyny, these women have become immune to society's idea of what a woman should be. Their courage extends from coast to coast, spreading a message of hope to our GLBT youth, empowering them to be whomever the hell they want to be! I personally salute your bravery, courage, and strength!

CONTENTS

ACKNOWLEDGMENTS

I'd first like to thank my Lord and Savior, Jesus Christ. I thank you for blessing me with compassion, love, and grace throughout my life. My love for you and faith in you will never diminish.

To my friends—I could not have made it without your support and encouragement throughout this journey. I cannot thank you enough for your words of encouragement and delightful sarcasm. You all have been an integral part in helping me achieve a lifelong dream.

I'd like to give a special thanks to my friend Ms. V. Bell: You will always hold a special place in my heart. You were the one who kept me excited about writing. I cannot tell you enough how important our friendship means to me. I learned to dare to dream because of you, and for that, I am eternally grateful. I wish you all the happiness life has to offer.

Last but not least, I want to thank the women in my FB group. Each of you have touched my life in such a way, providing inspiration and laughs.

CHAPTER ONE

Reflections

Living in Portland, Oregon, the past two years afforded me the opportunity I so desperately desired, a desire to be free from the suffocating pain inflicted on my unwanted heart. Its relentless torture inhabits my soul, leaving me timorous. I will ever escape its cold and dark clutch. The irony is my misfortune became a symbol of hope, ushering me to excel in life far beyond my wildest dreams. I have been given a rare opportunity to start life anew away from all remembrances of Zoe and the love we once shared. In the process, a newfound sense of freedom grew within me, sparking a clarity I'd have never known had I remained in Austin, Texas.

For the first time in my life, I am able to view my relationships not only with Zoe but my mother, Rose, and sister, Jaylon, as well. My eyes have been cleansed of coercion, leaving me able to view them without prejudice. I see now my life was never truly my own. I was merely a puppet in a sick, twisted play orchestrated by the very people who claim to love me. I am unashamed to admit I take pleasure in the recess.

Zoe abruptly ended our two-year relationship, leaving me severely depressed and full of unanswered questions. After deep prayer and at my mother's behest, I soon departed Austin, abandoning my life, striving to put my pain behind me. I refused to allow my heart to continue to be enslaved by Zoe's. The mere thought of her being near yet intangible to me was unbearable.

Rose dreaded the thought of me leaving but realized placing some distance between us would be good for me. I'd only been away from Rose once, at the age of sixteen. She had feared for my safety and shipped me off to New York. I lived there for a year in seclusion in a small Manhattan apartment before I was allowed to return home.

One foot off the plane in Portland and inhaling the clean, crisp air, I knew I had made the right decision. I was fearful of living in a strange city, not knowing anyone. I don't know why I chose Portland, perhaps fate. I believe it is in God's plan, relieving of my troubles, and as such, I turn to Christ for guidance. I read a Bible verse every day for a month when I first arrived. As each day passed, my broken heart began to heal, leading me out of my depression. My new life grew more satisfying as time went on. Looking back, I know God saved me from myself.

Exhausted from a frustrating night and upsetting morning, the plane ride to Austin is a welcome distraction. On board, I take my seat and buckle myself in. I stare out the window at the tarmac, waiting impatiently for takeoff. Once in the air, I recline my seat, making myself more comfortable. In a matter of seconds, I drift off to sleep, where my subconscious takes control, inducing my mind to reflect on my life, the good, uncomfortable, and the uncontrollable.

In my late teens, I got a job at a local credit union. I didn't want my past indiscretions aired, thereby making it difficult to attend college. Honestly, I had no desire to attend. I wanted a job to afford my own place away from Jaylon. I remember a feeling of euphoria when I moved into my first condo. Working for someone else was a means to an end. I had higher aspirations for my life. My goal was to become a real estate investor. My first and only job, along with the help of my mother's business associates, helped me gain the necessary knowledge required to become a real player in the industry. In my spare time, I researched areas around Austin being considered for development. I used my college fund to purchase land, commercial and residential real estate. It was often implied my methods of acquiring real estate were unethical, bordering criminal. I was young and ambitious and didn't care about perceptions. I was privy to inside information and capitalized on it. In five years, I acquired numerous properties in and around the Austin Metro and Downtown areas. The repercussions of my actions rarely entered my mind. If landed into any legal trouble, Rose, along with a team of attorneys, would bail me out. She would never allow anything to happen to me. I took advantage of the fact she was a judge in Travis County. It didn't hurt either when Jaylon became a police officer for the APD. By age twenty-three, I had made upward of ten million in real estate alone. It was easy money, especially in Austin. I regret placing my family in a situation that could have jeopardized their careers and status in the community for my own gain.

I made every effort to pay back every penny Rose had given me. She never accepted a dime, reminding me it was an investment in my future. Even though it wasn't the future she had intended, she said I made a wise choice. Rose not only helped me but used her influence helping Jaylon get into the law degree program at the University of Texas.

It was my senior year in high school. Rose informed me I had the option of attending any university in the country. She had dreams of me attending a prestigious school to pursue a law degree following in her and Jaylon's footsteps. Seeing the disappointment in her eyes when I informed her I wasn't attending college saddens me still. It was the first time I went against her will. As difficult as it was to disappoint her, I couldn't see myself wasting her money and my time sitting in a classroom when I could be out in the world making my dreams come true. I later discovered Rose did some savvy investing of her own in the early eighties. She had a feeling Austin would eventually become an economic boomtown, making her investments worth millions. She couldn't have been more right.

Although we lived in the affluent West Austin area, our lifestyle was modest. Rose taught us the value of a dollar and to how to be appreciative of our good fortune. As a judge, she was surrounded by greed and corruption yet remained steadfast and humble. On rare occasions, she would pamper herself and a few of her closest friends, taking unexpected trips overseas or surprising them with lavish gifts for no reason at all. Rose has always taken great joy in sharing her wealth with others, especially those in need. I can't count the number of charitable organizations she was involved in. She insisted Jaylon and I be involved in charitable work growing up, stressing the importance of helping others and doing good deeds. She reminded us if we want to be in God's good favor, it is imperative we help others. "Ask not nor expect anything in return for doing a good deed" was her creed. I was in awe of my mother when I learned she opted to remain anonymous for her monetary donations, teaching me genuine humility.

Her generosity extended itself to me on my twenty-fifth birthday. I remember her calling me into her study for a private mother-daughter moment. She took a seat at her desk then motioned me to sit. She smiled at me with a sense of pride and admiration in her eyes sharing her amazement at what I had been able to accomplish at such a young age. She stood up from her chair and walked around her desk and stood directly in front of me. Her warm, delicate hand cupped my cheek as she continued to smile at me. She picked up a beautifully wrapped package from off the top of her wooden desk, placing it in my hand, saying, *"Caiden, I have no doubt you will know what to do with this. Happy birthday, and I love you."*

A shy smile crossed my face as I unwrapped the package to find the deeds to her properties. She explained she bought them for Jaylon and me to have something to fall back on after she is gone. Humbled by her gesture, I managed to utter a quiet thank-you. Still unable to speak clearly, with tears flowing down my cheeks, I stood and gave her a loving embrace. She shared she had given Jaylon her remaining properties a few months prior for her twenty-eighth birthday. She said she was hesitant to do so out of fear Jaylon may not appreciate the true value in her gift. It was never about the value of her properties more than it was about keeping it in the family. Mom was livid when she discovered Jaylon sold some of the land to the Lycan Group LLC, an investment firm, after only a few months. Jaylon, Mr. Know-It-All, took the first offer, not bothering to have the land appraised. She only cared about the money, not how it would upset our mother. It took a long time for Rose to forgive Jaylon for her betrayal.

A flight attendant interrupts my thoughts, asking if I need anything. I reply *"No, thank you"* and continue my thoughts. I fulfilled my dream of opening both an upscale GLBT nightclub named Beautiful and a charming little coffee house on southwest Naito Parkway near southwest Hawthorne Bridge called Slow Grind in Portland. The life I have built here is most certainly aiding me in my attempt to move past Zoe. I can't imagine living anywhere else.

Just nine months in the city, I meet a young Dominican woman named Rheia Santos. She is intelligent, witty, understanding, and most of all, comfortable in her own skin. The only thing I would change is her insecurities about my feelings for Zoe. I blame myself for her perceptions considering it's difficult to deny the feelings I still harbor for her. I admit Rheia is a far cry from the type of woman I am typically attracted to. She's a few inches taller than me with short black hair. Her hazel eyes are striking, but I'm partial to blue-green. She's a bit slender for my taste. Nonetheless, she seems to be just the remedy I need to take my mind off Zoe. We met at Slow Grind one rainy Saturday afternoon. We were busy that day, so I pitched in and waited on her. She ordered an iced cappuccino, and I remember her remarking the cappuccino was absolutely disgusting. I was a bit perturbed by her candor considering I prided myself on serving the best coffees in Portland. I smiled cordially asking, "What could I do to make it right?" Without responding, she glared at me from her barstool, handing me her empty cup. As I reached to remove the cup from her hand, her glare now intensified. She leaned in closely, caressing my finger, whispering, "Can I have something hot?"

I chuckled at her request, removing the cup from her hand, promising the macchiato would be the hottest drink to ever grace her juicy lips and equally as disgusting as the cappuccino. She smiled approvingly at me as she sat back in her barstool. We talked for hours that afternoon. I found myself laughing for the first time in months. She was so easygoing and playful I couldn't help but ask her out. We have been dating ever since. I was upfront with Rheia, making it clear I wasn't looking for anything serious. She confessed she had recently ended a horrible relationship and preferred to take things slow. It worked out perfectly between us.

The plane jolts from turbulence shifting my thoughts to returning home. My trip back was as abrupt as when I first left. My mother wasn't in the best of health when I left. Her condition grew worse about a year ago. She is vague about her illness, not allowing me to speak directly with her physician. I visit her in secret once a month, carefully avoiding everyone, especially Jaylon. I couldn't risk her upsetting Rose in her condition with her foolishness. She always finds a way to piss me off, which upsets Rose. Sometimes I think she lives just to make my life miserable.

I hired Nurse Patterson a little over nine months ago when I became concerned for my mother's well-being after one of my visits with her. She seemed disoriented and agitated by my presence. I knew then she couldn't be left alone to care for herself. Jaylon's schedule is unpredictable, and I couldn't rely on her to take care of Rose regularly. Nurse Patterson agreed to sign a confidentiality agreement, making me comfortable about my visits. She took very good care of my mother, tending to her every need. Unfortunately, two months ago, she herself had taken ill. Unable to care for Rose anymore, she recommended a Nurse Woodward as a replacement. I agreed to hire her based off her recommendation. Although we never met in person, I instructed her to keep me abreast as of any changes in my mother's condition. I knew I would be home in a couple of months and discontinued my monthly visits.

Mom's condition seems to be deteriorating more rapidly than expected. Not knowing her illness left me to assume she had dementia based on the symptoms she displayed. Nurse Woodward shared with me that Rose's memory fades in and out regularly. She is having difficulty recognizing familiar faces. She doesn't even recognize her own home at times. I convince my mom's physician, Dr. Chen Fischer, to at least tell me how long he thinks she has. Reluctant to release any information regarding my mother's condition, he shares he would be surprised if she survives another month or two. Prior to her illness or shortly after, Rose gave Edwina Miller power of attorney over her estate. I would have to consult with Ms. Miller if I am to obtain any information regarding my mother's health. However dire the prognosis, I remain hopeful she will recover. After all, she is only sixty-three and much too stubborn to leave me. I find it difficult to comprehend Rose in such a frail state. I keep a mental image of her in my mind of when she was younger. In her prime, she was one of the most beautiful women I had ever known. She was tall and slender with the smoothest vanilla-toned skin. Her wavy long dark-brown hair was soft to the touch. Her almond-shaped eyes were the oddest green or blue depending on how the sunlight struck them. They possess an air of mystique, even haunting at times. I love how her eyes glow, especially when she smiles. She was always poised and full of confidence. She joked I was exactly like her.

Rose has always had the natural ability to seduce an audience. Men and women were helpless under her magnetic charm. She was a woman who knew how to get exactly what she wanted. She was at her most glamorous at the private parties she hosted at our home. Her evening gowns were always elegant but form-fitted, accentuating her feminine curves. She took great care to ensure we were prepared to interact appropriately with her guests. Her galas, as she like to call them, usually consisted of colleagues in her inner circle, judges, attorneys, politicians, business owners, and the like. Jaylon and I spent countless hours learning correct grammar, pronunciation, etiquette, and most importantly, when to keep our opinions to ourselves. We both dreaded having to learn so much, but in the end, it became a valuable asset.

At every party, we were sent to our rooms at eleven o'clock. It wasn't until we reached our late teens when the curfew was lifted. I imagine Rose shielded us from a life we were ill-prepared to comprehend. One night my curiosity got the better of me, and I decided to investigate. I slid out of my bed, opening the door quietly. I stuck my head out into the hall, confirming the coast was clear. I tiptoed down the hall until I reached the stairwell. I crouched down onto the wooden floor, pressing my body against the wall at the top of the stairs, out of view. I could see the entire first floor from my post. It didn't take long for the mystery to unveil itself as I saw a young couple running up the stairs hand in hand. They must have been anxious, because neither of them noticed me as they rushed past me, smelling of alcohol. I heard the young woman giggle briefly as they entered a guest bedroom. They didn't bother securing the door, leaving it slightly open. The giggling ceased as moans ensue, further piquing my curiosity. Finding myself at the crack of the door, I peered in to see the couple engaged in a kiss. At first glance, it looked as if the man in the tuxedo was hurting her. Upset at the sight, I swallowed deeply, placing my hand on the door, preparing to go to her rescue. I laugh at the thought in hindsight. How could a seven-year-old child ward off a man four times as large?

At second glance, the woman appeared to be enjoying his kisses, responding to him with equal force. His hands moved over her breast, firmly grasping them in his hand. Her moans escalated the harder he fondled them. My mouth gaped open in shock, seeing his hand move underneath her dress, between her thighs. I watched her moisten her lips with her tongue, causing me to lick my own. I knew this was wrong, yet I could not pull myself away. I continued to watch her reaction as his hand moved up and down underneath her dress. He ceased once the young woman cried out.

Startled by footsteps coming from the stairwell, I dashed back to my room, leaping into bed. As my heart raced, my bedroom door opened. I lay perfectly still, pretending to be asleep while managing to control my breathing. Rose's lavender-scented perfume loomed in the air as she stood at the door in silence for a moment. She entered quietly, taking a seat on my bed. I could feel her staring at me. I was terrified I had been caught spying on the couple in the other room. Suddenly, I felt her soft hand caress my cheek as she leaned down, kissing me gently on the forehead. She exited my room, gently closing the door behind her. I listened to her footsteps until they faded down the hall.

A few moments later, loud muffled voices spurred me to get out of bed. I quickly entered the hall to check on Rose. As I rubbed my eyes, I softly called out to her. Startled by my presence, she turned toward me, briefly cutting her eyes sharply at the couple now standing in front of her. My act continued as I groggily walked up to her, wrapping my narrow arms around her leg. She caressed my back as she explained her acquaintances were just leaving. I looked up at the young woman, extending my hand to her. She glanced at Rose first before politely smiling at me, remarking how adorable I am. She knelt down, facing me, introducing herself as Valerie. She cordially accepted my hand and asked my name.

I respond, yawning at first, "Pleasure to meet you, Ms. Valerie. I'm Caiden Westphal." I glanced up at Rose to see her eyes as they narrowed staring at Valerie. I could tell she was not pleased with the young woman. Rose placed her hands on my shoulders, turning me away from the woman and toward my bedroom. She taps me on the behind, saying good night. Back in the comfort of my bed, I lay gazing up at the ceiling, picturing Valerie's pretty face until I fell asleep.

My eyes open, and I find myself gazing out the window, into the clouds. I chuckle, remembering Rose having several gentleman suitors knocking at her door. I find it odd she never took a romantic interest in them. She never remarried either. None seem to rival her first love, Jaylon's father. I was always afraid to ask any questions, fearing it would dredge up painful memories for her. I only know she had a deep love for him. She never talked about him when we were growing up. To me he is a nameless man whom my mother adored. If she had a picture of him, she kept it hidden from us. Only once did she share a memory of the amazing love between them. There was pain in her eyes when she spoke of him that once. After that, I never dared bring him up again. I found it strange Jaylon seemed uninterested in wanting details about her father.

Rose didn't have many close friends. The only one I can recall is Edwina. She was as beautiful as mom. I never understood how two beautiful and eligible women never married. They spent a lot of time together when we were young. She even babysat us when Rose decided to go out on a date. They could easily have passed for sisters. I use to call Edwina my aunt. I haven't seen her in years. It is unclear to me why she faded out of our lives years ago.

I'm startled by more turbulence, prompting me to glance at my watch, noting we've only been in the air forty-five minutes. As the plane settles, I relax again in my seat, continuing to reminisce.

Jaylon and I had a fairly normal relationship until Jaylon reached her preteens. Something caused her to transform into a hateful and unfamiliar creature. I have often wondered what tragic event she uncovered to alter her personality. She grew to despise my very existence. For the life of me, I can't understand why she loathes me. For Rose's sake, we keep our distance from each other as much as humanly possible. The rare times we are in each other's presence, we try to maintain some remnant of civility. It eats at me, knowing we break Rose's heart every time we encounter each other. How must she feel as a mother that her only two children can't bear to be in the same room with each other?

I was adopted when Jaylon was three years old. Part of me believes Jaylon resents Rose for taking me in. I admit she did pay special attention to me, perhaps slighting Jaylon unknowingly in the process. Maybe she felt she was being replaced. Regardless, her animosity and contempt toward me grew more hostile as the years progressed.

My parents, Nadine and David, were killed in a car crash by a drunk driver. I was nine months old at the time. By the grace of God, I survived, suffering only minor abrasions with a small one-inch gash on my left arm. I can still see the question mark–shaped scar. It's a constant reminder that life presents circumstances out of your control, often providing no answers, a lesson I continue to struggle with today. I have so many unanswered questions about my parents, why I survived, why my sister hates me, and why Zoe cast me aside so easily.

The flight attendant asks again if I need anything. I smile, saying "No, thank you" as I shut my eyes once again. Rose and

Jaylon are the only family I have. Rose loved Nadine as if she were her own sister and David, her brother. She didn't hesitate to adopt me. She told me once that she never regretted her decision and loved me as if she gave birth to me herself. I will always be eternally grateful to Rose for the love and care she bestowed on me. Jaylon and I didn't make life easy for her, but she managed to keep our family together with love and tolerance. She knows there is a possibility that Jaylon's heart will be unable to love me. She will never give up on Jaylon, remaining faithful in her belief that one day, we will be the loving family she has always dreamed of.

Now, regrettably, returning home is the only option I have to make her life more comfortable. I pray time and distance apart have, softened Jaylon's heart, allowing us a chance to make amends. I love my sister and wish nothing but the best for her, yet she makes it impossible for me to even want to try to make things right between us. I have extended an olive branch a few times over the last two years, but she has yet to reciprocate.

Strangely enough, I used to admire Jaylon. I wanted to be just like her. She had focus and determination, always managing to get what she wanted no matter the cost. I recently found out she made detective for the Austin Police Department. Not a bad accomplishment for an openly gay, thirty-three-year-old stud lesbian. For as long as I can remember, she has always wanted to be a cop. The few times we did play together as kids, she was always the cop and I, the criminal. For the sake of the city of Austin, I hope she has changed from the bully I remember. Jaylon could be malicious, downright hateful toward me.

One time, we were playing cops and robbers; she pointed her toy pistol at me, ordering me to freeze, stating if I didn't, she would shoot my fucking head off. Stunned by her vulgarity, I hesitated for a moment then continued to role-play. I froze as she requested, holding my hands up in surrender. She walked over to me, aiming the pistol at my head. Before I could react, she struck me in the face with her backhand so fucking hard, I stumbled to the ground. She proceeded to kick me violently in the stomach and ribs. All I could do was plead for her to stop while trying to block the blows. I was a scrawny kid, and Jaylon was a hulk in comparison. Luckily, Rose heard my screams and rushed out of the house to my rescue. She screamed at Jaylon to stop, but Jaylon heard no sound, continuing her mission to destroy me. Rose finally yanked her off me, ordering her into the house and straight to her room. She dashed over to me in a panic, wrapping me in her arms, crying, asking me if I was okay. Okay? Hell, I was mortified! The only thing I could do was wrap my arms around her neck in pain and hold on for dear life. Jaylon beat me so bad I had to be taken to the hospital. After it was all said and done, I left with two cracked ribs and bruising on my stomach. The doctor reported the incident to Child Protective Services to investigate, believing I had been abused. How my mother managed to keep that out of the news is a mystery to me still. CPS placed me in foster care for about three weeks after the incident. I suppose, depending on your perspective, CPS determined it was safe for me to return home.

The moment I returned home our lives where never the same again. Rose kept a watchful eye on the two of us. She made sure we were never alone together. I think the incident made Rose realize Jaylon was never going accept me in her life. She did what she could to make homelife bearable for us, but you could tell no one in that house was happy. Rose finally arranged for Jaylon to get psychiatric help. I withdrew myself from interacting with Jaylon with the exception of dinnertime. Even in therapy, she acted as if the beat down was normal child's play. She never admitted to any wrongdoing. It took some years for me to forgive her for how she treated me growing up.

I remember her words to the letter: "Caiden, you fucking little pussy, can't even play like a real man." I asked myself, *Real man, what the hell does that mean?* Her comment eluded me until I hit puberty.

At age eleven, my attraction for feminine women began to display itself. I had no sexual interest in the opposite sex or women who looked or acted like men. Jaylon and I were both tomboys, so it was only natural we grew up to be homosexual. We share this one commonality between us.

I am hoping something positive will come out of Rose's illness, bringing us closer to each other.

"Excuse me, excuse me. How are you doing over here?" The flight attendant asks politely, drawing me back to the real world.

"Sorry, you caught me daydreaming. I'm doing well. May I have a vodka tonic with a twist of lime?" I respond.

"Yes, of course, Ms. Westphal. I will be back in a moment."

I interrupt her as she starts to walk down the aisle of the first-class cabin, asking, "Excuse me, miss, could you refer to me as Mr. Westphal? If you are uncomfortable with the *mister*, call me Caiden!"

She smiles a shy smile, responding,"My apologies. Caiden is a beautiful name. I won't forget it!"

She continues back down the aisle to prepare my drink. I can't help but admire her backside as she walks away. I have three hours to go, and after last night with Rheia, I am sexually frustrated, to put it mildly. I need to focus on something other than her nice, round ass. I grab my *GQ* magazine out of my briefcase and begin flipping through the pages. My eyes wander back to the flight attendant over the top of the magazine. I can't help it—she is gorgeous. Her thick, curvy frame, straight shoulder-length brunette hair, narrow green eyes, and juicy pink lips—she's just my type. I find it difficult to take my eyes off her. Her ethnicity is hard to pinpoint.

"Caiden, Caiden, your drink," she says, snapping me out of my daze yet again.

"Thank you, miss?" I reply, briefly glancing at her nametag, hoping she didn't notice me eye-fucking her body.

"You're welcome, Caiden, and it's Ashley Guerra!" she informs me as she walks past to check on the other passengers, gliding her hand across my shoulder. I envision the two of us alone in the first-class, having a raw sexual encounter. I smile at the thought as I turn my head to stare into the clouds.

A voice in my head laughs while reminding me of my commitment issues. Can Ms. Guerra be a one-nighter? I wonder.

Frustrated over the indecent thought, I continue to stare out the window, thinking of home once again.

I have been so out of touch with everyone, including my good friend Brianna. The last time I saw her was about a month after I moved to Portland. I shudder at the memory of our last encounter as I take a sip of my drink. She literally saved my life. We met through Zoe, quickly becoming good friends. She is cute and witty, so full of life. She is definitely eye candy with naturally wavy black hair, round gray eyes, and fair skin. We used to go out to the clubs, pretending to be a couple when she wanted to ward off women she wasn't interested in. I would tell her she needed to be upfront and let them down easy. She hated the thought of hurting someone's feelings.

She would have been good for Jaylon had Jaylon kept her hands off her. The two of them dated for about a year. After Jaylon's last attack on her, she had finally had enough of the abuse and ended it. To my knowledge, they have not spoken since. Jaylon and I got into a huge fight over her beating Brianna one night after we came from a downtown bar. Jaylon, allowing her insecurities to get the better of her, accused us of fucking each other behind her back. In true Jaylon fashion, I was to blame for all her failed relationships. I was determined not to repeat the multiplex of ass-kickings I endured as a child. She was always the victor. Unknowingly, I gave her power over me, giving her the advantage in battle. I made the mistake of magnifying her ability to defeat me, focusing on her size and strength versus my own. I should have viewed her as the pitiful bully she truly is, removing her power to defeat me.

It's strange how the mind reacts to different stimuli. My classmates insulted me almost as much as Jaylon did, except it didn't bother me. They referred to me as a nerd and a geek. My nickname became Slimphal because of my awkwardly slender frame. How fucking original, right? I can attest that compared to most of my classmates, I was the intellectual type. I aspired to make good grades and stay out of the principal's office. Basketball was the only cool activity I participated in, and surprisingly, I was good at the sport. Jaylon and I played together when I was a freshman and she a senior. Given our relationship, we managed to put our differences aside, going on to win the state championship that year.

My sister and I are polar opposites yet the same in some ways. It's peculiar we resemble each other to some degree. She sports a low fade, and her skin is the color of milk chocolate. Her dark brown eyes slant downward. Her physique is shapely, more feminine than she prefers, with wide hips and thick legs. Unlike me, she isn't comfortable in her own skin. It contradicts her idea of being a *stud* lesbian. In her mind, it means to be all male, all macho all the time. I believe if the opportunity presents itself, she would have the sex reassignment surgery. I, on the other hand, enjoy being a woman even though I have male tendencies. I am not fond of the term *transgender*, but it is often used incorrectly to describe people like us. Her drinking over the years coupled with an unhealthy lifestyle has taken a toll on her. She has aged considerably beyond her years. The night we fought, I wasn't the frail little girl she used as a punching bag growing up. I stood a few inches taller and was in good physical shape. To Jaylon, I was still the sheltered little pussy she beat down as a child. I abhor violence to solve problems, but she deserved an ass-kicking for what she did to Brianna. She beat her so bad, Zoe and I had to take her to the hospital. She suffered a concussion, sprained wrist, and a black eye. I tried convincing her to call the police on Jaylon, but she refused, noting she did not want to ruin Jaylon's career. She promised us in the parking lot of the hospital she would leave Jaylon.

Zoe, Brianna, Jaylon, and I were out celebrating my twenty-sixth birthday. I didn't want to celebrate, especially with Jaylon, but Zoe convinced me this birthday would be different, and against my better judgment, I agreed. Any birthday I ever had involving Jaylon turned out miserably. I had become so frustrated with birthdays that at some point, I decided to stop celebrating them altogether. We were club hopping on West Sixth Street, actually having a really good time. Brianna had given me a birthday hug and kiss on the cheek when Jaylon witnessed it. She went ballistic, yelling all types of profanities, calling us liars and cheaters, but what set me off was when she called me a weak-ass faggot. I lost it and charged at her. Brianna jumped between us quickly, turning to Jaylon, trying to calm her down. Zoe grabbed my arm, redirecting me to another area of the club in an attempt to defuse the situation. Brianna finally convinced Jaylon to leave. She instructed Zoe to take me home, and she would drive Jaylon home since Jaylon was obviously intoxicated.

Worried Jaylon might harm Brianna, I instructed Zoe to drive by Jaylon's house to make sure Brianna was okay. Jaylon was most abusive when she had been drinking. I asked Zoe to park across the street a few houses down so Jaylon would not see me and grow more irate. She complied, and we sat there, watching at three o'clock in the morning to make sure they got into the house safely.

Jaylon exited her car first, walking to the driver's side. As soon as Brianna stepped out of the car, Jaylon charged at her, knocking her down onto the concrete. She began punching Brianna over and over, calling her a bitch, a slut, and a useless piece of shit. I could hear Brianna's cries for Jaylon to stop. Instantly, when I saw Brianna hit the ground, I leaped out of Zoe's car, racing across the street, yelling at Jaylon as I approached, "Son of a bitch, get off of her! Come pick on somebody your own size, you insignificant little bastard!"

Years of rage and anger began to surge through my veins. I was praying Jaylon would come at me. I wanted to tear her fucking head off her shoulders and feed it to the pigs.

Jaylon looked up at me with Brianna still pinned to the ground and started to laugh hysterically, ranting, "Caiden, you really want to do this, little sister? I mean, really, you want your ass kicked again?"

Jaylon stands wobbling toward me, still talking shit. "Hail to the king, defender of whores and sluts! You would fight your own sibling over this bitch?"

I grew weary of her ramblings, rushing toward, her grabbing her by the shirt and pushing her backward into the passenger's side of her car. I began punching her repeatedly in her face, stomach, neck—anywhere my fists could land. Blood spewed onto me as I reveled in it, embracing the downpour of red rain covering me. I wanted her dead! I became a maniac turned loose and would not rest until I see Jaylon's head on the ground separated from her body. I was consumed by my own rage and contempt for her. My heart was pounding, pumping blood through my veins, supplying me the energy needed to continue my attack. Zoe and Brianna were tugging at me, trying to pull me off. I heard a scream: "Caiden, you are killing her! She is not worth it! Please stop this now!"

I am not sure if it was the grace of God, the voices returning me to sanity, or both, but I suddenly stop, and all was silent around me. Out of breath and gasping for air, I looked down at the pavement to see Jaylon sprawled out, drenched in her own blood. Her face, shirt, pants—everything was bloodred. The scene looked like a Picasso to me. Zoe took my hand, guiding me away from Jaylon toward her car, bringing me back to consciousness. I followed in silence. Brianna sat in the backseat, badly hurt. I glanced again to see Jaylon still lying motionless in the driveway. I slowly glanced over at Zoe from the passenger's seat then at Brianna from the rear view. I told Zoe to leave the drunken son of a bitch. Zoe started the car, and the three of us headed to Seton's emergency room to have Brianna treated. I could not go into the hospital soaked in blood—it would raise too many questions. Zoe caressed my face, hesitant to leave me. I kissed her on the hand to assure her I would be fine. I left them at the hospital and returned to Jaylon's house.

As I drove up, I checked if she was still lying in the driveway. I saw no sign of her. I pulled behind her white BMW 335i and turned off the engine. I got out of Zoe's black Mercedes and headed toward the house, noticing a blood trail leading up to the front door. I approached cautiously, and as I reached the front door, it is slightly open. I called for Jaylon as I pushed the door open slowly in preparation for an attack. As I entered the house, I heard what sounded like ice cubes clinking against a glass. The noise was coming from the kitchen. I called again for Jaylon but still no answer.

I reached the kitchen to find my sister sitting at the breakfast table with a bottle of vodka and a glass of ice. She had wiped some of the blood from her face. I could see she had been badly bruised. Her eyes were black and swollen. Her arms had cuts and scrapes from hitting the pavement. She was holding a frozen bag of peas against her face. I did not realize the damage I had caused until this moment. I struggled for words, now ashamed of what I had done, asking, "Jaylon, are you okay? I'm sorry. I . . . I don't know what came over me."

Jaylon looked up at me with a blank stare and spat blood on the floor at my feet. She got up slowly, and I could see she was in pain. She took her glass and bottle of vodka with her to her bedroom, slamming the door, leaving me alone in the kitchen. I washed up at the sink, cautious she might return. I grabbed an old T-shirt and a pair of Levis from her guest room and prepared to head back to the hospital to check on Brianna and Zoe. Brianna kept her word and broke it off with Jaylon a few days later. The incident was never reported to the police. The staff at the hospital wanted to contact the authorities, but Brianna convinced them it was a mugging. She said she couldn't identify her assailant and wanted to put it all behind her.

"Mr. Westhpal, how are we doing over here? Would you like a blanket?" the flight attendant asks.

I respond with a smile. "Mr. Westphal is it now? Why so formal all of a sudden, Ms. Guerra? A bottle of water would be nice."

She looks at me slyly as she heads toward the front of the plane. Upon her return, I am curious of the now formal address. I ask if I have offended her in some way.

She answers in a whisper, "No, not at all, Caiden. I am fairly new on the job, and the head flight attendant insists we maintain a professional relationship with our passengers. I think it has to do more with me serving a sexy dread-head while she's stuck with Mr. Comb-Over for the flight."

I chuckle and respond with a grin, "Please give her my apologies."

She laughs, handing me a bottle of water along with a napkin containing her cell. "I will be in Austin for the next three weeks. I would love to give you a personal tour of the city," she says quietly. *I'd love to personally tour you,* I think in silence as I smile at her.

The captain's voice comes over the intercom, announcing we would be landing in twenty minutes at Austin-Bergstrom International Airport. As I exit the plane, I head toward the bagging area, pulling out my cell to call Brianna.

She answers on the first ring. "Hello, stranger! I am outside at the Delta pick-up area in a black Audi A6."

Hearing her voice, I laugh as I grab my bags from the luggage belt and head outside to meet her. She is already standing at the back of her car with the trunk open. She greets me warmly with a big hug and kiss on the cheek. I embrace her with the same warmth, squeezing her tight, lifting her slightly off the ground. "Brianna, it is so good to see you. Thank you for picking me up. You look beautiful!"

She replies, "Wow! Caiden, you look great! Portland is good for you, or is a special woman_giving you this glow?"

"Portland is good for me, Brianna," I reply.

She suggests we grab a bite to eat downtown before she drops me off at Rose's. I load my bags in the trunk, and we head over to 291 West, a trendy bar and lounge we used to frequent. It's only been two years, and I hardly recognize parts of Austin anymore. I usually bypass downtown, taking the I-30 Toll when I visit Rose. As we head downtown, I notice more and more condos going up. It reminds me of Portland, in a way—only the air is thicker and the weather much warmer in Texas this time of year.

We arrive at the restaurant and grab a table on the patio. The waitress takes our order, and I sit back, taking notice of the now larger and more modern design. As we sit waiting for our food to arrive, we order a couple of Mexican martinis for old times' sake. We stare at each other oddly for a moment then suddenly, Brianna asks, "Caiden, have you contacted Zoe? Does she know you are here?"

I take a deep breath, pausing to think how I want to respond. "Brianna, I am not sure I am ready to see Zoe. I mean, I am not sure I can handle seeing Zoe. I just want to focus on Rosemary while I am here."

Brianna takes my hand and squeezes, saying, "I understand. Your mother is the primary reason you came back."

"My mother is the only reason I came back! There is nothing left for me here with the exception of you, of course," I remark.

She seems saddened by my response as she excuses herself to go to the ladies room.

While I have a moment, I find myself reflecting on Zoe. We grew up together from the time we were six. We lived a few blocks from each other and met playing in the park one Sunday after church. The two of us became best friends instantly. As young adults, we shared almost everything with each other with the exception of my sexuality. Zoe and her family are devout Christians, making it uncomfortable for me to discuss parts of my personal life with her. She didn't seem to mind the fact that I was openly gay. I didn't want to complicate her already-strained relationship with her parents with my life, so I made the decision to keep parts of my life separate from hers. Her parents never approved of our friendship, fearing I was a bad influence on her.

Looking back, we should have left things at best friends. Somewhere along the way, strong feelings developed between us, and we fell in love. We were twenty-six when we began dating. We kept our relationship a secret for about a year until Zoe grew comfortable with the idea of dating a woman. I wasn't thrilled about the secrecy. At the same time, I didn't want to rush her into something she wasn't capable of coping with.

Even today she is the most strikingly beautiful woman I have ever known. I love her wavy shoulder-length brunette hair, her remarkable almond-shaped ocean-blue eyes, olive-toned skin, shapely, curved five-foot-four body, and soft pink lips. She is compassionate, witty, and successful. I always thought we were meant for each other.

Brianna returns to the table as our food arrives. We catch up on each other's lives as we dine. After dinner, I grow anxious as we approach the house. In gratitude for a lifetime of love and care, I built Rose a mansion on ten acres on the outskirts of Round Rock, Texas, about six months after I moved to Portland. West Austin is beautiful, but she only moved there for the betterment of our education. Jaylon continues to occupy the residence. Rose loves the countryside, and Round Rock is a quiet, peaceful little town. This is my gift to her for taking care of me all these years. I employ contractors to maintain the landscape and pool and a maid service to take care of the interior. I knew Jaylon wouldn't help, so I took it upon myself to ensure Rose didn't have to lift a finger unless she wanted to. I feel a sadness when I think of how useless my sister is when it comes to our mother.

We arrive at my mom's, and I ask Brianna if she would like to come inside to say hello. She notices a Mercedes CL65 AMG coupé in the driveway. Not wanting to run the risk of it being Jaylon, she said she would come back another time. I take her hand in mine, squeezing gently to let her know I understand. We hug each other as we say good-bye. She pops the trunk. I grab my bags and head toward the house.

CHAPTER TWO

Rheia's Proposition

Although Rheia and I have been dating nine months, we have yet to indulge in sex. She wants to wait at least a year, ensuring I am with her for reasons other than sex. I enjoy her company, so I agree to her terms. I never imagined she would actually make me wait the entire year. I am not sure why I willingly agreed to her request, considering I had options. Maybe it was a safe move under the circumstances. I had the company of a nice woman without the complications of sex. I wouldn't have to pretend to enjoy it, knowing I wanted someone else. In order to abstain from temptation, I pour my energy into working out in my spare time, four to five times a week. The exercise seems to help release my sexual tension. CrossFit and I develop an intimate love affair over the past few months. Rheia and I aren't exclusive, but to my knowledge, we have not dated outside our relationship.

"When does your flight leave, honey?" Rheia asks while crawling into bed.

"I would have to check my itinerary to be sure. I think it leaves at noon tomorrow," I reply.

Rheia usually gets in bed in one of my T-shirts and a pair of panties. Tonight she ups her game, wearing a Vic Secret panty-and-bra ensemble. I am in bed, shirtless, with a pair of pajama pants as usual. She slides into bed and snuggles up to me, running her hand across my face then slowly down the center of my chest. Kissing me on the cheek, she mentions how much she will miss me while I am away. I gently kiss her forehead and tell her likewise, I will miss her too. Resting on her elbows with her chin in her hands, she stares at me, slightly biting her lower lip.

I am enthralled in *The Help* but take pause to ask her what she is doing. She smiles as she slides the book out of my hands then removes my geeky framed glasses, laying them on the nightstand. She begins to gently kiss me on the abdomen while running her hand across my chest. I stare at her oddly, wondering what has gotten into her. She straddles me as she massages my chest then starts to kiss and nibble on my neck and earlobes. Her warm breath against my skin arouses me. She softly whispers in my ear to make love to her. Still straddling me, she kisses my lips slowly, seductively. My response is more aggressive as I pry my tongue into her mouth. Is she finally ready? I ask silently.

I begin to run my hands up and down her backside, squeezing her tight butt and pressing her body close to mine as we continue to kiss. Our bodies roll around in bed until I am on top of her. My body moves between her legs, and I begin to slowly grind against her. Instantly, she begins to moan, running her fingers through my dreads, slightly tugging at them, arousing me further. The more we grind, the more passionate our kisses become. My lips move to her neck, down to her breast, stroking her nipples with my tongue. I stop to look at her to get approval to remove her bra and panties. She nods as she licks her lips in anticipation of me taking them off. I unsnap her bra from the front and slide it off her shoulders, revealing perfectly round 36C-cup breasts. I sit up slowly, sliding her panties off, tossing them to the side.

Staring at her naked body, I wonder to myself, *Why now?*

Sensing my hesitation, she sits, looking me in the eye, asking, "Caiden, do you want me?"

"Of course, Rheia, I am just surprised," I explain.

She smiles and again begins to kiss and suck on my neck. I push her away, warning not to leave any passion marks. I dislike hickies and the insecurity they represent, a character flaw I find extremely unattractive.

Her hand finds my cheek as she begins to explain, "Caiden, you are leaving, and I am not sure how long you will be gone. Tonight is a perfect opportunity for me to show you how much you mean to me. Caiden, I . . . I . . . I am falling in love with you."

I sit facing her, not knowing how to respond. I swallow deeply, and before I could speak, she leans in to kiss me. I cave at her advances and willingly accept her tongue into my mouth once again. I am asking myself, *Is this right?* I bury the thought and slide my hand down her side and over to her Venus. I hear her moan softly at my touch. It grows moist in between my fingers. Her body starts to move to the rhythm of my caress. *Caiden, what in the hell are you doing? You shouldn't do this. Not now!* I blurt out in my head. She feels and smells so inviting. My mind is screaming I shouldn't be doing this to her. She is a good woman. She deserves better. I pull myself back to the present, finding my fingers have a mind of their own as they glide in and out of her slowly and gently. My desire is overpowering. I won't deny myself the pleasure of being with this woman.

She whispers for me to push harder inside her, and I oblige. The harder my fingers penetrate inside her, the louder her moans grow. Her body begins moving faster and faster.

She runs her fingers down my back, pulling my hair, panting heavily. "Please don't stop, Caiden. Please, baby, I am about to cum!" Her voice continues to rise as she cries *oooh*s and *aahh*s, letting out a scream as her body quivers underneath me. My fingers exit her body, moving to her clit, teasing it. I begin to slide downward in preparation of tongue-fucking her clit.

Stopping my advance, she pulls me up toward her, kissing me on the lips, murmuring, "Caiden, I'm ready."

I smile at her comment and once again attempt to reach my destination. Rheia reveals to me she has never reached climax orally. My first thought is, *how strange*.

She has only been sexually involved with three other people I am aware of. She looks down at me, asking how she can reciprocate. As my chin rests on her stomach, I smile, not answering her question.

I begin kissing her belly button, moving up toward her breasts, gently tugging each nipple with my lips, and continue until I reach her soft, silky lips. I stare down into her eyes and kiss her softly. "Rheia, I want to be inside you," I comment.

The women she has been with never used adult toys. Naturally, it will be a new experience for her. She looks at me cautiously, thinking, before she responds, "Caiden, I am not sure I am ready for that. I want to please you, but toys seem over the top. If I want to be penetrated with a penis, I would be with a man."

Instead of outwardly alerting her to my growing frustration, I calmly exit the bed and head to the bathroom, speechless. I take a cold shower to avoid an argument over sexual preferences. Sensing my angst, she decides not to pursue a conversation. After I shower, I return to the bed, bidding her good night.

She snuggles up to my backside, kissing me once on the shoulder. "Caiden, I am sorry if I have upset you. I am just not ready for twisted sex," she whispers.

I pull away from her, hoping my body language relays I don't want to hear it. After about thirty minutes, still sexually frustrated, I pop a clonazepam to help me sleep.

The next morning, I wake to the smell coffee and eggs coming from the kitchen. I look at the clock, and it is seven thirty in the morning. *What the hell is she doing up at this hour?* I wonder. I lay in bed, still frustrated, wondering if Rheia is a good fit for me. I am going home, and it is unclear as to when I will return. My plan is to remain in Austin until—

A sudden sadness comes over me as I think of Rose. What if she doesn't recover?

Rheia enters my bedroom with a tray of coffee, OJ, a veggie omelet, and blackberries. She smiles and says, "Good morning, honey! I made you breakfast."

I sit up, propping the pillows against my back. "It smells great. Thanks for breakfast. How considerate of you," I respond, still aggravated from last night.

"Caiden, please don't be upset with me. Honey, I am trying to wrap my head around your request. I just need more time to process it," she responds. We sit in bed, eating breakfast in silence. Afterward, I throw on a pair of black sweat pants, white muscle T, and running shoes. I want to get a run in before I depart and clear my head. I hate eating before a run, but she took the time to prepare it. I grab my cell and armband and head for the door.

Rheia, still attempting to communicate, says, "Enjoy your run!"

I head out the door, not responding.

I run into Abby, the manager of Beautiful, while jogging. "Hey, Abigail, how are you?"

She looks at me awkwardly, replying, "Obviously, not as well as you."

What the hell does that mean? I wonder. "Hate to be so brief, but I have a lot to do before my flight leaves later this morning. I will call you to check on how the bar is doing in my absence."

"Okay, C, talk to you soon, and have a safe trip. Hope all goes well with your mom!" she yells as I fade deeper into the park.

After an hour, I return home, hoping Rheia has left. As I enter, I notice a handwritten note on the kitchen counter. I pick it up as I walk into my bedroom, tossing it on the bed.

I have to be at the airport by eleven. I had packed a few nights ago in preparation. Rheia has laid out one of my black suits, a white pocket square, black shoes, and a white shirt along with my favorite Rolex. Earlier in the week, I mentioned Texas is hot even in October; still she wants me "looking dapper," as she put it, especially sitting in first class. I thought it silly, but it seems to make her happy to dress me. Good thing she has no idea who gave me the watch. I doubt she would have been inclined to lay it out. I smile, picking it up for a second, remembering the day Zoe gave it to me.

In the bathroom, I turn the shower on and begin to remove my sweaty T-shirt. I am livid as I look in the mirror. *"What the f——!"* I scream in outrage. I am looking at my reflection and see fucking hickies all over my torso, even my fucking back. "Rheia, you sneaky little witch!" I yell in anger. Knowing damn well I despise passion marks, she waits until I pass out and intentionally molests me. "Fucking insecure b——!"

Upset, I slam my fist into the bathroom door, leaving a small dent. My first inclination is to call her, giving her a few choice words. I think this is exactly what she wants me to do. I refuse to give her the satisfaction. "She thinks this is a fucking game! Some sick-ass joke!" I yell at my image in the mirror.

Suddenly realizing I am short on time, I calm myself with deep breaths and finish getting ready. Luckily, the marks aren't noticeable with my shirt on. I grab my bags, car keys, and Rheia's note and head to the airport. I still have an hour before boarding. My assistant, Riley, is meeting me at the airport to pick up my SL500. No way am I leaving Midnight alone in a strange, dark garage unattended.

Riley Garrison has worked for me since I came to Portland. She is smart, talented, and at times naive. I invited her into the coffeehouse one rainy afternoon after noticing her hanging around the area, looking like a lost puppy. Her dreads looked as if they had not been maintained in months, and her clothes were battered, to put it mildly. She looked like she hadn't eaten in days. Somehow my heart was touched, and I felt a strong urge to help her. I sat down with her to make sure she was okay, offering her a cup of coffee and a sandwich. She told me she needed to get away from her past life. She was looking for a new start away from her family and friends. Her story was a familiar one to me.

I remember our first conversation asking about her talents, that I might have a job for her. She looked at me with an odd expression looming across her face. Assuming she thought the worst, I immediately cleared the air. "What skill sets do you possess?" I asked with a smirk.

"Oh, I work with computer security, programming, and software," she responded.

I eyed her curiously. She informed me she used to work for one of the largest software firms in the country back in California. My stare required more information as she went on to explain she had a penchant for hacking. She made it clear she never stole from the company but intentionally disrupted systems and acquired information meant to be secure just for the hell of it. She admitted she was a computer whore in so many words, addicted to the thrill of going places she was forbidden to go. She spent five years in the Air Force as a tactician. Strange as it seemed, I somehow felt instantly responsible for her. Right there on the spot, I offered her a job as my assistant. I was no computer genius, but she taught me a lot about computer software, access, operating systems, and data manipulation. We even hacked into a few corporate computer systems together for fun in our spare time. We developed code words and encrypted messages in the event those types of services were required.

She was actually a brilliant young woman. My advice to her was to start up a legitimate security firm. I told her I would assist her in any way I could if she so chose to do. Riley is of great use to me, becoming a close friend and confidante. She reminds me of what a sister should be. I hold my keys in the air, ordering her to take my baby straight home and park her.

She looks at me with a crooked smile and says, "Of course, CW."

I drop the keys in her hand and tell her I will check on the two of them in a few days. I am at the boarding gate, but before boarding, I decide to read Rheia's note. "Caiden, last night, you were amazing. You have no idea how much I love you. I hope you can forgive me for what I have done."

On the ride over to the airport, I decide it is best to end things with Rheia. Texting to break up seemed cowardly, so I call and get her voicemail. I make another attempt, and again straight to voicemail. I make one last attempt with no success. Normally, I won't break up via voicemail, but under the circumstance, there is no other option. "Rheia, I accept your apology. However, I think it best we end our relationship. I wish I could have told you in person. I know what it feels like to love someone and not have that love reciprocated. You deserve an explanation for my decision." I turn my cell to airplane mode and board the plane.

CHAPTER THREE

Home

I ring the doorbell of my mother's house. Not knowing her state of mind, I did not want to walk in unannounced. I wait a few moments, and no answer. I ring the bell once again and think maybe she is asleep. Still no answer, so I unlock the door and enter, saying, "Hello, Mom. It's Caiden. Are you here?" I hear a noise, maybe a TV, coming from the living room. I enter the living room to see my mother sitting in front of the TV, motionless. I look around for her nurse then return my gaze to Rosemary. My mom looks so fragile and weak, a shell of the former woman she once was. Before retirement, Rose was a judge for Travis County for twenty years. She is one of the most intelligent women I have ever known. My heart fell at the sight of her now frail self.

I move slowly toward the sofa, softly calling to her. "Mom, it is Caiden. How are you doing today?" I reach for her shoulder to touch her, and she turns to me slowly, staring at me blankly.

"Hello!" she replies. "Are you here to visit my kids? Jaylon is out playing, and Caiden is in the kitchen, preparing dinner. Are you staying for dinner, baby?"

She does not recognize me. I am paralyzed with fear. *How does a mother not recognize her own child?* I wonder in shock. I realize it has to be her illness causing her not to recognize me. Somehow I assumed she would recognize her baby girl! Tears trickle down my cheek as I stand frozen in disillusionment.

"Are you okay, baby?" Mom asks.

"Mom, it's Caiden, your daughter," I reply sadly.

She looks at me, expressionless, before turning her attention to the TV. I brace myself against a chair in silence. Suddenly, I hear faint music coming from the kitchen. As I approach, the sound of dishes clanking around drown out the music. At the dishwasher, I see a woman standing with her back facing me. She must be my mother's nurse.

"Hello, excuse me, miss."

She can't hear me with the earphones plugged in. I approach the woman, placing my hand on her shoulder. Startled, she jumps and drops a bowl of salad on the floor. I nervously go to her aid, picking up the broken bowl and spilled food off the floor.

"Sorry I startled you, miss."

She is on the floor next to me, telling me it is okay, she'd take care of the broken dish. Seeing my hands trembling, the woman caresses them gently, telling me everything will be okay. I thank her for her kindness as I sit, staring at the marble floor.

Still holding my hands, she responds, "Caiden, your mother is doing fine under the circumstances."

The woman's voice is familiar. I soon recognize it belongs to Zoe. I look deep into her beautiful blue eyes, finding it difficult to look away. "Zoe!" In barely a whisper, I reply, "I didn't recognize you. Your hair is . . ."

"Auburn," she replies, completing my sentence.

As I gaze at her, all the anger and resentment toward her dissipates in an instant. She takes her hand and places it on my cheek, wiping the teardrops falling from my eyes. Recognizing the fear in my expression, she draws closer to me, allowing my head to rest on her shoulder. She caresses my back as she holds me, promising once more that everything will be okay. I wrap my arms around her, holding on tight, not wanting to ever let her go. As we sit there, huddled on the kitchen floor in each other's arms, no words need be spoken.

I pull myself together and begin to stand, assisting her on the way up. We stood facing each other, struggling to find words. I caress her face, automatically leaning in to kiss her. Realizing what I was about to do, I quickly pull myself away from her. As I do, a shy smile moves over her face.

"What are you doing here, Zoe?" I ask quietly. She informs me she has been coming by regularly to visit with my mother. "I had no idea. Thank you, Zoe," I reply gratefully. Rose nor Jaylon mentioned this to me. "Does Brianna know you come by?" I ask.

"Yes, she comes by as well when she can. We discussed it when Jaylon told me your mother was ill. Brianna and I both agreed to do what we could to help," she explains.

"Why was I not told about this?" I ask, aggravated.

"Caiden, when you left, you made it perfectly clear you wanted nothing to do with me. Brianna could not bring herself to tell you because she thought you would be angry and cut her off too!"

My aggravation turns to guilt. I selfishly abandoned everyone I care about. Feeling ashamed, I ask myself, how could I have been so egotistical and uncaring? Zoe sees the disgust for myself in my eyes and gently rubs my arm. I can barely look at her. I manage to say, "Zoe, I am sorry for my behavior over the past two years. Had I known you and Brianna where helping to take of her, I would have come home sooner. Now my own mother doesn't recognize me. I should have been here. It is my responsibility. Can you forgive me?"

"Caiden, there is nothing to forgive. You didn't leave entirely on your own. I share some responsibility for your departure. The important thing is you are home where you belong. Once your mother spends time with you, I am sure she will recognize you."

The doorbell rings, interrupting our conversation. Zoe heads to the front door. A petite African American woman in her late fifties walks in, greeting her. "Hello, Zoe! How is Rose doing this evening?"

Zoe responds, "Hi, Eva. We were just about to have dinner."

As the woman enters the living room, she notices me standing by the sofa, looking me up and down. Suddenly, I feel like I am in a lineup. She walks casually over to me, stating "Caiden Westphal! I have heard a lot about you," and smiles. She reaches up to give me a huge bear hug. Despite being petite, she sure is strong. I look over at Zoe, mouthing *"Help!"*

She chuckles and throws her hands in the air, shaking her head. "I finally get a chance to meet you in person. Your mother speaks very highly of you. When she told me she had a handsome daughter, I thought she was losing her mind. I have to admit you are a handsome woman. Who would have thought? Honey, if I were a lesbian and a few years younger, I'd snatch you up!" she states as she continues to check me out.

"What the hell?" I mouth again to Zoe.

"Caiden, Eva Woodward. It is a pleasure to make your acquaintance."

I politely extend my hand to shake hers and reply, "It is a pleasure to finally meet you in person, Ms. Woodward."

She shakes my hand and with a big, charming smile, responding, "Handsome and well-mannered!" I blush at her comment. She turns her head, looking over at Zoe, and mouths *"This one is a definite keeper"* as she winks.

Zoe's face turns red, obviously embarrassed at the comment. She smiles that big, genuine smile I love so much, mouthing back, *"I definitely concur!"* I pretend not to notice the silent conversation in the room. Nurse Woodward walks over to my mother giving her a hug. My mother smiles as if she knows her.

"Caiden, I am about to give your mother her dinner and prep her for her bed. You two kids go somewhere and catch up. Caiden, don't worry. Your mother is safe with me." She must sense my hesitation at the thought of leaving the room. "Go on now. She will be fine. You can visit later if she feels up to it."

An employee telling me what to do—now this is a first! I stand in awe of this petite five-foot woman. She is a charmer to say the least. I look over at Zoe, motioning her to walk outside to the veranda. She follows my lead as we head out toward the backyard. It is unusually cool outside for it to be early October. I take my jacket off, placing it around her shoulders, when I notice she is shivering. We sit next to each other on a chaise longue and stare into the blue water of the pool. A small breeze catches her hair, blowing pieces of it into her face. I push the hair away from her eye, staring at her for a few moments. I take a deep breath of air and exhale, stretching my arms out, then ask Zoe to tell me how my mother is really doing. Her blue eyes are filled with sorrow when she explains Dr. Fischer doesn't think she has much longer. He thinks she may hold on two to three weeks. My heart sinks into the pit of my stomach at the news. I try to process what I just heard, but nothing can prepare me for news of this magnitude.

"Caiden, I am sorry to be the bearer of bad news," Zoe adds.

"It is okay, Zoe. I asked for the truth," I respond as I look down at the pavement.

She moves close to me and wraps her arm around mine as we sit there in silence, watching the ripples in the water. I remind her again how thankful I am for what she has done for Rose.

She replies, "Caiden, I love your mother as much as I love—"

At that very moment, I hear a loud yell coming from the veranda door. "Caiden! What are you doing here with Zoe?" It is Jaylon.

I respond, "Jaylon, how are you? It is good to see you."

She looks at me suspiciously as I get up to approach her to give her a familial hug. As I reach to hug her, she leans back with arms in defense, saying, "Caiden, you know we don't hug." She extends her hand out and shakes mine, tapping me on the shoulder, and I do the same. "Hey, Zoe, what are you still doing here this late? You are usually gone before I get here." Jaylon inquires.

I am thinking to myself, *I would be gone too if I had to deal with you all day.* I see an attractive young woman standing behind Jaylon trying to pass her to come outside. I introduce myself and extend my hand to her. She smiles, shaking my hand in greeting. "Hello, I am Detective Ericka Sawyer, Jaylon's partner." She looks over at Zoe then turns her attention back to me. "So you are Caiden? Glad to finally meet you. I have heard a lot about you," she informs me as she winks at Zoe.

Why has everyone heard about me, but I don't know a damn thing about anyone? I think. I notice Jaylon is brooding as usual and ask,

"Jaylon, I would like to talk to you about mom when you have time, maybe over a glass of wine?"

Jaylon looks at me, responding sarcastically, "Sure, Caiden, a glass of wine with you! Fantastic!"

Detective Sawyer smiles, interjecting, "Caiden, tonight a few of us from work are going out for drinks. If you would like to join us—"

Jaylon looks sharply at her as if she wants to slap the shit out of her. I see Jaylon's aggravation and politely decline her offer. "Thank you, Detective, but it has been a long day. I_am going to watch a movie and relax here for the evening. Some other time perhaps?"

"Call me Ericka. We are all family here, right?" she replies. Ericka walks over to Zoe, giving her a friendly hug, asking how she is doing.

Jaylon eyes them closely as she asks, "You are coming tonight, right, Zoe?"

Zoe quickly glances at Erika then back at Jaylon. She clears her throat, buying time to come up with a response. "I, uh, sent Erika a text earlier this morning to say I would not be able to make it tonight. Ericka, you did get my text, right?"

On cue, Ericka replies, "Yes, Zoe, I did, but I accidently deleted. Jaylon, I meant to tell you. It just slipped my mind."

I wonder why Erika is covering for Zoe. Jaylon asks Ericka what time Zoe texted. Ericka, aggravated by the interrogation, bluntly answers she can't remember.

"Caiden, what time did you get into town?" Jaylon asks rudely.

Great, Detective Westphal has just entered the building. I am in no mood for her bullshit. I respond superciliously, "Detective Westphal, why don't you just get to the point. Ask me if I have been with Zoe all fucking day and be done with it! That's what you really want to know, isn't it?"

Zoe and Erika chuckle lightly underneath their breath. Jaylon appearing aggravated ignores my remark. She turns back toward Zoe asking if they can meet up later. Zoe looks confused by Jaylon's question but notes she has other plans. Upset she didn't get the answer she desired, she barks at Ericka, "Let's go now!"

Before they leave, Jaylon warns me to stay away from Zoe. I decided to take the high road, giving her a warm smile wishing her a good night. The fucking nerve she has at times, unbelievable! Zoe says good-bye to them, and I wave good-bye to Ericka. Jaylon had already disappeared back into the house. I tilt my head back, thanking God we are not blood related. It is close to eight o'clock, and the effects of a long day are beginning to show. We go back inside, and I look for my mother in the living room. Before I step five feet into the house, I am met by Nurse Woodward informing me Rose is resting comfortably and shouldn't be disturbed.

"Caiden, I don't mean to appear uncaring, but understand your mother is in a delicate state and needs consistency. Is there somewhere else you can stay for a few nights until we can ease you back into her life?" she asks.

I am stunned at her request. You can get lost in one wing of this house, and no one would notice. After a brief internal hissy fit, I realize it's not about me. I go along with her suggestion to minimize the risk of Zoe finding out about my visits. I inform her I will rent a suite at the Westin near the Domain for a few days.

Zoe chimes in. "Caiden, that won't be necessary. I have plenty of room at my condo. Stay at my place for a few days, then see how things go. Besides, your mother would never forgive me if I allowed you to stay in a hotel."

Tired and outnumbered, I reluctantly accept her proposition. Maybe this is a chance for us to rebuild our friendship. I glance at Nurse Woodward surrendering the battle but not the war. "Nurse Woodward, I will be back tomorrow at three o'clock to spend time with my mother. Is that understood?" I state firmly.

Nodding, she lets out a sigh of relief as she ushers us to the front door. "See you tomorrow, Caiden, and good night, Zoe," Nurse Woodward replies as she closes the front door behind us.

CHAPTER FOUR

Zoe and Caiden

I offer to drive to Zoe's place out of old habit. She willingly agrees as she heads to the passenger side of her car. It is about a thirty-minute drive from here to Downtown Austin. We buckle up, smiling politely at each other as I start the car. I sit idle in the driveway a few moments staring into space thinking about Rose. Zoe reaches over, placing her hand on mine, offering comfort from my sadness. I pull out of my mom's driveway and head toward IH-35 South. We barely speak to each other on the trip. She seems distracted in her own thoughts as she gazes out the window. I begin to reminisce about our relationship, pondering how it all went so horribly wrong. Maybe we were young or immature, unable to handle a serious relationship. I wonder if we will ever discuss in detail why it ended. As we drive, I remember the first time she expressed an interest in me.

* * *

I knew my feelings for her were stronger than I imagined when she called me one day, sounding excited about a guy she had been wanting to date. As a friend, I offered my support, but deep down, I wished for the relationship to fail. After a month of dating, Zoe broke it off. When I inquired what happened, she fed me some bullshit story, telling me he moved away. Something in her tone led me to believe she wasn't being completely honest. I did some research of my own and found out he didn't move and wanted very much to be with Zoe. Needless to say, I was disappointed she lied and even more determined to figure out why she felt the need to. Outwardly, she put on a good show, appearing to be happy. Deep down, I knew she has never been happy in any of her romantic relationships. She would always find a reason to end it with someone.

Zoe had been on my mind constantly as of late. I fantasized about us being in a relationship. One day, I orchestrated a plan to test the waters to see if she had the slightest interest in me. I had nothing to lose and everything to gain. I had been dating Kyra for almost a year at the time. She was a student at UT, working on her doctorate in psychology. We had recently split because she cheated on me with my supposed best friend Trace. I had plans to meet with her later that evening after Zoe and I hung out to give her a chance to explain herself. I sent Zoe a text: "Great news, been dating someone. Would love for you to meet her. Can't wait to tell you about her."

It was a perfect June day with the temperature hovering around seventy degrees. We were to go on Town Lake to catch up then to our favorite wine bar for a couple of drinks. We arrive at the lake around three o'clock. Zoe looked beautiful in a navy blue sundress and sandals. Her brunette hair was bone-straight with bangs. I wore a pair of denim shorts and fitted V-neck T-shirt with slip-on sneakers. We exit my truck and walk toward the lakeshore. As we walked, she said, "I want to ask you a question about this woman."

I replied, "You mean Kyra?"

"Her name is Kyra?" she asked, looking over at me.

Looking straight ahead, I said, "Yes, that is her name, and you can ask me anything, Zoe."

She took a deep breath and asked, "Do you feel like she could be your soul mate?"

This is not the question I expected. I thought for a moment and replied, "Zoe, you only get one soul mate in life, and I already have mine."

Looking at her from the corner of my eye, I waited to see her reaction. She was about to speak but paused as if in thought then smiled as we continued our walk. We walked in silence for a couple of minutes. Then Zoe stopped suddenly and grabbed my arm, causing me to stop. I looked at her with a confused expression on my face.

She asked "Caiden, do you trust me?"

I thought to myself, *Where is this going?* and responded, "Zoe, I trust you until I can't trust you!" She again smiled as she turned to face me, taking my hands in hers.

Feeling her hands trembling, I gave them a reassuring squeeze. I had never seen her so anxious before.

My concern was growing as I watched her having difficulty breathing. I asked, "Zoe, what is it? You are starting to scare me. Is everything all right?"

She blurted out, "Caiden, you shouldn't continue to date this woman!"

"What, Zoe? Why?" I asked in surprise.

She replied, "Caiden, the fact you mentioned her to me means you are serious about her."

I responded defensively, "Why do you care all of a sudden Zoe?"

She tensed in frustration, saying, "Caiden, you never discuss the women you date with me._As your best friend, I feel it is my responsibility to tell you if she is not your soul mate, you shouldn't pursue her. It will only lead to heartbreak, and I don't want to see you get hurt."

I turned my head to face the lake, smirking. I took pleasure in knowing she was jealous. I turned back toward her, "While I can appreciate your concern for my well-being, I haven't had problems finding nice women to date in all these years. My heart can bend, Zoe, but it has yet to break. What is really bothering you Zoe?" I asked.

"Caiden, why are you making this so difficult? I am just concerned about you. I mean, you are doing well financially. You're smart, honest, well-built, and even kind of sexy. I mean, if I were a lesbian, you would be very sexy. Caiden, I don't want some gold digger taking advantage of you!" she replied.

I wanted to defend Kyra's reputation but could only focus on Zoe's comments. "You think I am sexy?" I asked jokingly as I smile at her.

"Caiden! Did you not hear all the things I said about you?" she responded in frustration.

I chuckled and replied, "Yes, I did, and I am flattered, but the *well-built* and *sexy* captured my attention the most!"

"You are exasperating, Caiden Westphal!" she exclaimed.

I smiled and replied, "Zoe Michelle Payne, all kidding aside, will you please tell me what has gotten into you?"

She looked at me with anguish in her eyes and began to explain. "Caiden, what I am about to say is really difficult for me. I have thought about this for months, probably years. I am trying to say, Caiden, I think—no, not think—Caiden, I know I have feelings for you in a way I know I shouldn't."

My heart began to beat rapidly, making me feel I was about to have a coronary.

She continued. "You are my soul mate, and I know I am yours. I have been denying my feelings for you since we were in our teens. Caiden, I don't know what to do." She covered her face with her hands, burying her head into my chest, sobbing.

Everything in that moment seemed surreal. I wrapped my arms around her, trying to console her, not knowing what else to do. Still in my grasp, she removed her arms, wrapping them around my waist, holding me tight. A few moments passed, and I looked down at her as she raised her head and I stared into those beautiful deep-blue eyes. They had always captivated my heart, and that day was no different. Zoe moved her arms, positioning them around my neck. She tiptoed up toward me, placing a delicate kiss on my left cheek then the right. Her soft lips were now in pursuit of mine. Once she seized them, we kissed each other with an intensity I had never felt before. Whatever fantasy I might have imagined our first kiss to be was nothing in comparison to what I was experiencing in that moment. It was the most sensual and intimate kiss imaginable.

I knew then, she would be the woman I would spend the rest of my life loving.

After our kiss, we gazed at each other, smiling uncontrollably. She rested her head against my chest, commenting, "It was as I always imagined, perfect!"

I looked down at her, commenting, "Perfect is an understatement!"

We walked back to my Rover hand in hand, both agreeing to skip the bar and go to her lake house to talk. We didn't say much to each other on the drive over. We were both nervous in anticipation of what might happen once we arrived at our destination. I wondered what it would be like making love to Zoe. What would it be like to hear her call my name in the heat of passion? Would this ruin a great friendship? Were we making a mistake? All possible scenarios raced through my mind. I wondered if she was contemplating the same thoughts. I never strapped up when I was with Zoe—I never had a reason to. In anticipation of meeting Kyra later that evening, I did wear my harness and dildo. *What the heck am I thinking about a dildo and harness for? We are just going to talk this through, not make love. Snap out of it!* I kept telling myself.

We were nearing Zoe's house on the lake.

Zoe is wealthy but doesn't act like some of the rich assholes I have encountered over the years. She is humbled by her family's wealth instead of feeling entitled because of it. I have always respected her for that. She has a fantastic five-bedroom, four-bathroom white stone villa that sits on four acres about a hundred yards from the lake's shore. The view of the hill country is amazing, and the custom-made pool that stretches the length of the villa is beautiful.

I pulled into the long driveway and parked not far from the front door. She unbuckled her seat belt and proceeded to exit my truck. As I opened my door to get out, I noticed Zoe walking around toward me. She was smiling as she neared me, placing one hand flat against my chest and the other on my cheek and began to kiss me even more passionately than earlier. I insatiably responded to her kisses with fervor. Breaking from our kiss, I grabbed her hand quickly, leading her to the front door. Once the door shut behind us, we couldn't stay off each other. I pressed her body against the wall, kissing and caressing her. She moaned as she reached to pull my T-shirt over my head and sling it to the floor. As she slipped off her sandals, she held her arms up while I slipped her dress over her head, tossing it on the floor. I unsnapped her bra with ease, still attacking her lips, invading her mouth with my tongue. I slipped my sneakers off in the midst of our passionate exchange. Never have I known such excruciating pleasure in anticipation of making love to someone.

Almost simultaneously we came to an abrupt stop, standing in her hallway, panting heavily. Zoe's eyes began to assess my bare upper torso. Her hands began to stroke my shoulders, moving to my chest. She ran her fingers across my abdomen, following my happy trail, stopping at my waist. She took a step back, perhaps to get a fuller image. Zoe had never seen me shirtless—not since we were kids. "Caiden, your body—it's picturesque. I had no idea you were in such great shape," she proclaimed as she bit her lower lip.

Blushing from embarrassment, I stood motionless for a moment, allowing her to quench her visual thirst. I outstretched my arm, clasping her waist, pulling her close to me, asking, "Zoe, are you—"

She placed her hand across my lips, preventing me from continuing, and whispered, "Caiden, I want this. I want you!"

Smiling, I scooped her up, cradling her in my arms as she squealed in surprise. She looked impressed. I was successful in my efforts. I grinned as I carried her through the walkway, into her living room, placing her down gently near her double-sized white leather sofa.

I stared at her enticing body for a moment then slid her panties down as she stepped out of them. I stood in awe, gazing at her in disbelief. This was actually happening.

She was, by far, the most beautiful woman I have ever seen. At five foot five, she was voluptuous and toned, shapely with a nice, thick bottom. Her breasts were a picture-perfect 36B. Those beautiful almond-shaped blue eyes burned through me as I gazed into them.

Zoe unsnapped the top button of my shorts. Nervous, I flinched. She smiled as she led me into her massive bedroom, taking a seat on the end of her king bed while I stand in front of her. Again she reached for my shorts to unbutton the remaining buttons, letting them fall onto the floor. She stood eyeing me, and I felt my body temperature rise and my body tingle in preparation for what was about to transpire. I was exposed, even vulnerable, under her watchful eye. She peered down at my harness and dildo for a second then back into my eyes with a devilish stare.

My head lowered as I giggled. Seeing her expression, I felt the need to explain my little invention. The harness is custom-made to fit the contour of my body, fitting snuggly around my thighs and waist. It is made with thin durable spandex encased in a fleshlike silicon material to match my cinnamon-toned skin. It is unlike any harnesses on the market, created and specifically designed to appear as a natural part of the body. A special mechanism was added to allow the dildo to be erect or recumbent. One simply clicks up, locking it in an erect posture, and clicks down to return it to its reclined state. The design is flawless and simplistic in nature. I call my little creation click-a-dick. It is patented; however, I have no interest in marketing it at the moment.

"Very impressive, Mr. Westphal. Only you would go to this extreme," she noted.

We both laughed as I explained, "It is all in the details, Ms. Payne."

The laughter eased the anxiety I was feeling. I gently moved closer to her, causing her to lean back onto the bed. Leaning on top of her, holding my body weight with my arms, we began to kiss each other, gently gliding our tongues in and out of the other's mouth. Our moans grew as the intensity of our kisses increased. Our hands were gliding over every inch of each other's body while unwilling to break away from our seductive kiss. My fingers discovered Zoe's clit, massaging it in a circular rhythmic motion. Excited by my touch, Zoe let out a tantalizing moan as we gazed into each other's eyes. My fingers moved down to her

Venus, gliding in and out of her. I could feel her Venus continuing to moisten with each stroke.

"Oh Caiden, yes, yes, I have ached for this for so long! You have no idea how bad I've wanted to be with you like this!" she murmured in between our tongue grind.

Her remarks only heightened my need to be inside her. Anxious to penetrate, I removed my hand from her Venus, positioning my body in between her legs. Still holding my body weight with one hand, I used my free hand to place my dildo on the edge of her Venus. I glanced at her for approval as she stared back at me with desire dancing in her eyes, willing me to continue. With the weight of my body, I slowly eased my dildo inside her. She tensed for a second, prompting me to pause. She then looked at me, nodding to continue.

Once I am completely inside her, Zoe clutched my back, digging her fingers deep into my skin. I stared down at her incredible blues while my body moved slowly with long, deep strokes in and out of her. My eyes closed and I inhaled her scent, shivered at her caress, the feel of my dildo gliding inside her and pressing against my own clit. I was moaning as my pleasure built, wanting to erupt.

In a low, sultry voice, I managed to whisper, "Zoe, you feel amazing."

My heart rate quickened as I felt my body gaining momentum, moving faster and harder in and out of her. My natural inclination was to fuck the hell out of her. I quickly erased the thought out of my mind, realizing this was no ordinary experience. I silently convinced my body to slow its pace, and as I did, Zoe's body met my present stroke in perfect harmony as she moaned in ecstasy.

Zoe pleaded, "Caiden, don't stop. Please don't stop! Harder, baby, please! Harder, go deeper. Oh, Caiden, yes, baby, yes. Caiden it's yours."

I lifted her legs onto my shoulders, giving me deeper access inside her. I was in a sexual frenzy, not wanting this experience to end. Suddenly my body refused to obey my will as I heard her voice rise. Her body tensed, alerting me of her impending climax. In perfect unison, we cried out in unadulterated elation.

"Caiden! I love you!" she exclaimed with shortness of breath.

"I love you too, Zoe!" I replied as my body fell next to hers in utter delight.

* * *

"Caiden, Caiden." I hear Zoe ask, releasing me of my thoughts, "Everything okay?"

Clearing my throat, I answer, "Uh-hmm, I must have wandered off to my special place."

Before Zoe advises I take the Sixth Street exit, she glances at me, puzzled.

I smile and remark, "I assume this is the correct exit, yes?" She smiles as she nods and instructs me to continue to Holy Street. We pull into her condo, and I look up at the towering twenty-story building. "Nice digs!" I comment.

I park in her designated spot, grab my bags, and we head up to her place. When we reach her condo, she unlocks a massive metal door. Upon entry, I see her condo is modern with stained concrete floors, and the floor plan is open. A granite wall separates the large living room from the kitchen. One side of the condo facing the lake has tempered glass windows from floor to ceiling. It is definitely Zoe's sophisticated style.

"Mr. Westphal, here is your sleeping quarters," she says jokingly.

"Thank you, madame." I chuckle in reply.

The room is immaculate. The king-size bed has a dark-chocolate tufted leather headboard with side and foot rails. She had a mahogany bedside table with antique brass on the pull drawer and corners, a matching dresser, and three African masks lined vertically hanging from the wall.

"I could get use to this, Ms. Payne," I comment.

"If I'm ever in Portland, I'm sure you would have equivalent accommodations," she remarks.

It has been a long day, and we decide to order delivery and watch a movie. Zoe leaves the room and heads down the hallway.

I look out the window to admire the view. I can see Lady Bird Lake from here. I unpack, shower, and change into pajamas and T-shirt and settle in. As I head to the living room, I see Zoe stretched out on the sofa and searching for a movie on Netflix. She looks at me oddly, commenting on the passion marks showing from my T-shirt. I explain the circumstances surrounding the marks and the repercussions. She seems satisfied with my explanation.

"I ordered Thai. Hope that's okay?" she informs me.

"Yes, sounds great," I reply.

Zoe suggests two of my favorites, *Titanic* or *300*. I laugh and pick *Titanic*. "*Titanic* it is," she comments.

It is going on nine thirty, and our food arrives. We eat and clean up then hop back on the sofa to start our movie. About half an hour in, I can barely keep my eyes open. I look over at Zoe, and she is glued to the screen.

"Zoe, I hate to bail on you, but I am beat. I am going to turn in for the night. Sorry, beautiful, the *Titanic* will have to sink without me tonight," I announce.

She looks at me with puppy-dog eyes and yawns. "It has been a long day. I think I will call it a night as well," she states.

As I get up from the sofa, I thank her for her hospitality and lean down to give her a kiss on the cheek. "Good night, Ms. Payne," I say as I walk down the hallway and head to bed.

After a few minutes in bed, I hear a subtle knock at the door. I turn on the lamp next to the bed and see Zoe standing outside the door. She peeks her head in, looking at me again with puppy-dog eyes. Laughing at her, I pull the duvet and sheet back, motioning her to hop in. She giggles and enters the room, quickly crawling into bed, wearing a T-shirt and a pair of boy shorts. She never liked sleeping alone. I look over at her as she snuggles next to me, kissing me on the cheek in gratitude for allowing her to share my bed.

"Caiden, I'm glad you are here," she remarks.

I smile at her then switch off the lamp. I lie in bed with my hand behind my head, staring at the ceiling. Zoe is resting her hand on my chest. I can feel her warm breath against my skin. I glance down, noticing she seems at peace lying here next to me. It makes me happy to know I can still be of comfort to her on some level.

It's been two hours since we lay down, and I am restless, unable to fall asleep. I realize I forgot to pack my sleeping pills. I look over at Zoe, who is sleeping like a baby. I gently remove Zoe's arm from my chest, trying not to disturb her. It is close to midnight when I ease out of bed and head to the kitchen to get a drink of water. I notice Zoe's cell phone is blinking and think, *Who could be calling at this hour?* I dismiss the thought as I finish my water and head back to my room.

As I attempt to slip back in bed, Zoe drowsily asks, "Is everything okay?"

I apologize for waking her and assure her everything is fine. I ease back in the bed, and she assumes her position again next to me with her face at my cheek. She kisses me tenderly on the cheek as she rubs her hand across my chest. I place my hand on top of hers, intertwining our fingers, and turn to face her. I see piercing blue eyes staring back at me. Instinctively, I kiss her on the lips, gazing at her. I lean in once more to kiss her as she willingly responds, kissing me softly yet full of passion. My body automatically rolls on top of her, and I begin stroking her neck with my tongue while my hands roam freely over her body. She graciously accepts my advances, kissing my neck, chest, mouth—every sensual spot she is aware of—purposely arousing me.

She positions herself on top of me, still caressing my body with her tongue. Pausing only for a moment, she sits up, straddling me below my waist. I watch as she removes her T-shirt exposing her well-sculpted breasts. She lets down her hair from its ponytail. I watch as it falls loosely past her shoulders. She stands at the foot of the bed, tugging at my pajamas, sliding them off. I sit up to remove her boy shorts. I lick her navel and caress her back. I tug delicately on her nipples with my lips. My hands slide down to her butt, firmly squeezing her cheeks, pulling her closer to me.

An overwhelming desire to devour her Venus with my tongue consumes me. Her fingers are twisting into my dreads, pulling at them, causing my head to tilt back. She leans forward, commanding my body back on the bed. She lies over me and begins to move her hands across my breasts, rubbing her thumbs over my nipples, then slowly she lowers her head down to my Venus. My body is painstakingly awaiting her enticingly warm touch. I feel my Venus growing wet as her fingers glide in and out of me gently.

I moan softly, "Zoe! What are you doing?"

I am excited to have her tongue on my clit once again. While her fingers are inside me, she kisses my abdomen until she reaches my navel, swirling her tongue in and out of it. She knows my body all too well. Fuck, she is driving me insane with desire! I feel her fingers exit while she runs her tongue along my happy trail. I am tense, nervous at the thought of her going down on me. She is the only woman I have ever given the privilege. Her warm lips are upon my Venus, kissing it slowly, taunting me. She moans, parting my lips, then proceeds to tongue-stroke my clit. My body, reacting, moves in unison with the slow and steady circular stroke of her tongue. My hands are pulling at her hair, causing her to moan.

Implacable at her task, she continues increasing her pace with every long satisfying stroke. I hear the sucking and licking sounds exuding between my legs, along with her moans growing more and more audible. Grasping my hips, she stops my motion, teasing me further, not ready for my pleasure to exhaust.

I lie motionless, dually frustrated and intrigued, surrendering to her will. Sensing she is the victor of this match, she delivers her final blow, pressing her mouth firmly against my clit, swirling her tongue hungrily. I am helpless to defend myself against her assault. Unable to resist, my body clenches as I reach my apex, crying out her name, relinquishing my body to her. This match goes to Zoe by TKO. She slides up next to me, smiling as if she has just won the heavyweight title. I glance at her, still reeling from my orgasm, unable to articulate into words my feelings. Looking into my eyes and caressing my face, she whispers "This is much healthier for you than a sleeping pill. Good night, sexy."

I have no response except an appreciative smile. I cradle her in my arms as we fall fast asleep.

CHAPTER FIVE

Reawaken

Around eight o'clock in the morning, we awake to a pounding at Zoe's door. I tussle in bed, still drowsy from our late-night sexcapade. Zoe jumps out of bed, throwing her T-shirt and boy shorts on and kissing me quickly on the lips, and instructs me to go back to sleep. After she leaves, I attempt to tune out the pounding at the door. A few seconds pass when the sound of muffled voices from the living room prevent me from going back to sleep. As I move to get out of bed, I hear a door slam. Concerned, I throw on my pajama bottoms and head into Zoe's living room. I see Zoe standing in the kitchen, brewing coffee.

Seeing a worried look on her face, I ask "What's wrong?"

In an obvious attempt to redirect, she asks what I would like for breakfast. It is unclear at this point if I should pursue an answer to my question. I decide to drop it for now and inform her I would be cooking her breakfast in gratitude for helping me get to sleep. I survey the fridge, making sure I have everything I need to make her favorite breakfast. She loves an omelet with spinach, feta cheese, tomato, and onion. I'm still concerned but make an effort to pretend nothing is wrong.

As she adds whipping cream to her coffee, it accidentally spills. "Damn it!" She blurts out in frustration. I grab a towel hanging from the dishwasher and wipe up the spill. I examine her hands, ensuring she has not been burned.

"Zoe, who came to the door this morning?" I insist.

"Caiden, can we talk about this later, please?" She asks.

Reluctantly, I respect her wishes and begin to prepare breakfast.

While chopping veggies, I notice Zoe's mood soften. She walks up behind me, placing her hands on my shoulders, planting butterfly kisses affectionately on my back. I pause from chopping a few moments as I smile, embracing her affections. She wraps her arms around my waist, squeezing me tightly as if it were the last time she would see me. I have not forgotten about the visitor but did not want to upset her, seeing her mood has improved. Releasing me, she reaches into a cabinet and pulls out two small glasses, filling them with orange juice. She takes a sip from her glass then offers me the other. I stop what I am doing and accept her offering, finishing the juice in one long swallow, placing the empty glass on the counter.

"Thirsty?" she asks.

"Very!" I reply.

I pin Zoe against the counter and begin to kiss her passionately, only pausing to slide her shorts off. I move my hand down to her Venus gliding my fingers inside her. Zoe's mouth gapes, as she grabs the counter to brace herself and begins to moan wiggling her body around my fingers.

"Oh, Caiden," she murmurs.

Kneeling onto the floor I begin to kiss her Venus, parting her lips with my fingers giving me full access to her clit. My tongue methodically licks her, causing her to moan softly.

Zoe's moans grow more intense as her body reacts, moving side to side, up and down. "Yes, sexy! Oh, you feel so good. Don't stop, Caiden. Oh god, oh god, Caiden! Caiden! Aaaahh, yes, yes, yes!" she cries out in orgasm.

As I stand, our eyes meet. Wrapping her arms around my neck, she stares up at me, and our mouths embrace into a deep, sensual kiss. Once our lips part, she stands in silence, gazing into my eyes for a moment, she then remarks, "Caiden?"

"Yes, Zoe?" I respond.

"I will always love you!" she whispers as she hugs me tightly. The tone in her voice gives me great concern.

Breakfast was quiet, with neither of us saying much to the other. We gaze at each other smiling and giggling like two teenagers in love. Afterward, we clean up the kitchen and go over each other's plans for the day. Zoe informs me she has a few errands to run and would be out for most of the morning, returning in time to take me to visit Rosemary. I insist on taking a cab to my mother's. I didn't want to inconvenience her any further.

I need to make a few calls to Portland; other than that, I will be at my mom's. I have not checked my cell since I arrived yesterday. I try to remember where I put it. While I am searching for my cell, Zoe dashes into her bedroom to shower and get ready for her busy day.

I locate it on the kitchen counter. I reach for it to check my messages when a call from Jaylon comes in. I attempt to enter my code to unlock then realize this is Zoe's cell. Why would Jaylon be calling Zoe? I ask. While in thought, I see my phone on the coffee table. I check it, and there are several texts from Riley and Abby. I notice there were no calls or texts from Rheia. I review my texts and respond to each of them, letting them know I arrived safely.

After making a few calls regarding permits and licenses for my club here in Austin, I finally get a chance to call Brianna.

"Hi, stranger, how are you this morning?" she asks.

"Brianna, how are you? Do you have any plans today? There is something I would like to discuss with you over lunch," I ask.

She informs me she won't be available until after five. I suggest we meet for dinner around seven at my one of my favorite restaurants on Fourth Street.

I decide with all this free time on my hands to gear up and go for a morning run. Great thing about Zoe's condo, it is right on the jogging trail on Town Lake. It is a cool October Friday hovering around fifty degrees, perfect weather for a run. It is now around eleven in the morning, and I have worked up a nice sweat when I begin to analyze what is happening between Zoe and me. I realize at some point we'll have to discuss *us*. I am enjoying reconnecting with her and in no rush to derail our progress. It feels good having her in my life again.

Out of the blue, my thoughts shift to Rose. I say a silent prayer, hoping she will regain her memory even if only for a brief moment. According to Nurse Woodward, we have very little time remaining. The odds of her retaining any memory are slim, yet I am steadfast in God's good grace. Rosemary instilled the power of prayer and faith in us at an early age. I have always believed in God and remain faithful no matter what my circumstance is.

As I continue my jog, I start to feel hopeful about my mom, Zoe, and my life back home. I miss Austin more than I realize. It is good to be back even under these conditions. I head back to Zoe's apartment around twelve thirty. She gave me her spare key to come and go as I please. I unstrap my armband to check my phone and see a text from Zoe: "Sexy, can't stop thinking about you!" I smile and text back, "I miss you already, beautiful!"

I schedule a cab to pick me up in an hour. I want to make sure I get to my mom's in time to meet with Dr. Fischer. I take a quick shower and throw on a pair of jeans, oxford shirt, blazer, and converse. Grabbing my watch and wallet, I head down to meet the cab. Thirty-five minutes later, I arrive at my mom's. I ring the doorbell, and a few seconds pass when Nurse Woodward opens the door. She is smiling as we greet each other. I walk in, passing her at the doorway in haste.

"How is my mom doing today, Nurse Woodward?" I ask.

She looks excited as she grabs my hand, pulling me into the living room, where I see my mom sitting on the right edge of the sofa. I notice Edwina sitting out by the pool through the patio door. She looks upset or sad—it's hard to determine. I look back at Rosemary as she looks at me with her green-blue eyes and a smile crosses her fragile face.

"Caiden, honey is that you?" she asks in a soft, weak voice.

She recognizes me. I look upward, praising God for this amazing gift.

I rush toward her when I see her arms open in preparation for a hug. I lean down, embracing her tightly in my arms. Tears of joy begin to trickle down my face I am so overjoyed. "Mom, how are you doing? I am so happy to see you!" I utter.

As we release each other, she motions me to sit next to her, patting her hand on the sofa the way she did when I was young. I am about to ask her more questions when she interrupts. Her facial expression turns serious, and I feel I have lost her again. She reaches her frail hand to my face, gently touching my cheek. "My baby, you look so beautiful. Caiden, I love you so much. You will always be my special gift from God. Caiden, I need you to listen to me."

I sit motionless, giving her my undivided attention. I nod my head, letting her know I understand.

She begins with an apology, admitting she should have told me sooner, then asks for my forgiveness. Her voice is soft, barely audible as she struggles to continue, "Caiden, I adopted Jaylon when she was six months old. Nadine is Jaylon's mother not yours. Your father, Edward, and I tried to have a child of our own without success."

I am listening in astonishment as she speaks. I rationalize she is confused and doesn't realize what she is saying.

"Prior to Nadine's death, we had decided to adopt Jaylon long before you were even born. Nadine was mentally unstable, and CPS threatened to place Jaylon in foster care. David, Edward's older brother, wasn't prepared to care for a child. Edward and I agreed it must be a sign from God since we had been unsuccessful in our efforts to produce a child. Twenty-one months later, we were pregnant. The pregnancy was difficult, and things between Edward and I had become complicated. We maintained a relationship until you were born October 27, 1983."

I am sitting next to my mom in complete dismay, wondering if she is telling the truth.

Seeing the confusion on my face, she touches my hand. "Caiden, you have to believe me!"

I look into her eyes, trying to uncover the truth in her words. It can't be right! Why would she keep something like this from us?

"Caiden, I am sorry there isn't enough time to explain it all" she said as she places a key in my hand. "This key is to my safe deposit box. You are the beneficiary of my accounts. When you are ready to know the whole truth, use this key. Caiden, promise me you will not open it until I am gone. Baby, I am so tired. Tired of the lies. I am ready to go home," she whispers as she looks at me with weary eyes.

I reluctantly promise as I place the key in my jean pocket. I shrug her comment off, not wanting to think about losing her.

"Caiden, do you trust me?" she asks.

My head is bowed as I hear her question. A faint smile befalls my face as I raise my head to look at her and reply "Until I can't, Mom."

She smiles at me once again. "Hello, you here to see Caiden or Jaylon?" she asks. My Rose is gone once again.

Nurse Woodward, who is standing nearby, comes over to assist her. She looks at me with sad eyes, placing her hand on my shoulder to try to comfort me. I look at her, half-smiling, and place my hand on top of hers, giving it a gentle squeeze. "Caiden, Rosemary, was only trying to protect you and Jaylon," she states.

I wonder in my mind, *Protect us from what?* as she moves her attention to Rosemary. I get up from the sofa, taking another look at Rose, and shake my head. I decide, to wait outside, by the pool, for Dr. Fischer to arrive.

I step onto the patio and am greeted by Edwina, one of my mother's longtime friends "Caiden, are you okay?" she asks.

Still in shock from my mother's confession, I don't reply. I take a seat near the pool, gazing into the water, when Edwina sits down next to me. I ask if she is going to tell me the truth about my mother's condition. She takes a deep breath and sits up erect, pondering her response. She informs me she is unable to share Rose's condition with me and offers her apologies. She lets me know she is here for me if I ever need to talk.

"What happened between you and Rose all those years ago?" I ask.

She half smiles, responding, "Caiden, one day I hope to explain everything to you and to Jaylon." She places her arm around my shoulder, pulling me closer to her, whispering, "Caiden, you do know I love you as if you were my own?"

I hug her back, nodding my head. "I know." I feel safe in her arms as we sit there in silence.

I check my watch, and it's three o'clock. The doctor should be arriving at any moment. Edwina reminds me I shouldn't be present during her meeting with Dr. Fischer. I let her know I would be in Rose's office while she meets with him. The doorbell rings, and I assume it to be Dr. Fischer. I head toward my mom's office to give them some privacy. Eva lets him in, directing him to the kitchen were Edwina is waiting. I introduce myself as we pass each other in the hall. I see him first check Rose's vitals and discuss something with Nurse Woodward. She points him in the direction of the kitchen. Desperate to have answers about my mother's condition, I stand in the hallway, out of view of Edwina and Dr. Fischer. I hear Edwina ask, "So Dr. Fischer, what can you tell me about Rose's condition?"

"Edwina, I understand this is a difficult time for you. Please understand we are doing everything we can to make Rose as comfortable as possible. I wish I had better news for you," he says.

"Is there anything more I can do to help her Dr. Fischer?" she asks, exasperated.

"Unfortunately, Edwina, we have to let nature take its course. I am sorry," he replies.

I walk quietly into my mother's study, reflecting on her words. I am her daughter. I search to find any legitimate reason why she would keep this from us all these years. I wonder if Jaylon somehow knew. This would explain why she hates me so much. She is a detective after all. All sorts of thoughts invade my mind, leaving me to ask myself, what am I going to do? I hear Dr. Fischer leaving and reenter the kitchen. Edwina is preparing to leave. We say our good-byes, and I am left alone in the kitchen with my thoughts.

I hear Jaylon's voice conversing with Nurse Woodward. She sounds in a seemingly decent mood. They exchange a few words, and the tone in her voice changes instantly. I look up to see her body tighten. She looks over toward the kitchen where our eyes meet. She walks over and stands in front of me and begins to speak. "I hear Mom was herself today."

I reply, "Hello, Jaylon, and yes, Mom was herself briefly."

Jaylon seems a bit out of sorts even vulnerable. She places her right hand in her pants pocket and strokes her cheek with her left. I have seen that posture once before when we were young. At the time, Jaylon was sincere in her apology for something horrible she had done to me. She has done so much over the years, I can't recall what she was apologizing for.

"Listen, Caiden, I know you and I are not on the best of terms. I understand Mom came back to us briefly today. Did she mention me?" she asks with tear-filled eyes.

I have never seen Jaylon cry before. I reply, "As a matter of fact, Mom did mention you. She said she loves you very much."

As much as I dislike Jaylon, I could not bring myself to tell her the truth or what may be the truth. Not until I have a chance to confirm the information. I detect a sense of relief in her expression. Jaylon tells me she was working near this area and stopped by to check on Mom, but she needs to get back to work. As she turns away and begins to walk toward the front door, she stops without looking back at me, saying, "Hey, a few of the guys are going out tomorrow night for a drink around nine. If you would like to join us, we will be at the usual spot."

Surprised by the invite, I reply, "I will be there nine o'clock sharp."

She heads out the front door.

I turn my thoughts to Zoe as I check my phone. I missed two of her texts: "Caiden, I can meet you at your mom's?" and the second, "Wish I were with you." I reply, "Leaving my mom's. Will meet you back at your place, see you soon." I call a cab, and it arrives at my mom's within fifteen minutes. It is nearing four o'clock as I head back downtown. I forget how bad traffic is on IH-35 at rush hour. It takes me over an hour to get back to Zoe's.

I am anxious to see her. I enter her condo, and she is on the phone. She looks at me, giving me a big wave, mouthing *"Be off in a sec!"* I nod and head to the leather sofa, taking off my blazer and laying it on a chair. I sit on the sofa and unbutton my shirt, rolling up the sleeves. I scan the room, noticing two wineglasses and a bottle of Pinot Gris on the coffee table. Zoe loves her wine. I, on the other hand, am no connoisseur of wine, but I enjoy a good glass from time to time. I look back at her, still chatting on the phone, and she mouths *"Pour us a glass, please, sexy!"* I see the wine opener next to the bottle. I uncork the wine, allowing it to breathe before pouring. Zoe walks to the sofa and sits down, placing her legs underneath her. I hear her tell whoever is on the other end of the phone, "I have to go, but I look forward to seeing you tomorrow evening."

Zoe mutes her phone and tosses it on the far end of the sofa. I notice she is wearing a high-waist black skirt with a hemline just past her knees and a sleeveless white blouse. Her hair is loose and wavy. She looks very corporate exec / naughty school teacher. I see her black leather pumps neatly placed on the side of the sofa.

"You look great!" I comment.

She leans in and starts giving me mini kisses on the lips and cheeks. "I have missed you today, Mr. Westphal," she states. I smile and reach to retrieve the glasses of wine on the coffee table. I offer her a glass. She smiles at me graciously, receiving the wine. I lean back on the sofa cautiously with glass in hand. We look at each other, clinking our glasses together, and take a sip. "How did your visit go with your mom?" she asks, concerned.

"It went well actually. She remembered me. We had a brief conversation," I reply. I was not ready to share the conversation between my mom and me with Zoe or anyone. I still need to process and validate if what she told me is true or if she is imagining it all because of her illness.

Zoe's eyes widen as she smiles at the news. "Caiden, that's great! I know how important it is to you," she remarks as she caresses my arm.

I take another sip of wine and place my glass back on the coffee table. I lean in to kiss Zoe on the lips. Her mouth opens slightly giving me access to her tongue. I let out a low moan as we kiss. My body is craving to make love to her. Zoe, still holding her glass of wine, leans into my kiss, moaning softly. She finally places her glass on the coffee table next to mine and pulls her skirt up to her thighs then straddles me. She places her arms around my neck, and we kiss each other passionately. My hands are firmly caressing her thighs and back. She manages to slide my shirt off my shoulders then reaches to unbuckle my belt. Her soft hands return to my shoulders and chest, caressing my body, sliding her nails gently down my neck to my navel. Her body begins to grind against mine. I slide my hands under her skirt, reaching for her panties.

"You naughty girl!" We laugh between our kisses in amusement as she has none on.

Her hands move back down to my groin area to unbutton my jeans. "Oh, you naughty boi!"

She giggles as she pulls my dildo outside my jeans. I push my body into the sofa to give room to slide my jeans lower to my thighs. While holding my dildo, she positions her Venus over it and inserts the tip. She removes her hand, placing both arms around my neck, then I watch as her body glides slowly up and down on me, moaning softly in my ear. My hands grab her waist as I savor the sensation I feel each time her body presses down on mine. Our bodies begin a dance, mine moving up when hers is moving down—up and down, we continue to the dance. Our enthusiasm grows as our bodies press harder and harder into each other with every stroke.

"Oh, Caiden!" she cries as we continue our sexual ballet.

"Ahhh, Zoe, don't stop," I instruct.

As her body moves up and down in my lap, my eyes close and my head tilts back on the rear of the sofa as I enjoy every lustful moment. My eyes reopen to see her beautiful eyes gazing at me, inaudibly indicating her desire for my touch. My mouth is agape, waiting impatiently for her tongue to infiltrate as she leans in, seductively biting her lower lip. Our bodies nearing the brink of pleasure, her hands are upon my cheeks as we kiss. I feel my body clinch in anticipation. Her head tilts back as her muscles tighten, and she lets out an enticing lament, propelling me into an explosive eruption.

"Zoe, baby, oh!" I moan, out of breath with my head resting against Zoe's breast. I place my arms around her, squeezing tightly.

Gasping for air with her arms wrapped around my neck, she holds me close. We sit in each other's arms, consumed by each other, motionless for a few minutes. After she stretches and lifts herself from my lap, lying back on the sofa, placing her feet in my lap. I reach for our glasses of wine, handing her a glass. She takes a few sips and winks at me. We both break out in laughter after realizing we didn't bother to disrobe. I take a sip of wine and look over at Zoe, smiling at her. I tickle her on the foot, causing her to quickly pull her foot away as she laughs. I love to hear her laugh.

We sit, enjoying our wine and company. I want to ask what really made her break up with me. I refrain from asking in fear that it would open old wounds that have not had time to heal. I wonder if what we share now will be enough to erase the painful memories.

"Caiden, are you hungry?" Zoe asks, snapping me back to reality.

It is six thirty; I have not eaten since breakfast. "Famished!" I reply, looking over at her.

"Main course or dessert?" she quips.

"Dessert, of course!" I reply, smirking.

"Caiden, you are insatiable!" she says as she laughs.

She squeals as I part her legs. I lean down about to kiss her Venus when we are interrupted by the doorbell. "Damn it!" I scream, perturbed by the distraction.

My face drops off her lap onto the sofa as she laughs at me jokingly. It dawns on me: I am to meet Brianna for dinner at seven. I immediately hop up off the sofa, giving Zoe a quick smack on the lips. Scrambling for my cell, I grab it and text Brianna I would be a few minutes late. As I head toward the bathroom to take a quick shower, Zoe is moving to answer the door.

Brianna texts, "Still at work. Is nine OK?"

I text back, "Nine is perfect!"

I am about to turn the shower on when I hear shouting. The yelling grows louder and louder.

"Who the fuck is in there, Zoe? Open the fucking door or else! Damn it, I know you hear me, Zoe!"

Boom, boom, boom are the sounds from the constant pounding. The voice is muffled, and I cannot make out whom it could be. I grab my shirt off the bathroom sink, tossing it on, and head down the corridor. I then move toward the front door, finding Zoe sitting with her back against the door, sobbing with her hands covering her face.

"Zoe!" I yell as I instinctively move toward her, kneeling on the floor in front of her, grabbing her hands as the banging still persists.

She looks up at me with tear-filled eyes, sobbing uncontrollably. I pick her up, taking her to my room, and order her to stay put.

"Caiden, don't! Please don't answer the door," she pleads as her voice cracks.

"Zoe, stay here. I will be right back, I promise."

I return to the front door and open it, staring into an empty hallway. I scan the hall left then right, but no one is there. I hear the elevator door and run toward it. By the time I reach it, the doors are shut. The elevator starts moving downward. I bang my hands on the outer door of the elevator in frustration.

My attention quickly turns to Zoe. I rush back to her condo, and upon reaching her door, I scan the halls once more before entering. I lock the door and walk to my room. Zoe is sitting in the middle of the bed, crying, resting her head on her knees with her arms wrapped around them. I have only seen her this upset once before—the day she broke things off with me. I have to find a way to get her to open up and tell me what is wrong. I take a deep breath to calm myself and walk calmly toward her, sitting at the foot of the bed. I ease down onto the bed and pull myself close to her, wrapping my arm around her. My touch only intensified her sobs as she wraps her arms around my neck, squeezing tightly, still sobbing.

"Caiden, I am sorry, so so sorry for everything!"

I hold her close to me, caressing her hair attempting to reassure her everything is going to be all right. I lie in bed with her in silence for about an hour until she falls asleep. I can't sleep, and my mind is racing. I rewind my thoughts, trying to piece together what is going on. Who is Zoe afraid of? How did they know someone else is in the condo? I slide out of bed, quietly heading into the living room. I grab my cell phone and keys and head outside. I did not want to disturb her. I need to find out what is going on with her and the mystery freak at her door.

I call Riley in Portland. "Riley, Caiden. Listen, something has come up. I need you to do something for me. I am texting you the details now. Let me know if you need anything else and get back to me ASAP!" I hang up to send Riley the text and go back inside. I place my cell on the bar and check to see how Zoe is doing. I peek in the room and find her sound asleep. Unable to sleep myself, I lie on the sofa, praying Riley finds something soon.

CHAPTER SIX

Amends

"Caiden, hey, how long have you been out here?" Zoe asks, shaking my shoulder.

I wake drowsy. "I must have fallen asleep late last night. How are you doing, beautiful?" I ask, concerned.

She looks at me with sadness in her eyes as she sits next to me on the sofa. I move to sit up, but she gently touches my chest, instructing me to lie back down. She places her hand softly on my chest as she stares at me. She wants to tell me something, but she is afraid.

"Zoe, I need you to trust whatever is going on we can get through it together," I state in the hope that she will confide in me. I see her eyes beginning to form watery droplets. Her left leg is shaking rapidly. It pains me to see her like this.

"Caiden, we need to discuss the real reason I broke it off with you. We can't move forward until I make amends for the past."

She is about to tell me everything when my cell rings. I ignore it, urging her to continue. She places her hands on her knees, staring out the patio door as if searching for the strength to confide in me. My cell rings again, interrupting us.

"You should answer that, Caiden. It may be news about your mom."

I want to argue the point, but I know she is right. I get up from the sofa, grabbing my phone off the bar.

"Hello!" I answer, sounding irritated.

"Caiden, this is Nurse Woodward. I need you to come to your mother's house immediately," she states.

"Is everything OK?" I ask, my voice shaky.

"Caiden, I do not think your mom has much time. Please get here as soon as you can," she says sadly.

I inform Zoe I need to get to my mom's quickly.

She immediately replies, "I am coming with you."

We both dress quickly, throwing on T-shirts, jeans, and sneakers, and head to her car. I am too nervous to drive, so I hand her the keys. We get in, and she reaches over to grab my hand to assure me everything will be OK. I hold her hand tightly, still thinking the worst. I grab my cell to make a call to Jaylon.

She answers on the first ring, sarcastically saying, "Caiden, what do I owe this pleasure?"

I respond "Jaylon, I do not have time for your bullshit. I just got a call from Nurse Woodward requesting to come to Mom's immediately! Are you on the way?"

"She called you?" Jaylon snorts, sounding surprised.

"Of course, she called me, Jaylon. Did she not call you?" I ask, frustrated.

"Uh yes, she did. I will be there later on today. I am tied up right now and can't get away."

Unwilling to allow Jaylon to piss me off, I dropped the call. *That fucking son of a bitch!* I think.

Zoe rubs my forearm gently to keep me calm.

Thirty-five minutes later, we arrive at my mom's. I dart out of the car and into the house.

"Where is she?" I ask.

"She is in her bedroom," Nurse Woodward responds.

I rush past her, heading straight to my mother's room. I open the door and see my mom propped up on a pillow. Her head turns toward me as I walk into the room. She is staring directly at me.

"Mom!" I whisper.

She lifts her frail arm and motions me to come sit by her. I obey as I sit on the edge of the bed. I grab her hand, placing it in mine and squeeze gently. I caress her face softly, smiling at her. She reaches her free hand to my cheek stroking it lovingly only the way a mother can.

"Caiden, my baby, it's time for me to go home. I am going to miss you most of all. You are my greatest achievement, and I love you. Remember, you were created out of love. Your father made so many sacrifices to keep you safe. We only wanted to protect you from our mistakes," she whispers in a tiny frail voice.

"Mom, I love you. Don't leave me, not yet!" I cry in panic as I watch her struggling for air.

Looking into her glossy eyes, tears begin to flow from me uncontrollably. I was losing her, and there was nothing I could do to stop it.

"Caiden, remember the key?" she mumbles.

I look at her, confused, then suddenly remembering the key she gave me the other day. "Yes, Mom, I have the key," I answer, still weeping.

"Good. Baby, do you remember Romans 12:2?" she asks.

She loves the Bible and made Jaylon and me, recite the King James Version often. "Yes, Mom, I do," I reply, trying to stifle my tears.

She nods her head gently, signaling me to quote the verse. "And be not conformed to this world: but be ye transformed by the renewing of your mind, that ye may prove what *is* that good, and acceptable, and perfect, will of God." My voice cracks halfway into the verse. I am rocking back and forth, holding on to her hand, begging her to hang on. She looks at me and smiles for the last time, then her eyes slowly close. After hearing her final breath, I collapse onto her bosom, holding her close to me, crying uncontrollably. I have lost my oldest and dearest friend. The pain is intolerable, making me sick to my stomach.

After a few moments, Zoe and Nurse Woodward enter the room. I could hear sniffles and feel Zoe's hands squeeze my shoulders. Her touch is warm and supportive, providing me comfort. She sits on the bed behind me with her voice cracking, telling me how sorry she is for my loss. I refuse to leave my mother's side. She is still here with me. Her body is still warm. I will not let her go. Eva is attempting to remove my grip from my mother, but before I could react, Zoe intervenes. I feel her rise up from the bed, speaking to Nurse Woodward, asking if she would give me a few more minutes. Eva must have agreed, leaving the room quietly. Zoe returns to my mom's bedside and again sits behind me, resting her head on my back, caressing my arms and shoulders. It is a comfort to have her near me.

After about an hour, I manage to pull myself together and away from Rose's body. The coroner arrives, waiting patiently in the living room.

Zoe politely asks, "Caiden, are you ready to go, or do you need more time?"

I look back at her to give her a nod of "Yes, I am ready to go." Slowly, I rise from my mom's bedside with swollen red eyes and turn facing Zoe. She instantly holds her arms out as I fall into them again, sobbing. "Caiden, everything is going to be okay, sweetheart. I am here for you," she utters as she holds me tightly, reassuring me we will get through this. She guides me to the living room, signaling the coroner to enter the bedroom.

I look around the room and see Nurse Woodward and Brianna both weeping. Brianna walks toward me to embrace me. I hold her tightly, thanking her for coming on such short notice. "It means a lot to me, Brianna, that you are here," I explain.

"There is no other place I would be, Caiden. I'm so sorry, honey!" she exclaims through mournful cries.

I scan the room, hoping Jaylon has arrived, but I do not see her. I release Brianna from my embrace and check my cell phone for a message or text from Jaylon. Where is she?

About five minutes later, Jaylon enters the house, stumbling around, smelling of alcohol. She is drunk and in a foul mood as usual. "Where is Rosemary?" she slurs.

I am watching my sister in disbelief. How could she show up here in a drunken stupor? It is taking everything in me not to knock the shit out of her. I take a deep breath, informing her Rosemary is gone.

Jaylon looks around the room when her eyes catch glimpse of Brianna. "What the fuck is she doing here?" she blurts out.

"Jaylon, that is enough! Don't start at a time like this!" I warn.

Jaylon, still wobbling, looks over at me then at Zoe. "Zoe? You got to be fucking kidding me! You are here with Caiden?" Jaylon asks.

"Jaylon! I said enough of your bullshit," I state, my anger mounting.

Zoe grabs my arm as she tries to redirect my attention to the matter at hand, whispering, "Caiden, now is not the time. Jaylon is obviously drunk, and neither of you need this right now."

I deduce Zoe is right and manage to focus on the details regarding my mother. As I am about to walk outside to cool off, Detective Sawyer enters the living room followed by two Round Rock police officers. She walks over to Jaylon to extend her condolences and gives Jaylon a firm handshake as she pats her on the shoulder. She then turns to head in my direction. I manage a polite yet small smile as we shake hands.

"I am sorry for your loss, Caiden. Your mother was a beautiful person," she offers. I thank her for her kind words.

I am about to turn my attention to the police officers when I notice them engaging in a conversation with Jaylon. Jaylon points in my direction and begins to blurt out, "She is the reason my mother is dead! Arrest her, arrest her!" Detective Sawyer intervenes, explaining to the officers Jaylon is under the influence and obviously at a loss.

One of the officers motions me to step outside. I follow, providing them a brief account of my mother's passing. They question Nurse Woodward, Zoe, and Brianna as well. They offer their condolences and wait patiently outside for the coroner to finish up. One of the officers suggests someone makes sure Jaylon gets home safely. I nod in agreement.

Ericka comes outside, apologizing for Jaylon's outburst. "She has been under a lot of pressure lately," she informs me.

"No need to apologize for Jaylon's behavior. I am used to it after all these years," I respond.

"Not that it's any of my business, but is there a reason your sister despises you?" she asks.

Looking her directly in the eye, I state "Detective Sawyer, you are absolutely right! It is none of your business" as I excuse myself walking back into the house.

The coroner and her team are moving my mother's body down the hall as I am entering. I take pause for a brief moment, looking at the body bag, and move to the side, allowing them to pass. I look down at the floor as they move by me, trying to erase the image of my mother in a body bag.

As they exit, I hear Zoe instruct them to take Rosemary to the Cook-Walden Funeral home in Pflugerville. She smiles at them, politely closing the door softly behind them. She looks over at me to see how I am holding up. I lift my head to look at her, assuring her I am OK. She moves toward me as Jaylon is coming down the hall with Detective Sawyer helping her to stand. "I am going to take your sister home. Caiden, about earlier, I was totally out of line, and I am sorry," she states.

"Apology accepted, Detective, and thank you for being a good friend to Jaylon," I reply.

Jaylon leers over at me, then Zoe, and remarks, "Zoe, you little bitch! I warned you what would happen—"

I charge at Jaylon, knocking her into the wall, and proceed to knock the shit out of her before she could finish her sentence.

Continuous blows from my fist meet her face until Detective Sawyer manages to get in between us, screaming, "Break it up! Caiden, that is enough! I do not want to have to arrest you. Please stop this!" she begs.

I stop punching Jaylon, but she is still pinned against the wall. I whisper to Jaylon, "Jaylon, if you come anywhere near Zoe or speak to her like that again, I promise, you worthless piece of shit, I will kill you!"

I back away from Jaylon, slowly looking her dead in her dark eyes, nodding my head, and mouthing, *"I mean every fucking word. That's a promise!"*

Jaylon looks at me and begins to laugh hysterically, stating, "You little shit, you don't know the half of it. Go ahead ask your precious Zoe to tell you the truth. You two deserve each other, and I hope the both of you rot in hell. At least, I am not a murderer like your whore of a girlfriend!"

I leap for Jaylon again, but Detective Sawyer is prepared for my attack. She is in between Jaylon and me, preventing a direct assault. She is holding her arm out, warning me to let this go.

Zoe grabs my arm, pleading, "Caiden, please, can we just go home?"

Detective Sawyer is trying to force Jaylon out the door as Jaylon stops, placing her hands on the doorway, responding to Zoe's comment, "Home? This motherfucker is living with you, Zoe? She is the reason you didn't want me to come in the other day, isn't it? Fuck you, you devious little cunt! You will pay for this, Zoe. I'll make sure of that!" Detective Sawyer manages to get Jaylon out of the house and into her car.

I am standing in the hallway, looking at Zoe for answers. My mind going to places I don't want to go. "Zoe, what is Jaylon ranting about?" I demand.

Zoe looks at me then turns to notice Brianna at the other end of the hall. Brianna sees the fear in Zoe's eyes and comes to her aid, holding her in her arms as Zoe begins to cry. As Brianna holds her, she is staring directly at me with bewilderment on her face. Brianna instructs me to take Zoe's car. She said they would meet me at Zoe's condo.

Brianna adds, "She just needs some time. Please, for me, just let this go for now."

I am livid, but looking into Brianna's eyes, I know this is difficult for her as well. Caught between her two closest friends. In order to protect one, she has to hurt the other. I stare back at her, hurt and confused. I nod, responding, "I will leave, but, Brianna, this is not over. I want answers!"

She nods sweetly as I head back toward the living room. After a few minutes, she convinces Zoe to let her take her home. Zoe, still obviously upset, doesn't even look at me as they exit.

Everyone has gone, and the house is eerily quiet. Walking back toward the living area, I see Nurse Woodward sitting at the kitchen table, quietly sobbing. I enter the kitchen, taking a seat across from her. I am saddened as I look at her grief-stricken face. Tears are running down her chubby little cheeks. I see a box of tissues on the counter and reach for a couple, placing them in her hand. She thanks me as I reach across the table to grab her hand in comfort. She looks at me with a slight smile, accepting my hand, holding it tightly. "You know, your mother was very proud of you, Caiden. All she ever talked about is how she raised a good one. I see a lot of Rosemary in you," she acknowledges.

As we sit across from each other, sharing a tender moment, I reply, "Thank you for taking such good care of her, Eva."

CHAPTER SEVEN

Zoe's Enlightenment

"Zoe it's been two days, and you have barely said two words. Caiden is worried about you. She has a lot on her plate, Zoe, and you are being really selfish," Brianna expresses.

Under the circumstances, I thought it best I stay at my lake house for a couple of days to sort things out. "Brianna, can we go for a walk? I . . . I could really use a friendly ear!" I utter.

Brianna agrees, so we head down toward the dock. "Zoe, I forget how beautiful it is out here," Brianna comments as she attempts to lighten the mood. Anxious to finally open up to someone, I make Brianna promise no matter what she wouldn't repeat it to anyone—especially Caiden! Reluctantly, she agrees.

I take a deep breath, saying, "I broke up with Caiden because I was ashamed of what I had done. Two weeks before Caiden left for Portland, I found out I was pregnant."

Brianna's eyes widen in shock.

"I lost my daughter eight and a half months into the pregnancy. She was stillborn, and I have been living with the guilt ever since,"

I couldn't bring myself to tell Caiden the real reason I couldn't be with her. Instead, I told her my feelings for her changed, and I no longer wanted her heart. Caiden refused to believe me at first. We argued for hours until finally I blurted out, "I don't want your heart! I don't love you anymore. Please let me go!"

I will never forget the look on her face the moment my words left my lips. It was tearing me apart to see the pain in her eyes. I never dreamed I could be so cruel to the woman I loved more than anything. At the time, I thought it was the best thing for us both. Either hurt her by telling her I had a one-night stand and risk her never looking at me the same way again, or tell her I didn't love her anymore and hope it would lessen the blow.

Brianna interrupts, asking why I didn't tell her the truth.

"I couldn't let her go through life thinking she is not enough for me, Brianna! I know Caiden and her pride. She would have never forgiven me for betraying her," I continue as Brianna looks off into the water in disbelief.

"How did all this happen, Zoe? Why didn't you come to me?" she asks, upset.

I respond, "Brianna, I am sorry, but my hands were tied. I wanted to come to you but—" I stop, suddenly contemplating if I should say anything else.

Brianna senses my hesitation and reassures me my secret is safe. Relieved to share my secret, I begin to cry uncontrollably. She places her arm around my shoulder to console me.

Tears are cascading down my face. I provide the details. I explain how Jaylon called me out of the blue one day, asking for help in mending things with Caiden. She said I knew Caiden better than anyone and could provide her insight. I agreed to meet Jaylon at the House of the Blue Martini to talk over dinner. I arrived at the restaurant to find Jaylon waiting at our table, sipping on a glass of wine. We talked for about thirty minutes over a couple of glasses. I remember feeling a little drowsy after my second glass. We continued our conversation over dinner, discussing ways she can improve her relationship with Caiden. About midway through dinner, two of her friends arrived. I assumed they were a couple. Jaylon introduced us then invited them to sit down and join us. I think their names were Jessica and Marcus. The rest of the night is a complete blur.

All I remember from that night is waking up the next morning to see Marcus ease out of my bed, putting his clothes on. He looked at me, saying "Thank you for a very entertaining evening" as he bent down to kiss me on the cheek.

I moved away from him quickly, keeping my sheet up to cover my naked body. He told me he was leaving, so I wrapped the sheet around me and followed him to my front door.

After my door closed behind him, I heard giggling coming from one of my guest rooms. I headed down the hall to investigate, and I found Jaylon and Jessica in one of my guest bedrooms naked. Turning my head, avoiding the view, I demanded they both leave. I shut the door and waited impatiently in the living room for them to go out, still trying to piece the evening together.

About fifteen minutes later, they entered the living room. I remember Jaylon, with a wicked smirk on her face, commenting, "Zoe, I didn't think you had it in you to be with a man anymore!"

I felt sick to my stomach and ordered them out of my house. Jessica left immediately while Jaylon hung around to taunt me. The sarcasm in her tone was evident as she spoke. "Don't worry, Zoe. I won't dare tell the prince her princess is a *whore*. It would absolutely destroy her! You know how overly sensitive my sister can be. Why, she just may get the impression she_really does have that horrible, unwanted black heart Rose warned her about. Hmmm, what to do, Zoe? What to do? My guess is she would never forgive you for this!"

I knew Jaylon would use this to her advantage. She warned me not to mention this to anyone. "Brianna, I felt literally at her mercy and hated it. I beat myself up, wondering how I could have been so irresponsible. I tried recapping the night but can only remember bits and pieces."

Brianna interrupts, "Zoe, you have to tell Caiden before Jaylon does. It would destroy her if she heard this from her. You have to know that!"

"Brianna, I have been trying to tell Caiden, but every time I get the nerve, we are interrupted. I thought I would be able to tell her before Rosemary passed—" I pause midsentence, realizing I have abandoned Caiden when she needs me the most. I am disgusted at myself, recognizing how selfish I am acting! In a panic,

I immediately call Caiden. I gnaw at my fingernails, nervously praying she answers. The voicemail comes on. "Caiden, it's me. I need to talk to you right away. Please call me back!" I say anxiously.

With my anxiety mounting, I send Caiden a text, "I'm so sorry! Please meet me tonight at the condo. I will explain everything."

Brianna, recognizing the urgency in my expression, pulls out her cell, attempting to call Caiden. She leaves a message. "It's me, Bri. Call when you get this message." She follows with a text, "Call me. It's important!"

Brianna and I hurry back to the grab my car keys and head out in search of Caiden. I contact the funeral home, hoping she may be there.

A woman's voice answers politely, "Smith-Walton Funeral Home?"

"Hello, this is Zoe Payne. I am calling in regards to Rosemary Westphal. I am trying to reach her daughter Caiden. By any chance, is she there?"

"I'm sorry, Ms. Payne, but Ms. Westphal left about thirty minutes ago," the woman replies.

"Can you tell me the date of the service?" I ask.

"Yes, of course. Thursday at three o'clock at our Pflugerville location," she responds.

"Thank you for your time," I reply.

The ride to my condo is quiet. Brianna is gazing out the passenger window in deep thought.

"Brianna, what are you thinking about?" I ask, startling her.

"Zoe, you said you only remember having two glasses of wine that night, right? I find it hard to believe you can't remember anything. It's not like you."

I have often wondered the same thing. I must have had more than I remember. We reach my condo and park. On the way up the elevator, I am wondering how and when to tell Caiden the truth. As we walk down the hall, Brianna locks our arms together, giving me a comforting smile.

Upon entering my condo, we find Caiden with an attractive young African American woman in my living room. A sense of ease covers me at the sight of Caiden. She is standing at the bar, staring in the direction of the young woman on the sofa. She must have just arrived from the funeral home, still dressed in slacks and dress shirt. Her head turns toward us as we enter, and a relieved smile crosses her face. She immediately greets me at the door, hugging me tightly.

"I am so glad you're here!" she exclaims.

Caiden releases me, turning her gaze to Brianna, thanking her for taking care of me. Brianna responds with a warm smile, taking a seat on the sofa near the young woman.

"Hello!" Brianna says to the woman.

She politely smiles at Brianna, preoccupied by whatever she is doing on the computer.

Caiden is holding my hand tightly, looking impatient.

"Caiden, who is your friend?" I ask.

"Zoe, Brianna this is my assistant, Riley."

Riley says a brief "Hello!" before continuing her task.

Brianna looks at me, signaling I should talk to Caiden. I nod in agreement and turn toward Caiden, informing her I have something important I need to discuss. We walk into my bedroom for some privacy. Caiden closes the door behind us, and before I could speak, Caiden leans down, kissing me on the lips. I give in to her advance, wrapping my arms around her neck, kissing her as if it were the last time I would have the opportunity. We move toward the bed, kissing each other tenderly. Visceral emotion engulfs my soul, rendering me powerless to her advances.

I look into her eyes, seeing a need for me more than a want. Underneath her desire, I see despair in her eyes. Her seductive light brown eyes are distracting me from my task at hand. Reluctantly, I place my hand on her chest, placing some distance between us, uttering, "Caiden, please, I need to talk to you. It's important!" I can't focus as my hands irrepressibly unbutton her shirt, revealing her smooth cinnamon skin. I gaze at her chiseled frame, thinking to myself, *She is beautiful on so many levels.* My mind selfishly gloats, knowing she is mine.

Entranced in the moment I revert back to a childhood memory of seeing Caiden for the first time. She appears to be biracial, half–African American, half-Asian. Her features are unique with big almond-shaped light brown eyes and bone-straight brown hair hanging just past her shoulders that flows easily in the breeze. Her lips are full and thick, and her smile is warm and inviting.

Zoe! I scream in thought, jerking myself back to the present.

Caiden is eyeing me, searching my soul, and out of nowhere, asks, "Zoe, do you love me?"

I reply without hesitation, "Of course, Caiden, with all my heart!"

Caiden paces the room slowly, tossing her dreads out of her face, turning to me, asking, "Do you want me?"

Puzzled by her line of questioning, I reply, "Yes, more than anything!"

She stares deep into my eyes as I answer. She draws closer to me, placing her hands on my shoulders, saying, "I know you feel threatened by my sister. Zoe, whatever it is, whatever you have done, I don't care! I don't need to know. I am sure you have your reasons for not telling me. Just be with me. Love me for the rest of my life. That is all I ask."

I stand speechless, feeling as if a boulder has been lifted from my chest. I look up at Caiden, placing my hands on her cheeks, with my eyes forming droplets at a loss for words. She wipes the tears from my eyes then holds me close to her, stroking my back. I begin to weep in her arms, praising God for blessing me with someone with a pure and forgiving heart.

Remorseful, I whisper, "I don't deserve you, Caiden."

"Zoe, we have all make mistakes. That's what's is so great about each of us. We are all perfectly imperfect!" Caiden explains.

She lifts my chin with her finger, gazing into my eyes, and gently kisses my lips. I am acting on impulse, surrendering my lips to hers. Butterflies in my stomach begin to flutter, and my Venus awakens, aching for her touch. I slide her shirt off her shoulders, running my fingers across her chest. Feeling the tension in her body, I grow eager to assist her in its release. I moan as she lifts me off the ground, wrapping my legs around her waist. She walks toward the side of the bed, moaning as she kisses my lips. Gently, she lowers me until my feet touch the floor. I turn with my back to her, grasping her hands, guiding them across my breast, down to my Venus, helping her massage my clit.

She moans in anticipation as she roughly pulls my body into hers, raising my shirt above my head, taking it off. My jeans and underwear follow as they hit the floor. She slips off her shoes, unbuckling her pants, letting them fall. Her hand glides over my breast, teasing my nipples. She lightly guides her hand down to my Venus, cupping it then slowly massaging my clit with her fingers. I let out a moan as my hands reach to caress her tight ass, pressing my butt into her pelvis, alerting her I am primed for penetration. My Venus is wet and tingling, inviting her well-endowed penis to enter.

"Caiden, don't hold back!" I quietly utter, giving her free reign over my body.

"I won't," she grunts through gritted teeth as her hand grasps the back of my neck, forcing me to bend over the bed. I outstretch my arms, burying my fingers into the duvet, bracing myself. I feel her sexy brown eyes scanning my backside as her hand slides down the center of my back, stopping on my buttock, giving it a swift smack. I utter in excitement. I feel the tip of her dildo on the outer edge of my Venus. I desperately want her inside me. The anticipation is almost unbearable.

"Caiden, don't make me wait!" I beg.

Her hands are clutching my waist, locking me in position. She is breathing deeply as she enters me with full force and expertise, thrusting me into a series of delicious cries of satisfaction. Every thrust I accept with pleasure as she dwells deep inside me with my body greedily pleading for more. Continuous moans depart my lips as I call out her name with each powerful, unyielding thrust. Her pace gains momentum, and her cries increase in volume, catapulting me into a magnificent orgasm. My body constrains, absorbing the sensation of unmitigated gratification. Caiden follows with an eruption of her own as she repeatedly cries out my name.

We collapse on the bed, gasping for oxygen to fill our lungs. Caiden lies behind me, caressing my arm with her finger, softly kissing me on my shoulder. I feel her warm breath against my skin, giving me goose bumps. A gratified smile crosses my face as I reflect on the pleasure I enjoy each time we make love. I face her, gently kissing her lips while caressing her cheek. She replies in turn with warm kisses of her own with her eyes fixated on mine.

"I love these beautiful blues," she whispers. I shyly smile, kissing her on the lips. My body still writhing from our sexcapade, I began kissing Caiden's chest as I roll on top, pinning her on her back. I look down at her, grinning wickedly, and she begins to laugh, knowing exactly what I plan to do.

"I don't have the will to stop you, Ms. Payne." She chuckles.

Curious to know what it's like to have Caiden's dildo in my mouth, I take the lack of resistance as a green light and proceed downward. I place my hand around the base, noticing it is still moist from my juices. Eager to submerge it into my mouth, I look up at her once more. She is looking down at me with a sensual smile. My eyes remain fixated on hers as I slowly lick around the tip with my tongue. She smiles brightly in disbelief, chuckling.

"Impressive, Ms. Payne!"

As my mouth opens, so does hers, as if assisting me on my journey. I smile and wink at her as I continue to place my mouth on her dildo, slowly allowing it to glide deeper and deeper into my throat. She continues to watch me curiously as she enjoys the show.

She explained once although she didn't have the sense of touch, her other senses provide her with a heightened sensation of pleasure. She has always taken pleasure in pleasing over being pleased. I am happy to see her aroused by my tongue play. Her body starts to move slowly, gliding her dildo in and out of my mouth carefully. She is tender and loving with me. My excitement builds, watching her bite her lower lip as she moves. She softly pulls her dildo away from my mouth then pulls me up to her, spreading my legs across her pelvis. Inserting her dildo inside me again, she rings an imaginary bell, saying "Ding, ding" as we move on to round 2. I love watching her muscles flex as she strokes. I lose myself in her as we make passionate love!

The intimacy we share is indescribable. I want don't want this feeling to end, willing my body to resist the urge to climax. Unable to oblige, I explode into orgasm, with Caiden's ensuing moments after.

She rests beside me, out of breath again, caressing me, holding me in her arms. While we lie exhausted in each other's arms, I take a moment to apologize for my absence during her mother's passing. Ushering my apology to the side, she expresses she needed time to be alone to mourn her loss, noting I have a lot on my plate as well and the time apart hopefully gave us a new perspective on our lives and relationship.

As we lie in bed, we realize Brianna and Riley are still in the living room. I attempt to lighten the mood, joking we are horrible hosts, leaving our guests unattended. She laughs in agreement. It is good to see Caiden smiling.

"Hmmm, we should be better hosts, Zoe," Caiden says as she turns to me with a stern look on her face. "One other piece of unfinished business before we return to our guests," she remarks.

My expression is of bewilderment, has she changed her mind about my secret? Caiden gingerly positions her body in between my legs, sliding downward, nibbling at my nipples as she continues her descent down south. "Caiden, your appetite is insatiable!" I insist.

"Only when it comes to you, Ms. Payne," she jokes.

"Mr. Westphal, somehow I seriously doubt that!" I say, laughing.

"Ms. Payne, this is no laughing matter!" she says with a smirk.

Caiden is at her destination gently, licking my clit with her tongue. My body flinches, feeling her warm soft tongue upon my clit.

"Ooh, Caiden, you feel so good," I whisper as my body begins to wiggle and press against her mouth. She takes great care in kissing and licking every inch of my Venus. She has a way of, making me feel I am the only woman in the world she desires.

"Are you pleased, Ms. Payne?" she mutters between tongue strokes.

"You'll have to keep at it, Mr. Westphal, in order for me to be absolutely sure" I joke. She feels, amazing! I close my eyes, relishing every moment. Her fingers ease inside me as she continues, seducing my clit. *Amazing* can't begin to describe how I feel in this moment.

I lie in bed, when suddenly, tears creep onto my cheeks as I think the pain I have caused her. How could I been so naive to let her walk out of my life? I have so many regrets about how I hurt Caiden, the loss of my child, the past two years of my life have been a nightmare. I have to tell Caiden the truth.

My impending climax brings me out of my thoughts. I pull Caiden's dreads as my back arches and head tilts back, enjoying my orgasm. Caiden teases me with her tongue, moving it slowly around my clit while my body jerks in response. She stops and looks up at me with vulnerability in her voice. "Zoe, promise me you will always be here. I don't ever want to be without you again," she pleads.

I reach for her placing my hands on her face. Crying myself, I cup her face and stare into her big brown eyes, reassuring her, "Caiden, I promise I will never let you go again. I love you."

My arms wrap around her, squeezing her as tightly as my body would allow, affirming I mean every word. She lay with her head buried in the pillow, weeping. Sadness fills me, knowing I am the reason for her pain. In this moment, I vow to prove to her she is the love of my life.

CHAPTER EIGHT

Resentment

"CW, hate to interrupt, but you have to see this!" Riley explains as she taps on the bedroom door.

"I will be right there Riley!" Caiden states as she gets out of bed, hurriedly throwing on her slacks and shirt as she heads to the living room. Still in bed, I begin to wonder why Caiden brought her assistant down from Portland. I hop out of bed and get dressed too, joining them.

My eyes meet Brianna's as she mouths, *"Did you tell her?"*

I shake my head no.

She looks at me, confused, mouthing, *"Zoe, you two have been in there for over two hours. What happened?"*

I mouth back, trying to contain my smile, *"I can't talk right now. I will fill you in later."*

Brianna leans back on the sofa with her arms crossed, with a smirk, mouthing, *"You two are nasty!"*

I can't help but giggle and nod in agreement.

Caiden and Riley are both staring at the laptop. Caiden's expression reveals she is not happy at Riley's findings. Her demeanor changes to anger, ordering Riley to download everything to her cell reconfigure the security settings, creating a loop of the host's objective. She sends a text with the addresses and cell numbers to set up surveillance. Lastly she informs her she will provide a diversion and warns, “Riley, I need you to be very careful. We are not dealing with corporate idiots this time.”

“Caiden, what is, going on?” I ask, concerned.

She purposely avoids my question, suggesting we go out for dinner.

“Will Riley be joining us?” I ask.

“Riley, how long before you finish here?” Caiden asks.

“Only a few more minutes, CW. I can take care of the rest on your signal,” she replies.

“Riley, would you like to join these two lovely ladies and myself for dinner?” Caiden asks.

“CW, I can’t believe you even asked!” she responds sarcastically. “How is it you seem to surround yourself with beautiful women?” Riley questions.

Caiden flashes a cocky smile, replying, “It is sheer luck!”

I roll my eyes at her, smiling as she winks at me.

“I wish I had that kind of luck!” Riley replies with eagerness.

Riley must have come straight from the airport, seeing her bags next to her by the sofa. I tell her she can shower and change in the spare bedroom across the hall from Caiden’s room. I pull Caiden to the side to inquire if Riley needs a place to stay. Caiden says she was putting Riley up in a hotel for the duration of her stay.

“Caiden, I have the room, and she did come all this way. I don’t mind if she stays here, really,” I explain.

She looks at me then over at Riley with a grin on her face then turning to Brianna, who is smiling. “I guess I am outnumbered here. Fine. Riley, the spare bedroom is down the hall on the right,” she offers.

Riley quickly grabs her bags with the assistance of Brianna as they head down the hall. Caiden is eyeing them carefully.

I nudge Caiden’s shoulder, giggling. “They would make a cute couple!”

Caiden looks at me out the corner of her eye, shaking her head grumpily, remarking, “Don’t go there, Zoe!”

Caiden calls ahead for reservations at eight o’clock at Perry’s. It is about five thirty, so we have plenty of time to prepare.

My thoughts return as to why Caiden brought her all the way from Portland. What are they up to? She is in deep thought, standing at the kitchen counter. I imagine the reality of her mother's passing is hitting home. I am leery. Two days is enough time to mourn her loss. Caiden is a private person, rarely showing her true emotions to anyone. I uncork a bottle of wine in the kitchen, holding it up to her, asking if she would like a glass. She nods yes as she stands there, still in thought. She manages to pull herself out of her daze and looks at me, half-smiling.

"What's wrong, sexy?" I ask.

She chuckles at her nickname, then her expression changes to sadness as she whispers, holding back from crying, "I miss Rosemary. Other than Jaylon, she is the only real family I have. I feel alone."

She must see I am thrown off by her comment while she walks up to me as I hand her the glass of wine. She leans down to kiss my cheek, noting, "If it were not for you, Zoe, I would be completely alone. I thank God for you every day. You make me so happy!"

I smile at her and caress her cheek, replying, "Caiden, you are stuck with me! I will never leave you."

"Is that a promise?" she asks.

I place my finger over my heart and draw an *X*. She chuckles as she places her arm around my waist, drawing me close to her.

Brianna and Riley return to the living room, both smiling like schoolchildren. I pour Brianna a glass of wine. She loves wine as much as I do. I offer Riley a glass. She looks over at Caiden, waiting for approval. Caiden eyes her firmly but says nothing. I pour a glass and walk it over to her, putting it in her hand. She thanks me and takes a sip as she sits on the sofa. Brianna signals me to go into my bedroom.

I excuse myself, telling Caiden, "Brianna and I need to get ready for dinner."

She knows it takes us a while, being femme girls and all. Jokingly she states, "Did you not just promise to never to leave me?"

"I don't think going into the next room constitutes leaving you," I reply back sarcastically.

She smiles then begins to converse with Riley.

Before I am pulled into my room, I overhear Caiden tell Riley she can borrow one of her suits because it was going to be a special evening. She wants everything to be perfect. Riley's eyes light up as she smiles brightly, excited to be wearing one of Caiden's tailored suits. I enjoy seeing her in a well-tailored suit fitting her sexy body to perfection. I am getting excited just thinking about the visual. I smile a big smile, remarking to myself, she is so damn *hot*! My girlfriend down below seems to agree as she begins to twitch.

Brianna plops down on my bed, staring at me, waiting for details. "Zoe, did you tell Caiden everything?" she asks.

"Actually, Brianna, Caiden prevented me from telling her anything," I comment.

I inform her about the conversation between Caiden and me. Deep down, I still felt the need to tell Caiden the truth. I will make it a point after the funeral service to sit her down and tell her everything. Jaylon is a loose cannon, and I won't risk her hurting Caiden. I am sure her version of events will be embellished.

Brianna sits in bewilderment, making the comment, "Zoe, do you even realize what you have in Caiden? Caiden is one of a kind. I would give my right hand to have someone love me the way she loves you—forgiving everything without knowing anything."

"You are absolutely right, Brianna. I am blessed to have Caiden. All I want now is to prove to her and myself that I am deserving of her," I respond. A bit of envy is reflected in her eyes as she looks at me for a moment.

Caiden interrupts, telling us she received a call from Detective Sawyer, informing us Chief Martin invited us to attend the policeman's ball this evening in lieu of our dinner plans. She said Chief Martin and Rosemary were old friends, and he would be honored if Caiden attends. He wants to present a plaque to Caiden and Jaylon in Rosemary's honor. I could hear the disappointment in Caiden's voice as she is telling us.

About an hour and a half later, Brianna and I go into the living room to find Caiden on her cell in the kitchen and Riley sitting at the bar. Luckily, Brianna still had clothes at my place from when we use to be roommates. She looks amazing in a black strapless dress just past her knees with black heels. Her hair is in an updo, with one tress falling to the side.

As we enter the room, Riley—looking very handsome in a black suit, white shirt, and dress shoes stands immediately, looking at Brianna, commenting with a huge smile, "Brianna, you look beautiful!"

Brianna smiles shyly, replying, "Thank you. You clean up very well yourself." She looks over at me, mouthing, *"Damn, she is a hottie!"*

I giggle, mouthing back, *"Indeed!"* There is definite chemistry between the two of them. It would be nice to see Brianna with someone who appreciates her.

Riley's eyes move to meet mine. She quickly glances over at Caiden still on the phone and unaware we have even entered the room and comments, "Zoe, you look incredible! I can see why Caiden is so in love with you. You two make a beautiful couple."

I blush at her comments and smile graciously, walking up to her, adjusting her pocket square and flattening her lapel, replying, "Riley, you are very sweet. Thank you. You look very handsome."

Brianna enters the kitchen to pour a glass of wine. As she does, Caiden is ending her call. Caiden sees her and comments on how lovely she looks. She gives her a kiss on each cheek and a quick peck on the lips, smiling at her in amazement. Caiden's beautiful brown eyes search the room until they find me. She smiles a big genuine smile, saying, "My eyes have never seen anything more beautiful than the sight before me. Zoe, you are absolutely stunning in that dress. Red is definitely my new favorite color. The black heels give it a very sexy edge. I approve, Ms. Payne!"

My heart is beating rapidly. I want so much to please Caiden tonight. It is an important night for her. She looks fantastic in a black three-piece suit, white french cuff shirt, black silk tie, and white pocket square with black oxford shoes. Looking at her, my Venus begins to tingle. I can feel myself becoming aroused, wanting to take her into my bedroom and seduce her.

"Mr. Westphal, I am utterly impressed! You are quite the dapper gentlemyn this evening. Every femme in the room will want to be me tonight," I comment, smiling at her.

It is close to eight o'clock when we arrive at the Austin event center. Once we reach the entryway to the ballroom we are asked our names. A young police cadet scans the list to find Caiden's name and immediately calls another cadet over to escort us to our table. He remarks to our escort, "These are special guests of Chief Martin. Please escort them to his table and notify him of their arrival."

Riley jokingly whispers to Brianna, "So this is what it is like to roll with CW, huh!"

Brianna giggles and replies, "There are perks when rolling with CW."

Always the gentlemyn, Caiden extends her hand out for Brianna and me to enter first. Riley and Caiden are close behind as we are led along a velvet rope leading to the red carpet area. There has to be five or six hundred people here this evening.

Photographers from the Austin *American Statesman*, the *Chronicle*, the *Villager*, and a handful of freelancers are all here, waiting for an important shot or blunder. Caiden motions Riley to escort Brianna onto the red carpet for a photo op. While we wait, William Monroe, a reporter from KXAN News, recognizes Caiden and directs the cameraman to turn in our direction.

William says, "Caiden, first off, we here at KXAN offer our deepest sympathy for the loss of your mother, the Honorable Judge Rosemary Caidence Westphal. The viewers are concerned—how are you coping with your recent loss?"

Caiden despises reporters and, even more, impromptu interviews. She, however, graciously thanks Mr. Monroe and the viewers for their condolences and support during this very difficult time. She goes on to say that, certainly, everyone can relate with this being a personal matter she is at a loss for words. She briefly shakes his hand, thanking him once again, and quickly takes my hand, heading reluctantly toward the red carpet. Pausing, she looks to see if there is another entrance into the event to avoid the hungry media. Unfortunately, our escort is directing us onto the red carpet, placing us in a direct path of the media storm. Caiden tenses briefly in frustration. I squeeze her hand, helping ease her anxiety. She looks into my eyes for a few moments before proceeding onto the red carpet.

Cameras are clicking, lights are flashing, and photographers are calling Caiden's name to look in their direction, hoping for a pic.

One reporter in the crowd yells, "Who is the bombshell in red?"

Another, "Do we hear wedding bells in the near future, Caiden?"

A third respectfully acknowledges, "I am truly sorry for your loss, Ms. Westphal."

Caiden, moved by the sincerity in the photographer's voice, graciously moves toward the crowd to shake her hand. As their hands lock, she gives Caiden a reassuring pat on the shoulder. Caiden smiles politely at her, thanking her for her genuine concern.

Caiden, in rare form, takes pause in making the following statement, "To answer the question of wedding bells. Sadly, in the great state of Texas, other citizens such as myself have been brutally raped of that liberty all in the name of DOMA and states' rights." Caiden moves closer toward the crowd in a regal fashion. Her voice is clear and concise as she continues, "We must ask ourselves whom this law actually protects." She stops for a moment, allowing her audience to ponder the question. Lifting her arm and pointing at me, she addresses the crowd, posing the question, "If I were to marry this beautiful woman, do we then become an imminent threat that warrants defending against?" Caiden's eyes fill with conviction as she speaks. "We can thank our legislature and the Conservative Party, who were successful in their efforts to amend the Texas Constitution, making marriage between one man and one woman."

You can hear a few utterings throughout the crowd in support of the marriage act.

Caiden, unmoved by the hecklers, continues, "I would be remiss if I forget to thank Democrats, some Republicans, and even Liberals who, even though in their own hearts and minds believe marriage should be between two consenting adults regardless of gender, fail to act, thereby allowing such a ludicrous law to pass. As you all know, my mother even acknowledged certain laws in this state are communistic in nature, archaic, discriminatory, and prejudiced toward certain demographic groups. The Texas Legislature doesn't even deny the fact they intentionally enact laws to deny equality and equal treatment under the law to the GLBT community and minorities abroad. As a matter of fact, it is one of their biggest political talking points come election time. We hear it repeatedly—we must protect family values, have less government, have the right to bear arms, et cetera, et cetera. Master manipulators of nomenclature, of smoke and mirrors, and quite frankly, ladies and gentlemen, master ass-kissers.

"Oh, believe me, we have had the wool pulled over our eyes time and time again with false promises, false truths, and deceit by our politically elite superheroes. I wonder how they would feel if their values, freedoms, and liberties were pillaged? Ask yourselves how many times have they altered the law in their favor? We as citizens should demand more from our politicians. We should demand they stand and fight for all Texans, not just a select few who line their political pockets. We should demand they stay out of our bedrooms, and in return, we promise to stay out of theirs. How proud we must be as Texas citizens to live in a state that openly condones and practices inequality and discrimination?

"The Texas Legislature, being cowards, hide behind the cloak of the Defense of Marriage Act and an amendment in the Texas Constitution to continue to deny citizens of this great state and of this great nation the right to fair and equal treatment under the law. When did it become the role of our government to dictate our personal lives? Luckily for us, it will be up to the Supreme Court to make this landmark decision. I guarantee you, not one politician has the stones to debate this issue openly and honestly, so I will leave you with this quote by Saint Augustine, 'An unjust law is no law at all.' And one final note—if Texas doesn't recognize my rights, then I cannot, in good conscience, recognize this law. Thank you."

I watch in awe as silence takes over the crowd as she concludes. After her last word, the crowd breaks out in roaring cheers and applause. She smiles, waving to the media, then turning to me. Enamored with her conviction, a sense of pride occupies my soul, ushering us into a deep, emotional kiss. The crowd goes wild with cheers and applause as we stand, kissing each other for what feels like an eternity. Breaking from our exchange, waving once more to our audience, we follow our escort into the ballroom to Chief Martin's table. As we enter, we are greeted with more cheers and applause. People of all races, nationalities, and genders are shaking our hands and patting us on the back in thanks. I have never been more proud of Caiden than in this moment.

We finally reach our table when Chief Martin waltzes over to Caiden with hand extended, remarking, "Your mother would be so proud of you right now. Great speech!" He then turns to me, remarking, "Ms. Payne, it is a pleasure to see you again. You must be awfully proud of this one."

We shake hands, and I reply, "It is a pleasure to see you again, Chief, and yes, I am extremely proud of Caiden."

The men at the table stand as they wait for Brianna and me to be seated. Caiden and Riley stand alongside them, being perfect gentlemyn. Brianna and I are seated next to each other with Riley on her left and Caiden on my right. Once we are all seated, I notice two empty chairs next to Caiden. The names read Detective Westphal and Ms. Santos. Caiden is conversing with the other dinner guests, unaware of our seating arrangement. The chief walks back over to Caiden, attempting to be discrete, informing her he has an urgent matter to discuss. He asks if she can meet him at the police station tomorrow at two o'clock, sharing his concern for Jaylon's career.

Caiden's expression is of curiosity as she agrees to meet with him.

"I am hoping you can assist us before things get out of control," he comments.

Caiden informs the chief she will do what she can to help. He walks back to his chair and takes a seat.

As the night progresses, we are having a good time, enjoying the music, entertainment, and of course, a lovely dinner. Riley and Brianna seem to be getting along well. I caught them kissing on the dance floor a few times. I am so happy for Brianna. Riley reminds me of Caiden in the sense she is caring and attentive to Brianna. Caiden doesn't seem to share my enthusiasm but does not interfere.

Chief Martin is standing at the podium and, over the loudspeaker, requests, "Everyone, please take a seat." He informs he has a few announcements to make, and afterward, we can all get back to enjoying the rest of the evening.

As we head back to the table, Jaylon is seated in the company of a very attractive dark-haired woman. Caiden greets Jaylon with lukewarm enthusiasm. Jaylon stands, extending her arms, giving me a hug. She does the same to Brianna. Brianna reluctantly hugs Jaylon, saying hello. Caiden introduces Riley as they shake halfheartedly. Riley appears to have the same disdain for Jaylon as Caiden.

Jaylon introduces her companion to us, saying, "Everyone, this is Dana Santos. Dana, this is my sister, Caiden; her date, Zoe; and friends Brianna and Riley."

Dana, in a quiet voice, says hello. She is hesitant, avoiding eye contact with Caiden.

We all take a seat as the chief begins his announcements. I glance at Caiden, and it appears as though she has seen a ghost as she looks at Dana out the corner of her eye. Jaylon recognizes someone from across the room, excusing herself to go speak. Dana eyes Caiden oddly as she sits uncomfortably at the table. As our eyes meet, she politely excuses herself to the ladies' room. Caiden's eyes narrow as they follow Dana until she is no longer in sight. Concerned, I reach for her hand, startling her. She smiles as she leans in to kiss my cheek.

Caiden turns her attention toward Chief Martin, who is preparing to speak about Rose. The crowd applauds respectfully as the chief asks Caiden and Jaylon up on stage.

It's about to get interesting, I think.

They both arrive on stage simultaneously. After a few kind words about Rosemary, the chief presents them with a beautiful teardrop-shaped crystal plaque in her honor. As they stand side by side holding the plaque, they smile cordially for the cameras. The crowd begins to chant "Speech, speech, speech!"

The chief hands the microphone to Caiden. She thanks the chief and everyone who offered their heartfelt condolences and support. She expresses they are honored to accept the plaque on Rose's behalf, acknowledging it befitting that Jaylon should have the honor and grace us with a few words. As she hands Jaylon the microphone, Caiden leans into Jaylon, whispering something to her while patting her on the back. Whatever Caiden said must have shocked Jaylon, because it took her a minute to recover.

She looks around the room for a few moments then begins to speak "I am grateful for the, outpouring of love and support I have received from my extended family here in this room. I could not make it through this ordeal without the help of fine people such as you. I am honored to accept this award on my mother's behalf. I know she is smiling down on me."

I sit in shock at the nerve of Jaylon to dismiss Caiden. I watch Caiden as Jaylon continues her rhetoric about her grief, her loss, her mother. Caiden is unmoved by Jaylon's words. She is stoic, standing beside her sister as she speaks. She is well prepared, knowing her sister all too well.

I want to go up to Jaylon and slap the shit out of her. I am so infuriated at the constant antagonism directed at Caiden. How can she stand to live with herself after all the horrible things she has done to Caiden? What happened to make her such a miserable, pathetic excuse for a human being? The crowd grows quiet as she ends her ranting, handing the microphone back to the chief.

Jaylon jumps down off the stage, yelling at some of her friends who are obviously as drunk as she is, giving her high fives and laughing. The chief's eyes fill with empathy, and he cordially smiles at Caiden. They shake hands as Caiden exits the stage while the chief instructs everyone to enjoy the rest of their evening.

Caiden approaches the table, appearing calm, when suddenly, out of nowhere, Ericka grabs her arm, suggesting, "We need to talk. This can't wait. Meet me in the hallway!" Caiden looks confused as she glances over at the empty seat previously occupied by Dana then back at Ericka who comments, "I can explain. Be outside in five, please?"

Caiden agrees. "Riley, time to go to work. You have a three-hour window. If things change, I will be in contact. I need this taken care of tonight!" Caiden exclaims.

Riley turns to Brianna and kisses her tenderly on the lips before she exits.

I turn to Caiden, demanding answers.

She replies, "Zoe, I don't have all the answers. I am working on it. Once I have proof, I will explain everything to you. Wait for me back at the condo. I will be home within the hour."

She turns to leave but stops, turning to me, expressing her love. I blow her a kiss, reiterating my love for her.

Caiden leaves the ballroom while Brianna and I are escorted to our limo. On our way out, we run into Dana. She appears drunk as she stops us, remarking sarcastically, "Well, well, if it isn't the infamous Ms. Absolute Perfection herself. Caiden described you as a goddess. She really should have her eyes checked."

Before I could respond, Brianna instinctively intervenes, pointing her finger in Dana's face, shouting, "Look, b——! You must be one of Caiden's little throwaways!" By this point, Brianna is about an inch from Dana's face.

Dana is standing firm with her hands on her hips, eyeing Brianna as she speaks, replying, "I wasn't talking to your skinny ass. I was, talking to this white b——!"

The heated exchange is drawing attention from passersby. I realize I have to defuse this situation and quickly. I pull Brianna to the side, reminding her this isn't the time or place to make a spectacle. I insist she calm down and let me handle it. I tuck my evening bag under my arm and calmly walk up to Dana, leaning in close to her and reply, "Dana, sweetie, really, the race card? Is that all your intellect will allow? Surely you can do better than that? I tell you what? How 'bout I give you another chance. *Go!*"

She looks at me dumbfounded and frustrated, unable to provide a clever response. Instead she mumbles something about snobby b——.

Brianna bursts into laughter, remarking, "Well played!"

We walk away, heading to our limo, leaving Dana standing speechless in the middle of the hallway.

The ride home is quiet. I am worried about Caiden, and I am sure Brianna is concerned about Riley. I wonder what Jaylon has done to make Caiden investigate? Why won't Caiden let me in? The driver startles us both, opening the door for us to exit. We hadn't realized the car stopped. We are standing on the sidewalk. I look across the street and see a police officer sitting in the car across from my building. I see officers on watch, but rarely parked in this area. He looks over at us, smiles briefly, and begins to work on his computer again. Brianna and I are exhausted as well as confused at Caiden, Riley, and Ericka's odd behavior. What does Dana have to do with all of this? Who is she to Caiden and Jaylon? So many thoughts race through my mind.

Brianna quietly remarks, "Zoe, I am not sure what is going on, but I get the feeling something bad is about to happen."

I look at her, reaching for her hand as we begin our stroll up to the condo.

Once inside, we change into comfy clothes and immediately open a bottle of pinot gris as we sit on the sofa, trying to console each other.

Brianna shares she encountered Jaylon at the ball. She said Jaylon approached her while she was going to the ladies room, pulling her to the side, telling her Caiden is about to pay for all the wrongs she has done to her. She said Jaylon keeps blaming Caiden for her mother's death, her father's death, insisting Caiden is the reason she and I aren't together.

The look on my face is of confusion. "Jaylon is delusional to think she and I could ever be together," I say, irritated.

"Zoe, have you and Jaylon ever—?"

I stop her before she can finish the question and reply, "Of course not, Brianna. How could you think that?" irritated she even entertained the idea.

Brianna mentioned Jaylon took a jab at her and Riley's relationship, commenting, "Brianna, still settling for second best, huh? Why settle for a wannabe Westphal, you had the real thing in your grasp? I'm curious, Brianna, when you and your little boi toy are fucking, who ultimately comes to mind?"

Honestly, her ego amazes me. There is no way on earth Brianna has any interest in Jaylon at all.

I look at the time. It's been an hour since we left the event, and still no word from Caiden. I am starting to worry even more. I remember Caiden mentioning to Riley she had three hours to complete her task. Brianna excuses herself and goes to bed. I remain on the sofa, sipping on my wine, pondering our discussion. I can't shake Brianna's last comment about her settling for a wannabe Westphal. I hear the key turn at the door, and Caiden enters, looking weary. She manages a subtle smile as she sits on the sofa next to me.

I ask, "Is everything okay?"

She turns to me, remarking, "Hopefully, in a day or two, it will be."

I want to ask her more questions, but I can see she is exhausted.

I grab her hand, expressing it has been a long day, suggesting we go to bed. She decides to take a hot shower to help her relax. While she is undressing, I turn the shower on for her. She startles me, placing her hands around my waist, kissing my neck softly.

"I am so lucky to have you, Zoe," she comments.

I turn to face her, and she is completely naked.

"Care to join me?" she asks sweetly.

I slip out of my clothes and take her hand as she leads me into the shower. The water is steamy; it feels so good against my skin.

"This feels great," she utters.

My arms are around her neck as we stand chest to chest. She leans down, kissing me, moving me up against the shower wall. I feel her hands caress my breast, teasing my nipples with her fingertips. I let out a sigh as my hands move across her shoulders, massaging them, helping to relieve her stress. She moans in appreciation as her head tilts back. My hand slowly glides down past her waist, reaching her Venus. My fingers fondle her clit as she continues to moan in enjoyment.

"Zoe," Caiden whispers.

"Caiden," I reply.

"I am sorry the night didn't go as I had planned. I have something important to ask you," she explains between moans.

"Caiden, you don't have to apologize," I reply, still stroking her clit.

Caiden slides down, resting on her knees, placing her warm wet mouth on my clit, stroking it with her tongue. My blood turns to fire at her touch. My fingers tightly entangle her dreads as my body begins grinding slowly against her mouth while her tongue continues to lick my clit. I need this more than I realize. Her tongue stroking and licking me feels exquisite. I am silently pleading to feel her fingers inside me. She must have read my mind as I feel them enter me, moving in and out as her tongue continues to stroke my clit. I moan each time I feel her fingers penetrate. God, she knows what she is doing! She knows my body is hers for the taking. I can't refrain any longer, crying out her name, reaching the apex of my orgasm.

Caiden rises, gazing at me, placing her fingers into my mouth one by one, she watches me enjoy my own juices. She kisses me in between my licks, sharing in the feast, sucking her fingers. "I love tasting you," she notes.

She reaches to turn off the shower, drying me with her towel, and I return the favor. As we get into bed, she looks at me intently, remarking, "I can understand why Jaylon wants you so much. You are so easy to love yet impossible to forget. I feel sorry for her in a way. I would do, anything to have you too!" She kisses me once more before we fall into a deep sleep.

CHAPTER NINE

Jaylon

"Arrogant little son of bitch! Marry Zoe? She has lost her fucking mind! Wait until she finds out her precious Zoe is a lying, fucking whore!" I mumble to the bartender.

Erika catches up to me at the bar. "You're drunk again! Jaylon, it is late, and we have a busy day tomorrow. Why don't you finish your beer so I can drive you home," she says.

"Why in the fuck would I let you drive me home? I saw you talking to my little piss ant sister tonight at the ball. Whose side are you on, Ericka?" I ask. Drunk, I decide to relinquish my keys to her. I am already in a shitload of trouble at work because of Caiden. I can barely stand, and my speech is slurred. I am enraged by my sister's comment at the ball.

"What has your sister done this time to place you in such a foul mood?" Ericka asks sarcastically.

"Caiden is right about one thing. No fucking wedding bells in her near future. No way in hell will I allow Caiden to marry the only woman I have ever loved" I mumble.

Ericka looks at me, confused, asking, "What are you rambling about? Why do you despise Caiden so much?"

I look over at her with my beer in my hand, saying, "Let's go."

We get into my car; I begin to enlighten her why I loathe Caiden so damn much. I have never shared my feelings regarding Caiden with anyone outside of my therapist. I am wondering to myself why I feel the urge to bare my soul tonight. Maybe I need to talk about it with a friend instead of a psychiatrist. I remember bits and pieces of my childhood. I am unsure at times if what I remember actually happened or if I imagined it. My shrink seems to think something tragic happened to me as a child. She says I am suppressing it. All I do know is my life was fine until Caiden came into the world.

Rosemary even named Caiden after her. You would think me—being the first born and natural child, she should have passed her name on to me. She treated that little bastard with kid gloves. Always coddling her as if she is her prize jewel. Always telling Caiden her heart is wanted and no one would ever unwant it. Never understood why she chose that word, but it never made sense to me. Rosemary attempted to explain it to us one day, I guess, when I was about ten or eleven and Caiden was seven or eight, saying if your heart is pure, it is wanted and loved. An unwanted heart is the worst thing a person can have inside them. It means no one can love you or care about you. Your heart is black and begins to rot and grow ugly inside.

I never took her words literally but Caiden sure fucking did. She believes everything coming out of Rosemary's mouth as truth no matter how much it sounds like bullshit. I used to tell her all the time that she did possess an unwanted heart. It would send her crying into Rosemary's arms like a little bitch every time. I can't count how many times I got in trouble for doing that. Rosemary told me I was going to scar her baby for life. If I kept on, she would punish me for it. Rosemary could be strict with me, so I knew she meant it. I stopped telling Caiden her heart was unwanted after Rosemary took a belt buckle to me one day. She did not hit me often, but she had had enough of me messing with Caiden. She whooped me so bad that day; I still have scars on the backs of my legs and buttocks from it. I found other ways to torment the little bastard though. I think I spent most of my childhood plotting ways to make her life miserable.

She was so gullible and easy to manipulate I couldn't resist. Caiden took all my bullshit because she is so afraid to have this unwanted heart beating inside her. I used to tease her about being adopted. I told her even her own mother and father didn't want her. That still cracks me up. I made sure her childhood was as miserable as mine. Rosemary battled against me, of course, to make sure Caiden's life was full of love and enrichment.

Rosemary did everything in her power to make sure Caiden wanted for nothing. She graduated from the University of Texas with a law degree and worked her way up the ranks at the Travis County DA's office, making a name for herself. She decided to make a difference in the community, so she ran for the Travis County District Attorney's office in 1988. Surprisingly, she won the election, serving only one term. Rosemary had her sights on a different prize and ran for the 147th Criminal District Court in Travis County in 1992 and won. She held that position until she retired in 2008.

Her passion for the criminal justice system inspired me in part to become a police officer. I went to public school from kindergarten up to the twelfth grade. I then attended the University of Texas–San Antonio and completed my bachelor's degree in criminal justice. Rosemary was very proud of my accomplishment. She insisted I attend college even though my dream was to enlist in the Air Force. She said if I wanted to join the military, it would be there after college. She did instill the value of a good education in me, and I am grateful to her for that.

Caiden, on the other hand, did not share her enthusiasm toward college. Rosemary sent Caiden to private school, growing up until high school. She felt the public school system would not stimulate her little darling's mind and encourage her to be all that she can be. All the money spent for her to go to private school, and Caiden never stepped one foot onto a college campus except to fuck naive college girls. Caiden had a way of manipulating Rosemary at will. I remember the two of them sitting down after Caiden graduated high school to discuss Caiden's options. Rosemary had Ivy League schools lined up for Caiden. She could have chosen any one of them and been accepted just because she was Rosemary's child. I remember being so damned pissed at her for throwing away opportunities I didn't have.

Caiden is highly intelligent and stupid at the same time. She would have done great at any school, but she was spoiled and had to do things her way, on her terms. Strange thing is Rosemary allowed her to do it. She gave her the option. She even helped Caiden purchase some local properties in Austin to help get her started. They had a connection that Rosemary and I never shared, and I always resented both of them for it. Caiden has always been Rosemary's favorite.

Growing up, I fought so hard to have Rosemary love me as much as she loved Caiden. I never understood why until I reached the age of fourteen, when things really got bad between us.

I remember, being in her office, pretending to be a judge about to sentence Caiden to death when I found some papers with our names on them. Curious, I read them. I was reading our birth certificates. You can imagine my shock when I read my birth certificate—"Jaylon Nadine Westphal; mother, Nadine Marie Richards, and father, David Bryan Westphal." Caiden's read "Caiden Bryce Westphal; mother, Rosemary Caidence Westphal; father, Edward Bryce Westphal." I heard someone coming down the hall and quickly put the birth certificates back in the folder, laying it on her desk.

Rosemary entered the room. She must have sensed something was wrong. She glanced at the folder lying on the desk then back at me. My facial expression must have alarmed her as she ordered us out of her office. Caiden and I scurried out, but I peeked back in to see what she was doing. She quickly grabbed the folder, placing it in her safe. I later went outside, walking the neighborhood, trying to make sense of what I had read. Caiden and I are related? How could this be? I was determined to confront Rosemary with my newfound information.

It was around nine o'clock when I strolled back to our house that night. She was sitting outside on a bench, waiting for me. I walked up the entryway, and she calmly patted the empty seat next to her on the bench. I remember her eyes were red like she had been crying. She sighed as she reached for my hand. "Jaylon, I see you found your birth certificate. I am sure you have some questions. I will tell you anything you want to know," she stated.

I sat in deep thought for a few moments. Every emotion you can think of was flowing through me. I did not know where to begin. I was not about to let her off the hook. She lectures me so much on the importance of being truthful and honest, I want to see how she explains this. I looked at Rosemary with troubled eyes and replied, "Since you kept this secret from me, I think_you should be the one to explain."

She smiled warmly at me, searching where to begin. Finally, she told me I was not going to like everything, but she promised to tell me the truth, how she remembers it. She knew this day would come and had already made up her mind that when it did, she would be completely honest. She had one condition, of course. She began, "Jaylon, I am going to tell you everything, but you have to promise me you won't mention this to Caiden. I need to explain to her just as I am about to explain to you. She may not understand all of this at her age. Can you do that for me?"

I stared at her for a moment, livid she was more concerned about how Caiden was going to react than the fact she has lied to me my entire life. I subdued my anger, knowing if I did not agree, I would be left in limbo. My voice cracked as I reluctantly promised not to utter a word to Caiden. I remember feeling sick to my stomach, having just agreed to protect the little bastard's psyche. I knew my world was about to be altered forever, yet she didn't seem to give a damn. She only wanted to ensure Caiden was safe from harm. She looked deep into my eyes, trying to assess if I meant it. I must have been convincing as she promised she would do everything in her power to help me work through my issues.

"It's true your uncle Edward and I adopted you after your parent's death. You were having a difficult time adjusting living with us. I doubt you'll remember most of it. You were very young. You rejected the idea of being adopted for several years, refusing to acknowledge the fact. Edward and I were in counseling with you for months after your parents died, trying to help you make sense of everything that happened. Your psychiatrist, Dr. Saxon, suggests you repressed all the traumatic memories relating to your parent's death, replacing them with pseudo or false memories, including us being your real parents. He also suggests you transferred your life experience to Caiden, convincing yourself she was the one adopted. At some point, we failed you as parents, Jaylon, giving into your reality. You had been through so much and didn't seem to be getting any better. Edward and I discussed it with Dr. Saxon and agreed we would go along, pretending, at least temporarily, until you were older, then we could try again hopefully with better results. At the time, we were so concerned with helping you we didn't stop to think how this would impact Caiden or our family."

"Jaylon? Helloooo, Jaylon! You okay?" Erika asks.

"Yes," I reply. I tuned out for a moment, recalling our conversation. I am desperately trying to remember my parents and my childhood. I still have night terrors of things I can't remember. Erika seems very interested in my tale so I continue, recapping Rose's interpretation of events.

"In high school, David and I were high school sweethearts. He was my first love until I met Edward. Nadine and I were friends but she was also in love with David. Even after high school, she tried everything in her power to make him love her despite the fact we were engaged and planning to marry. As you can imagine, it caused a rift between Nadine and me. I tried my best to love her and be a friend to her, but she wouldn't stand for it. She wanted nothing to do with me once she realized David's feelings for me were real. David and I did marry about a year after we graduated high school. We thought our marriage would end the controversy with Nadine.

"For several months, life went on peacefully until one day your father was out, drinking at a local bar with his friends after work. Nadine happened to be there that evening, and the two of them shared a few beers, so I am told. Your father didn't return that evening, and naturally, I began to worry. I called his friends, but no one would provide me any information. David came home about nine o'clock the next morning, still in the clothes he had on the day before. Barring the details, he ended up at Nadine's for the night. Nine months later, you were born. Your father swore he doesn't remember a thing, but the damage had already been done. I didn't believe him, so we divorced. Nadine finally got her wish when she and David decided to get married. He said he did it to make sure his child would grow up knowing she had a loving father.

"David adored you, Jaylon. It was the only thing that kept him going in that marriage. Family hood seemed to draw them closer together. I rarely saw or spoke to your parents and moved on with my life.

"Edward and I had become close once I divorced your father and, eventually, fell in love. We kept our relationship hidden from David. We felt it would be upsetting for him if he knew we were together. Once your father got wind of our relationship, they rarely spoke to each other. I remember David saying it was an abomination for us to be together, and he hoped we rot in hell for what we were doing.

"About two years had passed when David and I ran into each other, sparking a conversation. It was like the past two years never existed. One thing led to another, and we began to see each secretly again. During that time is when I became pregnant with Caiden. Even though your parents were in a very unhappy marriage, it is still no excuse for us to commit adultery.

"David made the decision after he found out I was pregnant to do the right thing and divorce Nadine. He didn't love Nadine how a man is supposed to love his wife, but he loved you dearly. He knew it wouldn't be easy, but he wanted custody of you, and with Caiden on the way, he wanted us all to be a family. He knew he would have to fight tooth and nail with Nadine to get custody of you. He sought an attorney, who drew up the paperwork for the divorce and had Nadine served. We did not hear from her for months after she had been served. His attorney advised him not to provoke the situation any further and to keep as much distance from Nadine as possible.

"Your mother prolonged the divorce for over nine months. Two months after Caiden was born, she finally contacted David, agreeing to sign the papers. She told him to come by her house to pick them up. David, following his attorney's advice, told her he would schedule a courier to pick up the papers for him. Nadine insisted if he wanted the divorce and custody of you, he needed to pick them up in person. He reluctantly agreed, informing her he would be over in a few hours. I wanted to go with him, but he refused, saying he didn't want to risk upsetting Nadine any further. He said it would only take a few minutes, and he would be back home in no time. He was happy Nadine agreed to give him custody of you. He feared she might not allow him to see you and dreaded the thought of not having you in his life. He went to Nadine's that evening and never returned home.

"The next day, I was informed your mother and father were gone. The police ruled it a murder-suicide. You were placed in foster care until the matter could be sorted out. Nadine shot your father through the heart the instant he walked through the door then, turning the gun on herself, fired a single shot through her heart.

"I am sorry Jaylon for all the pain I caused you, your mother, and your father," she said sympathetically.

Ericka interrupts my tale, commenting, "Jaylon, that is horrible. I had no idea. What happened to Edward?"

I look over at her from my passenger seat, slurring, "Who the fuck cares! Does this answer your fucking question why I hate Caiden? Everything is Caiden and that witch Rosemary's fault. Had it not been for them, my parents would still be alive and I'd be with Zoe, raising our child!"

Ericka pulls into my driveway. I get out, stumbling toward the house. She gets out, helping me to the front door. I'm so drunk I lean against her, walking to my bedroom. I plop down on the bed, staring at Ericka with drunken eyes, proclaiming, "Ericka, I will kill Caiden before she marries Zoe. She can't have everything."

I wake to a pounding headache, wondering, how the fuck did I get home? I smell fresh coffee brewing, so I get out of bed and go into my kitchen, finding Erika seated at the table, drinking a cup.

"What are you doing here?" I demand.

Ericka looks, shaking her head and replies, "Jaylon, you were drunk, so I drove you home. Do you remember anything from last night?"

I scratch my head and tell her all I remember is Caiden's punk ass telling me she was going to marry Zoe. The rest of the night is a blur.

"You need to freshen up a bit. You have a meeting with Internal Affairs this morning," Ericka reminds me. Ericka seems preoccupied with something, but I don't have time to worry about that.

Before we head to work, I down a cup of coffee and eat a slice of toast as I clean myself up.

CHAPTER TEN

Discovery

I wake and notice Zoe lying next to me, gazing up at the ceiling in deep thought. I lean over, kissing her on the cheek. She smiles as she rubs her hand across my cheek. Noticing she doesn't break her stare, I begin to stare at the ceiling with her, asking, "What are we looking at? It must be fascinating!" I chuckle.

She giggles, remarking, "Quite fascinating actually. We are watching our life together play out in front of us." She points her finger over to the right of the ceiling, commenting, "Over there is the beginning. We were young, naive, and reckless."

Moving her hand toward the left, she describes the different chapters of our life, detailing each one for me. Curious, I inquire what chapter are we in. With melancholy eyes, she faces me, remarking, "Caiden, I want a life with you. I want a family with you. I am afraid if I don't tell you the truth, our story will have an unhappy ending. I won't risk losing you again because of secrets."

I lie quietly a few moments, thinking if I can handle all her secrets. Am I ready to hear the truth about my Zoe? I turn to her, explaining if it is important to her then she should tell me everything. I agree we can't move forward if the past still haunts us. I brace myself in preparation, not knowing what to expect. I take a moment, praying in silence, asking God to allow me to listen with an open heart and mind. I kiss her once more, hoping to ease her anxiety. Zoe looks nervously at me as she clears her throat. I reach for her hand tenderly, squeezing it, assuring it's going to be okay.

"Caiden, I am truly sorry for hurting you. I don't know what I would do if I lost you again."

I look deep into her eyes and reply, "Zoe, I promise, you won't lose me."

She is struggling to find the words. I lie on my back, placing my hand behind my head, and pull her close to me. She rests her head on my chest and snuggles close to me, resting her arm on my stomach. She confesses she didn't want to end things with me. She said that against her better judgment, she followed poor advice, making a horrible mistake by not telling me the truth two years ago. I learned of her one-night stand and the pregnancy that ensued. I was saddened, hearing the news her child was stillborn. She was eight months into her pregnancy. As I listen, the pain in her voice is apparent. I doubt she has shared her experience with anyone until now. It is difficult for her to continue as she reflects on what could have been.

She pushes on, relieving herself of the pain and lies as she exposes her soul to me. I'm not surprised to learn Jaylon used her tragedy to hurt me. I am disappointed Zoe didn't have enough faith in me to be honest, from the beginning. Instead, she allowed Jaylon to weasel her way into her life and rejected me in the process.

The more I listen, the more enraged I become at the entire situation. The very thought of Zoe being intimate with a man has always sickened me. My heart is torn between feeling sadness for the loss of her child, angered by my sister's role, and betrayed by her. My heart is pounding inside my chest. Angry, I want to find Jaylon and the son of a bitch who impregnated Zoe and beat the living shit out of both of them. I can hardly breathe as I attempt to refocus my attention on Zoe. Wishing deafness upon my ears as madness takes root, I desperately try to conceal the harvest of repulsion that I reap.

"Caiden, Caiden, are you okay?" Zoe asks.

I close my eyes tightly, suppressing my true emotions. Refusing to take my anger out on her, I take a deep, calming breath to collect my thoughts. I reply, "It's a lot to take in at once, Zoe. I will be okay." Not wanting to believe her words to be true, I try to rationalize the evening she had with Jaylon, asking, "You said you only had two glasses of wine that night and can't remember anything?"

"Caiden, I honestly don't remember anything past my second glass. I have recounted that night over a thousand times in my head!" she responds frantically.

I think to myself, *There has to be more.* This isn't Zoe. She wouldn't have willingly done something like this. My thoughts quickly move to Jaylon, convinced she did something to her. *She had to!* I think, panicked, searching for a reasonable explanation for Zoe's behavior. I sit up in bed, breathing heavily, with the thought of Zoe fucking a man continuing to invade my thoughts. I am fighting desperately to control my rage. She is unsettled by my reaction as strokes my face. I want to lash out in anger at her, but I am rendered powerless, staring into her frightened eyes. Her stare softens, knowing she has succeeded temporarily in calming me down. I am calm, yet my heart continues to break inside. I look at her with helpless, grief-stricken eyes as she places her arms around me, holding me tight, caressing my back. I lay my head against her neck, squeezing her with all my might.

The longer we embrace, the more my contempt for Jaylon grows. I know she is responsible for all of this.

As she holds me, Zoe accepts the blame, expressing, "Caiden, everything is my fault. I am sorry. I wish I could take it all back."

I pull away from our embrace and respond, "Zoe, this isn't your fault! I blame Jaylon. She drugged you or something, Zoe! I know you, and what you describe is not the Zoe I know and love."

Tears start to fall down her face. My attempts to wipe them away fail as they begin to fall freely. I hate to see her in such agony. She lost a child, and I abandoned her when she needed me most.

I feel sick to my stomach all of a sudden, ashamed for leaving her the way I did. *Had I stayed, things could have been different*, I think to myself. I want to erase her pain from the loss.

After a few minutes, her tears cease. She watches me with sorrow in her eyes as I reassure her I am not leaving. "For better or worse, beautiful, remember?" I remark. She lets out a slight laugh, looking relieved I am still in the room.

We are sitting at the foot of the bed, next to each other, when she moves her body to straddle me, commenting, "I am blessed to have you, Caiden."

As she sits on my lap, my mind continues to torture me with visions of Zoe, giving herself to a man. She kisses me open-mouthed, using her tongue, searching for mine. I greet her tongue, yet I am still preoccupied by the thought of someone else touching these lips, caressing this body, and taking what is rightfully mine from me. I grow hostile in our exchange, grabbing her hair and forcefully jerking her head back. She moans as if it pleases her. I inspect her body as if to find some remnant of her sexual encounter. Her skin is flawless, breasts perfectly formed, nipples erect, waiting for my mouth to devour them.

Sensing my hesitation, she kisses my neck and nibbles on my ear, digging her fingernails deep into my back, leaving ridges on my skin. I can feel the sting as welts develop.

She whispers, "Caiden, I know you. I know your jealousy. Please don't let it consume you. Caiden, I need you so much right now!"

I perceive the desire in her tone. The urgency of the need to connect with me on a sexual level is apparent. My body warms at her request. I manage to push the unwelcome images out of my mind once again. I stand up with Zoe still in my lap, with her legs wrapped around my waist, and provide unyielding kisses to her lips. I want only to consume her body in its entirety, releasing the rage dwelling inside me.

She senses my aggression and utters, "Baby, take me. I am all yours. Caiden, please take me."

Her cries intensify my emotions, triggering my inner beast to surface. I thrust her up against the bedroom door, pinning her against it. She releases her legs to stand as we engage in a forceful tongue battle. My hands move across her breast, manhandling them. My fingers tug and pull at her nipples, feeling them grow harder against my touch. She moves her hands down my back to my waist, pulling my body into hers. I reach for her wrists, grabbing them, slinging them over her head, fastening them against the door. We stand eye to eye, panting heavily. My eyes move from hers again, scanning her naked body while fighting the images I tried to suppress earlier. The monster dwelling inside is alive, wanting only revenge for her betrayal, disputing my own thoughts struggling to keep the beast at bay. Its desire is overpowering my will to protect her from it. I release one of her wrists and uncontrollably plunge my fist into the door, barely missing her face. Her head turns out of fear for her safety as she shrieks aloud. She is trembling, yet she does not move. Pulling my fist away from the door, I slowly lift my head so my eyes meet hers. My heart breaks as I witness the horror on her face by my own hand.

After realizing what I have done, I quickly release her other arm, stepping away from her. "Zoe, I am sorry! I didn't mean to frighten you. I . . . I don't know what came over me," I explain, horrified by my own actions.

She looks at me as if I were a total stranger. She doesn't recognize me. Her body slides down the door as she sits, weeping, with her hands covering her face, yelling this is all her fault.

"No, no, Zoe, this isn't your fault! Zoe, I am sorry. Don't cry. I'm not going to hurt you! I take full responsibility for everything," I utter, sitting next to her, placing my arms around her. She leans into my shoulder, sobbing. I hold her as tight as I can, stroking her hair, pleading with her to forgive me.

Riley and Brianna are outside the door, asking "Is everything okay?"

Aggravated by the interruption, I bark, "Yes, everything is fine!"

Brianna is turning the doorknob, asking, "Zoe, honey, are you all right? Open the door, sweetie, I just want to check on you!"

Zoe responds, still in tears, "Brianna, everything is fine. I will be out in a minute."

Brianna, not convinced, insists Zoe open the door. I stand up and assist Zoe off the bedroom floor. I look at her and walk into the bathroom. She opens the door, allowing Brianna and Riley a glimpse of the aftermath. Brianna immediately gives Zoe a warm embrace. She escorts Zoe out of the bedroom, glaring at me as they exit. I look at her with frustration, shaking my head. Riley moves closer to the bathroom entrance, reminding me about the appointment I have with Chief Martin.

"Fuck! I don't need this shit today" I yell.

"CW, let's you and I go out for some fresh air. You look like you could use it. You left your cell on the bar. I took the liberty of answering your calls. The funeral home called and wants to do a final consultation with you before the service tomorrow. Ashley called to extend her condolences. She said she read about your mother in the paper, and if you didn't mind, she would like your permission to attend the service. Several friends of your mother's called as well to confirm the date and time of the service. Is it all right if I call Ashley back to let her know you would appreciate the support?" Riley asks.

"Yes, Riley, that will be fine. Thank you for taking care of that for me. You're a good friend. I apologize for my short-temperedness earlier. I am not myself today," I explain.

"No problem, CW. You know I have your back," Riley remarks with a smile.

Riley is right. I need some distance from Zoe. I throw on a blazer, T-shirt, and jeans with a pair of Converse shoes and we head out to grab brunch before my meeting with the chief.

Riley informs me of her findings at brunch, telling me she found several surveillance devices in Zoe's apartment, on her PC, and her cell. She even found a tracking device on Zoe's car. Last night, after the ball, I had her access Jaylon's security system, cell, and PC. I knew if I mentioned marrying Zoe to Jaylon, she would hang around to give me fucking "brotherly" advice. In reality, she wants details on the nuptials, probably to plan on how to prevent it from happening. Sick fuck.

Riley said the data she retrieved dates back to roughly two years ago. I ask her to pay close attention to the three weeks prior to me leaving for Portland. It is disheartening to discover Jaylon has been videotaping Zoe in the privacy of her home. Riley wants to provide me details, but I didn't want the extended version of what that sick bastard was viewing. I don't want Riley viewing it either, but at this point, I have no choice. She is just doing her job. I imagine Jaylon got an eyeful of Zoe. I shudder at the thought of that bastard even being near Zoe, much less stalking her.

I reach in my jeans for cash to pay for brunch when I come across the key my mother gave me before she died. Remembering what she said about finding out the truth, I squeeze the key tightly, thinking this was the last thing she gave me. I place it back in my pocket and turn my attention back to Riley.

"CW, I used the information you sent me on Friday to scramble the surveillance equipment in Zoe's apartment and her phone late that night. It was a temporary fix until I could get to Jaylon's surveillance equipment, disabling the primary source. The only thing she is able to monitor is a video feed of an empty condo," Riley says with pride in her voice.

"Damn! You are talented, Riley. Glad you are on my team." I chuckle.

I realize now Jaylon's little stunt at Zoe's apartment was an act. She has been watching us up until early Friday morning. She knew who was in the apartment the whole time. Fucking sick-ass psychopath! What type of freak watches their sibling having sex? I wonder. *Well, big sis, I hope the show was entertaining. It's the last one you will ever see,* I think to myself.

While at the restaurant, I contact the funeral home to go over the details of Rosemary's service. So much is happening, I have yet to truly reflect on my mother's passing. I take a moment, reflecting on her amazing life, taking pride in the fact of how much joy she brought to her friends, the community, and me. I know she wants me to celebrate her life and not mourn her passing. I will miss our long debates over love and life. The happiness I felt, celebrating the holidays and decorating the Christmas tree. Most of all, I will miss her wisdom, guidance, unconditional love, and the way she laughed at my silly jokes. Mom, you will always live on in my heart. It is nearing two o'clock, and I leave Riley at the restaurant to continue her research. The station is only a few blocks from here—in lieu of a cab, I walk.

On my way, I flash to the incident earlier with Zoe, hoping she can forgive me. What was I thinking? My jealousy can be overwhelming at times. I send a text—"Beautiful, sorry again for this morning. It will never happen again."

She immediately responds "Caiden, you weren't yourself. Of course, I forgive you. Can you forgive me?"

I feel relief after reading her text. I reach APD and head up the elevator to the administrative offices. As I exit the elevator, I see the chief talking, I presume, to his secretary. He smiles as he sees me heading toward him. We shake hands as he ushers me into his office. I take a seat in a comfortable roll-back leather chair, crossing my leg. His smile turns to concern as he sits behind his desk. He wastes no time on small talk, explaining he appreciates me coming by under the circumstances.

He tells me Jaylon is under investigation by IA for several charges stemming from official oppression, bribery, unlawful surveillance, blackmail, and other issues. He then asks if I know a Dana Santos or Marcus Roberts? I inform him those names are unfamiliar to me. "What about a Rheia Santos?" he asks.

My eyes narrow, wondering where he is going with all these questions. Unclear of his intent, I reply I didn't know her. He looks at me strangely, replying, "I see. Caiden, I can't say much, but Ms. Santos is key to IA's investigation."

I learn Rheia has filed a lawsuit against Jaylon and APD for official oppression. The chief shared she used to be one of Jaylon's informants. Jaylon arrested Rheia for prostitution a few years back, and she cut a deal to be a police informant to avoid jail time. She is here in Austin with her attorney, providing IA details about her involvement with Jaylon. He mentions she is in the interview room with IA as we speak. He makes it a point to share the city is doing everything it can to keep this lawsuit under wraps, stating if what

Rheia alleges turns out to be true, she stands to receive a large amount of money from the city and Jaylon could be charged on multiple counts. He goes on to warn me this could get ugly for the city and APD if this were to go public. He casually added this would not be good for me or anyone associated with the scandal. What he means is this could have an impact on the Payne Corporation as well.

This meeting isn't about Jaylon's well-being. It's about the city covering its ass, and they want to use me to help them do it. My mood has hardened toward the situation as I rise from my seat, saying, "Chief, I'd appreciate a courtesy call if you have any new information. Jaylon is, after all, family."

As I leave his office, I begin feeling nauseated at the thought of Rheia being a prostitute. Questions flow through my mind. How did she end up in Portland? Why was she there? Did we meet intentionally? I probe the offices, trying to catch a glimpse of Rheia without any luck.

I decide to wait in the lobby for her to exit. I am more determined than ever to find out the connection between Jaylon, Rheia, and this Marcus Roberts. It is nearing three thirty, and still no sign of Rheia. My patience is running low. I opt to walk back to Zoe's. As I'm about to leave, the elevator door opens, and out walks Rheia. She is escorted by a white-haired gentleman, presumably her attorney. I follow them out onto Seventh Street. They have a brief conversation, and the older gentleman gets in his car, leaving Rheia alone. Rheia waves good-bye and begins to walk up the street toward Congress Avenue. This may be the only chance I get to talk to her.

I quicken my pace to catch up to her. "Rheia! Rheia!" I call.

She looks back to see who is calling her. By the time our eyes meet, I am at her side. She looks surprised to see me. I smile while grabbing her arm, forcing her to the edge of the sidewalk near the grass.

"What the hell are you, doing? Let go of me!" she says through gritted teeth.

"Rheia, I am not here to hurt you. I just want to talk," I say as I let go of her arm. She looks around suspiciously to see if we are being watched. I try to ease her mind, telling her I am alone and no one else knows I am here. A taxi is coming, and I wave it down. Opening the door, I instruct her to get in before someone does see us. She huffs and reluctantly gets in. I advise the driver to head toward Barton Springs and South Lamar near Zilker Park.

"Did Jaylon put you up to this?" she asks with fear in her tone.

"Rheia, hell no! I need you to tell me what is going with you and Jaylon. Rheia, it's important. I am not working with the police either," I reply. I inform her I am aware of the IA investigation on Jaylon and know she has a role in assisting them in the matter. "Rheia, please! I don't really care at this point what IA wants with Jaylon. I care about you and your involvement with my sister!" I exclaim.

"Why do you care what happens to me? Last time I heard from you, it was to break up with me!" she says bitterly.

I inform her I did try to reach her and even sent Riley by her apartment to check on her.

The driver interrupts, "Where to now?"

I instruct him to pull over on the corner. Paying him, Rheia and I exit the cab, walking toward the park.

I have to use all my resources if I am going to get any information out of her. It is a chilly October afternoon, and Rheia has always enjoyed long strolls in this type of weather. As we walk, I attempt to gauge her demeanor. I realize I need to make her feel comfortable, so I inquire how she has been since we last spoke. The more we walk and chitchat, the more her demeanor warms up to me. The breeze makes her shiver as she wraps her arm around mine to keep warm. I stop for a moment to remove my jacket, placing it around her shoulders. She thanks me, and we continue on with our walk. I tell her I am glad to know she is doing well. I go so far as to apologize for breaking up with her the way I did. Rheia apologizes again for the passion marks. We look at each other as we walk, laughing and joking, reminiscing on the time we shared together.

She stops walking once we reach the bridge leading over the lake and rests her arms on the railing, looking out into the water.

"I love it down here. Don't you?" she asks.

"One of my Austin favorites, Rheia" I reply.

"Caiden, I have done things in my life I am not proud of. One of the biggest regrets I have is losing you. I wish I had met you under different circumstances. Maybe things would have turned out differently for you and me" she confesses.

I look over at her for a moment then face the water in silence.

"Jaylon forced me to go to Portland," she admits.

She goes on in detail, describing her mission was to find someone willing to seduce me, making me fall in love with them to get Zoe out of my system. Jaylon instructed her to follow me for a couple of months, get to know my habits so when the time came, it would be easy to seduce me. She knew a young woman who agreed to help her for the right price. Rheia adds, after she watched me for months, she started developing a connection to me. She said she didn't have the heart to allow someone to swoop in and hurt me. She contacted her accomplice and called the deal off, feeling if she took the job, she could protect me in some way. Her plan didn't go as she anticipated when she fell in love with me. She says she didn't have the heart to keep manipulating me and lying to me. The pressure started to wear on her, so she devised a plan, ensuring I would end things. She initiated sex, knowing I hadn't been with a woman since Zoe. She created additional drama by denying me the use of my toy, knowing it would frustrate me, causing me to question our relationship. Her final act of molesting me in my sleep, applying passion marks before my trip home would seal the deal. She gambled I would be upset, calling the relationship off. She could report back to Jaylon it was me who ended things in hope Jaylon would leave her alone.

I process her every word, feeling the disappointment develop within me. I question her in a hurtful tone, "Rheia, how could you be so deceitful?"

She replies, "Jaylon said if I didn't do what she asked, she'd make sure I did jail time. Prostitution isn't the half of it. Jaylon has evidence that could send me to jail for at least five years. I didn't have a choice, Caiden."

"Rheia, you could have come to me. I would have helped you. Instead you used me!" I exclaim. I couldn't contain the hurt any longer, lashing out at her, "You fucking, lying whore! What is it, Rheia? Your money run out in Portland, so you come back to Austin to ride the APD money train? I trusted you, and you deceived me! You subjected me to God knows what, yet you claim to love me! What a fucking joke! You know what? You and my faggot-ass sister both can go to hell!"

She takes a few steps back, staring at me in shock by my tone, responding cruelly, "You know what, Caiden? Here is the whole fucking truth! Your own sister paid me to be with you so she could play baby daddy to Zoe's child! With you out of the way, your precious blue eyes was willing to be with Jaylon and start a family because she was convinced you didn't want kids."

My eyes widen in shock as she rants.

"That's right, Caiden, she made a choice, and she chose her child over you. That's the_fucking reason she dumped you! For months, I lied to Jaylon, telling her we were sexing it down and you were wrapped around my little finger so she would leave you alone."

I yell at her to stop lying to me.

She continues, "Jaylon made it sound as if you were a fucking monster, and I believed her until I walked into Slow Grind and fell in love with you almost instantly. You stood there, poised with a bright-ass cocky smile. You were a femme's dream. You were intelligent, charming, kind, and successful. I thought, 'This woman has her shit together.' I knew the moment we met that you were nothing like what Jaylon described."

She pauses, staring at me with tears in her eyes, before admitting she came back to Austin hoping we could work things out and she could rid herself of Jaylon once and for all. She said it was never about the money even though she deserved it after what Jaylon put her through.

After listening to her, I begin to understand she is as much a victim as Zoe and I. I want to be angry with her, but deep down,

I feel sorry for her. We stare in the water in an awkward silence. I apologize for lashing out at her, asking if she has reported to IA.

Rheia expresses she doesn't trust IA and so far hasn't provided them any tangible information they can use against Jaylon. I see I am not the only one who feels something is off with this entire investigation. I make Rheia a proposition, requiring her to stall the investigation. In return, I assure her no one from APD, including Jaylon, could harm her.

She concludes, still looking at me with tears in her eyes, apologizing for her actions. I feel bad seeing the hurt in her eyes. I tell her I understand now why she did what she did and I wish things could have worked out differently. As I gaze into the water, a thought enters my mind, and I ask, "Rheia, how is it Jaylon doesn't recognize you?"

"Honestly, I don't know. I haven't seen Jaylon in a few years. We only talked via cell phone when she needed something from me. Maybe she does know, and she is just playing along," she replies.

My cell beeps, interrupting us.

A text from Zoe—"Worried about you. Coming home soon?"

I text "Soon."

I look at Rheia, not knowing what to say. I find myself leaning in, giving her a gentle hug. She squeezes me tightly, still in tears, warning me to be careful. She notes her concern that Jaylon is unstable, capable of anything. I offer her a cab, but she politely declines, remarking she will be okay. She hands me my blazer and requests I apologize to Zoe on her behalf. My expression is of confusion. She chuckles, remarking she will know what it's for. As I am turning to walk away, she adds, "Caiden, she is beautiful, and I am sorry for your loss."

On the walk home, I text Riley, checking to see if she has come up with any information on Marcus Roberts.

Riley quickly calls. "CW, you are not going to believe what I found on Jaylon's computer files. I will be at Zoe's in fifteen minutes."

I reply, "See you in fifteen."

Riley has already arrived by the time I reach the condo. I enter to find Zoe's parents sitting in the living room. "Mr. and Mrs. Payne, it's a pleasure to see you," I state as I give them each a warm embrace.

"Caiden, how have you been? It's so good to see you. We are both terribly sorry to hear about Rose. She and I were dear friends," says Mr. Payne.

I thank them both for their condolences as I move toward Zoe, giving her a quick hug, then greet Brianna and Riley across the room.

"Mr. Payne, where is Cassie?" I inquire.

He replies, "Caiden, please call me Robert."

Cassie Payne is Zoe's older sister. She was involved in a hit-and-run accident over three years ago, which left her paralyzed from the waist down.

Mrs. Payne responds, "She is at our hotel with our adorable granddaughter. The flight tired them out, and they are resting comfortably. She said to tell you hello and she looks forward to seeing you tomorrow, so she can introduce you to her daughter."

My facial expression is of confusion, thinking Cassie was unable to have children after the accident.

Robert interjects in response to my expression, "The accident left her paralyzed, not infertile as the doctors determined." A sense of pride graces his face as he speaks.

I glance at Zoe, seeing her reaction to our conversation. She seems uncomfortable with the conversation yet manages to disguise her discomfort, excusing herself to the ladies' room. I want to follow but, at the same time, don't want to raise suspicion. I don't think her parents are aware she was ever pregnant. I ask the baby's name and age in an attempt to redirect the focus off Zoe's exit. Carolyn tells me the child's name is Chloe Bryton Payne. She is about to turn two in a few months.

I remark, "What a beautiful name."

Mr. Payne looks at me oddly then chuckles. I pause for a moment, wondering if I said something wrong. Mr. Payne chuckles again as he looks over at his wife. She also begins to laugh.

Carolyn explains, "Cassie has always had a fondness for you, Caiden." Carolyn said Cassie named Chloe after Zoe and me, hoping somehow it would bring us back together. I stand dumbfounded—Cassie would fashion her child's name after me? I can understand Zoe, but me? I look at them both, smiling, saying, "I am humbled. I can't wait to see them!"

Zoe enters back into the room briefly then escorts me into the kitchen. I inquire if she is okay, considering. She nods she is fine. Zoe informs me she took the liberty of contacting a caterer to serve food at my mom's house after the service tomorrow. It completely slipped my mind. I kiss her cheek, hugging her tightly as I thank her. Her parents unexpected arrival is throwing our evening plans to spend some alone time together off. Zoe's personal chef, Mathew McGee, should be arriving within the hour to prepare dinner for six. She lets me know it shouldn't take long, and everyone should be gone by around nine. Brianna and Riley are staying at Brianna's to have some alone time of their own. We sit, enjoying a deliciously prepared meal with garlic-rosemary roasted chicken, wild rice, and asparagus. I look around the dinner table, happy to see everyone enjoying each other's company. It is a welcome distraction after the week we've had.

After dinner, I request to speak with Mr. Payne, but first inform Riley she has the rest of the night off. She needs the down time as much as I do. Riley's discovery can wait one more day. I did not want ruin a perfectly good evening with negativity. Robert and I step onto the balcony, taking in the chilly breeze and view of the lake. He mentions how well Zoe has done for herself. I concur, remarking how proud I am of her accomplishments. I glance down from the twentieth floor and am surprised by his candor. He explains he knows things between us have not always been pleasant. He reminds me of the grief he and his wife gave Zoe and me over our relationship.

He says looking back, they realize they were wrong to interfere. He notes that as parents they only did what they thought was best for Zoe. They naturally wanted her to live a normal, productive life with a young man who could make her happy. Robert acknowledged after I left they saw a drastic change in Zoe. She became disconnected, cutting them off entirely. He joked of the time when Rosemary warned him, either he accepts the fact Zoe is in love with a woman and supports her, or face the alternative and risks losing her. He admits he was stubborn and prideful, ignoring her warning. They thought that after I left, given time, Zoe would snap out of her homosexual phase and date men again. Zoe did as my mother warned, withdrawing herself from them. I learned they just recently reconnected a few months ago.

Robert remarks, "We have decided to embrace our daughter's lifestyle with open arms. We realize Zoe is happiest with you in her life."

I am floored by his admission. It makes what I am about to ask him much easier.

"Mr. Payne—" I start, but he quickly interrupts.

"Caiden, from here on out, I insist you call me Robert."

Clearing my throat, I explain, "Uhm, Robert, I brought you out here because I love Zoe with all my heart. She is the most important person in the world to me. I am asking your permission for her hand in marriage. It is important for me to have you and Carolyn's blessing. I believe I speak for Zoe as well."

He is resting his arms on the railing of the balcony, looking out toward the lake. I move close to the balcony door, bracing myself for his response. He looks down at the street then looks back out toward the lake. He lets out a long sigh, stands erect, turning to face me. His expression is unreadable, and I begin to question myself as to why I brought him out on a twentieth floor balcony to ask him to marry his daughter.

As he looks at me, his blue eyes soften as he speaks, "You know, Caiden, most men lack the character or guts these days to even consult the father when considering marriage. You are a traditionalist. It's a fine quality to possess, especially when you are about to marry my daughter. Caiden, Carolyn, and I would be honored to have you as a member of our family. To answer your question, yes, you have our blessing!"

He moves toward me with open arms, hugging me so tight I can barely breathe. He releases me from our embrace, and I vow I will spend my life making sure Zoe is happy and loved. He nods with a smile in agreement. I make him promise not to mention this to anyone, not even his wife, until I ask Zoe. We head inside with the others as they are preparing to leave. Zoe and I bid everyone a good night as we usher everyone out the door. I begin to yawn as I head into the bathroom to take a hot shower. Zoe remains in the living room, tidying up. I make a mental note to myself, "Hire Zoe a maid after our wedding."

I exit the shower, drying myself as Zoe enters turning the shower on and hopping in. She looks as exhausted as I feel. It has been a difficult and informative day. I hop in bed, picking up a *GQ* magazine to flip through, waiting for Zoe.

About fifteen minutes pass before she enters the bedroom, wearing a Vic's Secret panty and bra. "See anything in there you may want for your birthday?" she asks as she slides into bed next to me.

"My birthday?" I ask.

She laughs, reminding me of my birthday this month. So much has been happening in the past seven days that I forgot. "Sorry, it must have slipped my mind. No, there is nothing in here I want," I reply, smiling at her.

"Well, birthday boi, what do you want?" she asks.

"I have everything I want right here," I respond, pointing at her heart.

She looks at me with frustration and mumbles something under her breath.

"What did you just say?" I ask, laughing.

She looks back at me, giggling, saying, "I was thinking out loud. Don't worry about it."

I place the magazine back on the nightstand and pull my towel from my waist and toss it on the side of the bed. Zoe looks my body up and down devilishly, biting her lower lip. I slip under the sheet and duvet, pulling them up to my neck, eyeing her cautiously.

She takes the covers slowly, peeling them back down to the end of the bed.

"Zoe, what are you up to?" I ask curiously.

She smiles mischievously as she straddles my lap, taking my wrists and pinning them up over my head against the headboard, then leans down and kisses my lips. My mouth greets her lips in a welcoming fashion. I try to move my hands, but she forces them back against the headboard. I am aroused by her aggression. I lie subdued, allowing her free reign over me. She sits up, gazing at me. I am hypnotized, staring at her, unable to speak. I ache to make love to her. She releases my wrists, and my hands move slowly to touch her smooth, soft skin. She leans in, whispering in my ear, "I want to taste you," as she nibbles my ear lobe with her teeth. She rises up, unfastening her bra and dangling it in front of me, smiling. I attempt to rise and kiss her, but she obstructs my attempt, forcing me back down onto the mattress. Her teasing is driving me insane.

Slowly guiding my hands to her waist, placing them on her panty, she mouths, *"Rip them off."*

Obeying her command, I tear them off as she lets out a moan. My body heat rises as I grow more excited. I wait impatiently for her next command. She caresses my breasts and gently pulls at my nipples with her teeth, causing them to become erect. "Are you enjoying this?" she asks.

"Me? No, I'm not enjoying this at all," I tease.

I feel her warm mouth cover my nipples, sucking them while her tongue circles. My back arches at the sensation, pushing my breast deeper into her mouth. My fingers are gliding down her back, reaching her waist, clenching it, drawing her closer. Her mouth slowly moves up my chest to my neck, kissing, sucking, and licking me, making the most tantalizing sounds as she continues to harass me. I sigh, calling her name, yearning to have her. She kisses me, gliding her tongue across my lips, moaning. A carnal craving develops, inflaming my desire to satisfy her.

Our lips part as Zoe rises, panting heavily, gazing into my eyes. Our desire for each other is undeniable, moving beyond just the physical. She maneuvers her body, facing away while still draped across my lap. I rise, pulling her long hair, forcing her head back, and whispering, "It's yours," in her ear.

She grins salaciously, leaning forward toward the foot of the bed. I lie back toward the headboard, grabbing her thighs, pulling her Venus toward my mouth. Her hands grasp my lower legs as she assumes the position. I can feel her lips cover me as her warm tongue begins to lick my clit. I jerk suddenly at the sensation. A moan passes my lips as I look down, seeing Zoe's Venus is moist and eager for me. I find it difficult to reciprocate, distracted by her tongue on me. A chill passes through me as I quiver in delight. I grind against her mouth, inhaling the pleasure. Shaking my head in order to refocus my attention, placing my mouth around her Venus, my tongue moves back and forth over her clit whilst her body follows my rhythm. Zoe presses her pelvis firmly against my mouth as I grab her curvy ass, keeping it firmly in place. I ease my fingers inside her. She lets out a moan as her head rises briefly. My fingers are covered in her juices, moving slowly in and out of her. Her excitement builds as her body begins to sway around and around. I am helpless to delay my pending fate as my muscles tighten.

Reaching my apogee, I cry out Zoe's name in jubilation. Her body mimics my own, and I feel her tense as she clenches my ankles, moaning over and over as she reaches her apex. Her arms give out as she collapses on the bed, trembling atop me.

We lie still, relishing in the aftereffects of our passion. Later, Zoe lifts herself up on her forearm, looking back at me with a sultry grin. I know that grin all too well as I smile at her. My nymph's appetite is not yet sated. She moves her pelvis to meet mine. Her enflamed clit is pressing against mine as she begins to grind back and forth, round and round. My eyes close as my teeth clench. I feel our bodies grinding against each other. Moaning lustful cries while my body forms it rhythm to flow in contradiction to hers, I reach for her hips and press my body even closer to hers, guaranteeing optimal gratification. I amend my rhythm, remaining in sync with her movements. Our bodies seem perfectly designed to intertwine one with the other. I reach behind my head, squeezing my pillow as my head tilts back from our dual collaboration. I listen to her soft voice weeping my name between moans in pure enjoyment. I govern my body to postpone the inevitable joy it craves to safeguard Zoe's imminent climax. Once more, I feel her body arch and quiver as she moans in delight. The sound of her voice lifts me to orgasm.

Still reeling from our experience, Zoe moves toward the head of the bed, beside me, kissing me with sexual desire. I reciprocate, caressing her face, running my fingers across her soft lips, dipping them in and out of her mouth, uttering to her over and over how much I love her.

CHAPTER ELEVEN

Apprehension

It is eight o'clock when I wake, feeling rejuvenated. I know Caiden has a lot on her mind, and I want today to be stress-free as possible for her. I peek in to check on her, and she is sound asleep. This is probably the most sleep she has had since her arrival last Thursday. She looks so peaceful and relaxed, curled within the duvet. I creep through her luggage, avoiding waking her, looking for her cuff links. I remember that she had a beautiful pair of black pearls encased in silver her mother had given her for her birthday, which she only wears on special occasions. They will look perfect with the suit I got her. She keeps them in a black velvet box. Rummaging through her luggage, I find the box, grasping it. I want to polish them for her. I enter the bathroom, searching for a cloth, and peek out the door, checking if she is still sleep. I open the box, expecting to find cufflinks. Instead I discover a beautiful princess-cut diamond ring sitting atop a platinum band filled with smaller princess-cut diamonds closely knit together halfway around the band. It is at least three carats. My heart stops as my mouth gapes open while I stare in awe.

I think back to when Caiden and I first started dating. She asked me to describe my engagement ring. I thought she was joking, so I played along and drew her a sketch of my dream ring.

She took the sketch, eyed it for a moment, and asked, "Zoe, are you sure this is the ring you want placed on your finger when you marry?"

I took the sketch from her hand, eyeing it again, and handed it back to her, replying with an emphatic "Absolutely!"

She laughed, placing the sketch in her wallet. We never discussed it again.

Oh my god rings out in my mind. My hands tremble as my heart races. Startled when I hear Caiden stirring in bed, I dash back to her luggage, putting the ring in its box back into her bag exactly where I found it. I ease back into the bathroom, hoping she didn't notice me. I am having trouble controlling my excitement. I can't let her find out I know about the ring. Is she going to propose? Is this why she wanted the other night to be special? The private conversation with my father? I am freaking out! I can't breathe! I coax myself, saying, "Breathe, Zoe. Nice and easy, inhale then exhale." Finally, I am at a point I can breathe normally.

Caiden enters the bathroom, kissing me softly on the lips. She pulls away, smiling with a boyish charm, saying, "Good morning, beautiful!"

What an odd mood to be in on the day of her mother's funeral. She looks at me coyly, remarking, "Today is a good day, Ms. Payne. My mother's spirit lives on inside me. Shhh, quiet. Do you hear that, Zoe?"

I listen intently for the sound she is referring to.

She continues. "I can hear her voice. Listen, Zoe, do you hear it? She is overjoyed!"

I watch Caiden having a conversation with her deceased mother, placing me on high alert. I assume this is her way of coping. She tells me her mother visited her in her dreams last night, asking her to take care of Jaylon, sharing that Jaylon is the way she is because of her and Caiden and Caiden should forgive her. I am concerned, to say the least, by her mood. She has a tendency to hide her emotions, but this is peculiar even for Caiden.

I take her hand, leading her into the kitchen, where I have breakfast waiting: eggs over medium, oatmeal, toast with strawberry jam, and a side of mixed fruit. I pour her a cup of coffee and a glass of orange juice.

"Nice! What are you, going to eat?" she asks jokingly.

Helping to keep her spirits up, I playfully nudge her shoulder, whispering, "You!"

Caiden, looking reticently, offers a few naughty ideas.

I can't help to laugh at her proposition, asking, "What has come over you this morning?"

She replies shrewdly, "The better question is what 'came' over me last night!"

"Caiden Bryce Westphal, cut it out!" I order.

Caiden laughs, nodding and saying she will behave. She pops a strawberry in her mouth and rolls it around with her tongue, chewing it slowly, commenting, "Very sweet and juicy, mmmmh, just the way I like it."

I look at her with firm eyes, trying not to laugh and demanding she behave. She crosses her heart and explains she will do her best. We finish breakfast, and she helps me with the dishes. She glances at the time—almost nine o'clock. She reminds me she has an errand, gives me a quick kiss on the lips, and heads to the shower. I'm glad to see her in a playful mood, but the timing is strange. Her life has been in a tailspin since she arrived.

I start to wonder how she got along in Portland. Was she happy? Did she have good friends to look after her? Did she miss me while she was away? The doorbell rings, breaking me from my thoughts. I answer and wish I hadn't when I see Jaylon standing in the doorway. I stand with the door partially closed.

"What can I do for you, Jaylon?" I ask sharply.

"Well, hello to you too, beautiful. I am actually here to see Caiden. We are meeting at the attorney's office to settle our mother's estate in about an hour. Did she forget?" she asks.

"I am afraid she is tied up at the moment and can't be disturbed. I will have her call you," I reply. I attempt to close the door, but Jaylon forces her way in. "Jaylon, what the hell do you think you are doing?" I shout.

She looks around the condo to see if anyone is around. She hears the shower running and, assuming Caiden is preoccupied, she moves toward me. "Finally, I have a moment alone with you, Zoe. We should talk, you know, like we used to after my sister abandoned you. If memory serves me correctly, she left you pregnant and alone. You remember that, don't you, Zoe?"

She reminds me how she took care of me while I was pregnant and how I turned to her for support. God, how I wish I could turn back time, erasing that part of my life. She moves nearer to me as I back away from her. She stops and begins to eye my body, sucking on her teeth as she asks, "You like teasing me, Zoe? Answering the door wearing hardly anything. Nipples peeking through the shirt, begging for me to touch them."

I feel disgusted wearing only a T-shirt and Brazilian-cut panties in front of her. "Jaylon, I think you should leave before Caiden gets out of the shower," I suggest.

She continues, moving toward me, backing me up against the fridge, pressing her body close to mine, and smells my hair. I push her, trying to free myself, but she overpowers me. Still pinning me against the fridge, Jaylon utters in my ear, "Zoe, how quickly you forget."

"Forget what, Jaylon? I have no idea of what you are rambling about," I explain, still trying to free myself from her grasp.

Rubbing her hand across my cheek, she murmurs, "Caiden and I had a long talk after the ball the other night. Didn't she mention it to you? This nonsense between you and her has gone on long enough, and it's going to stop! You two will never be married, Zoe. It just doesn't make any sense why you think I will let you go so easily."

I tell Jaylon I didn't know anything about a marriage, asking what is wrong with her. I manage to free my hand, scratching her in the face, drawing blood. As she steps back in shock, I reach for a knife, lying on the cutting board. Clutching her face, she snarls at me with evil intent.

I warn, "If you come near me again, Jaylon, I swear—"

She cuts me off midsentence, yelling "You know what, Zoe? We can settle this once and for all. Caiden, come out here. Zoe and I have a few things to discuss with you!" I wonder if Jaylon has completely lost her fucking mind, knowing Caiden wants nothing more than to beat the hell out of her.

In a matter of seconds, Caiden charges into the living room in a pair of sweatpants and T-shirt, looking for me. I place the knife back on the counter before she could see it. She turns to Jaylon, fuming. "I thought I made it clear the last time that you are to stay the fuck away from Zoe! Are you fucking delusional, Jaylon?" Caiden bellows.

Jaylon looks confused at Caiden's command. She stands, smiling, and replies, "Caiden, you are not good enough for Zoe. She needs a real stud to love and provide for her. I'm the only one who can give her what she really needs," sounding convincing only to herself.

Caiden, noticing the blood on Jaylon's face, turns to me, reaching for my hand, examining it for injuries.

I reply, "I am okay."

I can see the rage building as she turns to Jaylon, advising her she has one opportunity to walk the fuck out the door on her own accord. Caiden's fists are clenched as her body tenses, ready to kill Jaylon. Jaylon notices Caiden's demeanor and wisely excuses herself, stating she has a funeral to attend, but we would continue this lovely exchange at a later date.

"Caiden, we have an appointment with the attorney in an hour to go over Rosemary's estate. Zoe, I will see you later at my place tonight. I have something very important to ask you," she states as she turns to exit the condo. Caiden is furious at her remarks, rushing at Jaylon, slamming her into the wall. "If it were any other day, Jaylon, I would—"

A knock at the door interrupts the two of them. Erika and a young cadet in uniform enter, seeing the front door ajar. "Jaylon, we came up to see what is taking you so long. I see we have interrupted yet another family reunion," she quips.

The young cadet places his hands on Caiden's shoulder in an effort to separate them.

Caiden, still holding Jaylon hostage against the wall, looks at the young cadet, demanding, "Get your damn hands off me!"

The cadet, not taking Caiden's request kindly, reaches for his taser.

Ericka quickly stops him, signaling him to stand down. "Uh, Caiden, this is becoming all too frequent a scenario. I am going to ask you nicely to release Jaylon and step away," she insists.

Caiden slowly releases her grip from Jaylon's jacket and steps away. Caiden looks over at Ericka and tells her she would like to make a request. Ericka looks at Caiden curiously.

"It seems my sister is obviously under duress or simply psychotic. Pick one, I don't really give a damn! Her actions, however, are becoming a nuisance, causing a negative impact on our quality of life. Her obsession with Zoe has surpassed a schoolgirl crush, bordering on insanity. Zoe and I would like to file a restraining order against Jaylon," Caiden states in anger.

Caiden smugly explains to Erika that while she is no expert on the law, she believes a verbal request in front of two of Austin's finest would be sufficient to get the ball rolling.

Erika looks aggravated at Caiden then turns her stare to me. I look at her and respond, "Ericka, I agree with Caiden. I don't feel safe around Jaylon anymore."

Ericka turns to Jaylon, advising her not to return to this residence or any other residence owned by us, our places of business, or come within one hundred yards of us with the exception of attending the funeral service today. She did instruct Jaylon to maintain a safe distance at the service. Erika questions Jaylon if she understands.

Jaylon barks, "I am a police officer, you sell out!"

Ericka guides Jaylon out of the condo, instructing the cadet to escort Jaylon off the premises. Ericka waves, telling me she will see us at the service, and closes the door. Caiden sits on the sofa, staring out the window in a daze, oblivious to the fact they have gone. I have no response, shaking my head in confusion at the entire incident.

"Why did you let her in?" Caiden asks, irritated still, sitting on the couch.

"Caiden, I didn't! She forced her way in," I reply defensively.

She moves off the couch and, growing more and more frustrated, comes toward me, replying, "I'm sorry. Are you okay? Did she hurt you? Did she put her fucking hands on you?"

Hoping to defuse the situation, I caress her face, staring into her eyes, answering, "Caiden, she didn't hurt me. Don't let Jaylon ruin today, please?"

Her forehead wrinkles as her eyes narrow while she considers my request. We stare at each other while she exhales, letting go of her anger. I kiss her lovingly, urging her to focus her energy on what is important, her mother.

Wanting to lift her spirits, I decide to give her one of her birthday gifts early. I ask that she shut her eyes and wait in the living room. I grab her gift from my bedroom, holding a box in both hands, presenting it to her. "Open your eyes, handsome. Surprise!"

Caiden looks down to see a small box wrapped in chocolate paper with white ribbon. She looks confused by my gesture. I order her to open it.

"Zoe, you didn't have to buy me a gift," she states, sounding frustrated.

I nod, acknowledging her comment, and again motion her to open it. She sits on the sofa, motioning me to sit beside her. I watch with anticipation as she opens the box and looks inside.

"Zoe, oh my god, an Oyster Perpetual Rolex! Zoe, it's beautiful, but I can't accept this."

Determined to make her understand she doesn't have to be the giver all the time, I pull the watch out of the box, placing it on her wrist, "Caiden, you don't get a say in the matter. You know, there are perks in dating a millionaire. Caiden, you have had a tough week, and I want to give you something special to bring a little joy back into your life. I know how much you love Rolex watches. Is it so wrong for me to spoil you as much as you spoil me?" I ask.

Seeing the determination in my eyes, she graciously accepts, kissing me softly on the lips and thanking me. We sit back on the sofa, in each other's arms, in silence, sharing a tender moment. Caiden admires the watch, promising me she will learn to accept gifts more freely.

She looks at the time, informing me she has to run by the bank but that she will be back in time to get ready for the service. The limo is scheduled to pick us up at two o'clock and escort us to the funeral home. Caiden is looking around for her sneakers and glances over at the armoire and sees the suit. She looks puzzled. I smile and explain I have gotten it for her to wear today.

She eyes it, responding, "You do have exquisite taste, Ms. Payne. Thank you again! Have I told you how amazing you are? By the way, last night was incredible. I will never get enough of you, Zoe!"

My cheeks are flushed at her words. I walk up to her, kissing her on the cheek in response. I have a few errands of my own I need to take care of. As Caiden prepares to leave, she looks over at me, making me promise to stay away from Jaylon. I promise I will stay as far away from Jaylon as humanly possible. She laughs and heads out the front door, locking it securely as she leaves.

Brianna is meeting me around ten so we can swing by the hotel for a quick visit with my sister and her daughter. I feel bad I have not spent as much time as I should with her and my niece. Since I have lost my own child, I find it difficult to be around children, especially one near in age as mine would have been. The circumstances surrounding my child's conception can't negate the fact that I loved her. While I wait for Brianna to arrive, I contact the caterer and funeral home, checking to make sure everything is running as planned. Noticing it is ten thirty, I send Brianna a quick text, "Where are you?" As I wait for her to respond, I look through my closet for something appropriate to wear.

I start to think about Jaylon and her obvious obsession with Caiden and me. Why does she think Caiden and I plan to marry?

Did Caiden put that in her head? The doorbell rings, startling me. I look through the peephole and open the door for Brianna. She enters, apologizing for being late yet seeming excited about something. We greet each other with a warm hug. I notice Riley is not with her, and she explains Riley is meeting with Caiden. They have some unfinished business prior to the service.

Brianna is beaming, sparking me to ask, "Well, don't keep me in suspense. How did things go last night between you and Riley?"

She giggles and replies, "Riley was a perfect gentlemyn. Oh, Zoe, we had the best time talking and laughing. She is really a sweet person underneath her brooding exterior. We talked until three in the morning."

I respond, "I am so happy you two hit it off. You make a great couple!"

She goes on to explain that Riley really has a lot of respect and love for Caiden. She shares Riley does not know where she would be right now if not for Caiden. They really look out for each other. Brianna mentions Riley and Caiden are a lot alike. I get the same impression. I know Caiden is very fond of Riley even though she will never admit it. Brianna tells me she wanted to make love to Riley last night, but Riley declined, noting Caiden will kill her if she takes advantage of Brianna. Riley has explained to Brianna that she likes her but prefers to get to know her better before they take it to the next level. Brianna continues her recap of their evening together, noting she was slightly disappointed, but it shows Riley has respect for her. I smile at her comment although I am still distracted by earlier events.

My cell beeps as we are getting dressed. It's Caiden informing me she is with Riley. Brianna and I meet my family at their hotel for brunch. We should plenty of time before we meet up with Caiden and Riley around one o'clock.

CHAPTER TWELVE

Revelations

Exiting Zoe's condo, I scan the halls for any signs of Jaylon. Once convinced she is gone, I head over to my mother's bank. Upon entry, I greet the receptionist, explaining I want to access a safe deposit box. She signs me in and asks me to be seated.

"Someone will be with you shortly, Ms. Westphal," she explains.

I wait impatiently until an older gray-haired woman appears to greet me warmly. I explain to her my reason for being here and provide her the necessary paperwork to give me access to my mother's safe deposit box. She offers her condolences and leads me into the vault area of the bank. She enters an access code to the vault. She searches to find my box number and inserts a bank key in one side of the box and instructs me to insert my key into the other. We turn the keys simultaneously, unlocking the safe. I pull out the box as the elderly woman ushers me to a small area with a desk for privacy, noting she will be right outside if I need anything, adding I could take all the time I need.

I place the box on the counter and take a seat in the chair provided. Sifting through the box, I notice a large sum of cash in two stacks, a vintage Rolex tucked away safely in a jewelry box, a picture of my mother, a man who seems familiar in a way, and an infant. On the back of the picture, the date reads October 27, 1985. My birthday! The infant in the picture must be me. The gentleman and my mother look so happy and proud. I see a newspaper clipping from December 1983. I open it up to read the headline "Mother of One Kills Estranged Husband and Herself." I read further, discovering the article is about my parents, Nadine and David. The article describes a two-year-old child was present at the time of the dual murders. I think for a moment then realize the infant in the article couldn't be me. I hadn't even been born. I continue reading, learning the child was placed in the care of Health and Human Services until a family member could be notified. I sit in dismay, wondering why Rosemary never shared this with me. I was under the impression my parents were killed in a car crash by a drunk driver. Why would Rosemary lie? Short on time, I text Riley to research this information. As I continue to search through the box, I find a letter written by Rosemary addressed to me dated October 27, 2008. My hands begin to tremble as I hold it. I remember Rosemary saying my questions would be answered after her death. I gulp as I open the letter nervously.

> My Dearest Heart,
>
> Caiden, as a parent we oftentimes make mistakes we can never recover from. One simple lie to protect your children turns into a landslide, overshadowing the light. I am a coward, too ashamed to look you in the eye and tell you the truth. Your father, Ed, and I have made mistakes no parent wants their child to realize. Not a day has gone by of me wanting to share my truth. I have been haunted by my lies for years. I'm afraid my choices have corrupted your relationship with Jaylon.
>
> Jaylon is the child in the newspaper article. She is the daughter of Nadine Marie Richards and David Jalen Westphal. Nadine and I were both in love with David simultaneously. His feelings were not mutual toward Nadine. She refused to accept he didn't love her and vowed

to be with him no matter the cost. One day, they ran into each other at a local bar, resulting in a one-night stand, inevitably producing a child. David and I were married at the time, and naturally, tensions were high between us because of his adultery. The deception ultimately led us to divorce. We agreed the right thing for him to do was be there for both Nadine and his child.

I moved on with my life, falling in love with Ed, your father's sibling. We wanted to start a family, but having a child between the two of us was complicated. Two years after David and I divorced, we found each other again rekindling old emotions. Although I was in love with Ed, I had a brief affair with David. The affair ended as quickly as it started, with me becoming pregnant with you. David automatically assumed the child was his and wanted us to be a family, but I had other ideas. I told him I was in love with Ed, and we'd raise our child together. David's pride and ego were bruised, turning him into a spiteful man. He grew enraged, threatening to take you away from me if we didn't do what he wanted. He said he'd make our lives miserable, and he had the power to do it. He gave us an ultimatum: either we end our relationship, demanding Ed leave Austin, never contacting me again, or he would make sure I never saw you again. Ed knew David would destroy us before he'd allow us to be together. Your father made the difficult choice to leave to prevent David from destroying our family. I begged Eddie to stay and fight, but our secrets would ruin our lives as well as our careers, and Ed wouldn't allow that to happen. Once David got what he wanted from Ed, he filed for a divorce from Nadine and forced me to be with him. He wanted us to raise both you and Jaylon together. I agreed to his conditions, feeling it was the only way I'd be able to be hold on to you. Ed had gone, leaving me heartbroken. The only thing I had left was you to keep me sane.

Jaylon has known about this since she was fourteen. I made her promise not to mention a word to you until I could explain it to you myself when you were older. I need you to understand I kept this from you because I was terrified of what Jaylon may have done to you in her condition if you knew. Jaylon has been mentally unstable even before she found out about her parents, and I couldn't risk her hurting you anymore. You unfortunately have been the recipient of her anger and feelings of being unwanted and unloved for years. I placed her in therapy after she learned about her parents, hoping to help her sort through her feelings. It didn't seem to help with her feelings towards you or me. She blames the two of us for her misery. I have no justification for my actions, only the love of a mother trying to protect her child. I know you understand how that feels. I hope you can find it in your heart to one day forgive me.

Love always and forever,
Your mother

P.S. The watch belonged to your father. I'm sure Eddie would want you to have it.

Tears cascade down my face after reading her letter. I am filled with mixed emotions of betrayal, love, and disillusionment. I stare at the picture of the three of us and an unexpected smile crosses my face. I have a father who loves me and gave up everything to protect his family. I pick up the watch, admiring the craftsmanship, simple yet refined. I check my own watch and realize I need to get back to Zoe's. I place the letter in my pocket and return the watch to its box and into the safe deposit box along with the other items and notify the attendant I am finished. It is eleven o'clock as I walk idly down the street, drifting in and out of consciousness, unaware of the world around me.

I remember my mother's letter and the newspaper article when a thought comes to me. I call Chief Martin, hoping to catch him in the office. His assistant answers. I inform her I have an urgent matter to discuss and would be obliged if she put me through right away. He answers, and I explain my situation and what I need from him.

I check my cell, and there is a text from Riley: "CW, I have everything you need. Can you meet me at the police station ASAP?"

I text, "On my way now."

I reach APD and head to the administrative offices. Upon arrival, I see Riley sitting in the waiting area. I advise her to hold off providing any information to APD. She looks at me, confused, and I tell her I will explain later. I ask Riley to wait for me outside. I need a moment with the chief. She picks up her laptop angrily and heads toward the elevator. Prior to leaving, I ask the chief one final favor. He tells me to stop by the lab, and they will assist with my request. He promises he will put a rush on it and be in touch as soon as he gets the results. I shake his hand and thank him for all his help as I exit his office.

It is one o'clock, and I decide to send Zoe a text: "At APD headquarters. Be home soon!"

Pressed for time, Riley and I grab a cab back to Zoe's. I can tell Riley is upset with me, so to ease the tension, I ask how her evening with Brianna had gone. She smiles, telling me they had a great time. I eye her suspiciously, wondering if she and Brianna had sex. She must be reading my mind as she instantly informs me she did not touch her in that way. I smile at her comment then stare out the window. "I know I have given you a hard time but I can't think of anyone I'd rather see Brianna with. Riley, if you hurt her, you will have me to deal with. Got it?" I snap jokingly.

Riley laughs and replies, "CW, I really like Brianna, and I am glad you approve. I give you my word, I will respect her. She's a special girl."

"Yes, Riley, very special," I add.

We arrive back at the condo, and I hand Riley the key to let herself in. I need a moment to myself to regroup. The reality of my mother's passing is starting to settle in. I am overcome with anxiety. My chest is tight, and I am having difficulty catching my breath. I take a few deep breaths, leaning against the wall outside Zoe's door. I hear Riley and Brianna laughing, excited to see each other. It brings a slight smile to my face. I have so much I want to tell Zoe, but I do not have enough time. I make it a point to tell her everything tomorrow once the dust settles. Hopefully the news will bring her peace, and we can focus on our future together. I walk in to see Riley and Brianna engaging in a passionate lip-lock. I clear my throat as I enter, greeting Brianna with a warm hello. She looks at me, trying to gauge my reaction to her and Riley. I smile at her as I walk into the kitchen.

I rummage through Zoe's liquor cabinet, finding a bottle of tequila and pour a shot. I look in the fridge and grab a bottle of domestic beer. I twist the cap, looking at Riley and Brianna as they look at me in surprise.

I ask, "Where is Zoe?"

Brianna points to the bedroom.

I take the shot of tequila and chase it with the beer. Zoe enters the room, surprised to see me chugging a beer. Spotting the empty shot glass and bottle of tequila next to me on the counter, she walks over to the bar, placing the top back on the tequila bottle, and returns it to the liquor cabinet. She asks me if I am okay. I nod yes, walking toward her, kissing her on the cheek, then head into the bedroom, taking a seat on the chair, swallowing the last of my beer. I think, *This is exactly what I need.*

I am alone in the room with my thoughts. Making myself comfortable, I lean back in the chair, placing my legs on the ottoman, turning my head toward the ceiling.

Zoe enters and sits on the bed, asking, "What are we watching today?"

I chuckle, responding "Zoe, today we are watching a tale about lies, deceit, and betrayal."

She responds, "Caiden, is this something you really want to watch on a day like today?"

I grimace as I turn to face her. She looks perturbed, informing me the funeral director called and the driver is going to be later than expected. A wreck on IH-35 Southbound has traffic at a gridlock. The driver managed to detour over to MoPac before traffic reached a halt. The service will be pushed back an hour as a concession. The limo will arrive around two thirty. I laugh out loud, telling myself nothing about today will surprise me. I motion Zoe to come sit next to me. She reminds me we have to get dressed. My clothes are hanging neatly alongside hers in her closet. I'm curious to know what she is going to wear, I peek behind my suit, and see a black sleeveless dress past the knees, stopping at the calf, with a low neckline and black four-inch heels on the floor. *Simple yet elegant,* I think to myself. She heads into the bathroom to do her hair and makeup. The effects of the tequila are beginning to hit. I stumble slightly as I rise from the chair and head into the bathroom.

Zoe is standing in front of the mirror, straightening her hair. I walk up behind her, placing my arms around her waist and kiss her neck. She smiles and continues working on her hair. I look at the mirror and comment on how beautiful she is. She again smiles but orders me to start getting ready. I can see she has her defenses up against any advance I attempt to make. I walk out into the bedroom and lie across the bed. I am feeling lightheaded. I have not eaten since breakfast this morning, and I am starving. After a few moments, I go into the kitchen, hunting for a quick snack to tide me over until we reach my mother's house. I grab an apple, a slice of muenster cheese, two slices of turkey breast, and a couple of green olives. Sitting alone at the bar, I devour my food. I notice my cell is flashing.

"How are you?" I answer.

"Hello, Caiden. I wanted to call and inform you of the results. They are as you expected," the chief replies.

"Thank you again, chief. I will see you at the service," I reply as I hang up.

Brianna and Riley enter the room dressed and ready to go.

"You two look very nice," I comment.

Brianna asks, "Caiden, shouldn't you be getting ready?"

Slurring slightly, I tell her I am on my way to do just that. Wobbling as I stand, I recognize the need to pull my shit together. What was I thinking, drinking? I open the fridge to grab a bottle of Gatorade and chug it down along with two ibuprofen. Riley enters the kitchen and directs me to the guest room. She instructs me to sit on the bed, and she would be right back. Upon her return, she hands me my clothing, remaining in the room to make sure I get dressed, helping me fix my tie and cuff links.

"CW, what is going on with you?" she asks, irritated.

I reply, still intoxicated, "Riley, you don't know the half of it, my friend."

After a few minutes, I manage to pull it together, and we head toward the living room. I see Zoe looking at me, perhaps a bit aggravated at my behavior as well.

I ask, "How was your visit with your sister and niece today?"

She remarks sharply, it went well. There is a quiet awkwardness in the room as we wait impatiently for the limo to arrive. It's two forty when a knock at the door breaks the silence. Riley answers to our driver apologizing profusely for the delay as we exit, heading downstairs.

Once we are all in the car, I lean over to Zoe and whisper "I'm sorry for my behavior earlier. It was inappropriate. I was being a complete ass" then lean back to my seat.

She leans into my ear, whispering, "I'm not very happy with you at the moment."

As she leans back to her seat, I laugh slightly. I test the water, placing my hand next to hers, resting on the seat. No response. I inch my hand closer to hers, brushing my pinky on the side of her hand. Zoe moves her hand into her lap. I guess I am not in the clear yet. I ponder what I can do to get back in her good graces.

Riley inadvertently offers me aid by commenting, "Nice watch, CW!"

I respond, "Thank you, Riley, it is an early birthday gift."

I look over at Zoe out the corner of my eye to see if she winces. Success! A subtle smile crosses her lips though she attempts to deny it.

Brianna teases, commenting, "And you wonder why she is such a spoiled brat, Zoe!"

I joke, "I'm wouldn't necessarily use the term *spoiled* per se."

Looking at Brianna, Zoe lets out a giggle, replying, "I may have to rethink things per se!"

We chuckle, continuing on our journey. Zoe reaches for my hand, squeezing it gently. Traffic is still a nightmare north and south on the interstate, and we are barely moving. I doubt we will make it to the funeral home by three thirty."

I stare out the window, recapping the day, wondering the right time to talk to Zoe. I think about Jaylon and all the horrible things she has done. I doubt she will comply with the restraining order. A chill comes over me, thinking what she may do to Zoe if given the opportunity. I shrug off the thought and begin to wonder how Zoe would like Portland. How should I propose to her? What type of wedding would she like? I am hoping she loves the one-of-a-kind ring. I remember the day she drew me the sketch. The drawing is still in my album. Does she want kids? Surely she does.

Zoe rubs my shoulder, startling me. I look over at her in wonderment at how beautiful a person she is. Riley and Brianna sit quietly, gazing into each other's eyes. Maybe they are made for each other? Riley is more at ease when she is around her, not at all the geeky nerdster she is around me. She obviously brings out the best in Brianna. It has been a while since I have seen Brianna truly happy. Jaylon screwed her up so bad, I never thought she would be able to love or trust again.

I feel Zoe sliding closer to me. She asks, "How are we doing over here?"

I respond, "Better now that you are closer."

She giggles as she caresses my cheek. She intertwines her arm in mine, leaning her head on my shoulder, remarking, "Caiden, everything is going to work out. I love you!"

My heart melts at her words as droplets begin to form in my eyes. I rest my head next to hers, squeezing her arm tightly, praying she does not see me crying. I have to be strong. I subtly wipe the tears from my eyes, replying, "Zoe, I love you. Thank you for being you."

Finally, at three twenty, we arrive at the funeral home. As we pull in, I am in awe of the multitude of cars in the parking lot. I wonder if there are two services going on at the same time. I ask the driver as we exit the limo.

He replies, "No, Ms. Westphal, there is only your mother's service being held today."

There has to be over four hundred people present. The driver pulls up on the side of the building, giving us access to the front of the chapel. I previously requested the first three pews for close friends and family. There would be more friends since Jaylon and I were the only family remaining. Prior to allowing us entry, the funeral director, Mr. Williams, informs me all three pews were full. He tells me Jaylon assured him the guests occupying the seats were approved by me.

I take a moment, closing my eyes, breathing deep slow breaths. I respond, "I see."

I signal him to open the door. Zoe, Brianna, and Riley look for me to enter first. I motion to Riley and Brianna to enter. I take Zoe's hand as we enter together.

The room is completely full of people, some I recognize and others unfamiliar to me. I am touched so many people came to pay homage to Rose. We reach the three front pews. I notice Jaylon sitting in the front row with her drinking companions from work, all in uniform. They have filled the majority of the first three rows.

I politely whisper into Zoe's ear to please stand here with Riley and Brianna for a moment. I pull Mr. Williams to the side, telling him there will be a slight change in the seating arrangement. I look across the room, pointing out individuals who will be exchanging seats with the party sitting here. I show him Nurse Woodward, Abby, and Ashley. Luckily, they are seated near each other, on the back row. I look for Chief Martin and his wife, sitting in the third row from the back. I scan the room to find Zoe's parents, sister, and niece, all sitting together in the fourth row to the back. On the other side, I point out Edwina Miller. I motion Riley to come over and instruct, "Please help Mr. Williams gather the following people and bring them up to the front."

I walk over to the front pew with Jaylon eyeing me closely. I address the officers, "Excuse me, officers, there seem to be a misunderstanding with the seating arrangements. I would be obliged if all of you sitting on the first three rows, with the exception of my sister and Detective Stewart, be so gracious as to offer your seats to a few very close friends of my mother?"

One of the officers, a captain, immediately stands, looking at the rest, and directs them to rise in formation and relinquish their seats. He walks over to me, looking me directly in the eye, and shakes my hand. They all line up in the middle of the aisle and walk graciously toward the back of the chapel, lining up against the wall. Mr. Williams is escorting Chief Martin and his wife, placing them on the third pew. I instruct him to bring them to the first.

As they are about to be seated, I extend my hand to Chief Martin and state, "You and your wife were good friends of my mother. She would be honored to have you sit here today, and so would I."

The chief, beaming with pride, offers his wife a seat as he takes a seat between her and Jaylon. As Riley escorts Abby down the aisle, I hug her fondly and instruct Mr. Williams to seat her on the third pew. I am headed toward Nurse Woodward and Ashley. Ashley stands, and we embrace. I thank her for coming and explain I will be escorting her to her seat. I turn to Nurse Woodward, smiling, extending my hand to grasp hers and aid her from her seat.

She smiles as she hugs me tightly, joking, "What took you so long to come and get me?"

I laugh at her comment and offer my apologies. I extend both my arms out, one to Nurse Woodward the other to Ashley, escorting them slowly down the aisle. My eyes search for Zoe as she watches me. Reaching the third row, I offer Ashley a seat. Eva and I continue to the first row, where I offer her a seat next to the chief's wife. She smiles at them politely then looks at me, patting my cheeks, remarking "Always the gentlemyn. Your mother would be so proud of you, Caiden" as she sits.

Mr. Williams is now ushering Zoe's family and Edwina to the second pew. Once everyone is seated, I motion Zoe to sit next to her mother. I take my seat next to her. Riley allows Brianna to sit next to me as Riley sits on the end. Mr. Williams is anxiously waiting for a sign to continue with the service. I nod my head, signaling we are now ready to begin. My mother did not attend church regularly. When she did, she was fond of Pastor McClintock of Great Mission Baptist Church. I contacted him and asked if he would perform the eulogy, and he willingly agreed. Rosemary would not have wanted a big fuss over her passing nor would she have anticipated a turnout like this. My mother was humble, and I am sure she is looking down at us, shaking her head.

As Pastor McClintock begins, I rest my arm behind Zoe on the bench. She moves close to me, resting her hand on my thigh, giving it a gentle squeeze. Her gaze, however, is fixed on the pastor. I look up toward the platform where the pastor is delivering his eulogy, and my eyes catch sight of my mother's casket. The silver casket is draped with a spray of red and white roses, her favorite. A framed picture of her dressed in her judicial garb is sitting on a tripod behind her casket, slightly elevated. A multitude of flowers surround her casket. The room grows quiet as I reflect on memories of her when I was a child, daydreaming about the lectures she would give me on matters of right and wrong, good and evil, love and hate, and most importantly, the power of forgiveness. Thinking back, I wonder if she was preparing me for the truth of my lineage.

My eyes move to Jaylon immediately as the thought crosses my mind. I watch her as tears pour down her face. I can hear her fighting back the cries escaping her mouth. *Is this all a show to Jaylon?* I ask myself.

The pastor, finishing his sermon, offers the floor to anyone who would like to say a few words about Rosemary. Chief Martin and the mayor both offer a few kind words on my mother's behalf.

As they finish, Jaylon stands and requests to say a few words. My first instinct is to prevent her from making a mockery of this service.

Zoe, feeling my body tense, calmly turns toward me, caressing my face, shaking her head, and whispering, "Do not give Jaylon power over you, Caiden. Look around you. She would be insane to embarrass herself in front of her superiors and peers."

Jaylon is insane, but Zoe is right. Jaylon, loves the attention on her; she always has.

She stands at the podium, looking out over the crowd, and begins to speak. "I personally want to thank each and every one of you for attending this service today and sharing in our grief._So often, we take for granted the people closest to us. I am ashamed to admit I fall into that category. My mother and I have shared some difficult times together, but we somehow managed to weather our storms. Rosemary is the reason I became a police officer. She inspired both_Caiden and myself to always be better than who we are. My sister, Caiden, a successful young financier, and myself, a dedicated public servant—we may have chosen different paths in life, but I can assure you, we are both extremely happy in our choices. I owe that to our mother, and I, thank her for her gift." Jaylon steps down and quietly goes back to her seat.

What fucking game are you playing, Jaylon? I think.

She looks back at me quickly and produces a smirk.

You are up to something, Jaylon? Her speech has placed me on high alert. That person speaking was not Jaylon Westphal. The pastor and the funeral director, as well as everyone in the room, have their eyes fixated on me.

Zoe shakes me, snapping me back out of my daze. She whispers in my ear. "I think everyone is looking to you to say a few words."

I look at her taken aback. I hate crowds, and I hate giving unrehearsed speeches. Fucking Jaylon knows this. This is her game to put me off mine. I knew she would get back at me for embarrassing her earlier by moving her entourage. I swallow deeply and look at the pastor as I move to the podium to speak. Who expects a grieving loved one to speak at the funeral? I wonder.

I grasp the microphone, moving it closer to my mouth. Looking out at the audience, I offer a cordial greeting. A few moments pass as I ponder what to say. I bow my head, asking everyone to bow with me for a moment of silence, giving me a few seconds to gather my thoughts.

"As I survey the room I take special notice of the demographics here today. We are all different, all unique! Be it our careers, our history, our ethnicity, our socioeconomic status—even our belief systems are all different. What is amazing is the fact that despite our differences, we have all come together as one, as a community, joining together for a common purpose: to pay homage to Rose Westphal. Looking at all you beautiful people brings me great joy in knowing my mother's lifelong goal has been achieved. As my sister pointed out earlier, Rosemary Caidence Westphal not only inspires her children but her peers, her adversaries, and the community to be better than we are. This is a true testament to her hard work, her dedication, her sacrifice, and her courage. I want to thank each of you for bringing her dream to fruition." Stepping away from the podium, I pause for a moment, seeing the crowd stand in applause.

I move to take my seat when I am interrupted by Mr. Williams informing me they are about to open the casket for a final viewing. He suggests I stay and be the first to say my final good-bye. I turn toward the second pew, searching for Zoe. She has already begun walking toward me with tears in her eyes and reaches me with her arms open, embracing me with a loving hug, whispering, "I am proud of you, and your mother would be too!"

The announcement is made, "The repass will commence." I stand in front of Rosemary's casket, squeezing Zoe's hand tightly as she caresses my back. I look for Jaylon, finding her, standing next to Zoe. She stares at me with tears flowing from her eyes. I have never seen my sister cry before. Moved by her sincerity, I wrap my arms around her, hugging her tightly as she reciprocates. It is an unforgettable moment for me to have Jaylon finally embrace me with love and compassion. We separate, and she looks at the casket and again at me. I signal to Mr. Williams to proceed with opening the casket. Once open, I immediately begin to tear up as I look down at my mother's body. I place my hand on top of hers then lean down to whisper in her ear, praying my words find her soul, "Mom, I read your letter. I now know the truth, and I forgive you. I will love you always and forever."

I rise from her casket and stand with my head down, glancing at her one last time. Zoe leans in to kiss her forehead to say good-bye. The reality of her death hits me like a ton of bricks. I can barely breathe; the air is stifling as I tug on my shirt collar. The horde of people and lack of circulation in the room begin to suffocate me.

Zoe quickly takes my hand, leading me through the crowd to the side exit for some fresh air outside. I struggle to loosen my tie and unbutton my shirt, still weeping. She takes me by the shoulders, instructing me to take deep breaths as she slides off my jacket, loosens my tie, and unbuttons the top button on my shirt. Looking around, Zoe spots our driver and signals him to unlock the door to the limo. "Caiden, come with me!" she orders.

I follow her toward the limo, and we both get in, locking the door. The car is running with the AC on, and the air feels cool against my skin. My tears subside once I have calmed down. Zoe's eyes are filled with concern as she watches over me. I caress her cheek, assuring her I am fine. She sits beside me quietly, holding my hand, caressing it softly. I lean in toward her and begin kissing her passionately. Surprised, Zoe pulls away. I kiss her again with more intensity, pulling her onto my lap.

"Caiden, we shouldn't!" she cries.

"Zoe, I need this!" I exclaim.

She moans as my hands find her breasts, squeezing. Switching positions, she is seated with my body between her legs. I lift her dress to her waist, revealing her thighs then grasping her panties, pulling them off. Zoe pushes my shoulders away from her, pleading for me stop. Ignoring her plea, I begin to kiss her inner thighs, moving toward her Venus.

"Caiden! You can't! Please stop!" she screams.

Hearing the panic in her voice, I stop abruptly, staring into her blue eyes, ashamed of my actions. Feeling horrible at what I had done, I apologize profusely, returning her panties and pulling her dress back over her knees.

Hearing voices outside the limo, we quickly straighten our garments, checking each other.

I comment to Zoe, "I can't go to the cemetery and watch my mother be lowered into the cold ground."

Clasping my face, she replies, "Caiden, you can do this. I'll help you. We will get through this together."

Hesitantly, I nod. In the back of my mind, I knew if I did not go, I would regret it for the rest of my life. We exit the limo and head back into the chapel. We sit, patiently waiting for the last few people to pay their respects. About ten or fifteen minutes pass; the casket is sealed. The burial is restricted to family and a few close friends. The majority of people at the burial site are my friends and Zoe's family. Ericka represents Jaylon's sole friend. The burial is brief. Watching the casket being lowered, I pick a white rose off the spray lying atop it, inhaling the aroma. I kiss the rose once then gently allow it to fall out my hand onto the casket as it is lowered into the ground.

CHAPTER THIRTEEN

Exposed

A few close friends of Rosemary's were invited back to her house. I organized the catering service, realizing Caiden was in no condition to take care of it herself. The limousine ride to Rosemary's is quiet. Caiden is staring idly out the window, consumed in her thoughts. Brianna and Riley are in the first stage of new love, consumed by each other. I sit close to Caiden, resting my hand on top of hers. She is taking her mom's passing much harder than I anticipated. It is difficult to read her emotions at times. The past few days have been hard on her. She never really had time to grieve until today. Jaylon's antics have been a distraction, but there is more going on with her. I hope she will eventually confide in me.

We pull up to the house, and the driver opens our door. Brianna, Riley, and I exit the limo, but Caiden still in deep thought remains.

"Caiden, are you ready to go inside?" I ask.

She looks at me, motioning for the three of us to go ahead. Caiden tells the driver he is more than welcome to go in and grab a bite to eat. He accepts Caiden's invitation and considerately walks to the front of the car, turning the engine off, but leaving the back windows half-down, giving Caiden fresh air on this cool, sunny October day. We head inside to greet the guests.

Riley, concerned about Caiden, stays outside, telling Brianna she would be in shortly. I lead Charles, our driver, into the kitchen area to be served. I spot my parents and sister in the living room and go over to check on them. Brianna is moving around the room, checking on guests and sparking conversation. She has always had a knack for public relations. I excuse myself from my parents when I notice Abby. I want to officially introduce myself and see how she is getting along in a room full of strangers.

"Abby? Hi, I am—" I begin as she finishes my sentence.

"Zoe Payne! I know exactly who you are. How are you? It is a pleasure to finally meet you. Caiden has told me so much about you." She is a very enthusiastic young woman.

"The pleasure is all mine," I reply.

As we are conversing, Caiden enters the room. She looks like her old self—confident, poised, and charming—as she mingles with the guests. A soft smile graces her face as she moves through the throng of people, each vying for her attention to offer their condolences. Spying my family, she goes over to greet them. My father gives her a warm, hearty handshake and pat on the back. My mother hugs her, gently caressing her face. Caiden's eyes widen as she bends down to hug Cassie. Her eyes light up as she sees Chloe for the first time, asking Cassie if she can hold her. Cassie agrees, and Caiden picks her up, lifting her high in the air. I watch Caiden play with Chloe and see the joy in her eyes as she kisses her tiny cheeks. She would be a wonderful parent. My hands subconsciously hold my stomach as if with child. My heart grows sad, thinking about my own child.

Caiden is holding Chloe in her arms as her eyes skim the room. She catches a glimpse of Ashley talking—or rather, trying not to talk—to Jaylon. Caiden places Chloe back in Cassie's arms as she excuses herself and walks toward Ashley.

Seeing Caiden approaching her, Ashley's eyes light up. Jaylon notices she is distracted and turns to see Caiden, heading in their direction. Jaylon's eyes roll, appearing aggravated she has lost Ashley's attention. Ashley anxiously moves toward Caiden, and they embrace each other as if they had not seen each other in years.

Caiden lifts her from the ground, squeezing her tightly. She places her hands on Caiden's face, kissing each cheek, then hugs her again.

Brianna startles me suddenly, appearing by my side. "Who is that Caiden is talking to?" she asks abruptly.

I reply, "She is a friend of Caiden's from Portland, I believe."

"Looks like more than a friend to me. Do you see how she is flirting with Caiden?" she implies.

I look at Brianna and roll my eyes, chuckling. "Brianna, are you familiar with the term *trust*? A lot of women flirt with Caiden."

She looks at me again with a smirk, saying, "Zoe, you are too trusting. I would never let a woman that gorgeous anywhere near Riley!"

I laugh, telling her she needs to let go of her insecurities. Caiden's eyes find mine from across the room. Caiden reaches for her friends hand, escorting her in our direction. When they reach us, Caiden releases her hand and kisses me on the cheek, saying, "Zoe, I would like to introduce you to someone. Zoe, this is Ashley Guerra. Ashley, this is my Zoe."

She smiles at me politely, extending her hand. I reciprocate as we exchange salutations. She leans in toward Caiden, uttering, "This explains a lot. Caiden, she is stunning!" I blush at her comment as Caiden stands beaming with pride.

"Would you ladies care for a drink?" Caiden asks.

We simultaneously reply, "No, thank you."

Ashley checks her watch and explains to Caiden she has to leave for another engagement. She smiles, saying good-bye to us as Caiden walks her outside.

I look at my watch, not realizing we had been here nearly three hours. It is nearing nine o'clock, and the caterers are cleaning up, preparing to leave, and the guests have all gone, leaving only my family, Ericka and Jaylon, and the four of us.

I notice Ericka glaring at Riley and Brianna. It is no secret that Ericka tried to pursue Brianna, but there is no romantic interest on Brianna's part, I think in part because Ericka and Jaylon are coworkers and friends. Ericka is a nice woman but lacks the edge

Brianna enjoys in a partner. Brianna has explained this to Ericka on several occasions, but Ericka seems insistent on changing her mind. The one thing tying Jaylon and Ericka together is they don't know when to give up on a lost cause. I visit with my family, avoiding Jaylon's leering eyes upon me. I am unnerved by the way she often looks at me. I see that glimmer of hope in her eyes that one day she and I will be together.

I start to think back to my pregnancy when Caiden had gone and I was alone and had no one to lean on. I remember how sweet, kind, and nurturing Jaylon was toward me, not at all like the woman she is today. I regret ever trusting her during that time. I have no one to blame except myself. I often wonder why she has not mentioned our brief encounter to Caiden. I wanted so much to tell Caiden about our date, but after she freaked out about me sleeping with a man and knocked a hole in my bedroom door, I lost the courage. I know I have to find the right time to tell her. I don't want any secrets between us.

I am startled as Caiden walks up behind me, kissing my neck, placing her arms around my waist. I place my hands on her arms and squeeze tightly, inhaling her cologne. Her scent sends chills down my spine.

"Why is Ericka giving Brianna the third degree over there?" she asks.

I did not notice they had engaged in conversation. Caiden looks around for Riley and sees she is having a discussion with Jaylon.

"This can't be good!" Caiden jokes as she continues to eye Riley and Jaylon.

They seem to be getting along nicely from what I gather. I am more concerned with Brianna and Ericka. Ericka doesn't look happy. Brianna's arms are folded as she listens to Ericka. She is looking around the room when our eyes meet. She gives me the "help me" look, and I giggle softly. I tell Caiden I would be right back, but she is in a frisky mood and refuses to let me go.

"I miss you, beautiful. Stay here with your family and me. Brianna's a big girl. She can handle Ericka," she convinces me.

I smile at Brianna, letting her know Caiden is not letting go of me. She rolls her eyes then turns back to Ericka. I look back over at Riley, tilting my head toward Brianna. She immediately understands my message and politely excuses herself from Jaylon, heading to Brianna's aid.

Riley places her arm around Brianna's waist and introduces herself to Ericka. "I don't believe we have been formally introduced," Riley states as she reaches out to shake Ericka's hand.

Ericka grabs Riley's hand firmly, shaking it briskly. "Pleasure to finally meet you, Riley. I was just telling Brianna it is good of you to come all the way from Portland to support Caiden. When do you plan on going back?" Ericka asks.

Riley politely looks at Ericka then turns toward Brianna, smiling, saying, "I am not sure exactly. I can't see myself, leaving this gorgeous creature here alone in Texas."

Ericka's expression hardens as she tries to maintain her composure. "Well then, I guess I will_be, seeing you around," she quips.

Riley responds "Yes, I guess so. Have a good night, Detective" as Ericka walks off.

Caiden is enjoying my family's company. She can't seem to get enough of Chloe. As she sits on the floor with Chloe in her lap, she is asking Cassie how things have been. She tells her she misses her and it is great to see her little one. Caiden comments on how much she looks like her Auntie Zoe.

Cassie jokes to Caiden, "If I didn't know any better, I would swear this is Zoe's child."

Caiden laughs as she directs Chloe's tiny blue eyes toward me. "See your beautiful auntie_Zoe? She is the most beautiful auntie in the world. You are very lucky little one," Caiden states, teasing Chloe.

I look on in amazement at how Caiden has taken to Chloe and Chloe seems at ease in Caiden's care. My heart is filled with both love and pain at the sight of them together. My eyes begin to tear as I quickly head down the hallway to the guest bathroom before anyone can notice.

Unaware anyone was in there, I open the door to see Jaylon coming out. She sees me crying and asks me genuinely if I am okay. I nod, wishing she would exit so I could go in. She stands aside as I rush in, looking for a tissue to dry my eyes.

I can feel her still standing in the door way as she offers, "Zoe, I'm sorry. It must be difficult for you to see your niece, considering what happened."

For the first time in a long time, I believed Jaylon's words. She is sincere in her concern.

"If there is anything I can do to help, let me know," she adds softly.

My tears begin to fall out of my eyes irrepressibly as I stand with my back turned to Jaylon. She hears my cry and gently places her hands on my shoulders to comfort me. I turn to face her, knowing she is the only one who witnessed my loss, and fall into her arms, unable to control my tears. She hugs me tightly while I weep on her shoulder. She softly pats my back, telling me everything is going to be okay. My tears subside, and I pull myself away from her embrace.

"Do you feel better now?" she asks, looking concerned, with her hands resting on my shoulders.

Looking in her dark eyes, I reply "Yes, yes, I do. Thank you, Jaylon. I should be getting back" as I move past.

I look up to see Caiden standing in the doorway, not knowing how much she has witnessed. By the expression on her face, I knew she needed answers. She glances over at Jaylon then back at me. I can see her eyes filling with rage from what she just observed. Jaylon turns to Caiden, glaring at her, taunting her with a smirk. The sweet, caring Jaylon I know is gone in an instant.

"Caiden, Zoe and I were in the middle of a private moment. Do you mind, giving us a few minutes to finish our conversation?" she asks.

I interject, "Caiden, it's not what you think. Jaylon saw that I was upset—"

Caiden interrupts me midsentence, yelling, "Zoe, what the fuck is going with you two? Answer me, damn it!"

I shiver at her tone. I begin to explain the chain of events to her.

As I am trying to calm the situation, Jaylon starts in on Caiden, telling her had she not abandoned me, she wouldn't have to clean up Caiden's mess. "Caiden, I have said it before, and maybe this time, you will understand. I understand Zoe's pain, something you seem to be oblivious to. When she needed you most, you scurried off to Portland, leaving her pregnant and alone," Jaylon states.

"Jaylon, stop it! That is enough. Please don't do this!" I scream.

Jaylon begins to rant how Caiden and Rosemary continue to interfere in her life. How everything would have been better if Caiden had remained in Portland.

Caiden, furious, yells, "Jaylon, shut the fuck up. Her pain, her pain! You bastard, you are the whole reason she is in pain to begin with, you manipulative son of a bitch! Had it not been for your interference, this entire time, Zoe and I would be—" Caiden stops midsentence, looking over at me, realizing she has said too much. "Zoe, get your things. We are leaving!" she orders.

I attempt to exit the bathroom when Jaylon puts out her arm, preventing me from moving, saying, "Zoe isn't going anywhere. She belongs here with me."

Caiden, infuriated by her actions, pushes Jaylon aside and grabs my arm, yanking me out of the bathroom. By this time, everyone has moved to the hallway to see what is happening. Riley moves next to Caiden as Ericka moves next to Jaylon.

"It has been a long and frustrating day for everyone. Brianna, I task you with ensuring Zoe, her family, and Abby get home safely. I will call to check on you later," Riley instructs.

Brianna looks at me in shock as I look at my family in disbelief.

"Everyone, please leave now! Everything is going to be fine," Riley says, again reiterating we should leave at once.

Brianna quickly prepares everyone to leave the house. I am motionless, unable to move, wondering what will happen if I go. I stand my ground, stating firmly, "I am not leaving! If you two want to kill each other, then go right ahead!" As my parents head to the front door, I hear Chloe crying. I look over at her in Cassie's arms, reaching for Caiden.

"Caiden, baby, please! This fighting is upsetting Chloe. Please come home with me, and we can talk about this," I beg, praying Caiden is listening.

She looks over into Chloe's tiny blue eyes, seeing her little arms stretched out toward her. I can see in her eyes that her heart melts at the sight. Caiden, staring at Chloe, stubbornly tries to hold on to her rage, but to no avail. She glares at Jaylon and Ericka then back at little Chloe with outstretched arms. She surrenders to Chloe's cries, turning toward Cassie and grasping Chloe in her arms.

"It's okay, little one. No one is going to hurt you, I promise," Caiden whispers to her as she rocks her in her arms.

Chloe's cries lessen as she sniffles, pulling at Caiden's nose. Her tiny fingers touch Caiden's face as she cracks a smile, softening the mood in the room. I hurriedly take advantage of the situation, opening the door to allow my family and Caiden to exit. Caiden is captivated by this tiny soul, unable to break away from her spell.

On the drive home, I suggest Chloe stay with Caiden and me in hopes it would contain her mood. Cassie, uneasy about the arrangement, decides it would be best if Chloe stays at the hotel where she has her things. I am somewhat relieved by her recommendation. Caiden holds Chloe in her arms until she falls asleep then gently passes her to her mother.

Cassie smiles, remarking "Caiden, you have a way with her. I have never seen her so at ease with anyone other than my parents. You have a definite effect on her"

Caiden, still eyeing Chloe, replies, "I think it's the other way around, Cassie. This little one has a spell on me."

My heart warms, listening to Caiden speak so fondly of Chloe.

Halfway home, I look over to ask Caiden a question and notice she has fallen asleep. My parents have been quiet the entire trip.

Cassie looks at me, asking, "Zoe, do you realize how much Caiden loves you? Are you really going to jeopardize everything again for Jaylon?"

I am shocked at her line of questioning and reply, "Cassie, what are you implying? Of course I realize Caiden loves me!"

She sits quietly for a minute then responds, "What is going on between you and Jaylon? You realize you can't have them both."

I am angry at her implications, remarking, "Cassie, there is nothing going on between Jaylon and me. I love Caiden more than anything. I just feel sorry for Jaylon."

She replies, "Zoe, I love you and Caiden. I don't want to see you screw this up again! Take some sisterly advice and focus on you and Caiden. For goodness' sake, leave Jaylon alone. It is causing problems between you and Caiden."

I start to reply but sit silently, staring out the window as we pull up to the hotel. I get out of the car, assisting Cassie with Chloe. I hug my mother and father, bidding them a good night. They take Chloe inside the hotel while Cassie remains behind.

She looks up at me, saying, "Zoe, you are going to have to tell Caiden the whole truth about you and Jaylon's—whatever it is. I pray she can forgive you. Good night, sis."

We arrive at home as Caiden awakens from her slumber. "How long have I been asleep?" she asks.

I inform her she fell asleep not long after we left her mother's house. We head toward the elevator in silence. I am comforted, knowing she is home safe with me.

Entering the condo, Caiden immediately pours a glass of water and takes a sleep aid. She strips out of her clothes and heads toward the bedroom, collapsing face down onto the bed, not even bothering to get under the sheets. She is exhausted, and so am I. I manage to pull the covers from underneath her and lie next to her, staring at the ceiling, wondering how she is going to react when I explain to her about my brief encounter with Jaylon.

It's three o'clock in the morning when I hear Caiden in the kitchen, pouring a glass of water. Once she is in bed, I ask if she is okay. She nods yes drowsily, snuggling up to my back, wrapping her arm around my waist. Feeling her warm breath against my neck makes me quiver. The smell of her cologne lingers faintly in the air as she pulls me close to her. Aroused by Caiden's scent, I am unable to go back to sleep. I reach into my nightstand drawer, finding my mini vibrator. I am hoping to take the edge off my sexual tension from earlier. As I am readying myself I notice my cell blinking.

A text from Brianna—"Z, everything OK?"

I text, "CW is sound asleep. Is Riley upset?"

Seconds later, Brianna, texts "Upset? No, told her the truth. She is fine. Just had great sex!"

Even more frustrated, I text, "*Great!* At least someone is having sex!"

Brianna replies, "Sorry, Zoe. Tell Caiden the truth. Bye."

Easier said than done, Brianna, I think.

I am holding my vibrator in my hand, preparing to pleasure myself, when I hear Caiden groaning in her sleep, "Unwanted, she will never love me!" My heart breaks as I listen to her fears. How could she feel this way? What have I done to make her think I don't want her? I become frantic, unable to keep still. I ease out of bed, tossing my vibrator back in the drawer.

About to head into the living room, my eyes catch a glimpse of the box in Caiden's luggage. I move toward it, looking back to make sure Caiden is still asleep. Against my better judgment, I take the ring out of the box and place it on my ring finger. I stare down at my hand, admiring it. What detail and craftsmanship was used in designing it! Caiden didn't miss a single detail from my sketch. The diamonds, the metal—it is absolutely perfect! I wander aimlessly into the living room and sit on the sofa, staring out the window until I fall asleep.

The sunlight shining through the window awakens me. I sit up to stretch, wondering where I was for a moment. Hearing Caiden's footsteps, nearing realize I still have the ring on my finger. I quickly pull at it to take it off, but it won't budge. Seeing her coming toward the sofa, I reach for a pillow to cover my left hand.

"Good morning, beautiful," Caiden states, smiling.

"Good morning, sleepyhead," I reply.

She sits down next to me. Thank God she is sitting on my right side. She looks at me seriously and says, "Zoe, I think we need to have a talk, or I need to be a very good listener."

I nod, but I make a request for her to put on a shirt. It is less distracting this way. She chuckles, walking to grab a shirt from the bedroom. In her absence, I again attempt to remove the ring, and it still will not budge.

She sits down beside me again, stating, "Is this better Ms. Payne?"

"Definitely," I reply. I still ache to make love to her but refocus on our pending discussion.

"Well, Ms. Payne, you have my undivided attention!" she explains as she holds her cell phone in her hand, powering it off, and placing it on the coffee table. "Zoe, is something wrong with your hand?" she asks.

I reply, "No, Caiden, it is a bit cold in here."

She chuckles as she reminds me I am not a very good liar. "How does it look on your hand, Zoe?" Caiden asks.

Surprised by her question, I wonder, *How does she know?*

Smiling and staring out the window, she asks, "A better question, Zoe—how does it feel on your hand?"

She lets me off the hook, informing me she checks the box daily to ensure it has not been disturbed, and this morning, to her surprise, the crown jewel was missing. She deduces a thief must have snuck into her bag while she was asleep and stolen it. My actions this morning convinced her it was no thief at all but an inquisitive nymph who borrowed it. She looks at me, smirking, asking with her hand out, "May I?"

Utterly embarrassed, I grudgingly slide my left hand from underneath the pillow, placing it in hers as we sit next to each other. Feeling horrible I ruined her surprise, I respond, "Caiden, I feel awful. I'm sorry I took the ring. I should have left it alone, but it is so beautiful I couldn't resist placing it on my finger."

She looks perplexed as she views the ring, replying, "Hmmm, something is missing."

Alarmed, I reply, "Caiden, its perfect."

"No, something is definitely missing. Stand up, please, and remove your underwear."

I look at her confused.

"Humor me?" she asks with a smile. She rises from the sofa and stands at the opposite end as I look at her dumbfounded after removing my underwear. She is eyeing my hand closely with her hand on her chin, remarking "Something is still not quite right! Remove your shirt, please?" Seeing utter confusion on my face again, she comments, "Humor me once again."

I slip my shirt off, watching her carefully, wondering what she is doing.

She asks, "Let your hair down for me, please?"

I do as she instructs as she keeps her focus on my left hand.

Her eyes then begin to move slowly across my body, examining every inch, always returning to my left hand. She nods her head and responds, "Now it looks perfect on you."

"Caiden, will you do something for me?" I ask.

She nods.

"Take off your shirt, please?" I ask.

She looks at me slyly, replying, "I thought it was a distraction."

"It was. Now humor me and take it off, please?" I reply.

Smiling as she lifts it over her head to remove it, she remarks, "I am not putting this back on."

I giggle, replying, "I don't want you to." I pause, staring at her bare torso, and state, "Hmmm, something is definitely missing."

She laughs at the mockery.

I demand she not move a muscle. I disappear into my room momentarily, returning with my hands behind my back.

"Zoe, what are you up to?" she asks with suspicion in her voice.

"Close your eyes," I instruct.

She looks at me, puzzled, but obeys my command, closing her eyes tightly. I move close to her, walking slowly around her in a full circle, running my fingers softly across her body as I go. Now facing her, I reach for her left hand, cradling it in mine.

"Don't open your eyes!" I order.

I raise her hand, covering her ring finger with my mouth, gliding it in and out to moisten it. I hear Caiden moan softly as she licks her lips.

"Are you trying to seduce me? If so, you are doing an excellent job, I might add," she jokes.

I slip a band on her finger, ordering her to open her eyes. She opens them, peering into mine with curiousness. She raises her left hand to view my gift, inspecting it meticulously.

She comments, "Hmmm! Ms. Payne, you have outdone yourself. A platinum band filled with solitary princess-cut diamonds. Another birthday gift?" she asks with a smirk.

Caiden never celebrates her birthday, feeling she is blessed all year long. She doesn't like to make a big deal about one day out of the year. The past couple of years have been difficult for her, and I want this year to be special. Clearing my throat, I explain how I plan on making this year the best birthday she has ever had. I want to shower her with anything my heart desires, and there is nothing she can do about it.

"So I have no say in the matter?" she questions.

"No, Caiden, no say at all. This year I am going all out for your birthday," I insist.

She looks at the ring again then back at me, saying, "Zoe, I only want one thing for my birthday. Do you have any clue of what that is?" she asks.

I ponder her question and respond, "Hmm, the black Bugatti you keep eyeing on my tablet?"

Using her index finger, she motions me to go closer to her. I motion her to come to me. She laughs, drawing a line in the air and splitting the middle, asking "Meet me halfway?" Our lips are narrowly apart, she leans down to kiss me. My body tingles as our lips touch. I caress her cheeks as we kiss, whispering "I love you" to each other.

During our exchange, Caiden remarks I am the only woman she will ever love. She sweetly whispers, "Ms. Zoe Michelle Payne, will you do me the honor of becoming Mrs. Caiden Bryce Westphal?"

Her words permeate through my body as I begin to weep out of sheer happiness. "Yes, Caiden, the answer is yes. I would love nothing more than to become your wife!" I answer crying.

She hugs me tightly, lifting me off the ground, replying, "You have given me the best birthday gift possible. I love you, Zoe. I love you so much."

I hear her voice cracking as she attempts to fight back the tears. I look at her beautiful brown eyes and begin to wipe her tears as I try to prevent my own from continuing to flow.

"Caiden, I am so happy. I love you more than you can ever imagine," I utter.

We stand, kissing each other intensely for what seems like hours.

Caught up in the moment, I respond, "Caiden, words can't express how happy I am right now!"

I continue on my quest, kissing her soft lips while caressing her body. Her defenses weaken as she gives into her desire, pulling me into her arms, staring into my eyes like a hungry wolf. I moan as our bodies collide, running my fingers through her dreads, listening to her moans. She bends to lift me over her shoulder, carrying me to the guest room, tossing me on the bed.

My body is excited to feel her caress. My Venus is pulsating, wanting to feel Caiden's sensual touch. I feel wetness in between my thighs at the sight of her glaring down at me. I extend my arms, welcoming her into them as she climbs on top of me, parting my legs with her body. "Oh, Caiden!" I cry as she kisses my breasts and strokes my body with her fingers. I feel her heart pounding through her chest as she lies on top of me, grinding between my legs.

She pulls her pajama pants off, continuing to stroke me with her body. "Oh yes, Caiden! Don't stop! God, you feel so good!" I proclaim.

Caiden presses hard against me as she grinds our clits together, the friction sending quivers through my veins. I wrap my arms around her, pulling our bodies even closer. She moans as she enjoys the sensation of our bodies meshing.

"Look at me," Caiden orders.

I stare into her big brown eyes filled with love and lust, enjoying her every move. Watching her body flex as she strokes against me only heightens my sensation. I am filled with joy as I reach climax. Looking at her, I watch in wonderment as she begins to explode. Her eyes still on mine, she lets out a cry of elation, calling my name then falling on top of me with her head resting on my shoulder as I gently caress her back. Nearly out of breath, she turns to me, assuring me she's not done with me yet. I smile, letting her know I am prepared to make love for as long as it takes to satisfy her appetite.

Moving to lie on her back, she replies "I hope you're prepared for a lifetime, Zoe. I will never lose my appetite for you."

Her words warm my heart as I lie next to her, watching her stare at the ceiling.

Before I can ask the question, she replies, "I am watching our wedding. I am admiring how beautiful you look in your wedding dress. Your father walking you down the aisle with great pride as onlookers stand watching with joy in their hearts."

Watching her, I notice she is showing signs of real happiness as she continues to stare at the ceiling. She glances over at me for a moment, whispering, "No matter what you tell me, Zoe. It won't change how I feel about you, I promise."

I wonder how she can be so sure. My secrets cost us our relationship the first time. I don't deserve Caiden. I've hurt her so much.

I close my eyes as I pray for the courage to be completely honest and hope she can forgive me. I feel her hand grasp mine gently, pulling it to her lips. She is still staring at the ceiling, waiting, hoping, or praying—her expression is difficult to decipher. I reiterate how much I love her, affirm how deeply sorry I am for hurting her.

She whispers softly, "I know, Zoe."

I think, where should I begin? Caiden must be reading my mind as she suggests I start from the beginning. How does she do that? Does she know me that well? My palms are sweaty, the temperature in the room appears to have gone up a few degrees. I look at Caiden—she is still fixated on the ceiling with her hands resting on her stomach.

I finally get the nerve to speak when Caiden sits up in the bed, resting her back against the headboard, stating, "Zoe, We just got engaged, and we should be celebrating, not dwelling on the past. You were going through a difficult time. For whatever reason, Jaylon became an integral part of your life, and I'm grateful you had support. We weren't together, and life for both of us went on. I don't need to know what happened between you and Jaylon. I just need to know if I am the person you want to marry."

Her declaration renders me speechless. I sit up, staring at her, thinking, what have I done to deserve this amazing woman in my life? I move onto her lap in tears, answering, "Of course, I want to marry you. Caiden, I love you so much."

Caressing my cheeks and smiling, she replies, "Mrs. Zoe Michelle Payne-Westhpal has a nice ring to it, wouldn't you agree?"

I laugh slightly as I wipe the tears from my eyes, remarking, "It is obsequious of you to consider. Nevertheless, I desire your name. Is that okay with you?"

She places her hand on her chin, stroking it as if pondering my question, replying with a chuckle. "Hmmmm, *obsequious*? Let me Google that." I tickle her underarm for teasing me. She laughs and responds, "Mrs. Zoe Michelle Westphal! You may have something beautiful!

"Yes! I concur! Mrs. Zoe Michelle Westphal it is." Her eyes light up as the words escape her lips. She pulls me to her, kissing me tenderly in a way I have not felt before. I realize, kissing her, she has exposed herself to me completely, yielding me full access to her heart, body, and soul. Overcome by raw emotion at her gesture, my tears flow freely. Remembering her nightmare, I manage to utter, "I want your heart forever."

CHAPTER FOURTEEN

Face-Off

I take a cab to my mother's attorney's office in Round Rock, arriving fifteen minutes early. I enter the two-story building and locate the office of Edwina Miller, PC. After I check in with the receptionist, I grab a magazine, taking a seat, and respond to a text from Zoe. Passing time, I flip through the pages until the receptionist informs me Ms. Miller is ready to see me. I look around, wondering, *Where the hell is Jaylon?* I follow the receptionist back to a conference room where she instructs me to have a seat, and Ms. Miller would be in momentarily.

"Can I get you anything to drink, Ms. Westphal?" she asks politely.

I say, "No, thank you, Miss—"

She fills in the gap—"Gabrielle."

Edwina enters the room, holding a file folder in her hand. We embrace then take a seat while she explains she knows my time is valuable and this shouldn't take more than an hour.

Clearing my throat, I apologize for Jaylon's tardiness. She cordially smiles, explaining Jaylon isn't scheduled to arrive until 3:30, p.m. She said Jaylon must have been out of sorts, thinking the meeting was yesterday. Edwina chuckles, saying, "Why would she think I'd schedule a meeting the day of Rose's"—She looks as if she is about to cry.

She eyes me closely, asking, "Caiden, how have you been holding up?"

I tell her I am managing the situation.

Edwina insists I not hesitate if I need anything and shares I am like a daughter to her. She sits, resting her arms on the conference table, not wasting any time, and states, "Caiden, your mother's estate is worth twelve million dollars in liquid assets. Her home in West Austin is valued at five hundred thousand dollars, and there is a trust fund for you worth three million dollars. You are the primary beneficiary of her estate. All you need to do is sign here and here and leave fifteen point five million dollars richer than you came in."

I glance at the paperwork then set it to the side, turning my gaze back to Edwina. Her eyes look tired and red, like she'd been crying. I ask her how she is doing since my mother's passing. The question seems to cause her deep pain as she stares off into the distance in silence. I call her name to gain her attention. She looks at me, wiping under her eyes, explaining it is difficult for her to accept. She is taking Rose's death very hard. So many years have gone by. I didn't realize they were still very close. I hadn't seen Edwina since we were teenagers.

She explains circumstances prevented her from keeping in touch with Jaylon and me but shares she and Rose remained in constant contact over the years. She is well aware of the intricacies of my relationship with Jaylon. She knows more than we do about David, Nadine, and Edward. Even the adoption, how life was for us growing up, the abuse, everything. As a friend, she was tasked with helping the two of us salvage our relationship. She is hoping to start today, by meeting with us together. She made a promise to Rosemary that she will do whatever she can to help.

"Ah-hah! Well, Edwina, my mother's good intentions have caused Jaylon and me a great deal of grief. Don't waste your time trying to salvage what can't be salvaged," I comment.

"I can see why she referred to you as the stubborn one," she exclaims.

Ignoring her snide comment, I ask if I need to be present when Jaylon arrives. She tells me it isn't a requirement, but personally, it will mean a great deal to her if I stay.

My mother wanted her to share with me that she set up a trust fund for Jaylon. Rosemary included provisions in Jaylon's trust. She went on telling me it was important to Rosemary that Jaylon not feel insubstantial. It was her final wish for it to appear we were treated equitably.

"Unbelievable, Edwina! Even after death, my mother is still manipulating our lives. What the hell is wrong with this picture? If she wanted things to be equitable, why didn't she give Jaylon half her estate? Why did she not think about that thirty years ago when she lied to us about who we were, who our parents were? Look, Edwina, I respect you, and I love my mother dearly, but I refuse to lie for her. Considering Jaylon and I don't speak, I am pretty sure her secret is safe!" I yell in anger.

"I'm sorry to have upset you, Caiden. I know this is difficult for you. Try to understand, we—I mean Rose did what she thought was best," she remarks.

As I am about to reply, we are interrupted by Gabrielle informing Edwina that Jaylon is out in the waiting room.

Edwina looks at me, asking again, "Caiden, I am just trying to fulfill a dear friend's dying wish. Will you please stay so I can do just that?"

I shake my head at her in utter disgust, contemplating my next move. I realize she is only doing her job and think, *What harm could come of it?* I look at her and reply, "I will stay on one condition." Her eyes widen as she waits for my terms. I continue, "Don't put me in a position to have to lie. Are we clear?"

She nods her head, signaling she understands. She has her receptionist escort Jaylon into the conference room as I angrily take my seat.

"Good afternoon," she says to Jaylon.

"Hello, Edwina," Jaylon responds, ignoring me completely.

Edwina motions for Jaylon to take a seat as she begins to inform her about our trust funds. I peer over at Jaylon for a moment, wondering how long it will take her to burn through $3 million. I look back at Ms. Miller as she explains to Jaylon that it was our mother's desire for us to salvage our relationship.

"Ms. Miller, not to be rude, but there is no relationship to salvage. As long as she"—Jaylon's voice rises as she points her finger in my direction—"continues to interfere with my relationship with Zoe!"

Livid, I slam my hands on the table, rising up, yelling at Jaylon, "What in the hell are you talking about, Jaylon? When will you get it through your thick head there is no relationship between you and Zoe!"

Jaylon blares back, "Caiden, you know damn well Zoe still has feelings for me. How could she not, Caiden, after everything we have been through together? I was there for her when she needed someone the most. Zoe is confused, Caiden, and you have your head so far up your ass you don't even see it! Everything between us was going great until Rosemary grew ill and you returned home."

I yell back, "Great! Great! Jaylon, if it was so damn great, why is she engaged to me and not you? Answer me that, Detective!"

Jaylon seems shocked at the news. How could she be? I told her the other night Zoe and I were getting married. Ms. Miller screams out for us to stop this nonsense and try to talk as civilized adults.

We both look at her, simultaneously aggravated at the interruption, but sit back down in our seats. I hear her commenting under her breath, "This is going to be harder than I thought."

I ask if we could move on to the provisions. I check my watch, and it is nearing four thirty. I need to meet with Riley and Brianna within the hour. Ms. Miller informs Jaylon she would receive monthly installments in the amount of fifty thousand dollars for the next five years until the trust fund is depleted, including interest. She will have to resume psychiatric counseling twice a week and show significant improvement over the next year. Jaylon's psychiatrist will report her progress to Ms. Miller on a routine basis. If Jaylon fails to make an appointment and does not reschedule or decides to discontinue her sessions, the funds will then be automatically transferred over to me.

Way to go, Rosemary! I chuckle to myself.

How well she responds to treatment determines how long she will have to continue. She will have to go, at minimum, two years before an evaluation can be requested on her behalf, releasing her. The final clause in the will caught my attention. It states specifically that if any unnatural harm or death befalls Zoe Michelle Payne or Caiden Bryce Westphal, her funds are stopped automatically.

Edwina asks Jaylon if she understands the terms set before her. Jaylon's eyes are filled with rage as she informs her she understands. Edwina places the paperwork in front of Jaylon, requesting her signature. She signs the documents, pushing them back at her. She concludes the appointment, reminding Jaylon she will be in touch. We both rise to leave when she asks me to hang on a moment.

Jaylon glares at me closely then, turning to Edwina, inquires if I have any provisions on my trust fund.

Edwina smiles at her politely, stating, "I am sorry, Jaylon, but I am not at liberty to discuss the matter. Gabrielle will see you out."

Jaylon glares at me again with her eyes filled with rage. She wants to leap over the table and kill me. I resist the temptation to taunt her as I watch her exit the room.

Edwina turns to me, thanking me for staying.

I politely smile and ask, "Is there something else you need to discuss?"

She replies, "Caiden, do you mind if I enlist Zoe's assistance. I may need her to talk with Jaylon's psychiatrist."

"Yes, I mind very much! Zoe has nothing to do with this. I do not want her involved!" I exclaim.

She looks at me oddly, replying, "Caiden, I mean no disrespect when I say this, but Ms. Payne is an adult capable of making her own decisions. I asked you out of courtesy, hoping you would help this process, not hinder it. I will leave it up to her to make the call."

I reply, "I can see why my mother enlisted your services. I hate to disappoint you, Edwina, but Zoe will not go against my wishes."

She remarks, "Caiden, let's let Zoe make up her own mind without coercion from either of us, shall we? If you are right, you have nothing to worry about. If I am right, then she may be the key to helping your sister get better! That is the desired outcome in all this, isn't it?"

I think I am not sure what the desired outcome is. Getting up from my seat, I ease into her personal space, whispering in her ear, "Edwina—and I mean no disrespect when I say this—but stay the fuck away from Zoe!"

She turns, staring me directly in the eyes, replying, "Caiden, I will do what I feel is best to help your sister. What is the harm in seeking Zoe's help?"

I reply, staring back at her, "The harm, Edwina? Jaylon is psychotic, unstable, and emotionally imbalanced. I believe she will cause Zoe harm in order to hurt me. I will not allow you or anyone else to risk her safety to help Jaylon! If you and my dearly departed mother think dangling a carrot to the tune of three million dollars is going to fix the problem, then you are sadly mistaken."

Realizing my contempt for Edwina is growing, I know I need to get away from this woman before things get out of control. I inform her I will have my attorney get in touch with her office early next week after they review the documents as I exit her office.

Heading out of the building, I am about to call a cab when I see Jaylon. She walks up to me, nostrils flaring, and out of nowhere, lands a right cross against my jaw, knocking me back against the door. Disoriented by the blow, I can only sense her moving in to attack again, punching me in the gut, causing me to lose my breath as I fall to the ground on one knee. Struggling to get up and gasping for air, I manage to get on my feet before she could throw another punch.

I hear her screaming, "Come on, you son of a bitch! Get up so I can knock your ass back down!"

I look at her and begin to laugh in her face, infuriating her even further, taunting, "Is that all you got, Jaylon? You crazy sick bastard, surely you can do better than that!"

She charges me again, throwing another right cross. I deflect and counter with two consecutive jabs to her face—one landing above her eyebrow; the other, on the jaw. She stumbles to the side, obviously dazed by the blows. I stand, knees slightly bent, motioning to her with my hands to come and get me. She wipes the blood dripping from above her eye and charges at me with her body bent, trying to tackle me. I am shoved against the building as I pound my elbow into her back over and over until her knees hit the ground. I punch her on the side of the face, striking her lip, causing blood to spew as she falls to the side, bumping her head on the pavement. It is hard for me to catch my breath.

I move to deliver more blows when I am blindsided by a three-hundred-pound security guard forcing me to the ground. I look up to a crowd of spectators watching in disbelief. I demand the security guard to release me.

She says, "Not until you calm down."

I steady my breathing as I lie on the ground, looking over at Jaylon, who appears unconscious. I hear someone say the police are on the way.

A familiar voice instructs the guard to release me. Edwina is standing over me, stressing "You two are pathetic! You're acting like heathens! Your mother would be so ashamed of you two right now!"

The guard disperses the crowd while Edwina instructs me to go inside, to her office, and wait. Once the crowd clears, the guard returns to check on Jaylon. She is coming to as I walk back into the building. I head to Edwina's office as she instructs. I am convinced I will need legal representation once the police arrive.

I am in the conference room when Gabrielle brings me a towel filled with ice, placing it gently on my jaw, saying, "This should help ease the swelling."

I smile at her and flinch from the pain, thanking her for her kindness. She smiles at me, still holding the ice pack to my face. Jaylon is escorted to another room in Edwina's law firm. I see Edwina enter her office, followed by one uniformed officer from Round Rock PD and Detective Stuart. She doesn't have jurisdiction in Williamson County. What is she doing here? Erika and the RRPD speak briefly, maybe fifteen to twenty minutes. After they are done, the uniformed officer leaves the building.

Erika glares at me through the glass wall of the conference room as she and Edwina walk toward me.

Closing the door behind them, Erika sits down as Edwina explains the situation. "Caiden, I have every mind to have you and your sister hauled to the police station!" Edwina yells.

In a superior tone, I ask, "When did attorneys start threating their clients, Ms. Miller?"

She looks at me, wondering what I am talking about. I explain, "As of about twenty minutes ago, I became your client when you instructed me to go to your office and wait. I know probate is your law of choice, but you're licensed to practice criminal law, aren't you?"

Aggravated by my smugness, she replies, "Caiden! You're impossible! This incident is not going to be reported. You and your sister have been given a reprieve thanks to Detective Stuart. Can you just be grateful? It wouldn't hurt to say thank you to Detective Stuart."

I chuckle, replying, "Edwina, I am grateful. Grateful my sister has friends on the force that will overlook a crime when it is one of their own!"

Annoyed, Erika asks, "Caiden, have you always been so arrogant? I used to think Jaylon was exaggerating. Now I am not so sure."

I lean back in the chair, resting my arms on the table, and clasp my fingers. I eye Erika and remark, "Me arrogant? Detective, I didn't just influence a public servant to walk away from his sworn duty. You did, and you call me arrogant! Oh, and since we are sharing opinions of each other, if you believe anything coming out of Jaylon's mouth, then I have to question your mental stability as well. Am I free to go, Detective?"

Motioning with her hand, she points toward the door. Gabrielle is sitting next to me now, applying the ice pack on my swollen hand. I stand again, thanking her for her attentiveness. After bidding good-bye to Edwina and Erika, I walk past them through the door, I text Riley, informing her I am running late.

I am calling a cab when Erika walks outside, ordering me to get in her unmarked car, remarking it isn't a request. She is beginning to annoy me. The cab will take longer, so I decide to humor her and hop in on the passenger side.

"Zoe's condo, Detective," I state.

"Do I look like your fucking limo driver? Unbelievable, the arrogance!" she comments out of frustration.

I reply, ignoring her comment, "Detective, let's cut to it. What is it you want?"

She turns to me, rolling her eyes, obviously irritated at me for whatever reason. I learn from Erika that Jaylon has been in and out of psychiatric care the majority of her adulthood. Erika explains that Jaylon found out about her lineage in her early teens as my mother's note suggested. Jaylon was too young and ill-equipped to handle the information, so she rebelled against Rose and me, causing even more problems within our household. Erika poses the question, how would I feel if my mother killed my father and then killed herself, leaving me alone in the world, feeling unwanted? She goes on to tell me when Jaylon is going to therapy regularly and taking her meds, her life is productive. "Jaylon continues to blame Rosemary and you for her problems."

She feels sorry for Jaylon and wants to help her. She knows more about Jaylon than I ever will and seems to genuinely care. She is like a sister Jaylon seems to want. After speaking with Ms. Miller and Jaylon's psychiatrist, they believe that together they can help her get better. Erika insists the psychiatrist is interested in meeting Zoe and me to help her work through her issues. I begin to see Edwina has enlisted the services of Detective Stuart.

I listen to her as we ride down MoPac to Zoe's condo for a while. Halfway on our trip, my mind wanders off until she nudges me, asking, "Caiden, you are wealthy, right?"

I comment, "It depends on your definition of wealthy."

Still frustrated with me, she states, "You know what I mean. You have means to easily purchase any car of your choosing, yet you insist on riding Pedicabs and taxis wherever you go like regular people."

I laugh at her question, replying, "I am regular people, Detective. Do you think money makes a person different? If so, then, Detective, you have a lot to learn."

She glances over at me, asking if I am being serious. I look back at her and tell her, yes, I didn't think I was any different from her or anyone else.

She burst out laughing at me, almost crying, asking "Are you on drugs? Caiden, people treat you differently because you are wealthy, or do you not recognize that?"

I try to explain in simpler terms, hoping she will understand my logic. "Anyone will treat you differently if they believe you are of benefit or threat to them. Take you, for example. When you go out without a shiny badge hanging from your neck, people treat you like a regular person. When you go out and they discover you are an officer, how do they treat you then?"

She ponders the question then chuckles, agreeing I may have a valid point.

I remind her of the original question, saying I enjoy supporting locally owned and small businesses. "It helps keep the local economy growing, which helps people keep jobs in order to feed their families. That, to me, Detective, is more important than a car?" I share that I do have several vehicles sitting in my garages.

She looks at me, grinning, remarking, "You surprise me, Westphal!"

I exit the car and thank her for the candid conversation.

CHAPTER FIFTEEN

Indulgence

I lie in bed, drained from making love to Caiden all afternoon, wondering if my body can live up to her sex drive. If I had to describe it, the word *unquenchable* comes to mind. I joke she is addicted to sex. She counters she is addicted to my sex.

"Good answer, Westphal," I tease.

Laughing to myself, I think how many women would love to have this dilemma? Caiden is showering, preparing to meet with Jaylon and their mother's attorney to go over her last will and testament around three o'clock. She isn't thrilled having to see Jaylon. After what happened between them at the funeral, I am praying they can rebuild their relationship. I wish there is, something I can do to help.

Afterward she is meeting with Riley and Abby, preparing for the grand opening of her new nightclub. What is it with her and nightclubs? I am curious about the name as she refuses to tell me, saying it is a surprise. Abby will manage it for her until Caiden can find a suitable replacement. Riley, of course, will handle security. Neither are anxious to return to Portland, so it is working in Caiden's favor.

I reach over to my nightstand, grabbing my cell, scrolling to find my calendar. I enter today's date: "Friday, October 11, 2013 – Eight o'clock a.m. - Caiden proposes – Eight o'clock a.m. Zoe accepts." Eyeing my engagement ring I am glowing, wondering whom to call first with the news, my friends or family? I opt for the latter, calling my mom and dad. Luckily, I catch my parents and Cassie together and share the news. My parents are ecstatic and suggest we have dinner to celebrate. Cassie and Chloe are equally happy for us and want to speak to Caiden. Explaining Caiden is unavailable at the moment, I schedule a dinner date for Sunday evening to celebrate. I have to remember to tell Caiden to clear her schedule.

I am about to text Brianna when I hear Caiden from the bathroom, asking me to look in her bag for her Tag Heuer watch. I rummage through, wondering if she is ever going to unpack her luggage, when I come across a set of keys. There has to be over ten keys on the ring, and half are similarly shaped. What is she doing with all these keys? I shake my head, asking myself, do I really want to know? Tossing the keys to the side, I find her watch and take it to her in the bathroom. Wearing only a towel around her waist, she smiles as I enter. I am immediately turned on as I view her body. I walk up behind, caressing her back, placing her watch on the sink. She says thank you, smiling at me from the mirror as she brushes her teeth. *How does this woman make my pulse rise without doing anything?* I ask myself.

"Busy day?" she asks.

I look at her, giggling, and reply, "Actually, yes. I am meeting with some old friends. It's a good time to inform them we are engaged, maybe get some wedding ideas."

"Oh, I see. Sounds fascinating! I'm sure you and your besties can sort out the details over dinner and cocktails," she replies, chuckling. Caiden is, dreading the engagement announcement. She thinks it will be a media circus.

I kiss her on the back, telling her I love her as I exit the bathroom hastily. I quickly text Brianna, "*Caiden and I are officially engaged!*"

Not thirty seconds lapse when my cell rings. Brianna is screaming in my ear, excited at the news. She offers to take care of the engagement announcement and help plan. She informs me we will discuss the details over dinner tonight with our friends. I hang up to prepare for date night with the girls. I am distracted as I admire my future wife looking very suave in a light gray suit with a pair of cognac monk-strap dress shoes and soft-blue shirt. She smiles at me, asking if I approve. I look her up and down, biting my lower lip. She laughs, saying she takes my lip bite as a definitive yes! As Caiden is, preparing to leave I ask her to try to play nice with Jaylon. Rolling her eyes, she says she will be on her best behavior. Kissing me on the cheek, she grabs her cell to make a call.

I head to the shower, undressing as I go, anxious to jump in. Still overjoyed from this morning's event, I begin to fantasize what life will be like as Mrs. Westphal. We have a lot to discuss. Where will we live? Do we want a big or small family? So many questions flow through my mind. I refocus my thoughts, enjoying the hot, steamy water racing over me. As I wash my hair, I pause, hearing a noise. The water feels so good against my skin, I ignore the distraction and continue to shower. I scream when I see Caiden standing at the shower entrance.

"You startled me! I thought you left."

"Sorry, beautiful, didn't mean to scare you. I want to kiss my future wife good-bye before I leave," she replies as she kisses me softly on the lips, commenting, "Wet and naked! You make it difficult for me to leave you in this state."

I bite the side of my bottom lip, wrapping my towel around me, stating, "Does this make it easier for you to leave?"

Caiden chuckles, replying, "No, not at all!" Kissing me again she tells me a package was just delivered. She placed it on the bar for me.

Drying my hair, I am wondering what package it is—I haven't ordered anything. It is a chilly day, so I grab my gray wool loose-neck sweater, black leggings, and a pair of black closed-toe heels. I am looking around and can't find my purse. I think for a minute, *Where did I have it last?* I walk into the living room, to see if I left it there. The oddest thing—I can't find it anywhere. Frustrated, I sit on the sofa, trying to backtrack where I last had it. Maybe I left it in the limo?

I look on the bar, seeing a very large, unmistakable chocolate-brown bag and a package wrapped in black with a white bow sitting next to it.

What has Caiden done? I wonder, smiling. I unwrap my gift and immediately recognize the Rolex crown on the white box inside. An Oyster Datejust in white gold with diamonds encircling a pink face. "Very gracious Mr. Westphal," I say aloud to myself as I place it on my wrist. Staring at it, I begin to think of Caiden. I move to the LV bag, pulling out a large box. I open it and remove a W PM tote bag from the cloth. I read the note enclosed—"There's more." I peek back into the bag to discover a smaller box. Opening it, I find Insolite trunks and lock wallet with a note, "Open me."

As I open the wallet, I see my driver's license, a black card, and a stack of bills. I shake my head, giggling at Caiden's generosity. I look over to my right, noticing a handwritten note from Caiden. *"Zoe, hope you love your surprises. Your 'other' tote is under the bed. I remember someone telling me not long ago there were perks to dating a millionaire. Well, Ms. Payne, there are also perks when engaged to a millionaire stud boi! I love you."*

I sit back and laugh as Caiden teases me for my comment earlier when I gave her the watch. I send a text, *"To my stud millionaire with great taste! Thank you."*

Caiden texts, *"To the lovely and charming heiress of Westphal Inc., you're welcome!"*

It's a little after four o'clock by the time I arrive at Nine Two-West, a local hot spot we frequent downtown. Immediately, I hear a group of women yelling congratulations to me as I enter the restaurant. I see Brianna, standing, waving me over to our table. I see Ashley, Sherry, Ginger, Peyton, Tonya, Christina, and Melanie. I haven't seen them in over a year or two. We all greet each other warmly. As we all sit down everyone leans into the table, waiting anxiously to see my engagement ring. I giggle at their anticipation around proudly, placing my hand in the center of the table, exposing. Loud screams and squeals fill the restaurant as they gaze.

Ginger remarks, "Zoe, this ring is amazing. It has to be four or five carats!"

Peyton remarks snidely, "Congratulations, Zoe! Who would have guessed you and Caiden would end up together?"

I take pause for a moment at her comment, deciding envy is circling the wagon and her comment is not deserving of a response. Peyton and Caiden used to date well before we got together.

As I understand it, she wanted more than Caiden was willing to offer. I was surprised to hear they dated, considering how pretentious she is. Outside of her physical attributes, she is not Caiden's type. Not to mention her feelings on interracial dating. She often reminds us how complicated a relationship like that could be. I am quickly reminded why I haven't seen Peyton in over two years. I'm wondering why she is even here. I certainly didn't invite her. Brianna nudges my arm, mumbling under her breath that she didn't invite her. I shake my head and laugh, assuming she sees the confused look on my face.

Brianna orders a round of Mexican martinis and appetizers for the table. As we enjoy our food, we reminisce on old times, enjoying our evening. I was able to catch up with Tonya, Christina, and Melanie. They all seem to be doing well but still looking for Mr. or Mrs. Right. I didn't want the focus to remain on our engagement. I want Caiden and me to discuss our wedding plans first. Tonight is about catching up with friends and enjoying an evening out.

We have been at the restaurant for a little over an hour when an attractive metro stud approaches our table. She is tall, maybe five foot nine medium build with scruffy blonde hair, wearing dark jeans, a white button-down, a gray blazer, and boots. She introduces herself as Tracey Young—Trace for short. We say hello as she asks if we are celebrating anything special.

Everyone looks around the table curiously when out of nowhere, Brianna crassly asks, "What can we do for you?"

Tracey, clearly taken aback by Brianna's tone, clears her throat and politely replies, "I couldn't help noticing this blue-eyed knockout from my table"—she was looking at me—"nor resist the temptation to come over and ask her out!"

As she was speaking, I was sipping on my martini and began to choke as she finished her sentence. After catching my breath, I cordially decline her offer.

Her eyes narrow as she stares at me, commenting "I see. Well, if you change your mind, I_will be in town for a few days," and hands me her business card.

Brianna snatches the card from my hand, ripping it up, and informs her I wouldn't need it as she waves her off. Ms. Young eyes Brianna oddly as she walks off. Everyone, surprised, is wondering, what in the hell was that about?

Excusing myself to the ladies room, I bump into Tracey exiting. She stands in the doorway, blocking me from entering. I step back for her to exit, but she doesn't move. Irritated, I push my way past her. While in a stall, I hear the bathroom door close and assume she has left until I hear whistling. I think, *Oh god, not another psycho. Jaylon is all I can handle.*

I exit the stall, moving toward the sink to wash my hands, when she remarks, "I apologize if I offended your girlfriend."

I look at her blankly, replying, "She can be a tad possessive."

I return to our table, continuing our evening, when our waiter approaches. He is explaining that the blonde woman sitting across the way is paying our bill. We look over, and it's no other than Trace. I give her a fake smile and instruct the waiter to bring the bill to our table. The girls offer to pay, but I explain my fiancé insists on treating us this evening. They are flattered as they offer their gratitude to Caiden.

It's ten by the time we leave the restaurant. Brianna shares they are taking me to the House of the Blue Martini nightclub to celebrate. After walking a couple of blocks, we reach the front entrance of the club, only to realize the line stretches around the block. I suggest we go to another bar, but everyone insists this is the place to be.

The doorman notices us and walks over, asking, "Is this the Payne party?"

The girls all yell in unison, "Yes, yes, it is!"

He asks, "Which one of you is Zoe Payne?"

"I am," I reply.

He makes a call on his headset, explaining our party has arrived. Once he finishes his conversation, he immediately apologizes for the inconvenience and escorts us to the side entrance of the building. I never knew there was a side entrance into this place. If I went out more often, I would know these things. We go up a flight of stairs into a lavish room filled with velvet gray sofas and armchairs, teal and white drapes from ceiling to floor, and soft lighting, and the cement floors glow with flashes of rainbow-colored lights. You can see the entire lower level of the club.

Our waitress approaches, introducing herself, sets up bottle service on wrought-iron tables, saying if we need anything to please let her know.

The DJ pops his head out, asking do we have any special requests. Of course, Brianna provides him a slew of artists to play throughout the evening: Rhianna, Beyonce, Katy Perry, Sam Smith, Disclosure, and a host of other artists. He laughs at her request, suggesting she come into the DJ box to spin a few.

The manager of the club, John, introduces himself, checking to see if we were having a good time. Tonya and Christina are bouncing up and down, yelling to him they are having a blast. He turns to me and remarks, "Congratulations, by the way, on your engagement. I wish you and Caiden the best. Enjoy your evening, Zoe!"

Everyone is having fun, but I find myself missing Caiden. I stare at my phone, hoping for a text or call from her. I shoot a text, joking, "Westphal so much influence, impressive!"

She texts, "Having fun?"

I reply, "Wish you were here!"

Brianna bumps me with her hip, stating, "Somebody has the Caiden blues!"

Embarrassed, I nod yes as I laugh.

A couple of hours have gone by, and we were feeling the effects of the alcohol. We are yelling down at the crowd, dancing, acting silly, and taking hundreds of selfies. I forgot how much fun it is to hang out with my friends and be wild.

John comes over the loudspeaker, apologizing for the interruption, stating he has an announcement. The DJ cuts the music. "Good evening, and welcome to the House of the Blue Martini. I hope you are enjoying yourselves." The crowd roars.

He continues, "I have a special announcement to make. I would like to introduce to you all the new owner of the House of the Blue Martini. Please give it up for none other than Caiden Westphal."

Caiden walks on stage, shaking John's hand, and waves to the crowd. John passes her the mic as she begins to speak. "I'll be brief. As you may have heard, I very recently became engaged to an extraordinary woman." Caiden points toward the VIP lounge as the crowd bursts into cheers. Caiden looks toward the lounge, finding me, and continues, "Zoe, when you said yes, you opened the door for me to share my world with you. As you know, part of that world is my love of nightclubs. I thought to myself and said, 'Self, what do I give Zoe as an engagement gift?' Then it came to me: give her something I love. With that, studs and femmes, tops and bottoms, ladies and gentlemen, and everyone in between, I am proud to announce Austin's newest GLBT bar and lounge opening soon: Zoe Rose! Happy engagement, beautiful! I love you."

My jaw hits the floor as I stand in shock at her announcement. Everyone is jumping up and down, screaming and yelling, hugging each other in the background as if they'd won the lottery.

Brianna puts her arm around me, noticing my reaction.

"I'm dumbfounded Caiden bought me a nightclub!" I utter to Brianna.

"Zoe, come on. You can't be that surprised," she remarks.

Still in disbelief, I stand in silence, resting my arm on the rail, watching as Caiden starts to walk off the stage. I see women near the stage screaming and reaching for Caiden like she is a rock star. She looks into the crowd, smiling brightly, flashing those shiny thirty-twos and waving as she exits. I take a seat on the sofa, fixing myself a stiff vodka and cranberry. I am flattered, embarrassed, excited, overwhelmed; so many emotions leave me paralyzed.

Riley enters the VIP room and takes a seat next to me, asking if everything is okay. I look up at her and nod, unable to speak.

She smiles, commenting this isn't the first club Caiden has named after me. "Beautiful in Portland—you knew that, right?" she asks.

The urge to be with Caiden is overwhelming. I look toward the entrance, hoping to see her walking in. Anxious, I decide to go downstairs to look for her. Riley stops me telling me Caiden will be up momentarily. She is in PR mode, working the crowd for Zoe Rose's grand opening. I look down on the lower level, seeing Caiden conversing with some bar patrons. She looks happy, casually easing through the crowd, making sure to shake a hand, give a high five, or provide idle chitchat.

Women are pushing and shoving each other to try to speak with her. I imagine speaking is the last thing on their minds. One short-haired redhead grabs Caiden by the arm and begins to whisper in her ear, resting her arm on Caiden's shoulder. Caiden entertains her for a few moments then moves on through the crowd. The redhead looks disappointed as she walks away. A drunken brunette falls into Caiden's chest. Caiden braces her against her until she regains her balance. After Caiden checks to see if she is okay, she nods at Caiden, attempting to engage in conversation, but Caiden is prompted by a beautiful African American woman with long dark hair.

At first glance, she appears familiar. By Caiden's expression, she knows her. She excuses herself from the brunette and approaches the other woman, who has her arms out to greet her. Caiden seems hesitant to offer a hug, instead takes her hand. A conversation between them ensues for several minutes. She has Caiden's attention, making me curious how they know each other. I watch Caiden carefully as she seems nervous around her, continuously pushing her dreads out of her face.

Standing near the bar, the young woman turns to the bartender, ordering drinks. When he returns, she gives one drink to Caiden. They clink glasses in a toast, taking a sip of their cocktails.

Caiden leans in closer to her as she speaks into Caiden's ear. Caiden laughs at her comment as they continue to stand amidst the crowd. People in passing stop to hold idle conversation with Caiden. The woman seems agitated at the intrusion as she pouts each time they are interrupted. My green-eyed monster creeps out of me. I want Caiden away from this woman. Caiden motions the young woman to walk with her as she continues her stroll, heading toward the staircase.

A young blonde, obviously drunk, stops them. She places her arms around Caiden's neck, attempting to kiss her. Maybe it is the alcohol or my jealously, but I have seen more than enough.

I move toward the staircase when I am interrupted by Ginger remarking excitedly, "Zoe, this is great! Every femme in this club wishes she were you right now!"

Flattered, I manage a smile, thanking her. I am distracted at the moment, unable to fully engage her conversation, by Caiden and this woman. Impatiently, I pace back and forth, looking down at the two of them heading in this direction. Caiden must be bringing her upstairs.

Caiden appears at the stairwell, heading toward me. As soon as she reaches me, I wrap my arms around her neck, giving her a loving hug, not wanting to let go. She holds me tightly, caressing my back, squeezing me. I look up at her and notice her jaw is badly bruised.

"Oh my god, Caiden, what happened to your face?" I ask, shocked.

She chuckles, replying, "I was playing nice with Jaylon as you requested!"

Automatically, my lips softly kiss her bruised face as she jokes she will live. I ask if she is going to be okay. She nods yes.

"Happy engagement!" Caiden whispers.

I remark, "You are amazing. Do you know that?"

Caiden blushes, replying, "Zoe, we are about to embark on a lifelong journey together. I want every day with you to be amazing!"

How can a girl argue with that? I ask myself.

In between kisses, I tell Caiden I want her to take me home and fuck me.

She comments jokingly, "Did you say what I think you said?"

I look her in the eyes, asking her to read my lips. Her eyes move to my lips as I mouth slowly, *"Take me home and fuck the shit out of me!"*

Her eyes light up once she fully comprehends my request. A little taken aback at my boldness, she stands in silence with her eyes still gazing at my mouth. Distracted by my request, Caiden momentarily forgets Ms. Dark Hair is standing next to her. Clearing her throat, she tells me she would like to introduce me to someone.

"Zoe, this is Kyra Mitchell. Kyra, this is my wife-to-be, Zoe Payne."

Seeing the woman up close, I remember meeting her at the Find-a-Cure gala over a year or two ago. She looks at me closely, asking, "Haven't we met before? Oh, oh, I remember we met at the FAC gala. You were dating a police officer at the time. Hmmm. What was her name? Jayra? No, Jayson."

Caiden blurts out "Jaylon," glaring at me as she says Jaylon's name.

"That's it! Jaylon!" Kyra states.

I reply quickly, "Yes, I remember. Good to see you again." I glance at Caiden, noticing her jaws are tight with anger, yet she maintains her composure.

As if things can't get any worse, Jaylon appears, firmly grasping Caiden's shoulder in greeting. "How's it going, sis? Zoe, how are you?" she asks.

Caiden tilts her head back, taking a deep breath, replying harshly, "Jaylon."

Jaylon introduces herself to Kyra, informing her she is Caiden's older sister. Kyra looks confused, shaking Jaylon's hand as she turns to Caiden, who looks likes she wants to kill someone. Kyra offers her a sympathetic smile. Caiden reminds Jaylon of the restraining order, asking, "Shouldn't you be a few hundred yards away from us?"

Jaylon looks at Caiden, telling her she is not concerned about her threat. She reminds Caiden she does have friends on the force, further aggravating Caiden.

"Caiden, are you ready to go?" I ask hesitantly.

Jaylon intervenes, insisting we stay and celebrate the engagement. Jaylon looks at Caiden, commenting how swollen her jaw is, asking "Does it hurt?"

Caiden looks back at Jaylon, commenting on how the cut over her eye improves her look. "It makes you pretty," Caiden snips.

I cover my mouth, attempting to hide my laughter.

Awkwardly, the four of us stand near the railing, watching the people below, when it dawns on me that Kyra is the woman Caiden dated right before we started dating. How many women has Caiden been with crosses my mind. *What is she doing here?* I wonder. Not wanting to look at Caiden considering Kyra just outed me, I continue to scan the lower level of the club.

"Zoe, I heard you," Caiden roughly answers, acknowledging she heard my request. She excuses herself, saying she will be back in a few minutes, leaving me with Kyra and Jaylon.

I reach for Caiden, but she angrily pulls away from me.

"So when is the big day?" Kyra asks, breaking the uncomfortable silence between us.

"We haven't set a date yet. We only got engaged this morning," I respond.

"I am happy Caiden found her soul mate," she adds.

"Kyra, how do you and Caiden know each other?" I ask.

She looks surprised, responding, "We used to date. I always thought we'd end up together."

We both sip our cocktails as our conversation continues for another thirty minutes.

Jaylon is surprisingly quiet, leaving me troubled. Eyeing the cut above her right eye, I notice she has stitches. I further examine her face, seeing a bruise on her jaw. Those two are going to kill each other one day.

Caiden is off doing PR not far away, keeping a watchful eye on the three of us.

Kyra boldly admits she hoped to reconcile with Caiden. "I always thought we made a perfect match. We would have been good for each other," she asserts.

Jaylon starts laughing, now alert, and replies, "Kyra, you and a hundred other women feel Caiden is the perfect match. I feel sorry for any woman who gets caught in Caiden's web."

Kyra doesn't acknowledge Jaylon's comment. Listening to the two of them rant, I wonder why I am still here. I excuse myself, telling her to enjoy the rest of her evening.

Brianna motions me to come over. Once I reach her, she asks jokingly, "What the hell are you three discussing? Why is Caiden's ex here? Have you completely lost your mind, Zoe?"

"Please don't start in on me. As my bestie, I need your support for the night," I reply, frustrated.

She smirks at me as she taps her glass to mine, making no further jokes. We watch the people below when Brianna points out Ericka in the crowd.

"Great, more drama!" I say, exasperated. All I want is to be at home with Caiden. I turn around and see Kyra flirting with her. She is persistent. Caiden's eyes meet mine as she continues her conversation with that witch. I think she is rather enjoying seeing me jealous.

I head downstairs, removing myself from the situation. I reach the ground floor and feel someone grab my arm. Bothered by the encroachment, I pull away, noticing it's the woman from the restaurant.

"If I can't take you out to dinner, can I at least buy you a drink?" she asks.

Seeing Caiden isn't ready to leave, I accept her offer. She grabs my hand as we squeeze through the crowd up to the bar.

"What are we having?" she asks.

"Martini," I reply.

She orders our drinks, commenting, "Where is your fiancé?" I point toward upstairs. "Oh, VIP. Why am I not surprised?" She laughs.

Instinctively I cross my arms, giving her an annoyed glare.

She adds, "You look like the type!"

"Oh, this is where I am supposed to ask, 'What type is that?' right?" I fire back, cutting my eyes at her.

The bartender brings our drinks over, and Trace hands me my martini "Sarcastic and beautiful—my type of woman." She chuckles as she takes a sip of her drink.

Realizing I am taking my frustration out on her I giggle at her comment in an effort to be cordial. She inquires how long have I been with my partner.

"A while," I answer.

She looks disappointed by my response. After her second martini, she opens up about herself, telling me she moved back to Austin a few weeks ago after a recent breakup with her ex of five years. I look at my watch, noticing it is close to one thirty in the morning. I didn't realize I had been talking with Tracey for almost an hour. We happen to look up at the VIP lounge and see Caiden and Brianna staring down at us. By the blank stare, I can tell Caiden is not pleased at the view. Tracey smiles at Caiden, lifting her drink, toasting to her, sharing she and Caiden used to be best friends. I don't remember Caiden ever mentioning her. I thank her for the drink, explaining I should be getting back upstairs.

Tracey comments, "If you were with me, I wouldn't leave you alone for a second."

I stare at her, trying not laugh at the awful pickup line.

Talking with her for an hour gives me even greater appreciation for Caiden. Before I turn to leave, she grabs my hand firmly, replying, "I never caught your name, gorgeous!"

I reply, "Then you need more practice."

She laughs, releasing my hand.

I turn around, bumping into Caiden. "Are you ready to go?" I ask.

I hear Tracey behind me, remarking to Caiden, "Long time, no see, my old friend."

Caiden looks at Tracey, replying harshly, "I'm not your friend."

Tracey asks to speak to Caiden for a moment. Caiden tells her they have nothing to discuss, guiding me away from the bar.

"Come on, Caiden. It's been over six years since the Kyra incident. I did you a favor, C. She wasn't right for you," she exclaims.

Annoyed, Caiden starts to turn around to confront her when Jaylon appears, placing her hand on Caiden's shoulder, stopping her. Jaylon tells Caiden she owes her one, reminding Caiden about Scarface. Caiden looks surprised by her comment.

Jaylon chuckles, saying, "Didn't think I knew about that, huh?"

Caiden escorts me back upstairs, leaving Jaylon to deal with Tracey.

What was that all about, and who is Scarface? I wonder.

Caiden is already on her cell, instructing the driver to be out front. She asks Riley to make sure everyone gets home safely.

By the time we exit, the limo is out front. As soon as we get in, Caiden rolls up the privacy window. Craving her so badly, I straddle her lap, unloosening her shirt, kissing her aggressively. I bite her lip, causing it to bleed as she jerks from the sensation.

"Does seeing me bruised and in pain excite you?" she asks.

The taste of her own blood arouses her as she pulls my hair. Her hand covers my throat as she grasps it firmly, almost choking me. A sigh exits my lips, feeling her squeeze tighter. I can feel her hands move across my breast, rubbing my nipples with her thumb. I feel her warm mouth cover my exposed neck, biting, licking, and sucking it aggressively, making me moist. My hands flow through her dreadlocks, caressing her shoulders while I lick and nibble her earlobe. My mind is screaming, *Damn, I want to be fucked!* She starts to remove my blouse when we notice the limo has stopped moving.

Caiden opens the door impatiently before the driver steps out to assist. Grabbing my hand, we dash into the building toward the elevator. Caiden is pushing the elevator button, willing the doors to open. The sexual tension makes me want to fuck on the spot. I can't keep my hands off her. Finally the doors open. Wasting no time, we attack each other upon entry, unable to control our desires. Caiden lifts me off the ground and slams me against the wall. She kisses me with such lust and passion. Our tongues twirl in each other's mouths, licking and sucking the other's lips. My hands are in a frenzy, caressing her back, gripping and squeezing her ass, pressing her body between my legs. I pull at her dreads, forcing her head back, unveiling her neck. Overcome with raw emotion, I stake my claim to her, leaving noticeable passion marks. By her moans, she doesn't seem to mind. Reaching our floor, Caiden moves down the hall, carrying me as if I were light as a feather, the two of us still passionately locked at the lips. I fumble through my tote for the keys, opening the door clumsily.

Bursting through the door, Caiden slams me against the front door, releasing my legs. I rip open her shirt, sending buttons flying across the room. She steps back abruptly, removing her jacket and shirt, then demands I take off my clothes. Turned on, I remove every piece as she orders. Underneath her smoldering stare hides a dark and sinister craving I have never seen in her eyes. Her pants slide off her waist, onto the floor, revealing she is equipped to fulfill my request. I am moist at the sight of her favorite sex toy. My Venus yearns for penetration as it twitches and tingles at the thought. I eye Caiden, acknowledging nothing is off-limits. She can ravage me any way she chooses.

Her slender frame is upon me, forcing me to face the door. I am firmly pressed against it from her weight. I spread my legs while she runs her fingers across my clit, gliding them inside me. I'm so wet, so ready for her. Her fingers are soaked with my juices as they move slowly between my cheeks, reaching my opening. She slides them inside me, and I flinch momentarily from the intrusion. She waits for my body to relax and uses my juices as a lubricant. Her fingers move back to my opening, sliding in and out of me. She is prepping me, gliding a third finger inside. I am beginning to warm to this foreign feeling, moving my body up and down on her fingers, moaning as they glide deeper inside me. My arms are outstretched against the door as my hands begin to form a fist.

I moan, crying, "Fuck me, Caiden!"

Excited by my words, she thrusts her fingers as deep as they could go inside me. My Venus is still producing moisture, still craving her turn. I am enjoying this newfound feeling too much to share.

Caiden's body is warm against my skin as she kisses me, whispering I'm the only one. I feel her kisses on my shoulder, moving down my back to my buttock. She is on her knees, parting my cheeks when I feel her tongue licking me down there. My fists tighten, and my head drops, staring at the floor, as I enjoy her tongue. I moan louder and louder as I lick my lips, taking in her touch.

Our anticipation leads us into the bedroom and onto the bed. I'm on all fours as she climbs in behind me, pulling me into position. I feel her lubricated dildo barely grazing my flesh when she asks, "Why do you want this, Zoe?"

I reply, "I want to please you."

In a deep voice, she responds, "You do please me. Am I not pleasing you, Zoe?"

Before I could answer, Caiden thrusts her dildo inside me. I cry out as she continues to enter in and out of me with force. My hands twist in the sheets. I bury my head into the pillow to muffle my moans. I overwhelmed with feelings of pleasure and pain simultaneously, hoping she doesn't stop. Her brutality arouses me further. I hear our bodies colliding, making a slapping sound. Caiden continues, pulling me by my hips, bringing me closer to her body to penetrate deeper.

"Is this how you like to be fucked Zoe?" Caiden asks through gritted teeth.

I am so captivated by this wonderful torture I can barely utter yes.

"What were your words to me? *'Fuck the shit out of me!'*" Caiden remarks.

"Ooh, baby! Caiden, fuck! Fuck me harder! Ah! Ah! Oooh, I love the way you fuck me!" My body is swimming in ecstasy. My Venus is screaming at the top of her lungs for her turn. I feel my juices oozing down my thighs as Caiden continues to probe me.

"Your body belongs to me, Zoe!" she proclaims, pressing hard into me.

Through moans and cries, I utter, "Caiden, yes, yes, its yours!"

No sooner than the words leave my lips our bodies tighten as we cry out each other's name, reaching our climax.

Caiden roughly flips me over, lifting my legs on her shoulders. She is inside my Venus, pounding in and out of me like a beast. My eyes roll back at every stroke while I quiver uncontrollably. I can't get enough of her, grasping Caiden's back, digging my fingernails deep into her flesh, drawing blood as she groans. Feeling exhilarated, my body shatters into climax. I watch her beautiful body detonate on top of me. She falls onto the bed next to me, barely able to catch her breath.

Still not yet sated, I straddle her with my back to her, inserting her dildo inside me again, riding it up and down. Caiden reacts, pushing up in me as my body pounces down on her. We continue our fuck session, neither wanting to surrender to our exhaustion. Sensing she is near climax, I lean forward, grabbing her ankles, giving her eyes full access to my Venus, teasing her, moving slowly up and down her dildo.

"I like this side of you, Payne!" she whispers, slapping me hard on the ass.

Turning my head slightly toward her, I smugly ask, "You didn't think you'd be the only one, doing the fucking tonight, did you?"

I continue my slow, seductive journey up and down her until our bodies give way to our lust.

Turning to face her, I crawl on all fours until my pelvis reaches her mouth. Outstretched, barely able to breathe, she nods in acceptance. Teasing, I lift my body away from her lips.

"Taunting me?" She asks.

"Savoring," I respond.

I enjoy the anticipation of what's to come. Impatient, Caiden grabs my hips, forcing me onto her mouth, taking full control. I squirm in elation as her mouth envelopes my Venus and her tongue presses firmly against my clit, licking at it and grazing it with her teeth. It doesn't take long to bring me to my apex. I moan as she sucks and strokes my clit, giving me butterflies in the pit of my stomach. Almost to the point of exhaustion, my body graciously allows me one last glorious outburst. Grabbing the headboard tightly, bracing myself for the finale, I cry out her name over and over until my orgasm is complete.

CHAPTER SIXTEEN

Fruition

I awake to the front door shutting. Caiden has returned from her morning run.

"Good, morning!" she remarks as she heads to take a shower.

What time is it? I wonder, looking at the clock, seeing it is only 10:00 a.m. Does she ever sleep? We went to bed at four in the morning. Drained and sore, I lie in bed, reminiscing how exciting last night with Caiden had been. I enjoy being uninhibited. I think it just comes naturally for Caiden. My envy takes over, remembering Jaylon's words from last night, wondering how many women has Caiden been with? How many experienced what we shared last night? Kyra quickly comes to mind. She made it clear she still wants Caiden.

Interrupted by the blinking light from my cell, I glance at the number. It's unfamiliar to me, so I send it to voicemail. I sit up and stretch, noticing my phone blinking again from the same number. I answer as Caiden is entering the room.

"Hello, is this Ms. Zoe Payne?" the caller asks.

"This is she. Who's calling?" I reply.

The caller, Jessica Powell, briefly explains she is a real estate broker from the Lycan Development Group LLC. She states her client wants to make an offer on my condo. I advise her it isn't on the market. She insists her client is very interested in the property and willing to pay extra if needed. I remind her again my condo is not for sale as I end the call.

Caiden looks, wondering what is going on.

I give a quick recap, and she asks, "You must really love this place, huh?"

I reply, "Yes, it has sentimental value. I love being downtown, viewing the lake, and feeling the peace and quiet way up here."

Caiden looks perplexed, realizing how important my condo is to me. "Zoe, I'm curious. Since I have been here, I have never seen any of your neighbors. Do you know them?" she asks.

Stumped by her question, I have to think about it, realizing I haven't taken the liberty to meet my neighbors in the two years I have been here. Matter of fact, I don't remember seeing any of my neighbors other than entering and exiting the building. I eye her blankly as I have no response. Note to Zoe—"Find time to meet your neighbors."

Holding a towel around her neck, Caiden looks at me, shrugging her shoulders in disbelief, smirking. "Voted Ms. Congeniality in high school, huh, and you don't know your neighbors!"

I frown at her, wanting to laugh at her snide comment but not giving her the satisfaction.

She looks at me, smiling, and replies, "Come on, Zoe. You know you want to laugh!"

I can't hold my frown any longer, starting to laugh at her sarcasm.

Starving, I suggest we go out for breakfast at a local café off Highway 183. I want to get her away from downtown for the day. She hasn't had the chance to visit around town since she arrived. An excursion to our favorite spots in the Metro area will be good for us. I am looking forward to some one-on-one time with her outside of my bedroom.

"Sexy!" I call.

"Yes, beautiful?" she replies.

"I love you!" I exclaim.

She blushes as she shakes her head, going back to the bathroom to shower. I follow, needing to get ready for the day.

I ask Caiden if she ever plans on unpacking her luggage. She looks at me, informing me that at some point, she will need to return to Portland within the next few days. I grow sad at the thought of her leaving. She walks up to me, explaining she would love it if I return with her. We would only be there a few days—four tops, she explains. My sadness quickly turns to joy as I agree to go to Portland with her. We finish getting dressed and head out. Conscious of our conversation about my neighbors, I take the opportunity to knock on one of the doors. Caiden is standing behind me, teasing as I wait for the door to open. We wait a few moments, but no one answers. She knocks on the door next to my unit as she laughs at me. Tipping back and forth on her heels, she looks at me, shrugging her shoulders. Rolling my eyes at her, I grab her hand and head toward the elevator.

While we are waiting, Caiden looks around and notices a door leading to the rooftop. She points at it, asking if I go up there. I told her some rich asshole threw enough money at the builder, convincing them to sell that part of the property. Now the space is privately owned, so none of the residents can utilize the amenities. The few residents living here were each reimbursed a portion of the cost of the condo for the inconvenience. I did get the opportunity to use the space once when I first moved in. It was really an oasis up there, with a cabana, bar, chaise longues, pool, showering area, and other amenities.

Caiden remarks, "It sounds charming. Hope the bastards were overcharged!"

I laugh in agreement.

Caiden suggested we skip the limo or taxi and drive today. She wants it to be just the two of us as well. Concerned about last night with Kyra, I ask Caiden how she felt about Kyra mentioning I dated Jaylon. She stares at me, explaining she hates the idea and wants to erase the thought from her mind. She reminds me that she promised to forgive me regardless of what happened while she was in Portland. I toss her the keys, and we head out for breakfast.

After last night, I am famished. On our drive over, we discuss a few things in regard to our wedding. Caiden is relinquishing control of our wedding to me. She said a wedding is always about the bride, and I should have everything my heart desires on that very special day. Her only request is I consult with her from time to time on the progress. She also requests she pick at least one of the flavors for our wedding cakes. I inform Caiden my father insists on paying for our wedding, but he has a budget in mind.

Caiden looks over at me, smirking from the driver's seat, and says, "No offense to your father, Zoe, but money isn't a factor when it comes to our wedding. I appreciate his offer. I will talk with him, and let him off the hook!" she says.

I stare out the window and find myself wondering her worth. I know she is successful, but we've never discussed our finances with each other before. We never had a reason to. The more I think about the wedding, the more questions arise.

Pulling into the restaurant, I get a text from Ginger, "Seen today's paper?"

I text, "No, Why?"

She texts, "You & Caiden's engagement."

I text, "What, How?" Surprised, at first, I quickly realize Brianna mentioned she would take care of it. I text, "What pic?"

She replies, "The Ball Red Carpet, several photos in color 'nice'."

I grab Caiden's arm suddenly, informing her we need today's paper. She asks if something happened, and I shake my head no, yes, no.

"Our engagement announcement is in today's paper!" I squeal in excitement. She laughs, shaking her head, mumbling something under her breath. Luckily, there is a newspaper stand in front of the restaurant. Caiden digs in her pocket for change as I stand impatiently, waiting for her to get the paper. She looks at me like I am on drugs, laughing at me as she inserts the coins and pulls out the paper. I pry it from her hand frantically, searching for the lifestyle section.

I open it up, and there it is, a full-page color spread announcing *"Zoe Michelle Payne & Caiden Bryce Westphal are elated to announce their engagement and pending marriage. Payne, heiress to Payne Corp., and Westphal, a multimillionaire mogul & philanthropist, met in Austin, Texas. Payne is heavily involved in multiple charitable organizations throughout the US & abroad & Westphal is involved in real estate development, small business, & several charitable organizations. Their combined net worth is estimated at over $140 million."*

The pictures from the policeman's ball are amazing. There are four different photos of us from the evening. My favorite is of Caiden and me exchanging a heated kiss on the runway. I couldn't be happier as I show Caiden the announcement. She looks at the pictures, commenting how the cameras love me.

"You are very picturesque, beautiful. I'm glad Brianna didn't go overboard with the announcement!" she jokes.

My heart is beating out of my chest as I view the announcement, suddenly making our engagement a reality. Caiden informs the hostess we would like a table for two inside.

Noticing, I have yet to take my eyes off the announcement, Caiden jokes, "It's not going to change, Zoe!"

I hit her arm as I return to the paper. I am in awe at the pictures. "Caiden, you are so damn sexy!" I comment to her.

We are finally seated, and I am still glued to the paper.

"Zoe? Are you going to look at that all day?" Caiden asks—jokingly, I think.

I hold my finger up, signaling "Just a sec" as I read the announcement once again. I was so caught up in the pictures I skimmed past the announcement.

I place the paper in my lap and look at Caiden seated across from me, commenting, "How do they come up with an outrageous net worth of $140 million?"

Caiden looks back at me calmly, replying "I don't think they are that far off, beautiful" as she takes a sip of water.

I look at her again, confused, asking, "What do you mean they are not that far off?"

The waitress returns with our order, placing our food on the table. She smiles at us, asking if we need anything else. Caiden looks at me to see if I need anything before replying, "No, thank you, Robin. That will be all for now."

Surprised she knew her name, I am about to ask when Caiden interrupts, "Her nametag."

How did she know I'd ask? I laugh as I take a bite of my Eggs Francisco. I introduced Caiden to this restaurant a few years ago, and she fell in love with the dish. She has yet to try another item on the menu. I smile, watching her enjoy her breakfast. She did work up quite an appetite last night.

Robin returns to our table and kneels down, resting her elbow on the table, whispering "Congratulations, you two. I recognize you from the paper."

Caiden and I glance at each other, smiling as we thank her. Caiden orders another grapefruit juice and water.

"Thirsty, Mr.Westphal?" I ask jokingly.

She raises her eyebrows and begins to laugh, remarking, "Ms. Payne, as thirsty as you were last night."

A chill comes over me as I reminisce about our evening together.

The newspaper slips out of my lap, reminding me of the conversation we were having previously.

"Caiden, what did you mean by 'They are not far off'?"

She looks puzzled. "Oh, finances, of course. If I had to guess, you are worth, say, fifty to sixty million dollars, correct?" she asks. I nod in agreement. Nervously rubbing her hands across her thighs, she clears her throat, adding, "I am unaccustomed to discussing my portfolio. Hmmm! Zoe, last I checked, my net worth is roughly sixty million dollars, notwithstanding my inheritance and liquid assets. In all, I'd say I am worth around eighty to ninety million dollars, give or take. Now can we please change the subject?"

I am surprised by her admission. I can see by her fidgeting that she is uncomfortable, discussing the topic.

After breakfast, we go to Mount Bonnell. We've not been there in years. The view of Austin is breathtaking. We make the one-hundred-step climb, reaching the pavilion when Caiden comments the views are still amazing. As we look out toward the city, she stands behind me with her arms around me. I rest my hands on her arms as we enjoy the view of Downtown. She squeezes me tightly, kissing me on the cheek. Everything is perfect in this moment. I realize there is no one else I'd rather spend my life with.

"Zoe, how are you feeling, after last night?" Caiden asks quietly. I dwell on her question before responding, "Caiden, last night was better than I ever imagined. I love being with you. Why do you ask?"

She sighs. "I need to know I am enough for you. I hear the whispers when we are out in public. I know what some of your friends think of me."

I stop her from going any further, turning to face her, explaining, "Caiden, I used to care what people thought of me, of you, of us, but I was young and impressionable. I am not the same insecure girl anymore. I love you, and I don't care what people whisper. Caiden, I want to be with you. You do know that, right?"

She nods yes, but her body seems unsure.

A feeling of guilt sets in, knowing she hasn't forgotten how I treated her in the past. We concealed our relationship for the first two years. I was ashamed to admit to my friends and family we were together out of fear of rejection. Caiden became resentful and frustrated, having to hide her feelings. We began to argue, further straining our relationship. My family and friends kept questioning my relationship with Caiden until I finally told them the truth, praying they would understand. Instead, my parents forbade me to see her, threatening to disown me. My friends were no better, claiming I had been brainwashed into thinking I was a lesbian. Gradually, they disassociated themselves from me. Combining my pregnancy, it all became overwhelming, and I couldn't continue to hurt her anymore.

How can I blame her for her doubts with everything that happened between us? I should be the one asking am I enough for her? I'm suddenly sick to my stomach, thinking how much time we've lost because of my insecurities. I hug her tightly, trying to reassure her I am no longer afraid of the world and everyone in it, asking for her forgiveness. I feel her soft hand caress my cheek as she leans down, kissing me softly on the lips.

We sit for hours, talking about our past and future together. The more we talk and laugh, the more I am reminded how I miss our conversations. She has a way of bringing out the best in me. Realizing we had been out here a long time, Caiden suggests we head home.

Heading back down the steps, she adds, "Zoe, thank you. It's been great, spending time alone with you."

We arrive back at the condo, I comment, "Home sweet home."

Caiden replies, "You really do love this place. Could you ever see yourself living anywhere else?"

I explain I'd never given it any thought. I silently wish she loved it as much as I do.

As we go upstairs, Caiden teases me about the neighbors. She is knocking on one of the doors, pretending someone answered, introducing herself. I shake my head, grinning at her playfulness.

We unwind on the sofa, sharing a bottle of pinot gris, enjoying each other's company. Placing her wine glass on the table she kisses me on the lips, stroking my cheek. My hands automatically cup her face, kissing her equally as soft. My body aches to make love to her as she moves on top of me, whispering how much I mean to her. There is no attempt of seduction on Caiden's part as she tenderly kisses my lips. This is a purely spiritual moment between us, with Caiden revealing a softer more tender side. I am left hypnotized by her words, "I never want to be without you, Zoe".

My heart is filled with joy, and I utter, "Caiden! I will never let you go, I promise!"

Hugging me tightly, her body starts to tremble; she is quietly weeping. I squeeze her tight, caressing her back gently as tears slowly trickle down my cheek. I feel we have reached a new plateau, connecting spiritually as we lay intertwined in each other's arms.

CHAPTER SEVENTEEN

Unmasked

Caiden decides to postpone the, opening of Zoe Rose until November 2, after consulting with Abby. I'm excited to get a chance to see Caiden and her team in action. She jumps right in, rolling up her sleeves, working side by side with our staff, giving them full control of their responsibilities, and taking their ideas into consideration. I envy their relationship. The corporate world is doing whatever is necessary in order to please shareholders and increase the bottom line. I'm looking forward to a change of pace, taking an extended leave from Payne Corp. I appointed my father as the interim CEO until I return. He's eager to get back at the helm.

Watching Caiden with Riley and Abby is how a family business should be. They all are taking ownership and work as a single unit. I'm enjoying watching Abby order Caiden, Riley, and the contractors around like minions. None of them seem to mind, laughing at her as she barks out orders. She's meticulous, ensuring everything from the seating, lighting, sound system, restrooms, wall décor, bar, and liquor display is set up perfectly. Caiden jokes she hasn't worked this hard since her mother made her clean the house as a child. Abby spares no prisoners, assigning me the task of decorating our offices. She jokes Caiden's idea of an office consists of a cell, a desk, and a tablet. I gladly accept the task, wanting to add a feminine touch to our shared space.

Abby implies Caiden and Riley lack the ability to provide the correct ambience to lure women to their establishment, sparking a playful debate. Riley fires back, mentioning Caiden's club in Portland, noting it is doing very well. Abby jokes it's because Caiden had the good sense to hire her. A sense of happiness flows in me, as I see Caiden laugh and joke without a care in the world. I'm glad to know she has them in her life.

Caiden exclaims, "Women come out for an experience with the expectation of meeting Mr. or Mrs. Right who can and will take care of them."

Riley chuckles as she listens to Caiden, pointing out there are dozens of clubs in Austin women can go for the ordinary.

Caiden's excitement is evident when she states, "Zoe Rose is glamor. It's sophistication. It's sex appeal—a place people come to escape the mundane!"

Abby, Brianna, and myself are staring at Caiden with our arms folded, glaring at her.

Smirking and withdrawing her foot out of her mouth, she quips, "Riley, by the flared nostrils and wicked stares in the room, I've made my point. Seriously, Abby, what do you look for in a mate?"

Abby looks at Caiden coyly and responds, "Someone genuine and caring."

Caiden asks, "So they don't require a job?"

Abby, aggravated, replies, "I am quite capable of supporting myself!"

Caiden counters, "I have no doubt, but you didn't answer my question."

Brianna adds, "If they are capable of taking care of me, then it's an added value, not a necessity."

Caiden offers, "Look, let's be honest and admit finances plays a role in how people select a partner."

"Caiden, are you saying I'm with you because of money?" I interrupt.

Caiden looks at me, fighting back a grin, noting, "Zoe, not everyone is as lucky. You're wholeheartedly in love with me! You can't help yourself."

I can't fight back my smile, knowing it's the truth. I counter, trying to form a serious expression, "You sure about that, Westphal?"

Her eyes narrow as she looks at me with a self-assured smirk on her face.

Brianna promoted the event on local radio and talk shows, placing ads in the papers, setting up different blogs on Facebook, Twitter, Instagram, you name it. She rented billboards strategically, placing them along IH-35 north- and southbound, Ben White Boulevard, and 183 to catch the hundreds of thousands of commuters' attention. From one end of Austin to the other, you couldn't help but notice some reference to the club.

Caiden insists on having a photographer come in to capture my eyes.

Brianna jokes, "If your eyes have the same hypnotic effect as they do on Caiden, we should have no trouble seducing people into the club."

Caiden fell in love with the shots, having them displayed in frames around the club. Although flattering, I am having a hard time seeing the images displayed.

After completion, it looks amazing. The location is perfect, resting in the downtown warehouse district. We've been open for business nearly a month, and the support from the GLBT and heterosexual community is overwhelming. Since opening, we have grossed over $650,000. Caiden and I agree that a percentage of our net profits will go to local charities anonymously.

Now we are up and running, Caiden feels comfortable leaving Zoe Rose in the care of Abby and Riley while we head to Portland. We postponed our trip in order to get the club up and running.

It is late November when we decide to finally make the trip. I am excited to see where she has been living for the past two years. Our plan is to leave Thursday, November 27, returning on Sunday. Caiden and I decide to spend our last night in Austin home alone, packing and recovering from the very busy past few weeks. She seems anxious to get back to Portland. I think she misses it. We haven't heard a peep out of Jaylon in a month. I'm starting to actually worry about her. I imagine she is following the rules to maintain her trust fund. When I heard of all the provisions, I felt sorry for her. I admit Caiden is a lot more at ease without her around.

Everything is going great until Edwina Miller approaches me one day, asking if I would help assist in Jaylon's recovery. I naturally agreed, hoping it will help bring Caiden and Jaylon closer together.

Caiden wouldn't hear of it, saying the last thing Jaylon needs is to be near what she can't have. She went so far as to consult with several psychiatrists and psychologists in an attempt to convince me the best thing I can do for Jaylon is stay away. She can't understand Dr. Morrison's unorthodox approach, sarcastically suggesting both Dr. Morrison and Jaylon are insane. I reluctantly agree to her request not to get involved to save our relationship.

I remember the day I shared Edwina's proposition with Caiden. Needless to say, a three-day argument ensued over the subject. It was so heated I lashed out at her, asking how she can be so coldhearted and indifferent in regard to her sister. She was furious with me to the point we stopped speaking to each other to avoid another argument. I decided the best thing for us was to give each other space. I stayed with Brianna for a few days until we both had time to cool off.

Being at Brianna's isn't much better. She has a few choice words for me even after I explain Caiden has given me an ultimatum to be with her or help Jaylon.

I express to her that the Christian thing to do is to help someone in need. She quickly reminds me Jaylon isn't the only one suffering and I am being pretty damn selfish, acting like a spoiled brat. My best friend doesn't even agree with me. Admittedly, her comments hurt, but Brianna has never held her tongue. She explains it from Caiden's perspective, noting she has never denied me anything. All I have to do to get my way is bat my "beautiful blues," and she is putty in my hands. She says Caiden obviously has her reasons for wanting me away from Jaylon. She can relate, knowing how abusive Jaylon was to her. Brianna feels Jaylon is volatile and capable of hurting us. Caiden is only trying to protect me. She doesn't hold back, expressing I'm being selfish because I'm not getting my way.

She said, "Think about it, Zoe. Jaylon has Edwina, Erika, a psychiatrist, and support from the APD helping and assisting her. Who does Caiden have besides her friends? Who does Caiden need? As much as Caiden puts on a rigid front, this can't be easy for her. The one person she should be able to count on most is fighting against her for the one person who hates her."

She asks how I would feel if I were in Caiden's position. She reminds me that when you are involved with someone, you don't need to know or understand when they are passionate about something. Sometimes, you just need to be there and support them because it is the right thing to do. She goes on, suggesting one day, things between the two of them will change. They may even work things out, but until then, I need to be there for Caiden.

I am being given an earful from Brianna. She points out I have a tendency to fix things when sometimes it's not my place to fix them. She continues, explaining some people in the world are evil just as some are good and we can't change that. Jaylon is one of those evil people—walking the planet only caring about Jaylon.

"Think about it like this: Caiden has forgiven you without even knowing what you've done. She loves you unconditionally, even with your imperfections. Why is it so difficult for you to accept not everything is meant to be fixed by Zoe Payne? Caiden and Jaylon have had problems long before you ever entered into the picture. The best thing you can do for Jaylon without hurting Caiden is pray she gets better and be there for the person you say you want to marry."

To lighten the mood, I ask her, "When did you become so smart?"

She laughs, replying, "Years of heartache will make you evaluate what's important in life, Zoe. Maybe it is time you evaluate what is important in your life!"

I thought about everything we discussed, coming to the conclusion Jaylon isn't worth me losing Caiden. I followed Brianna's advice, saying a prayer for Jaylon to get well. I contact Caiden, admitting I am wrong in my haste to defend Jaylon and I should have been there for her. After our talk, I return home to find Caiden waiting for me with a handful of red roses.

We are lounging in bed that evening when Caiden says she has something to tell me. She said things have been moving so swiftly, there was never a good time to for us to talk. I sit up in bed, reaching for the remote, turning the TV off. Her look is intense as she explains, "I wish I didn't have to be the one to tell you this, but you need to know the truth."

Her eyes are full of sorrow and my heart is sinking into my stomach. "Caiden, please just tell me!" I say anxiously.

She sits up in bed, resting her back against the headboard, and begins to share the reason Riley is in Austin. Caiden used Riley's expertise to help her investigate Jaylon. She said after I told her about the pregnancy and losing the baby, something didn't sit well. She asked Riley to hack into Jaylon's computer and security surveillance. They discovered I never had a one-night stand with Marcus. Jaylon set the entire scenario up and kept a video diary. Caiden suspects Jaylon drugged me at the bar. It is the only explanation she can think why I can't remember anything about that night.

Jaylon brought me home along with Marcus and Jessica. Jaylon used Marcus's sperm to inseminate me while I lay passed out in bed. She made Marcus wake up in bed with me the next day so I would think we slept together. Marcus, an ex-con, is one of Jaylon's informants. Either he owed her a favor or she blackmailed him into being a part of her scheme. She played on my emotions, helping convince me to break up with Caiden. Jaylon knew there was a good chance Caiden would leave if she thought I betrayed her.

Jaylon sent Rheia to Portland in an attempt to make Caiden fall in love with her and forget about me. Caiden went on to informing me Jaylon set up surveillance in my condo and my phone and placed a tracker on my car, all in an effort to keep us apart. Jaylon thought I would eventually fall in love with her with Caiden out of the picture.

"Zoe, I know about the suicide attempt," Caiden murmurs quietly.

A chill went through me at the thought of her knowing I tried to kill myself after I lost the baby. I felt desolate after the loss of Caiden and the baby. I lost the will to live and took a bottle of sleeping pills. Jaylon stopped in to check on me one day and discovered me passed out on the floor. I somehow managed to text her for help. I don't remember much about that night. She rushed me to the emergency room, where the doctors were able to pump my stomach and revive me.

I look over at Caiden, noticing her eyes watering, filled with anguish at the thought, as she whispered, "Zoe, how, why would you do such a thing?"

I place my hands over my face, shaking my head, crying, "Caiden, I don't know. I thought I had lost you forever, and losing the baby, it was too much. I didn't want to live anymore. I'm so sorry. I never wanted you to find out."

After my attempt, I checked into a psychiatric facility for six months, coping with my loss. I blame myself for everything that happened. If I had gone to Caiden in the beginning, maybe all this could have been avoided. It is silly of me to believe Jaylon could be a loving, caring person. Caiden has been right about Jaylon all along. *How could I have been so gullible?* I ask myself, in tears.

Caiden reaches for a briefcase sitting on the floor next to her. Opening it up, she pulls out an old newspaper clipping her mother left along with a handwritten letter. She hands me the clipping and letter, instructing me to read them. After learning about Caiden and Jaylon's family secrets, my heart begins to break. Even after finding out all the horrible things Jaylon has done, I can't help but feel sorry for her. I ask Caiden how long has she known. She said she found out the day of her mother's funeral. I look at her with sorrow in my eyes, wondering how she managed to deal with everything on her own, wondering why she didn't confide in me sooner.

After reading the news clipping, I couldn't help but weep for Jaylon. I can't imagine having to witness my mother kill my father then herself in front of me. How horrible for any child to have to endure such a tragedy! Even at such a young age, it had to have left an impression. I wonder at how odd it is for a woman to take her own life in such a gruesome manner. How must she have felt, leaving her only child alone in the world feeling unloved and unwanted? How must Jaylon have felt all these years after learning the truth? This sheds light on Jaylon's erratic behavior.

My feelings for Jaylon are distorted. *She raped me!* I scream in my head. How could she lie and manipulate without remorse? I'm trembling as Caiden holds me in her arms. The tears rush down my cheeks as I scream in pain, cursing Jaylon for everything. Caiden continues to hold me, caressing my hair. I throw my arms around her neck, begging her for forgiveness. How could I be so stupid to have trusted Jaylon? I can't stop my tears from flowing. Caiden doesn't speak a word as my sobs continue.

The next morning, I wake, still curled in her warm, safe arms. Caiden stares at me with concern, asking if I need anything. I look at her, shaking my head no, and bury my head back into her chest. She squeezes me, assuring me everything is going to work out and she is there for me always.

A few days pass, and I still can't find it in my heart to forgive Jaylon for the misery she has caused in our lives. I'm trying to take into consideration how screwed up her life has been, yet it still doesn't justify her actions. I'm taking Caiden's advice, reading my Bible and praying to God for strength to put this all behind me. Deep down, I know Jaylon isn't well, making it difficult for me to continue to hate her.

Caiden enters the living room, sitting beside me. I tell her she didn't have to carry this burden alone, explaining she can confide in me always. She looks at me, expressing the need to absorb it all before coming to me. She couldn't share anything until she had a clear understanding of it all.

She turns to me with a serious look on her face, saying, "Zoe, our lives have been manipulated for far too long. We can't change the past. My hope is we grow stronger together, continuing to move forward with our lives."

There is a determination in her eyes as she speaks. She acknowledges the past couple of days have been difficult. She assures me she will be patient and understanding for as long as I need but expresses all she wants is to marry me and soon.

Hearing the sincerity in her voice, I break into tears from the joy of knowing she still wants to marry me. I ask, even after everything, is she sure she still wants me?

"More than anything, Zoe," Caiden replies sweetly.

Feelings of love and hope permeate me when I hear the certainty in her voice. I think we have been through so much and deserve to be happy. I take a deep breath and look into her beautiful brown eyes, stating, "I have wasted enough precious time denying my feelings and refuse to wait any longer. I'm ready to be Mrs. Westphal!"

Caiden's big, beautiful smile glows as she hugs me tightly, sharing she couldn't be happier.

CHAPTER EIGHTEEN

Impromtu

I'm beginning to wonder if we will ever make it to Portland. Caiden refused to travel under the circumstances, further delaying our trip. We use the time to analyze how we will move past all the hurtful things Jaylon has done. Caiden has enough evidence to send Jaylon away for a long time. I can't understand why she hasn't gone to the police. I assume that deep inside, she believes she can help her. Caiden has been cooperative in aiding in Jaylon's therapy, attending sessions, trying to understand how to cope with Jaylon's bipolar disorder. It's hard on Caiden, knowing what Jaylon has done. She never talks about their sessions, and I'm afraid to ask. I can never read her moods afterward. She is so good at hiding her true feelings that I find it difficult to read her at times. She holds so much internally, never wanting to burden anyone with her issues. I want so desperately to help ease her suffering. Perhaps after we are married, she will be more inclined to open up to me. For now, I continue to be supportive and respect her privacy.

In the end, we turn our attention on more positive aspects of our lives and begin discussing our wedding plans. I ask Caiden to promise we will not have sex until our wedding night. It's already been three weeks since we last made love, and I know this is not an easy request. I remember her eyes narrowing as she dwells on my proposition, standing at the edge of our bed and reluctantly agreeing, adding the proviso that kissing and foreplay aren't part of the deal.

She knows what her kisses do to me. As for her foreplay, I am defenseless. I accept her challenge, calling on all my defenses against her charm. I have a feeling she is going to do everything possible to make me give in to temptation as she nonchalantly climbs into bed with no shirt on, kissing me on the forehead and bidding me good night.

The next morning, on our way to the airport, Caiden asks if I mind taking a slight detour before we reach Portland. I nod okay, still groggy not fully comprehending her question.

On the way to the gate, I ask, "Where are we going?"

Caiden calmly answers, "Hawaii, to get married."

I stop in my tracks to make sure I heard correctly.

She laughs, noting, "What better place to get married?"

I shout, "Caiden, are you serious?"

She looks at me, grinning as she nods yes. Excited at the news, I leap in her arms, wrapping my legs around her waist, kissing her all over her face. She chuckles, kissing me in return, expressing her enjoyment at my response.

Next thing I know, we are in the air, on a ten-and-a-half-hour flight to Kauai, Hawaii. Caiden goes over the itinerary with me on the flight. We have two suites at the Sheraton Kauai Resort in Poipu Beach, Koloa, for the next two weeks. She had one of her assistants out of Portland set everything up. She didn't want to risk anyone interfering in our wedding plans. She says we will have a huge ceremony in the summer where everyone can attend, but for now, she wants me all to herself. Our itinerary is full of activities to keep us busy for the duration of our stay, including personal tours, sailing, shopping, hiking, and a wedding.

I ask her why two suites, and she explains this will minimize the risk of us breaking our vow of celibacy. I'm not happy with this part of the agreement. Caiden is right—it will help keep the sexual tension between us at bay.

We arrive late Thursday evening and opt to dine in one of the suites after our long flight. Caiden downloaded our marriage applications prior to leaving Austin, and we filed the applications early Friday morning with a marriage agent in Kauai. Caiden managed to pull a few strings, expediting the approval process. We decide on a quaint ceremony in the tropical garden of the hotel with an amazing view of the ocean. The ceremony is going to be performed by an ordained minister highly recommended by friends who married here a few weeks prior. Although our ceremony is going to be quaint, I convince her to wear a tux. I am going shopping for a wedding dress in the next day or two. The ceremony is scheduled for next Tuesday, December 10, at noon.

After the wedding arrangements are made, we spent the rest of the day shopping in Old Kola Town and took an aerial tour to view the Napali coast.

After our excursions, we head to the hotel for a late dinner. The cool weather is ideal for a romantic evening stroll along the beach. The sky is clear as the moonlight dances on the ocean while we walk hand in hand admiring the beauty of the island. As we stroll, she shares how she has dreamed of this day for as long as she can remember.

She comments, "Zoe, you are the most beautiful person I know. I thank God for placing you in my heart and my life. I feel like the wealthiest person on the planet, knowing I get the pleasure of sharing the rest of my life with you."

I squeeze her hand tightly as we continue our walk, thinking what an amazing person she is. I am blessed to have found someone who loves me as much as I love her. Moved by her sentiment, I face her, clasping her hands in mine, remarking, "Caiden, the first time we met on the playground years ago, I knew you would be an integral part of my life. I am sorry it has taken me so long to love you the way you deserve. God has been gracious enough to give me a second chance. Caiden, I will never make the same mistakes again. Nurse Woodward is exactly right_when she said you were a keeper. I promise to always keep you in my heart."

She looks down at me with tears trickling down her cheek and gently kisses my lips.

I reciprocate with great passion and desire, wrapping my arms around her neck, pulling her close to me, whispering, "I know we promised to wait, but I want you!"

Clearing her throat, she looks in my eyes, smiling shyly, expressing her desire for me as well. She admits she would love to give in to temptation but she doesn't want to break her promise. She smiles a sweet smile at me, taking me by the hand, guiding me back to the hotel.

The walk back is quiet, but I can feel love in her touch. I shyly smile, seeing the happiness beaming from her face. I love this side of her, relaxed and worry-free from the day-to-day tasks of running her businesses. Being here, she seems somehow different, comfortable and vibrant. She's gone islander, wearing linen shorts, flip-flops, and floral shirts.

When we reach the suite, she says a personal shopper and assistant will be meeting me at eleven in the morning to take me out for last-minute wedding preparations. She reaches into her pocket and pulls out her wedding band, giving it to me, saying it's for safekeeping. She asks for my ring, stating she wants to have it engraved before the wedding. We never discussed what we want to put on the rings. She sees my anxiety and calmly assures me she is confident that whatever it says, she will know it is from the heart. I ask what her plans are for tomorrow and when will I see her. She tells me she has some last-minute planning of her own and we will meet up around five here at the hotel.

I grow sad at the thought of, being away from her. I wish we could enjoy every moment together on this beautiful Island.

She reads my mind as she quietly remarks, "I will be thinking of you the entire day, beautiful. I will miss you too!"

"How—?" I begin when Caiden interrupts, finishing my sentence, "Does she do that?"

She chuckles at my curiousness, remarking "It's all in the details of knowing you, Ms. Payne!" and leaning in to kiss me good night.

As she draws near, my heart beats rapidly. My lips part, excited to feel her tongue caressing mine. Her lips are soft, warm, and inviting. I kiss her passionately, trying desperately to weaken her resolve.

My body aches to feel her touch as we stand at the door of my suite, still engaged in a heated kiss. Her hands move to cup my breasts, squeezing them firmly. I moan at her touch and begin to suck on her neck. Pressing me against the door, breathing heavily, her hands continue to roam my body. My hands glide down her back, to her firm round ass, squeezing it, pulling her body even closer into mine. I reach into her pocket, pulling out the key to the suite, and open the door, still using my free hand to hold her shorts at the waist, pulling her into the room. The door automatically closes behind us as Caiden brushes my hair away from my neck and begins to kiss and nibble from my neck down to my shoulders.

I am guiding her toward the bedroom, praying I succeed. I lift her shirt over her head, dropping it on the floor, admiring her physique as if it were the first time my eyes had seen it. I quickly undress, stepping toward her, pulling at the drawstring to her shorts, when she grabs my hand.

I whisper, "Caiden, this is one promise I can't keep. It was silly of me to ask. Please, sexy? I want this. Don't you?"

Staring at me, she bites the right side of her lower lip then licks her lips. They are moist and glisten in the dim light of the room.

Contemplating her next move, she releases her grip from my hand, allowing me to unloosen her shorts. They drop to her feet, revealing only her boxer briefs, and, to my dismay, harness-and-dildo free.

I tease, "You are doing your due diligence!"

Chuckling, she replies, "I hope this won't be a problem for you, Ms. Payne!"

I reply, "No, Mr. Westphal, you are quite adept with or without!" Smiling, I climb into the middle of the bed.

She notes, "It's always near if you change your mind."

"I'll keep that in mind!" I giggle.

She reaches for my ankles, pulling me toward the foot of the bed until my knees reach the edge. Standing over me, she rests my legs on her shoulders as she glares down at my Venus.

Her eyes are burning with lust as she asks, "Ms. Payne, do you mind if I say hello to an old friend?"

Excitedly, I utter, "Please do!"

She kisses my ankle slowly, licking down my leg as she moves southward. My Venus twitches, knowing that soon Caiden's perfect lips will greet her with a warm, sensual hello. My eyes are fixated on her tongue as it grows closer and closer to my Venus. Her eyes never waver from her destination as her tongue nears my inner thigh. I feel her kneel at the foot of the bed as her lips graze my Venus, triggering a subtle moan from my lips. My legs dangle helplessly over her shoulders while her lips press firmly against my Venus. Her tongue delicately glides across my clit, stroking slowly as she enjoys the flavor, moaning with each stroke as she becomes more aroused, feeling my juices, flowing onto her chin.

Closing my eyes I lie back, embracing each precious stroke until my body catapults itself to climax, leaving me breathless and weak. Caiden moves to climb on top of me when I rise up, sitting at the edge of the four-post king bed, signaling her to continue standing. She looks at me curiously as I stand and move behind her, taking her arms, and extending them out to the bedposts. She grabs the posts, holding them tightly. I reach around her body, cupping her breasts in my hands, and caressing her nipples with my fingers, feeling them enlarge. She flexes, excited by my touch. I kiss and lick her back while she moans in enjoyment. Playing on her weakness, I glide my hand down the middle of her chest until I reach her waist, inserting my hand in her briefs, reaching her soft, well-manicured hairline. She widens her stance, allowing me full access to her Venus. I grasp it firmly, running my fingers in between her lips, toying with her clit. Feeling her moistness, I grow excited, pressing my body close to hers, letting her feel my breasts against her skin. Massaging her clit firmly, I feel her body tensing, wanting to release the post to consume me.

I whisper in her ear, "Do you want to let go?"

Caiden lowers her head, squeezing the posts tighter, nodding yes.

Moving in front of her, I am lost, gazing into her beautiful brown eyes with only the desire to pleasure her. My hand moves past her clit, reaching her Venus.

She flinches, bracing herself for the inevitable. There is peace in her eyes as she gazes at me, at my body. She leans in, prying my lips open, kissing me as she whispers, "My body is your playground!"

Aroused by her words, my fingers glide inside her. Her moans are enticing, driving me to continue gliding in and out of her feeling her juices flow down my fingers.

She murmurs, "Zoe, yes, yes!"

Sucking her breasts and licking her nipples as she moans fills me with lust. In the midst of Caiden's climax, I am pleasantly surprised by my own eruption. I shout her name over and over as I cum, enjoying this unexpected bonus.

Caiden cries, "Zoe, cum again with me? Zoe, I want to hear you. Oh, Zoe!"

Hearing her voice sends my body into convulsions as we climax together.

Caiden stares at me, remarking, "I love these eyes!"

I stare back, responding, "Caiden, I never want to be without you. I love you so much!"

She lifts me up, placing me in the bed, kissing me gently on my cheek. She smiles shyly, gazing deep into my soul in wonder. I ask what she is thinking. She explains that she never imagined being loved by anyone, much less by someone as remarkable as me.

I blush at her flattery, caressing her adorable face. "I love to see you happy, Caiden," I whisper.

"It's because of you, Zoe" she utters.

We lie huddled next to each other in bed when Caiden expresses she should go back to her room. I hold her close, desperately wanting her to stay. The past night was almost unbearable without her warm body and loving arms around me.

"Caiden, don't go!"

Caiden rolls her eyes, mumbling I'm spoiled as she grabs me, kissing me playfully on the neck.

I smirk, kissing her on the lips, teasing, "it's your fault."

She laughs, attempting to get out of bed, when I grab her quickly before she has time to escape, wrapping her arms around me, joking, "I have you now!"

She relents, replying, "You have always had me, Zoe." She squeezes me, kissing my cheek.

We look out at the ocean lit by moonlight, admiring its beauty. I kiss Caiden on the forearm and tell her good night. She holds me close as she kisses me on the neck, bidding me sweet dreams.

* * *

My eyes open from the glare of the sunlight. I feel happier than I have ever been. I reach for Caiden only to find a note and her wedding band on the pillow. "GM beautiful, hope you slept well. Meet you here at five."

Starving, I order breakfast before hopping into the shower. While eating, I have a moment to reflect on the past few days. They have been incredible. I think about our wedding, wishing our friends and family were here. I know we plan to have a formal wedding next summer, but it would be great to have everyone we love share in our happiness. Everything is moving so fast, we never gave it any thought. A knock at the door interrupts my thought. I look at the time, and it is a quarter to eleven, remembering my appointment with the personal shopper.

I open the door to Brianna and Abby, screaming, "Surprise, Mrs. Westphal!"

My mouth drops at the sight of them.

"You didn't think we would miss the most important day of your life now, did you, Zoe?" Brianna jokes as she hugs me.

Abby, smiling her cheerful smile, joins in, making it a group hug, saying, "Hi, Zoe, how are you?"

Still in awe, I manage an OMG and ask, "You guys, how? When? What?"

Brianna, laughing, replies, "Compliments of your soon-to-be husbian. I'm so glad to see you, Zoe. You look invigorated!"

Abby comments, "Zoe, you look so refreshed and happy!"

"Yes, I am very happy!" I respond.

Lea and her assistant, Marco, arrive at eleven sharp, carrying two wedding dresses. They are the dresses I saw one day while Brianna and I were out having a BFF day. I made a comment on how beautiful they were. She obviously mentioned it to Caiden. Lea informs me if neither is to my liking she can have one designed and ready in time for the wedding. I tell her that won't be necessary. After seeing the dresses again, my mind is made up. Brianna suggested I have one custom-made. I explain I had fallen in love with this particular dress as I hold it up to me in the mirror. Why go through all the trouble of having the perfect dress designed if one is already waiting for you? The dresses came with the accessories I had picked out that day, so I saw no need to take up any more of Lea and Marco's time, sending them on their way.

I want to spend the rest of the day with Brianna and Abby doing femme things. We spend half of our day at the spa, being treated like royalty, and the other half engaging in sunbathing on the beach. I asked Brianna if she knew what Caiden and Riley's plans were for the day. She tells me they are going deep-sea fishing, kayaking, or golf—she isn't sure which.

Sounds harmless enough, I think to myself.

I peek at my cell, hoping for a text from Caiden. I feel like a schoolgirl with her first crush. Brianna asks me if I am okay. I smile at her and nod.

We arrive back at the hotel around five, and still no word from Caiden.

The three of us head back to the suite, enjoying a bottle of wine together as we make plans for the big day. I'm standing on the terrace, gazing into the ocean, when my cell rings. I quickly answer, "Hi, handsome!"

"Hello, beautiful. How's your day going?" Caiden responds.

I explain it is a wonderful day, thanking her for the surprise. She tells me something has come up and she won't be back to the hotel until late tonight. I ask how her day is going. By the tone in her voice, I feel something is wrong. I'm disappointed but explain I understand and I'm looking forward to seeing her later this evening.

Still conscious of Caiden's tone, I am unaware of my latest visitors. Abby startles me, motioning me to come inside. To my surprise, I see my parents, Cassie, and Chloe. I end my call with Caiden in order to greet them.

Concerned for Caiden, my emotions get the best of me, and I immediately hug my father tightly, burying my head in his chest. He holds me close, asking if I'm okay. Still hugging him, I tell him I'm happy to see everyone. My mother is smiling as she hugs me, expressing how happy she is to be included our wedding. I give Cassie a warm hug and ask how she is doing. I feel Chloe tugging at me leg. I lift her up, giving her sweet kisses on her little cheeks. She is giggling as I raise her in the air, telling her how much her auntie misses her. Her tiny arms are extended, squeezing my nose. She looks around at Brianna and Abby curiously, smiling at them. She turns back to me, wrapping her little arms around my neck, squeezing. I begin to tear up as she hugs me. I glance at Cassie as she smiles at the two of us.

"Wow! She really misses her auntie," Cassie teases.

My father has a knack for knowing when something is bothering me. He asks, "Where is Caiden?"

I explain she is taking care of last-minute wedding arrangements and will meet us later this evening. My family retires to their suites to rest after their long flight. Before they leave, Brianna informs us we have dinner reservations at eight o'clock at a local restaurant not far from the resort. Brianna is playing with Chloe as she walks my parents and Cassie to the door.

Distracted by my thoughts, I walk out onto the terrace, gazing into the ocean. Abby follows, asking if I am okay. I look at her for a moment then ask if she knows anything about Caiden and Riley's reason for missing dinner? She stares out at the beach, remarking she has no idea what they are doing. Teasing, she assures me nothing sinister is in the works.

Seeing we have a moment alone, Abby takes the opportunity to let me know she doesn't want to see Caiden hurt, noting she witnessed firsthand the devastation and heartache Caiden endured when they first met. She explains Caiden struggled for two years to work through her pain, managing to live a semblance of a normal life, and she'd hate to see her progress diminish.

I respect her loyalty to Caiden and can understand her concerns. At the thought of family, I remark to Abby that I wish Rosemary could have been here to witness the ceremony. Suddenly, an idea emerges, and I recruit Abby to assist. Brianna strolls onto the balcony, admiring the view, asking how things are between Caiden and me.

I reply, "Everything is great, and we are happier than we have ever been."

Later that evening, we ride over in the limo to dinner. Even though Caiden and Riley aren't present, we have a festive evening. I'm happy to have my family and friends here. During the course of dinner, Brianna asks what prompted the quick nuptials.

I reply, "We love each other and want to marry as soon as possible."

She looks at Abby then at me, telling me she understands we are in love but doesn't understand the rush. She points out we've only recently gotten back together and reminds me Caiden has barely had time to mourn her mother's passing. I didn't want to ruin a lovely dinner, so I advise Brianna we can discuss this later back at the resort. After some thought, she smiles back at me in agreement. We continue our dinner and return to the resort around eleven o'clock. My parents and Cassie go to their suites while Brianna, Abby, and I return to mine.

Bothered by Brianna's sudden resistance to our wedding, I ask Abby to give us a moment.

"Brianna, what is, going on with you? I thought you are happy for us?" I comment.

She raises her concerns, noting she didn't want to see either of us get hurt. She reminds me of how hurt Caiden was the first time and says how she didn't want to see Caiden go through that again.

I think, *She and Abby must have had one hell of a conversation on the flight over.* I assure Brianna I am not the same person I was two years ago and have no intention on breaking Caiden's heart, reminding her Caiden has forgiven me. Obviously by her remarks, she hasn't.

"I'm curious, Zoe. Four years ago, your parents threatened to cut you out of their lives if you stayed with Caiden. Now, all of a sudden, they love the idea. I'm confused about the whole, thing," she adds.

"Brianna, my parents realized they were wrong about Caiden! Where is this coming from?" I ask in frustration.

She admits she thinks we are moving way to fast. I can see I will not be able to convince her we are making the best decision for us, so I ask she just be happy for us and let us live our lives.

Brianna is still troubled by my parent's acceptance, continuing her inquisition into their sudden change of heart. Frustrated and tired, I share with her how my suicide attempt affected them deeply once they found out. They felt partly responsible, believing their decisions drove me over the edge. I shared that after Caiden left, I cut myself off from my parents, blaming them for everything.

One day, my father called, asking if I would meet him and my mother to talk. He said they missed me and wanted to work on rebuilding our relationship. My parents came by my place over five months ago. We had a long conversation about my sexuality, the reason I cut them off, and Caiden. I gave my parents a choice to either accept the fact I am homosexual or never see me again. I finally stood up to them because I was tired of living my life for everyone else.

Brianna looks at me with tears in her eyes, remarking she had no idea. She apologizes for her earlier comments, saying she misjudged me without knowing all the facts.

Noticing it is midnight, I decide to text Caiden, hoping for a response. After saying good night to Brianna and Abby, I lie in bed, restless. I open the terrace door, listening to the sounds of the sea until I fall asleep.

CHAPTER NINETEEN

Reluctance

It's ten in the morning as I sit in the hotel restaurant eating breakfast as I wait for Caiden to come down. I look out at the ocean, thinking, *What a romantic place to get married.* I am happy for Caiden and Zoe, but I have reservations. I plan on discussing them with Caiden on our excursion today. I think it will do my friend some good to get some distance from Zoe. I want to make sure she has a clear perspective on her decision to marry Zoe so quickly. Zoe makes Caiden happy; however, I am concerned they are moving entirely too fast into marriage. Just a few weeks ago, Caiden stood in front of reporters, claiming she couldn't get married until the laws in Texas acknowledges same-sex marriage. I've watched my friend struggle trying to get over Zoe. She was damn near broken behind a woman too ashamed to be seen with her.

I find it hard to believe out of nowhere Zoe has suddenly found herself. Considering the state of her company, I'd hate to think she is marrying Caiden for financial gain. She doesn't appear to be the type. Nonetheless, it's my job to protect Caiden's interests. I'm sure she won't be thrilled when she finds out I took the liberty of investigating Zoe's affairs. Caiden may not be able to see past her "beautiful blues," but they don't affect me. Caiden takes one look at her, and it's as if the two years of suffering never existed. I love my friend, but she can be impulsive and make irrational decisions. I'm afraid when it comes to Zoe, she doesn't think at all. It's as though she is bewitched. I've never seen her like this with a woman. Caiden is right when she says she can't resist Zoe's charm.

I've known Caiden for the past two years and never have I seen her so whipped. Back home, Caiden is a player extraordinaire. Her cool demeanor and swag hold women defenseless against her easy smile and charm. They will do anything she asks. Hell, even after she hooked up with Rheia, she still had women falling at her feet. She stays guarded, avoiding a serious relationship, allowing no one to get to close. I'm not sure how Rheia managed to stay for as long as she did. Maybe because she insisted they wait a year to have sex. I'll give it to my friend—she never minced words or played games with women. The Caiden I know seems to have vanished, leaving me wondering if one woman really will be enough for her.

Why would a mega-rich, smart, good-looking gay woman want to settle down with one woman? Caiden can be with a different woman every night of the week. She's peculiar and difficult to interpret. The crazy thing is Caiden has dated a lot of women but never seems sexually interested. I used to wonder if something is seriously wrong with her. Sex isn't her endgame. Hell, it's not even a bleep on her radar except when it comes to Zoe. Imagine my surprise when I arrive in Texas to Zoe and her going at it damn near 24-7. Abby and I were in complete shock. Seriously, our Caiden having sexual relations on a regular basis? No freaking way! Abby and I had a good laugh for sure.

I finish my OJ when Caiden enters the restaurant. I wave her over to my table. As she approaches, I stand to give her a firm handshake when she grabs me and hugs, greeting me as though we had not seen each other in years. I honestly don't know what to make of her behavior. She's not normally a hugger. I took the liberty of ordering one of her favorite power breakfasts: oatmeal, nine-grain toast, one egg over medium, and a glass each of milk and OJ. She's a stickler when it comes to her health regimen. I don't know of anyone more disciplined when it comes to eating clean and staying fit. I watch Caiden inhale her breakfast, joking she must have had an intense workout. She laughs, agreeing it was very intense.

Across the restaurant, I notice two very attractive women siting a few tables from us. They look like islanders, both with tan, dark skin and wavy brown hair. One has green eyes; the other, hazel. They are smiling at us, so I give them a friendly wave. Caiden notices me staring and turns to see the two women at the table. They giggle at her and wave. She smiles, waving hello, then quickly turns her attention to me. Amazing how indifferent she is to their flirting, instead asking how things are going in Austin. I tell her the club is a huge success, and her pet project for Zoe will be complete within a day or two. She seems pleased by the news as she moves on to inquire about Jaylon.

She is curious to know if Jaylon is going to pose a problem regarding the wedding. I assure her the situation with Jaylon is under control, noting she is attending therapy sessions regularly, and according to her doctor, she is making tremendous strides. She looks at me with concern, asking how the IA investigation is going. I explain that unfortunately, without Rheia's testimony, there is little IA can do. Not to mention, Jaylon has been working with the feds on a case for over two years. Turns out her partner, Detective Sawyer, is a federal agent posing as an APD Detective. She was "assigned" to Jaylon. I have yet to determine the object of their investigation. Whoever it is, the feds must want pretty bad to overlook all the corruption Jaylon has perpetrated.

"Riley, your talent has no bounds. Only you can break into the FBI database undetected," she comments. I'm surprised she is taking the news well. I thought for sure she'd be pissed Jaylon is making a clean getaway. She stares at me, remarking, "Basically Jaylon is untouchable?"

I reply with discontent, "Yes, for now it appears she has amnesty."

Caiden looks somewhat relieved at the thought. She sits back in her seat, staring out into the ocean.

As I am about to redirect her thoughts, one of the young women from earlier approaches us, saying, "Excuse me, but my friend and I would like to invite you to a party we are having tonight not far from here." She grabs my cell, typing in her name and address.

I thank her for the invite, noting we will make every effort to be there this evening. She looks at me, smiling, then over at Caiden still dwelling over the news about Jaylon. I lightly kick her leg under the table to snap her out of her daze.

She looks at me then at the young woman, clueless to what has transpired. Caiden, half-smiling at the young woman, extends her hand to greet her, saying, "Aloha, I am Caiden, and this is Riley."

She introduces herself while shaking Caiden's hand. "Aloha, I am Kai, and my friend over there is Melia. Hope you two can make it tonight."

As she walks off, Caiden looks at me for an explanation. I laugh as I explain about the party as she finishes her glass of milk.

Aside from the news about Jaylon, Caiden is in good spirits, even laughing. I ask her again about going to the party Kai invited us to. She looks at me, reminding me we have dinner reservations with my girlfriend, her fiancée, and soon-to-be in-laws, or did I forget?

I explain the reservations are for eight. We can have dinner then go to the party. I attempt to convince her she only has a few nights of freedom remaining. What better way to enjoy it? I stress to her that I need a break from Brianna and Abby. They are driving me nuts with constant girl talk. It will be nice to have some stud time with Caiden. We haven't hung out since we've been in Texas. I miss the old times when the two of us would go out and party until the wee hours of the morning. I act like a five-year-old, begging Caiden to go to the party. She doesn't realize it, but she needs a break from Zoe.

Oddly enough, it's been two hours, and Zoe hasn't made contact with Caiden. I wonder if Brianna had a chance to discuss her concerns about our wedding.

After breakfast, we hop in the jeep, heading to the marina to rent a speedboat for a few hours. I think it will be a good place for us to talk without interruption. Afterward, we are going to the beach to enjoy this great sunny seventy-six-degree weather and put back a few cocktails.

Once we leave the marina, we go out about five miles from shore and drop anchor. We pop open a couple of beers and sit back, floating in the ocean, enjoying the solitude. I ask Caiden if she and I can have a candid conversation. Looking at me curiously, wondering what I want to discuss, Caiden places her beer in a cup holder. She eyes me, reaching for a bottle of water, waiting for me to speak. I get straight to the point, stressing I think she is rushing into this marriage. I confess that, against her wishes, I had done some research on Zoe and her father's business. Caiden's jaws tighten as she prepares to blast me for my insubordination.

I interject, requesting she hear me out before she fires me. "Look, Caiden, I know you asked me not to look into Zoe's affairs, but I'm worried about you. You have been acting weird ever since we came to Austin. I think you are in overdrive when it comes to this wedding."

Caiden glares at me as she speaks. "Riley, you had no right checking up on Zoe or her family's affairs. What gives you the right to invade their lives, especially when I distinctly ordered you not to?"

I see quickly this isn't going as planned. "Caiden, I'm sorry, but ever since Bri—" I stop my sentence, not wanting to bring up Brianna's name.

Caiden asks, "What did Brianna tell you, Riley?"

I look out into the ocean, trying to gather my thoughts. Caiden asks again firmly.

"Caiden, look, I am trying to look out for your best interests since you don't seem to be doing a good job of it. Zoe has you wrapped around her finger. For two years, I watched you struggle to get over her. The minute you hit Austin, you are back under her spell," I reply.

"Riley, what in hell are you talking about? Do you think for one fucking second I'm not in control of my life? You should know me better than that, Riley! I'm beginning to wonder if you even know me at all!" she yells.

"Caiden, why are you and Zoe in a rush to get married?" I ask.

"Riley, how about we love each other? I have waited my entire adult life to be with Zoe. I don't want to wait any longer. Is that so difficult a concept for you to understand?" she asks.

I point out she is not acting like herself, spoiling the shit out of Zoe. "I've never seen you act like this. Caiden, I'm curious about the timing, man. Come on, think about it. You've shared with me all the hurtful things Zoe did to you. On top of all that, the relationship she had with your fucking lunatic-ass sister! You expect a sane person to believe she has done a one-eighty and everything is cool? What the fuck, Caiden? If any other woman would have done this shit to you, they'd be in the fucking wind! Have you even mourned your mother's passing?" I ask.

Caiden moves toward me, getting in my face, growling, "Riley, this is none of your damn business. I am going to marry Zoe whether you or anyone else likes it or not. Damn it, Riley, don't you trust me?" Caiden looks me dead in the eye as she asks.

"Of course, I trust you, Caiden, but—"

She interrupts. "But nothing! Riley, I appreciate your concern. Trust me, I know what I am doing. I have never wanted any woman except Zoe. It's been this way since I first fell in love with her. I know she has done some seemingly unforgiveable things, but I have forgiven her."

I remind Caiden she has been gone for the past two years, so how would she know Zoe has changed?

Caiden sits back down on the bench as we float in the Pacific, quiet for a few moments. I look over at her, watching her gaze into the sea, looking hurt and disappointed. I am not sure what to say, so I sit in silence. Caiden turns to look at me and begins to explain that for the past two years, when she told us she was going out of town for business, she returned to Austin to visit with her mother and to check on Zoe. She let me in on a little secret, telling me she bought the condo next door to Zoe's. She kept tabs on her and Jaylon, noting it killed her to see them grow close.

I ask her why she never intervened if she loved Zoe so much. She says it would have made things more complicated. She didn't want that for Zoe, expressing she didn't leave Austin to get over Zoe. She left Austin in order for Zoe to get over her. She knew she would always love Zoe and running away wasn't going to change how she felt. Zoe was confused about her sexuality, her family, her friends, and it was too much for her to handle. Caiden felt that if she left, Zoe could sort things out clearly without feeling like she had to choose a side. Caiden needed Zoe to stand up for herself and figure out what she wanted without coercion from her.

Zoe's family, Jaylon, and even her friends were causing her enough grief. She didn't want to add to it. She said it was the most challenging thing she'd ever done in her life. Imagine watching the woman you love from a distance go through heartbreak, the loss of her child, and worst of all, try to commit suicide.

I ask Caiden if she was there when Zoe attempted to take her own life. She admitted she witnessed everything from her tablet while she was next door.

Once Caiden realized what Zoe had done, she went into her apartment to help her. She sent a text to Jaylon from Zoe's phone, knowing she would be there in an instant. Caiden then called 911 to report the incident so they would send an ambulance right away. She said Zoe doesn't remember, but Caiden took her into the bathroom and made her throw up the majority of pills. Caiden says she was frantic, praying to God for Zoe to be okay. Once Jaylon arrived, she hid in the guest bedroom closet until the coast was clear. Jaylon found Zoe in the bathroom before the ambulance arrived.

There is a lot I didn't know about my friend. She continues to share how Zoe's father came to her about a year ago, asking for money. He was near bankruptcy, about to lose his law practice. He had squandered all his money from Payne Corp and his law firm gambling. He sold all his shares to help pay off some of his gambling debts. Mr. Payne had too much pride to ask Zoe for help. His friends and business partners weren't willing to give him any financial assistance. He turned to Caiden as a last resort.

Caiden explains Mr. Payne offered to give her and Zoe his blessing if she would loan him the money to save his law firm.

It was all he had left after selling his stock in Payne Corp. After careful consideration, Caiden loaned Mr. Payne $2 million dollars—with stipulations, of course.

I am proud of my friend for how she handled the situation. She told Mr. Payne, "I would love to have you and your wife's blessing more than anything, but I won't buy it." She gave him the money because she didn't want to see his family destroyed by his addiction. Caiden instructed him to seek help for his addiction, and only then would she loan him the money. Caiden made it clear Zoe is never to know about their arrangement. Of course, he agreed and got professional help. In the meanwhile, Caiden hired a team of consultants and accountants to go in and help restructure, rebrand, and rebuild his law firm into the successful company it is today.

I am beginning to understand through Caiden's eyes what true love means. It's not all good all the time. My friend has sacrificed so much to protect the woman she loves. I don't know if I could have the courage to "let go and let God," as Caiden preaches all the time. I sit quietly, feeling ashamed of myself, unable to look at Caiden.

She sits next to me, remarking, "Riley, when you fall in love you will make sacrifices you never thought you'd make. You'll do things you never thought you'd do. At the end of the day, you realize it's all worth. Riley, I believe this is God's plan for me: to help people I love."

It is seven o'clock when we head back to the marina. I apologize to Caiden for being so hasty in my judgment and thank her for her candor.

She smiles at me at me, joking, "Do you still want me to postpone the wedding?"

I smile at her, punching her in the arm, replying, "After what you just shared, there is no way I'm letting you cancel this wedding!"

We hop back in the jeep and decide to stop for bite to eat. Though disappointed, we didn't get to hang out on the beach, I am happy Caiden and I got a chance to share an intimate moment. She is opening my eyes, showing me what real love looks like. If not for

Caiden, I don't think I would recognize love at all. I am grateful to have her as my friend.

Caiden and I forget about the time as I put back a few beers. By the time we realize it is nearing ten o'clock in the evening, Caiden pays our bar tab and suggests we head back to the hotel.

Aware of my drunkenness, she takes the keys and drives us back safely. I can barely keep my eyes open, and feeling sick to my stomach, I instruct Caiden to pull over. The bumpy ride from the jeep is more than my stomach can bear. Before I could even get out, I uncontrollably begin to vomit on the side of the road. My head is pounding, and I feel like I want to pass out. I hear Caiden, laughing at me in the background, teasing me. I finish discharging the excess alcohol out of my system, and we continue back to the hotel. I'm wondering how to explain this to Brianna. She hates it when I get like this.

At the hotel, Caiden has to practically carry me to my room. I am disoriented, barely able to remain conscious. I remember Caiden grabbing my wallet for the room key. Before Caiden could get my key, Brianna opens the door. Caiden escorts me to the bed, leaving me in Brianna's care. I hear Brianna, blasting Caiden for allowing me to get so drunk. I'm not worried about Brianna chastising Caiden. She's used to Brianna's wrath and is quite good at deflecting it. Caiden slaps me on the leg, wishing both of us a good night as she heads out of our room.

CHAPTER TWENTY

Admission

On my way back to my suite, I hear a child crying. I notice the sound is coming from Cassie's room. I tap softly on the door, waiting a few moments until Irene, Cassie's nanny, answers. Looking tired and holding a fussy Chloe in her arms, she apologizes for the noise. I assume she thinks I am here because I have been disturbed. I explain that no apology is needed. I was passing by and heard a baby crying. Chloe is reaching for me, anxious to be free from Irene. I look at Irene for permission to hold her. She eagerly passes Chloe into my arms. Cassie is in the background and asks Irene who is at the door. Irene replies, "Ms. Westphal, Ms. Payne."

Cassie insists I come in. Upon entering, I explain I didn't mean to disturb them. I just heard Chloe crying and wanted to check if everything is all right. Cassie, looking tired as well, explains Chloe has been unusually fussy this evening. I chuckle as I hold her, bouncing her up and down, hoping to calm her. She stops crying and begins to playfully plant her fingers on my face, repeating my name over and over.

Cassie smiles, seeing Chloe's mood change, remarking, "You would think she is your child, the way she interacts with you."

I laugh at her comment, still playing with Chloe.

They both appear exhausted, so I offer to take Chloe for a stroll on the beach to give them a break. Cassie looks at me, then at

Chloe giggling in my arms, and agrees. On the way out, I promise to take good care of her.

* * *

"It's past midnight, little one. You are a little night owl, aren't you?" I tease.

Chloe and I find a nice spot in the sand not far from my suite. I point toward the water's edge, noticing a huge turtle moving across the soft sand under the moonlit sky. Chloe's little eyes follow my finger, and upon seeing the turtle, she lets out a high-pitched scream. She grabs my arm in fear of the huge creature. I pick her up and calmly explain the turtle is not going to hurt her. Once she is convinced, she releases her grip and eyes the turtle cautiously.

She says, "Big turtle, Caiden! *Big* turtle!"

I laugh at her in amazement and reply, "Yes, Chloe, very big turtle."

Chloe is nestled in my arms while we watch the creature slowly progress on its journey. After a few minutes, I realize Chloe has fallen asleep. I didn't want to wake her, so I sit holding her, admiring the beautiful night sky.

I'm startled by the sound of footsteps drawing near when I hear a soft voice whisper, "Amazing view?" I smile, recognizing Zoe's voice.

She smiles when she sees Chloe in my lap and takes a seat next to me. I ask the time, not realizing it's near one o'clock in the morning. I apologize for missing dinner, explaining time had gotten away from Riley and me. Zoe accepts my apology without question, nudging me, teasing she hopes this won't be a habit. She is joking, but I can see in her eyes she is troubled. I ask if everything is all right. She sighs as she looks up into the starry sky. I can't help but notice how beautiful she looks under the moonlight.

I remark, "Zoe, I had a very interesting conversation with Riley today. I can only assume you had the same with Brianna and Abby. Do you think we are rushing into this marriage?"

She turns to look at me, replying, "Caiden, despite our friends' concerns, I don't think we are rushing into anything. We love each other. By all accounts, we have wasted enough time."

I let out a deep sigh of relief, receiving the answer I hoped for.

After reflecting on my conversation with Riley, I realize it is time to lay all my cards on the table. I need to confess my actions over the past two years. Ashamed, I look toward the ground, telling Zoe before we say "I do" there are some things she needs to know. She caresses my back for comfort, seeing the difficulty I am having, trying to form the words. A chilly breeze crosses us, interrupting my thoughts. I look down at Chloe, realizing I should take her inside before she gets sick. Signaling to Zoe, we rise to get Chloe out of the cool air. Zoe reaches for Chloe, resting the little girl's head against her shoulder. I smile at them, daydreaming what it would be like if Chloe were our daughter. I place my arm around Zoe's waist as we walk side by side to deliver Little Blue Eyes to her mother. After placing Chloe in her bed, Zoe gently kisses her on the forehead. She stares down at Chloe with wonderment in her eyes. I know how badly she wants a child of her own. I kiss Chloe goodnight then turn to Zoe, noting the change in her toward Chloe.

After we leave Cassie's room, Zoe takes my hand and intertwines our fingers, squeezing gently. Her head is down as we walk to our suite. I squeeze her hand, feeling she is having a moment of sadness, thinking about the child she lost.

We walk onto our terrace, inhaling the island air. Nervous, I run my fingers through my dreads, anxious of how Zoe will react to my transgressions. I clear my throat as she eyes me carefully, waiting for the ball to drop. Suddenly, I don't know where to begin. I think to myself, *I don't want any secrets between us.* How can I tell her the truth and not bring her father into it? I feel her hand caress my face, assuring me everything will be fine.

She says, "Caiden, nothing you tell me will make me love you any less. Everyone has secrets."

I begin to describe my activities over the last two years, explaining I purchased the condo next to hers, keeping an eye on her. I watched the relationship between her and Jaylon develop and progress. I explain I was there the night she attempted suicide and how I took her in the bathroom to make her expel the pills she had taken. I inform her I was the one who texted Jaylon from her phone and made the 911 call. I look at her for a moment to measure her reaction.

She stands next to me, looking out at the water, expressionless for a few moments then asks, "Why, Caiden? Why would you watch me all that time and say nothing! I don't understand. What type of person claims to love someone then does something like that? Caiden this is . . . this is crazy!"

My confession is upsetting. I continue to explain that I know my actions were immoral—hell, even irrational. I need her to understand that at the time, I was devastated at losing her. This was my way of holding on to her. She needed time to sort her life out. "Zoe, I never meant to hurt you. I admit it sounds insane, but it was the only way I could be close to you without being hurt by you." I remind her that she made it clear she didn't want me. We were over. I couldn't accept that. Hell, I didn't believe for a second she ever stopped loving me.

"Caiden, you hypocrite! You blast Jaylon for doing the exact same thing! You invade my privacy, you stalk me, and you expect me to believe it is out of love! Caiden, do you realize how all this sounds?" she yells.

"Yes, Zoe, I know how this sounds. I didn't know what else to do. I tried calling and texting you, but you never responded. I freaked out. I'm sorry, but you left me no choice. I couldn't let you go!" I yell in frustration then wait impatiently for her to speak.

She stands in silence, glaring at me with her arms folded. She points to the door and screams, "Get out! I can't believe you, Caiden. Please just leave."

I move to grab her, but she backs away from me again, ordering me to leave her alone. Angry and hurt, I storm out of her room, slamming the door behind me. In the hall, I pace back and forth, contemplating my next move, growing increasingly aggravated. Trying to reason with Zoe is futile at this moment. My chest begins to tighten as my blood boils. I need to get away before I lose control.

How could she react this way? Maybe Riley is right. Zoe isn't the woman I think she is. After all she has put me through, she has some fucking nerve. What have I done? Unwanted thoughts run through my mind. How dare she compare me to that asshole Jaylon! I wasn't the one who impregnated her—no, who raped her! I wasn't the one who manipulated everything so she would fall in love with me! Yet she can forgive that bastard so easily. I would lay down my life for her, and this is how she treats me? She tossed me away once. Now at the first sign I do something wrong, she readily tosses me away again. She can't possibly love me, kicking me out like that. How can we solve our problems if we can't even talk to each other?

My rage continues to build toward her. This is not what I want. How did we get here? I wandered a couple of miles away from the hotel, on the beach. Sitting on a fallen tree, I stare into the ocean, wondering, why even try to be honest? I have made so many sacrifices to be with her, to make her happy. I am tired of thinking, tired of trying to do the right thing, tired of being hurt. Nothing good seems to come out of it.

Not knowing what else to do, I drop to my knees in prayer, asking God to carry me because I am too weak to carry myself. Whatever plan he has for me, I will follow without question. I only ask for the wisdom to see the light of the path I am to follow. I ask for forgiveness for my sins and the courage to forgive those who have sinned against me.

My entire life begins to flash before me as if I were having an out-of-body experience. My life from this perspective is clear and void of bias. I have a vision of my mother standing in front of me in a white dress, with the ocean breeze blowing her hair. She is much younger, maybe in her twenties. She smiles at me, holding out her arms to give me a hug. I stand, moving toward her, when she stops me from coming any closer, saying, "Caiden, don't give up. It will all work out, I promise."

I don't know if I am hallucinating or dreaming, but seeing her in front of me feels real. I move to ask a question when she fades away like mist.

"Mom, don't leave. I need you!" I scream into the heavens.

I drop back to my knees, staring up in the sky, hoping to catch a glimpse of her beautiful face. I lie on the sand as tears flow down my cheeks uncontrollably, realizing how much I miss Rose. I spend the night dreaming of her, wishing she were here to comfort me.

The sounds of waves, crashing against the rocks wake me from my sleep. Glancing at my watch, I see it is ten thirty in the morning. I stretch, noticing unfamiliar surroundings. Quickly realizing I had fallen asleep on the beach, I rise and dust myself off, beginning my trek back to the hotel. As I reach the road, I see a jeep in the distance coming toward me. I laugh, thinking I can always count on Riley to look out for me.

As the jeep nears, I see Riley on the passenger side. I recognize the driver and third passenger. *What the fuck!* I scream in my head. I am livid at the sight of Jaylon and Ericka in the jeep as they park in front of me. I glare at Riley as she exits the vehicle, walking toward me. Jaylon and Erika are about to get out when I stop them.

Jaylon, with a fucked-up grin on her face, fails to listen, getting out, remarking, "Caiden, I don't have time for your bullshit."

Erika, hopping out of the back, utters to Jaylon, "Don't start this sibling rivalry shit! That's not why we are here."

Riley lifts her head, motioning for her and me to take a walk. She looks back at them, signaling to give us a minute.

We walk to the water's edge out of earshot.

"Why are they here, Riley?" I ask through gritted teeth.

"Caiden, I think I should let your sister explain."

Angrily, I bark, "I didn't ask my fucking sister, Riley. I am asking you again! Why are they here?"

Frustrated with me, Riley sighs then asks, "Have you been here all night?"

I snap, "Riley, this is my last time asking. What are they doing in Hawaii?"

She clears her throat to speak "Zoe is freaking," handing me her cell, advising I should give her a call. I push the phone away, not wanting to deal with Zoe right now.

Erika approaches, apologizing for interrupting, stating, "Caiden, we are not here to cause trouble. Jaylon has something important to discuss with you."

I reply flippantly, "Really, Erika! Are you fucking serious! You two flew all the way to Hawaii because Jaylon has something important to discuss! Three words, Erika: *cell-fucking-phone*!"

She half-laughs, irritated at my remark, replying, "*No shit*, smart-ass. You self-absorbed, arrogant little prick!"

"Detective, pulling the gloves off early this morning, I see!" I reply angrily.

Erika leaps toward me as Riley quickly stops her in her tracks. I order Riley to release her. If she wants a fight, I will give her one. By now, Jaylon has crept her way over to us. She stands in front of me, looking me up and down. It looks like she is struggling to find the words to speak, rubbing the back of her neck.

After some time, she exclaims, "Caiden, quit being so fucking stubborn and listen! I'm not here to mess up your little wedding plans. I'm here . . . I'm here because . . . I'm here because you are the only fucking family I have left. As much as I . . . I . . . I, um, hate to admit it, I fucking care about you! Happy now, Erika? I've admitted it!"

I begin to clap my hands slowly, chuckling at Jaylon, remarking, "Bravo, bravo! Excellent performance, Jaylon, simply excellent. Wouldn't you agree, Riley?"

Jaylon, frustrated, yells, "You see, Erika! I told you she wouldn't believe me!"

Erika intervenes, explaining Jaylon is telling the truth. She stresses that over the past few weeks, Jaylon has made extraordinary progress in therapy. She looks me in the eye, explaining it took a lot of courage for Jaylon to come here to make amends. She realizes it is difficult for me to believe, pleading with me to hear her out. I glance at Riley as she stands next to Jaylon, wondering if she believes this bullshit. Her expression is unreadable. I gauge Erika to determine if she is sincere. I glance at Jaylon. She is standing with her head down as if ashamed to look at me. I don't need this shit right now. I look back at Erika inquisitively, waiting for the ball to drop. Everyone is quiet. All you hear is the sounds of the ocean.

Jaylon lifts her head slightly, looking at me. In a low voice, she asks, "Caiden, can we go somewhere and talk without fighting, please?"

I'm not sure what the hell to think. Unconvinced of her sincerity, I quietly walk to the jeep and take a seat. They soon follow as Riley drives us back to the hotel. I get out not, uttering a word, and head to my suite.

Heading straight for the shower, I am stopped by my reflection in the mirror. I look like a homeless person, covered in white sand and smelling like I hadn't bathed in a week. I undress quickly, jumping into the shower. My skin welcomes the soothing relief of hot water. The sand falls to the marble floor, into the drain, as I submerge my head under the showerhead. I find myself wishing Zoe were here. My thoughts turn to Jaylon, wondering what she is planning. I don't believe her or Erika for a second. Jaylon hates me too much to want to reconcile our relationship. She said it herself: if I marry Zoe, there is no relationship to salvage.

A subtle knock is coming from bathroom door. I hear Zoe's voice asking if she can come in.

"Come in, please," I answer.

I rinse the soap from my eyes and stick my head out when I see Zoe. Her eyes are full of sadness. I shyly smile at her, motioning her to enter the shower. She rushes in, fully clothed, wrapping her arms around my neck, resting her head against my chest. I'm glad to have her in my embrace. I hold her close to me as the water continues flowing down my back.

Zoe cries, "Caiden, I'm sorry for the way I reacted last night. After you left, I realized I was wrong to shut you out. I thought I had lost you for good."

After her apology, I am chastised for making her worry. I turn the shower off and reach for my towel, wrapping it around my waist as I step out of the shower. She removes her wet clothing, and I toss her a towel to dry off. I look at her, perplexed, inquiring, "You still want to marry me after last night?"

Her head tilts and her eyes narrow as she replies, "Caiden, why would you think I don't want to marry you?"

I reply "I thought . . . I thought . . . You were so angry last night, I thought . . ."

She interjects, "Caiden, I was upset, shocked even. I didn't want to argue. I overreacted."

She explained we are going to have arguments, even have heated debates, but it doesn't mean she loves me any less. She asks me, does our past relationship have anything to do with how I feel? Terrified of losing her, I can't voice my fear aloud. The very thought makes my chest tighten. She walks up to me, asking if I am deliberately trying to sabotage our relationship.

Smirking, I answer, "Perhaps I am."

She jokingly punches me in the stomach. I fall to the ground, pretending to be wounded, pleading for her not to strike me again. She laughs as she sits beside me on the floor.

Zoe's eyes turn bittersweet as she takes my hand in hers, saying, "Caiden, I love you. You are the best thing to ever happen to me. Can you find it in your heart to believe in me?" Exhaling

I turn toward her, expressing my fear of losing her. She shares she has the same fear because of her mistakes.

I impress upon her that I will pour all I have into making our marriage a success. I admit to being spoiled and having a lot to learn about relationships. With all our secrets out in the open, we have a chance to begin anew if we leave the past in the past. I kiss her gently on the lips, stating we have a lot to do before our wedding tomorrow. She snuggles up to me, asking if we can sit here for a while, that after last night, she is afraid to let me out of her sight. I tease, noting once we are married there will be days she will welcome the day we have time apart. She giggles then asks if we are okay. I assure her we will have a long and happy marriage. She inquires how I can be so confident. I smile at her, sharing it's because my mother has assured me on numerous occasions.

I learn Jaylon stopped by earlier this morning to speak with Zoe. They had a long, in-depth conversation, ending with Jaylon apologizing and admitting to masterminding the plan to keep us apart. I am surprised how readily Zoe forgave her. She believes Jaylon is remorseful, wanting to make up for all the horrible things she's done. She's convinced Jaylon wants to work on rebuilding a friendship with her and make amends with me. I, on the other hand, am not convinced Jaylon is being completely honest about her intentions. Nonetheless, I continue to have faith she will turn her life around. Zoe is curious if I plan to allow her and Erika at our wedding. Everything is steamrolling, and I've not given it any thought. My sister and I have a long history of animosity toward each other. It's difficult to comprehend she wants a relationship with me now.

This day is flying by as I notice it's already one o'clock in the afternoon. I contact the concierge, confirming our wedding bands have been delivered on schedule. Next, I consult with the pastor regarding the ceremony. In the midst of planning, a message from Riley comes in requesting I meet her, Erika, and Jaylon in an hour at the hotel bar. Before I could respond to Riley, Brianna enters, giving me a quick kiss on the cheek while rushing Zoe to get ready. I'm quickly ushered out of our bedroom when I see Abby is standing in the living quarters. Delighted to see her, I embrace her warmly, lifting her off the ground. She laughs at me and asks if I am ready for tomorrow. I smile with confidence, assuring her I have never been more ready for anything in my life. She stands, smiling, remarking how happy I look.

I am about to reply when Brianna walks back into the living area, explaining she also had a talk with Jaylon. I see my sister is making her rounds. Naturally, I inquired. She too surprises me, stating she honestly believes Jaylon is sincere in her intentions. She added that Jaylon wants to attend the wedding. I look at her blankly, ignoring her last comment.

Short on time, I dash into the bedroom to throw on a pair of linen pants, sneakers, and tee as I get ready to meet Riley.

Zoe pulls me close, giving me a long and passionate kiss before I leave, commenting, "See you at noon tomorrow, Mr. Westphal. Please be careful today."

I smile at her, saying, "I can't wait. You and the girls enjoy your day. Abby, Brianna, Zoe, behave. Tonight is the bachelorette party correct?"

Brianna locks arms with me, making me promise not to pull a disappearing act. I tease that unless I'm kidnapped, I'll be there. I kiss her on the cheek, saying thank you for the concern.

Zoe seems reluctant for me to leave. I ask what's wrong. She shakes her head then hugs me tightly. Abby chimes in, hinting I'm in for a wild night. I chuckle as I shake my head, not wanting to put the thought of other women in Zoe's mind.

Zoe sees my smirk and smugly comments, "Look, but don't touch."

I ask, joking, "Touch just one?"

She pats me softly on the face, saying, "Careful, Westphal! Don't push your luck!"

I reach for the door and hear Zoe, "I know it is a lot to ask, but please give Jaylon a chance! What is the worst that can happen?"

Without, looking back I remark, "I will pray on it, Zoe. Is that good enough for now?"

She answers "It's a good place to start."

CHAPTER TWENTY-ONE

Sister's Keeper

Heading toward the lobby, I am stopped by Robert and Carolyn. "Good morning, Caiden. We are glad we ran into you. Do you have a few minutes? There is something we need to discuss with you before the ceremony tomorrow."

I bid them both a good morning and ask if they would give me a second. I text Riley, letting her know I am tied up and would be down shortly.

"Robert, Carolyn, so good to see you both!" I state.

Robert looks over at Carolyn, and she looks at me, remarking, "It is such a beautiful day. Why don't we take a stroll and chat for a bit?"

I gaze at Carolyn, admiring how attractive she is for an older woman in her early fifties. She has the same shoulder-length brunette hair as Zoe with shades of gray peeking through. Her build is proportionate to her five feet six frame, weighing around 160 pounds. If she were younger and slightly slimmer, she would be the spitting image of Zoe.

Looking at her takes me back to when Zoe use to be self-conscious about her weight. She worked extremely hard, losing over fifty pounds. She used to get so frustrated when people eyed us in public, swearing it was because of weight, commenting we didn't look as if we belonged together. I would joke, saying everyone was jealous of me because I had the most beautiful girl in the world. She couldn't be persuaded, believing it had everything to do with her being full-figured. I brushed it off to people being ignorant with their own self-esteem issues. It was two years into our relationship when she began her battle with weight gain. She was hard on herself, and it began to interfere with our relationship. She became jealous and possessive, accusing me of cheating on her. She went so far as to accuse me of sleeping with Brianna behind her back. I told her it was all in her head, but it eventually added more problems to our relationship.

"Caiden! Caiden did you hear me?" I snap out of my daze and reply to Carolyn, "I'm sorry, Carolyn. What were you saying?"

She begins to explain Robert confessed his gambling addiction to her. He told her about losing his share of Payne Corp. He added he would have lost his law firm had I not come to his aid. Robert confessed everything, even the proposition he made to me if I helped him. I glance over at Robert then back at Carolyn, not knowing how to respond. She calmly continues, reminding me she and her husband had not been kind to me in the past.

Matter of fact, they were quite ruthless in their efforts to keep Zoe and me apart. She admits that she is ashamed of their behavior, explaining they were only doing what they thought was best for Zoe. She told me about the heated debates she and my mother had over our relationship. She said Rose once told her no parent imagines their child will grow up to be homosexual. That is not how we are programmed in this society. She said Rosemary wanted her children to grow up and be happy and live fulfilling lives.

Carolyn explains, "Caiden, as parents, what we fail to realize is our idea of happiness for our children is quite often different from what our children see as happiness."

She reflects on the time when they set Zoe up with potential suitors. She laughs as she remembers how Zoe tried her best to make them happy by, dating men. She comments, "I watched Zoe when she dated men. I was hoping one of them would make her glow the way she does when she is with you. After a few attempts at dating, Robert and I realized how miserable our little girl was. At the mere mention of your name, Zoe's eyes would sparkle! We knew we had made a huge mistake in trying to impose our will on her."

She stops walking for a minute and looks me dead in the eyes, saying, "Caiden, your mother would be so proud of you." I look at her, dumbfounded.

She continues, expressing how impressed she was I did not take Robert up on his offer to buy their blessing. She expresses her wants for Zoe, noting she wants someone who will love her unconditionally and have her best interest at heart.

She states, "Caiden, you surpass my wildest expectations. I know Zoe will be happy as long as she is with you. We welcome you into our family, and we are truly sorry for how we treated you in the past."

Stunned by her candor, I am left speechless. *Is this really happening?* I question myself. After regaining composure, I reply, "I am grateful to have your blessing. I understand a parent's love more than you realize. I know the lengths they will go to protect their child. I promise to make Zoe as happy as she has made me."

A sense of relief moves across their faces as Carolyn embraces me with open arms. Crying, she whispers in my ear, "God gives us gifts in the most unexpected form. Caiden, you are one of those gifts, and we're thankful to have you in our lives."

We are heading back toward the hotel when Riley texts, wondering where I am. As we reach the hotel, I hug both Robert and Carolyn again, bidding them good-bye.

Robert walks with me, out of earshot of Carolyn, stating, "Caiden, thank you for everything. I am getting the help I need, and my business is thriving because of your assistance. I can't thank you enough for what you have done for my family. Oh, and, Caiden, if you hurt my daughter, I'm going to kill you!"

I look at him, chuckling at his remark, and walk into the hotel, toward the lobby. *Wow! What a start to the day!* I happily think to myself.

I reach the lobby to find Riley, Jaylon, and Erika sitting at the bar, having cocktails. I check my watch and see it is two thirty.

"A bit early to be, drinking isn't it?" I ask.

"We are on vacation. This is what normal people do on vacation. Loosen up and have a seat. Tonight is your last night of freedom. Bartender, a vodka with cranberry and a twist of lime, please," Jaylon states as she orders me a drink. I am surprised she remembers.

She hands me the drink and raises her glass to make a toast. "To my little sister and her bride: may your life together be filled with love and happiness!"

I glance over at Riley as she smirks, and we clink glasses. Erika spies the two young ladies Kai and Melai who approached Riley and me yesterday. She makes mention of how attractive they are. Jaylon turns to look at them and smiles, lifting her glass toward them, gesturing hello—her way of breaking the ice with a woman. The ladies giggle as they wave to us. Kai gets up from her table and walks up to us, remarking she missed us at the party last night. Riley quickly steps to her, informing her we were detained because of business and apologize for our absence. She smiles, but I see disappointment in her eyes. Riley comments we would love the opportunity to make it up to them for going to so much trouble.

She smiles at Riley then turns her attention to me, stating, "Caiden, is there something you would like to say to me?"

I look at her blankly, replying, "No!" Riley nudges me in the arm, and I continue, "Kai, I am sorry we missed your party. Surely, you ladies had fun with the other guests. We were probably an afterthought."

She looks at me again, smiling, stating, "We only invited you two."

I gulp and clear my throat, trying not to chuckle and reply, "Oh, I see. Is there anything we can do to make it up to you?"

She moves so close I can feel her breath against my face, insisting the four of us attend a luau they are having this evening. She says we are perfectly dressed, and she will be expecting us at seven sharp. I hear the three musketeers behind me informing her we would be there. She looks at them and smiles.

She again turns to me, placing her hand on my shoulder, squeezing firmly then moving her hand down my arm, commenting, "Hmm, very nice. You take good care of your body."

I reply, "I do my best."

Jaylon offers to buy her and her friend a drink. She calls her friend over, and they take a seat at the bar, between Jaylon and Erika with Riley, standing in front of them. A ridiculous sight if I must say so myself. Those three are definitely savages circling the wagon.

I hear idle chitchat between the five of them while I sit on the end, next to Erika. Checking my watch again, it is now three o'clock. Kai gets up from her barstool and moves to sit next to me. She is obviously flirting as she rests her arm on my shoulder, asking why I am sitting way over here.

Looking out into the ocean, I begin to chuckle. I am about to explain to her I am getting married in the morning when Zoe, Brianna, and Abby spot us sitting at the bar. The three of them walk over to us to say hello. Brianna eyes Riley with suspicion but maintains a calm demeanor. Abby speaks to everyone, saying hello. Zoe says hello to everyone then turns to face Kai and me. I stand and introduce them, explaining to Kai, "This is my fiancée." The two shake hands politely. I ask Zoe where they are off to.

Kai, shocked at the news, quickly remarks, "You two make a beautiful couple."

I thank her for her kind words as I walk with Zoe away from the bar as she explains they are on their way to the salon. Brianna and Abby quickly follow us toward the exit. I tell them to have a good time. I pull Zoe close to me and kiss her softly on the lips. She caresses my face as she leans into kiss me intimately in kind. I tell her I miss her already.

She smiles at me then leans in to whisper in my ear softly, "I can't wait to marry you, Mr. Westphal! You will officially be mine, then I can do all sorts of naughty things to you."

I smile, whispering in response, "I like the sound of that. What things?"

She ponders my comment, replying jokingly, "I promise it will hurt in a good way, Mr._Westphal."

I laugh in amusement and kiss her one last time. "You ladies enjoy your day." As they begin to walk away, I call to Zoe, "I love you, and have some fun tonight."

I look over at the bar, watching Kai work her magic on the three of them. She certainly knows how to work a room. I ease back into my seat next to Erika when Kai again approaches me, asking if I like dancing. I hear my companions burst into laughter, amused, no doubt, at the fact that I don't dance. I explain to Kai that I am not a very good dancer. I can't remember dancing ever. She tries to contain her giggles but to no avail, laughing as she asks me what music I like.

I smirk at her, expressing my love for R and B, hip-hop, rap, country, rock, pop, and neo soul.

"Who's one of your favorite artists?" she asks.

I think for a minute, telling her I'm a fan of Anthony Hamilton. She laughs, noting he's one of her favorites. She leans into the bartender, and next thing I hear is "Cool" coming from the speakers.

Kai motions with her finger for me to go over to her. I shake my head in panic as I tell her no way will I embarrass myself. She stands in the middle of the floor with her hands on her hips and lips twisted, posing the question of how I plan to dance with my bride. I ponder her question, realizing she has a valid point. Riley eggs me on, telling me I should be happy someone is willing to sacrifice their toes to teach me to dance. Jaylon and Erika are laughing hysterically. Jaylon reminds me I used to dance all over the house every time I heard a song playing. She jokes that I used to have some pretty good moves back in the day. I refresh her memory, teasing because of her lack of enthusiasm and appreciation for my dance skills, I lost the will.

Erika chimes in, "Are you going to let such a beautiful woman dance solo? Come on, Mr. Confident, grow a pair and dance with the lady!"

Aggravated at their assault, I find the nerve to get on the floor with Kai. She smiles as she places my hand around her waist and holds the other in her hand. She eases my stress, saying we can do the basic side-to-side steps until I loosen up. She tells me to look into her eyes and follow her movements.

In the process, she asks me about my personal life. I find myself at ease, talking to her, explaining how I started my first nightclub. I am talking her ear off, but she doesn't seem to mind. Before I realize it, we have danced to a few songs. I look around and notice the hotel bar is now full of people drinking, laughing, and dancing.

Riley hands me a shot of 1800 Coconut. We tap glasses, and down it goes. I look over at Jaylon to see her enthralled in conversation with an attractive brunette. Erika is chatting with a lovely dark-haired Asian woman.

Kai comments, "Caiden, do you realize you have been dancing the whole time we have been, talking? You are actually a very good dancer. Tomorrow, when you are dancing with your wife, don't think about the movements. Focus on how beautiful she looks. Your body will automatically do the rest."

I look at her, laughing, letting her know she is a very good dance instructor. Curious, I ask Kai, does she work for the hotel?

She laughs at my question, responding, "You could say that."

Looking confused at her response, I rephrase, "Do you own this hotel?"

She looks surprised, commenting, "In the three years my family and I have taken ownership, it has never dawned on anyone to ask." I apologize for my oversight. She lets me off the hook by acknowledging I am at least open-minded enough to realize the latter is a possibility. "I like you, Caiden. You're a bit peculiar yet very sweet and charming. I find it very easy to be around you," she mentions.

I thank her for the dance lessons, excusing myself to the restroom. On the way, I ask Riley if she is ready to go. She says everyone is having a good time here, and if I didn't mind, can we hang out for a while longer? She points out there are lots of women interested in getting to know us. I smirk at her, letting her know we can stay as long as they like.

Jaylon walks up, asking if she can have a word with me in private. I nod yes but ask she wait until I return.

A few minutes later, I return to see Jaylon, standing where I left her. She smiles at me as she motions for us to take a walk. Heading toward the beach, Jaylon has her hands in her pants pocket as do I. We walk side by side in a slow stroll when she begins with an apology encompassing everything horrible thing she has ever done to me. She realizes, after Rosemary's passing, how cruel and selfish she had been to us over the years, admitting she was a bitter and hateful person for most of her life. If she couldn't be happy, she wanted everyone else to be as miserable as she was. She admits she was wrong and understands my hesitation in trusting her now.

"Caiden, if the shoe were on the other foot, I can't say I would be so open to believe me either. I know it is going to take some time and a lot of hard work on my part to prove to you I want to change. I want my little sister in my life in a good way!" She pauses for a moment then remarks, "I am really sorry for the whole unwanted heart thing with Zoe. I knew that would eat at you, and it was wrong of me to use her to hurt you. I know you took Mom's words to heart, and selfishly, I used them against you."

We continue our walk when she mentions she ran into Danielle a couple of days ago. I can't remember who she is. She jogs my memory, explaining she goes by Dani. She said she is the woman who cheated with Alyssa when she and Jaylon where together. Jaylon laughs, telling me Dani told her something very interesting. I continue to walk in silence as Jaylon recaps the night Dani and Alyssa went out to the club announcing their new relationship. I remember Jaylon was devastated when she found out.

She goes on, explaining Dani said it was a night she would never forget. Dani shared she had been attacked in the alley when she went outside to smoke a cigarette that evening. Jaylon tells me she was hurt pretty bad. A couple of cracked ribs, a broken nose, a black eye, and a scar across her cheek still visible to this day. Jaylon stops walking and turns to me, asking if I knew anything about the incident. I look at her and shake my head no—I knew nothing of it. She eyes me suspiciously, telling me Dani knew who beat the shit out of her that night. As I continue to listen, I lower my head, saying nothing.

She places her hand firmly on my shoulder and states, "Caiden, thank you for sticking up for me." She laughs as she repeats Dani's comments. "No one fucks with a Westphal without consequence. Consider this a consequence for fucking over my sister."

I hear in her voice that she is getting choked up, mentioning she can't believe I did that after all the fucked-up shit she did to me. After a few moments, she starts to laugh uncontrollably at the thought, commenting she wishes she could have seen me in action. I laugh at it myself, remarking it was a foolish thing for me to do.

Jaylon switches gears, discussing her and Zoe's relationship. She admits they were together for all the wrong reasons. The few times they attempted intimacy, they couldn't go through with it. She adds, "Zoe is one hundred percent Team Caiden. I have never seen anyone more in love. You are blessed, Caiden. You always have been."

As I continue to listen to Jaylon open up about the past, I begin to see a transformation in her. I can tell she is trying to be better than who she is. She let me know she has been attending church since Rosemary's funeral. Oddly enough, Jaylon has been having visions of Rosemary. I let her know I have had visions of her as well. We agree she is still working to keep the family together. I thank Jaylon for her honesty, explaining I want to believe in her, but I still have reservations. The better part of me is willing to give her a chance. I take a deep breath, deciding to invite her and Erika to the wedding. She smiles brightly and thanks me. We embrace, squeezing each other tight. I can feel her body trembling as we embrace. I can tell she is crying.

She whispers in my ear, "Caiden, I miss my little sister, and I am so sorry for all the pain I have caused you. You don't know how much your forgiveness means to me."

I begin to choke up at her words, replying, "Jaylon, I have never given up on you. I pray silent prayers, hoping we would get to this point. I'm glad to have my sister back in my life."

We release each other and wipe away the tears. Looking at each other, we begin laughing and simultaneously say to the other, chuckling, "It's the sand causing my eyes to water."

I must admit, it feels good having Jaylon here. Despite our history, she is family, and I love her even when I've hated her. Jaylon throws her arm over my shoulder, placing me in a headlock like she used to do when we were kids, as we walk back to the hotel bar, only this time, it's not in malice. I wrap my arm around her waist, laughing, joking, "You don't want any of this."

We laugh and smile all the way back to the hotel.

I think to myself, *Today has turned out to be very special.* I have reconciled with my future in-laws. More importantly, Jaylon and I are on the path to building what I hope to be a solid relationship filled with love and trust.

CHAPTER TWENTY-TWO

Faith

Startled by the alarm clock at six thirty in the morning, I fumble to turn it off. Drowsy, still half-asleep, I lie in bed, staring up into the darkness, summarizing my life. Today is the day I have been praying for. I start to wonder what marriage will offer me that I don't already have. Will I be a good spouse to Zoe, a good parent to our children? Can I remain faithful to our vows? Why am I questioning myself? I shut my eyes tightly, focusing on happier thoughts, pushing all doubts out of my mind. I slowly sit up, rubbing the sleep from my eyes, looking around the faintly lit room, hoping for a vision of Rosemary. I wish she could have lived to see this day. I imagine her, sitting on the front row, smiling at me, assuring me I am making the right decision.

Rosemary was always a champion for Zoe and me, never doubting once our love for each other. Preparing to leave for Portland, I remember her telling me she understood my reason for leaving. I can still hear her voice: "Caiden, it may not feel like it, but you leaving is a blessing. Sometimes, in order to be seen, we have to make ourselves invisible to the ones we love."

I'll be damned if she wasn't right.

Distracted by my cell blinking, I grab it, reading a text from Zoe: "143."

Smiling, I get up to open the drapes and take in the view of the ocean. It's peaceful as I continue to reflect on my pending nuptials.

Maybe I'm having pre-wedding jitters as panic begins to set in. My heart begins to race, and I can barely breathe. I sit on the edge of the chair, trying to steady myself. What is wrong with me? Taking long, deep breaths to relax, I focus on all the reasons I love Zoe.

A knock at the door startles me. Still trying to calm myself, I ask, "Who is it?"

The voice on the other side is Kai's. What is she doing here at this time of morning? I wonder. The door opens as Kai peeks her head in, asking if I am dressed. Her eyes are fixed on the floor. Still sitting on the arm of the chair, I motion for her to enter. I grab my T-shirt off the floor and toss it on. Standing in my pajama pants, I ask "What can I do for you?" She reminds me last night that I requested a wakeup call this morning. Scratching my head, I look at her dumbfounded, not remembering the request. She smiles at me politely, inquiring if everything is okay. Still struggling to remember last night, I nod yes. She moves toward me when an uncomfortable feeling comes over me. The way she is looking at me is somehow different.

I quickly rise from the chair, thanking her for the personal touch. She is now directly in front of me, still smiling like a schoolgirl with a crush. I move away from her, nearly tripping over the chair, and take a seat on the sofa, asking, is she all right? She nods in response as she moves to sit next to me. I am about to ask her what happened last night when there is another knock at my door.

Feeling awkward, I hurriedly jump up from the sofa and answer the door. I'm grateful to see Riley, standing there wide-eyed and smiling. "Hey, CW! You have about thirty minutes before—" She pauses her sentence when she notices Kai in my room. "Oh, um, sorry. Didn't realize you had company. I'll come back in fifteen," she states.

I insist she come in and have a seat, explaining I will be ready in about fifteen minutes. Riley acknowledges Kai then looks at me oddly, tilting her head, her look implying Kai and I spent the night together.

I thank Kai again, telling her I will catch up with her later. She reluctantly stands, saying she will see me later as she leaves my room. The door barely closes when Riley immediately asks if Kai spent the night. Aghast she would even think of it, I look at her, shaking my head as I go to throw on some clothes.

While dressing, I hear Jaylon and Erika's voice in the living area. I'm wondering, did I invite everyone to my suite this morning? Still reeling from last night, I lean against the sink, trying to remember what happened. I am drawing a blank, only remembering kissing Zoe good night right before midnight then heading to my room. I came in alone, got undressed, drank a bottle of water, then fell asleep. Bits and pieces of the evening fade in and out of my mind. Growing frustrated, I walk into the living area, demanding someone provide me details of last night.

All three of them burst into laughter at my demand. I am not amused by their display.

Jaylon, attempting to speak through her laughs, remarks, "Caiden, um . . . um . . . you and Kai got 'close' last night."

The expression on my face is of sheer fear. Riley takes pity on me, explaining I had a few too many. Kai was gracious enough to tend to me in her bedroom while I recovered from my inebriated state. She says she found me passed out in Kai's bedroom while she sat next to me, making sure I was okay.

"I see?" I reply, still confused.

She reassures me we both were fully clothed when she found us and adds they let me sleep it off. It was around eleven o'clock when Kai escorted me back to the hotel, where I ran into Zoe.

Riley hints Kai is interested in me. That would explain her odd behavior earlier. "CW, you know she has been into you since we got here. Kai probably mistook yesterday's attention as something more. Don't worry about it. In a few hours, you will be off the market for the rest of your life!"

Erika looks at her watch then at me, joking, "Mr. Metrosexual, you have a seven thirty appointment at the stylist for your mani and pedi, or did you forget that too?"

I roll my eyes at her and reply, "That's Mr. Metrosexual Stud! It wouldn't hurt you to have those gnawed off nails and tarantula toes done. I see now why you are single."

"Pretentious asshole," she mumbles under her breath.

Jaylon interjects, reminding us we have a lot to do in only a few hours. I have to agree with Jaylon. We head out, finishing up last-minute details. As we head over to the salon, Riley goes over the details of the wedding. She asks why we didn't have a rehearsal. I explain it is a simple ceremony, and I didn't think one was necessary. *How complicated is it to stand there and say "I do,"* I think. I am sure our show wedding will have all the bells and whistles—we can rehearse then.

By the time we finish at the salon, it is ten o'clock. All remaining is to get back to the hotel and prepare for the ceremony. On the ride back, I stare out the limo into the ocean, wishing Zoe and I didn't have to return to Texas on Sunday. Payne Corp is undergoing a myriad of public relations issues. As CEO, it's critical she be present to dispel any rumors and keep the stockholders assured. She insists she can handle things from here, but I disagree. Riley taps my shoulder, gaining my attention as we pull into the hotel.

"You ready, CW?" she asks.

I nod in response as we exit the limo. Jaylon and Erika explain they have some official business to take care of but assures me they will be at the wedding on time. As we head to my suite, I notice Riley seems overly concerned, even protective of me today. She informs me she is going to remain by my side for moral support. I chuckle at her remark as we enter the suite. Anxious, I decide to get dressed, hoping to take my mind off everything. After dressing, Riley suggests one final toast as a single stud boi when we hear a banging at the door.

Brianna is pleading for me to open the door. Instantly, an uneasy feeling flows through me. The door opens when Brianna, half-out-of-breath, charges in, mumbling, "Zoe is freaking out! She doesn't think she can go through with the wedding!"

"Brianna, what happened?" I shout.

She looks at me, apologizing. I ask her what she is apologizing for. She explains she saw Kai leave my room early this morning and inadvertently mentioned it to Zoe. "What the fuck is wrong with you, Brianna! Why in the hell would you tell Zoe something like that? Are you deliberately trying to sabotage our wedding?"

She responds, "Caiden, I'm sorry. I didn't mean to mention it. It just slipped out in conversation."

Riley looks at me then at Brianna, asking, "Brianna, what exactly did you say to Zoe?"

Brianna turns to Riley, explaining their conversation. She tells Zoe she wishes she could have as much faith in Riley as she has in Caiden. Brianna's comment prompts Zoe to ask why she would say something like that. Brianna goes on to explain she saw Kai leave my room early this morning. Brianna assumed Kai spent the night. After Zoe heard, she went ballistic.

Riley sees my rage and asks Brianna, "Where is Zoe?"

She says she didn't know. Zoe left so quickly, Brianna didn't see which way she went, so she decided to come and alert me.

"Brianna!" I snap at her.

Riley intervenes, prompting me to go look for Zoe. She says she will remain here in the event Zoe comes to her senses and returns to the hotel.

I grab my cell, dialing Zoe's number. The call goes straight to voicemail. As I leave, I fight the impulse to lambast Brianna for her irresponsibility, but finding Zoe is more important.

"Brianna, I hope for your sake I find her in time!" I exclaim as I charge out of the room.

My first stop is Zoe's parents and sister. No one has seen or heard from her this morning.

Think, Caiden! Where does Zoe go when she is upset?

It's now ten fifteen and not a lot of time before our nuptials. I have to find Zoe and explain what Brianna saw. I run through the hotel lobby, toward the beach, scanning it, but there is no sign of her.

Come on, Caiden! It's a small fucking island! Where would she go?

Suddenly, I remember Zoe pointing out a small church a few miles down the road from the hotel. That's it! Zoe always turns to the church in a crisis. She has to be there! I summon my driver and inquire if he has seen my fiancée. He said he dropped her off at the Koloa Fellowship Church just down the road. Hastily, I hop into the limo and instruct him to drive me there as quickly as he can.

"Everything okay, Caiden?" the driver, Henry, asks.

I reply, "I'm not sure, Henry. I just need to get to the church!"

"Ms. Payne appeared upset this morning when I dropped her off," he replies.

"Yes, I am sure she was," I reply.

"If you don't mind, can I give you a bit of advice?" he asks.

Frustrated and anxious, I nod, waiting for his response.

"I have seen couples marry in haste, then a few years later, they divorce. I like to think I am a good judge of character when it comes to picking winners and losers, so to speak. If I were a gambling man, I would bet my entire life savings in favor of your marriage!"

I look at him as he looks at me through the rearview and smiles. I reply, "Henry, you must know something I don't to bet against those odds."

He chuckles as he explains, "When you have seen as much as I have, Caiden, you know what true love looks like. I have had the pleasure of watching you two interact in a way few people do. You look into each other's eyes when you speak, you hold each other's hands, walk side by side, play and laugh together. Looking at you, I see so much love and respect, each for the other. It is refreshing to see a couple truly enjoy being near each other for no other reason than it makes you both happy. I would wager Ms. Payne is having cold feet and turning to faith for guidance."

"I pray you are right, Henry. Thank you," I reply softly.

We pull up to the church. Upon exiting the limo, I am about to ask him to wait when he turns to me, smiling, motioning me to go inside. I hear the engine shut off as I walk toward the small wooden church. Reaching for the door handle, I quietly pull the door open and see Zoe standing at the front pew with her head bowed in prayer.

I walk slowly up the aisle and take a seat on a pew across from her, not saying a word. After a few moments, she raises her head, staring forward. I see her weeping. She is holding a handkerchief, using it to dab her eyes. Even with tear-soaked eyes she's beautiful. Her hair is pulled up in a bun, covered with a one-tier mid-length tulle veil with a golden headband filled with crystals and pearls. She's wearing a beautiful ivory fit-and-flare strapless gown with champagne beaded lace with a swoop train. It is accessorized by a single pearl necklace with matching earrings. I am speechless, taking in her beauty.

Sensing my presence, she takes a seat next to me and whispers, "Caiden, after a lot of soul searching, I have come to realize I don't deserve you."

I attempt to speak, but she silences me before I can get a word out.

She continues, "I have been selfish and hurtful towards you. I know you will never let go out of chivalry. I am letting you off the hook by doing it for you. You deserve someone who hasn't hurt you or lied to you. I'm sorry, Caiden, but I can't marry you."

My heart breaks as I listen. I gather my thoughts, replying, "Zoe, I didn't come here to convince you to marry me. I'll decide who I deserve—that decision isn't up to you. I want to spend my life with you, but I won't plead a case to convince you this is what you should do. Zoe, I had to take a long look in the mirror and not only forgive you but Jaylon, Rosemary, and myself. Zoe, until you can forgive yourself, I agree, we shouldn't get married. I am returning to the hotel to prepare for a wedding. Whether you show or not, I'll have my answer."

I turn to walk away and hear her voice cracking as she speaks. "Caiden, I'm afraid I will never be enough."

Everything inside me wants to turn around to hold her. I stand firm and reply without turning to face her, "You have always been enough, Zoe." I continue toward the door when I feel her hand grasp mine, pulling me toward her.

"Caiden, please stay and pray with me?"

Placing my hand on top of hers, I nod as we head back to the altar. We kneel and bow our heads. She begins by asking God for the wisdom and strength to allow her to forgive herself for her sins. She praises God for placing me in her life and thanks him for reuniting our families. She squeezes my hand tightly as she begins to weep. I thank God for his grace, guidance, and love in our lives. We pray in silence a few moments.

I stand, grabbing her hand, assisting her up. I look at her, inquiring if she feels better. Smiling up at me, she nods. I take her hand in mine and escort her back to the limo.

Henry is staring at us through the rearview, asking, "Where to?"

I look at Zoe, waiting for her response. She asks him take us back to the hotel, mentioning we have a wedding to attend.

He whirls the limo around and floors it, commenting, "I will have you there in no time."

Zoe reminds me it is bad luck for the groom to see the bride before the wedding. I tease, telling her a Westphal makes their own luck.

Our wedding takes place as scheduled. I am pleasantly surprised to see Nurse Woodward and Edwina at the ceremony. As a tribute to my mother, Riley and I wear a single white rose in our lapels. Our simple ceremony has turned into a full-blown wedding thanks to Zoe and Abby. Zoe flew in a few of her closest friends and, with Abby's assistance, managed to have a few of my employees from Portland make the trip. Chloe makes the most adorable flower girl, ushering in our wedding rings. We spend a couple of hours after the ceremony visiting guests, cutting a three-tier Italian cream cake, taking wedding photos, and listening to Riley, Brianna, and Jaylon roast us. Our first dance is to the sounds of Eric Benét and Tamia's "Spend My Life with You." Zoe and I can hardly keep our eyes off each other.

When we get a minute alone, we both agree it is time to retire to our suite. It has been a long afternoon, and we are anxious to be alone together as a married couple. We graciously thank our guests for celebrating this joyous occasion with us and bid them adieu as we retreat to back to our suite.

I open the door, lift her into my arms, and whisk her over the threshold. I think how happy I am, looking forward to this new and exciting chapter! I gently place her back on her feet in the living area.

She is smiling from ear to ear, gazing at me, commenting, "You look so handsome. I almost hate to see you take off your tuxedo."

I smile shyly, joking, "I can leave it on if you prefer."

She shakes her head, replying "I said almost, Mr. Westphal," as she walks up to me, placing both hands on my cheeks, kissing me softly.

"Mrs. Westphal." I smile as the words roll off my lips "I do love the sound of that."

Pulling her close to me, wrapping my arms around her waist, I notice a note on the bar, "Courtesy of Kai and staff, congratulations to you on this special day. We wish you a long and happy marriage." The room is filled with scented candles, a basket filled with fresh island fruits, champagne, cheese, crackers, and chocolates.

"How sweet of her to do all this for us," Zoe mentions.

She grabs her cell off the bar and moves next to me to take a picture of us. I laugh, noting we have hundreds of wedding shots. She smiles, commenting, "None like the ones we are going to take in this room." I chuckle as I smile for the camera.

After a few more playful pictures, she places her phone down and turns her back toward me, asking me to unzip her dress. Eagerly, I oblige and watch hungrily as she slips out of it, revealing a turquoise lace bra and thong. She steps out of her dress, slipping off her heels. Nearing me, she begins to assist in the removal of all my clothes. We stand, gazing at each other with love and hope gleaming from our eyes. I pull her into a passionate kiss that lingers.

As we move toward the bed, Zoe whispers softly in my ear how much she wants to make love. Her mouth finds my nipple as she slowly runs her tongue over it, sending chills through me, while gently tugging the other with her fingertips, causing gasps to escape my lips. It feels like the first time—every touch, every stroke, every kiss a new sensation. She slides onto the bed as I lie atop her, kissing her neck and arms, tasting her body. I pause for a moment as I hear "Beautiful" by Meshell Ndegeocello softly playing in the background.

"Caiden, I want you," she whispers in a soft, sultry voice.

Her fingers run through my dreads and down my back, exciting me. I look into her blue eyes, remembering our very first night together, praying it will always feel like this. Unsnapping her bra, I stroke her nipples with my tongue. They feel warm to the touch. My hands caress her body. Feeling her skin against my fingertips arouses me further. I glide effortlessly between her legs as she parts them readily. I slide off her thong, tossing it aside. I glance down at her naked frame, in awe of how beautiful she looks. Her delicate hands caress my cheeks as we gaze deep into each other's eyes in wonderment.

I slowly suck her fingers one by one. I watch her eyes close slowly as her tongue moistens her lips seductively. She is enjoying the foreplay. I lean in, kissing her soft pink lips gently, biting the lower. The scent of her is emotionally intoxicating as I move to her neck, inhaling deeper. Her pelvis writhes against me, inviting me in. Her hands ease down my backside as she pulls me close to her.

"Caiden, she is wet. She wants you," she whispers.

Eager, Zoe grips my dildo and inserts the tip into her Venus. Foreplay is no longer an option as my wife demands gratification. I thrust slowly into her and can feel her back arch as she gasps in delight. Her hands find the back of my arms, gripping them tightly as I continue to thrust in and out of her, going as deep as her body will allow. Dirty whispers fall off her lips, enhancing my excitement. I move her legs over my shoulders, pushing even deeper inside her still, moving in a steady rhythm. As the intensity builds, my body thrusts harder and harder. Every wonderful gasp and moan from her lips drives me faster and deeper inside her. I gaze into her eyes filled with lust and desire as they gaze back at me. Our senses at their peak amplify every touch, moan, and caress.

Feeling our bodies begin to tighten, I pause, delaying our pending implosion. She turns over onto her knees, provoking me to enter her from behind. Inserting the tip, I gradually ease into her once again. I watch as her hands grip the sheets, her head facedown into the pillow, moaning loudly. Seeing my dildo penetrate in and out of her sends me into unadulterated bliss, calling her name as I explode.

Zoe, turning her head to the side of the pillow, cries out, "Caiden, oh, Caiden, I love you, I love you so much!" while her body revels in enjoyment.

Once done, I remove my harness as she turns to lie on her back, motioning me to go closer. I lie on top of her and kiss her passionately, staring into her eyes as our lips touch and our tongues wrestle. She rolls on top of me, caressing my chest with her hands, moving down to my navel. Placing her mouth around it, she playfully rolls her tongue in and out of it, causing me to laugh. Her mouth finds my happy trail, and she glides her tongue down to my clit and strokes it delicately as my body flinches. She kisses it then begins to suck on it, twirling her tongue around and around. My body shivers at the sensation. I look down, seeing a devilish glimmer in her eyes as she stares back at me. My head falls back as I lie, impatiently waiting for her to pleasure me.

Bending my knees, she moves her head into position, gaining full access to me. I feel her warm mouth cover me as she uses her tongue to stroke my clit. I uncontrollably begin to moan at her touch. My hand rests on her head, grabbing her hair, pressing her head closer to my body. Her head bobs as she masterfully strokes me. I release my grip to grab a pillow, trying to stifle my moans. Feeling my body on the brink of climax, I scream Zoe's name loudly. Even after I climax, she isn't satisfied as she continues her quest to savor my juices. My body flinches as she continues her tongue-lashing. Unexpectedly, a second orgasm ensues, even better than the first. I beg Zoe to release me as my body can stand no more.

She lifts her head, smiling at me with a wicked grin. Sated and exhausted, I look down at her and smile. Licking my lips prompts her to come toward me. Her face is filled with excitement. She knows exactly what I want to do to her. She sits on my lap, and I can feel her warm, wet Venus throbbing against my skin. I run my fingers across her hard nipples as I sit up to kiss her, telling her how much I love her. She wraps her arms around my neck as we sit face-to-face.

She smiles, exclaiming, "Caiden, I love being your wife! You are my one true love."

I take pleasure in her comment. With love-filled eyes and shortness of breath, I whisper, "Zoe, you make me feel wanted. I am grateful you are my wife."

We lie holding each other when Zoe reminds me we never got a chance to read the engravings on our wedding rings. I signal her to go first. Sliding the ring off her finger, she reads the inscription "My Heart." After reading it, she gently kisses my lips, acknowledging she adores the inscription.

Eager for me to read my inscription, she assists me in sliding my ring off. As I glance over, I see her eyes light up as I read the inscription "Wanted Heart."

I am speechless as I gaze into her eyes, unable to find the words.

She rests my head against her shoulder and hugs me tightly, whispering, "Your heart will never feel unwanted again!"

ABOUT THE AUTHOR

T. J. Wolfe is an e-book author, political activist, member of the Human Rights Campaign and Equality Texas. A former business owner, Wolfe has a B. A. in Business Management and currently resides in Austin, Texas. "Unwanted Heart" was created in part to support the marriage rights of same-sex couples even after the Supreme Court ruling and bring greater awareness to the masculine and androgynous lesbians in the LGBT community.

Printed in the United States
By Bookmasters